Some Girls Do

Some Girls Do

....

LEANNE BANKS

WARNER BOOKS

An AOL Time Warner Company

This book is dedicated to all of you who say to me, "Yes, Leanne, you can do it." You know who you are.

Acknowledgments

I have been blessed with assistance and encouragement during the writing of this book and would like to thank the following people: Karen Solem and Karen Kosztolnyik, my two champions, thank you for helping to make this happen. Thank you to romantic suspense author Karen Rose for technical assistance, Binne Syril Braunstein, and longtime friends and colleagues Millie Criswell and Donna Kauffman for creative assistance. For professional and personal encouragement, heartfelt thanks to Cindy Gerard, Pamela Britton, Janet Evanovich, Joan Johnston, the Silhouette Desire loop. For real-world perspective, I don't know what I would do without the ladies-night-out group, my phantom general consultant, and my parents and family. To all of you, I'm humbled by your generosity and belief in me.

"A little restraint is fine . . . as long as you don't overdo it."
—SUNNY COLLINS'S WISDOM

Prologue

Her objective was plain, reassuring, and sexless.

Katie Collins ought to know. She achieved her objective every day before she took the train from Media, Pennsylvania, to Society Hill in the heart of Philadelphia's historic district. Everything hinged on her ability to be nearly invisible. She pulled her dark blond hair into a dated twist that immediately aged her five years past her twenty-five. She always knew she got the twist at its most unappealing because it felt too tight, like an unwanted halo. Skipping cosmetics, she pushed her arms into the sleeves of her shapeless gray jacket and glanced approvingly into the mirror at the immediate effect of the drab color. She almost seemed to disappear.

She looked like a sexless spinster with no life to call her own, certainly no threat to the sixth wife of a semiretired CEO who could have been a poster boy for Viagra. Katie was the perfect personal assistant for Ivan Rasmussen, aka Ivan the terrible, founder of the top computer software games company in America.

Sliding the black-rimmed glasses up the bridge of her nose to hide the baby blue eyes she'd inherited from her mother, Katie felt a twinge of longing for a taste of a life of her own and squeezed her eyes shut at the feeling. She'd had blips of those kinds of feelings more often lately and they always scared her. Those feelings reminded her of her infamous mother Sunny Collins. It was more important than ever that she not follow in her mother's footsteps. Sometimes, she could even hear her mother's voice offering advice from the hereafter, but she always tried to shut it out.

Katie had a job to do, and everything depended on her keeping her nose to the grindstone. Excitement wasn't part of the equation. Neither was romance. When her mother had been alive, she had taken enough lovers for ten women, so Katie just figured she was one of those ten who would go without.

Years ago, her name might have been Priscilla Sue Collins, and she might have been from Texas with a mother rightly labeled the town slut, but she'd left all that behind. Her Texas accent, her unfinished high school education, memories of her mother making peanut butter sandwiches with M&M's, and her youth, although Katie couldn't remember a time when she'd felt young.

She'd left everything belonging to Priscilla back in Texas. Except one thing. And that one thing was the reason Katie Collins rose every morning and disappeared behind a gray jacket and black-framed glasses.

*"Every once in a while, you meet a man worth
the trouble he's going to cause you."*
—SUNNY COLLINS'S WISDOM

Chapter 1

Ivan Rasmussen looked at his world as if he were the
Almighty himself. Katie supposed that in Ivan's creation
story, he looked at his hugely successful company and like
the Almighty, saw that it was good. He looked at his grand
house in exclusive Society Hill and saw that it was good. He
looked at his most recently acquired wife, who was able to
trace her ancestry back to the *Mayflower*, and saw that she
was good.

But when Ivan looked at his youngest daughter, Wilhemina, he saw that she was not so good. She was a mess. Wilhemina bore the influence of every woman who'd passed
through her life from her now-deceased Las Vegas showgirl
mother to the Slovakian housekeeper who'd once sneaked
cookies to her. Unfortunately Wilhemina had inherited her
looks from her portly father, Ivan. All her personal stylists
had quit, and although Wilhemina was eager to do charity
work, no one really trusted her to complete an assignment.

Staring at a recent photograph of Wilhemina, Ivan
pinched the bridge of his nose as he stood beside the full-
length window of his home office furnished in leather and
aged oak. "Patricia and I are finally taking a cruise to Europe," he said. "We'll be gone for six weeks."

Katie's palms grew moist. She prayed he wasn't going to release her. "Congratulations," she said, fighting her nerves. "You and Mrs. Rasmussen will enjoy the time together."

"Yes," he said with a lack of enthusiasm. "There won't be much for you to do while I'm gone, so I'm giving you a temporary assignment. There's a possibility for a bonus in it for you too," he said and glanced at her. "I want you to look after Wilhemina."

Katie breathed again, slowly. Wilhemina was odd, but not impossible. "You want me to keep her personal calendar organized?"

He shoved one of his hands into the pocket of his Brooks Brothers wool slacks. "In a manner of speaking." He stretched his sagging chin upward and nodded. "I want you to be her companion. When Wilhemina gets bored, she—" He sighed. "She eats."

Katie nodded, aware of Wilhemina's diet struggles. "Oh, yes, sir."

"It's no secret we've been hoping Wilhemina would find a nice young man to marry. Despite all our efforts, no one has been found."

"I'm sorry, sir," Katie said, unable to conjure another response. She knew Ivan had exhausted every possible means short of cosmetic surgery to find an approved husband for Wilhemina. He had employed high-class matchmakers and used on-line dating services with disastrous results. She heard he'd even consulted a love magic specialist in the French Quarter of New Orleans.

"You're a sensible woman, responsible, highly motivated, compassionate. How would you like a shot at it?"

Katie blinked. "A shot at what, sir?"

"At finding a husband for Wilhemina. The primary requirement is that the prospect will have to pass a security test."

Katie's mind reeled. "You want me to find a husband for your daughter?" she asked, unable to keep the disbelief from her voice.

He lifted his chin again, stretching his neck against his crisp white collar in a gesture that indicated his supreme discomfort. "I realize it's a long shot, but I'll make it worth your while if you can do it."

"How does Wilhemina feel about this idea?"

He shrugged. "I haven't told her, but she won't mind. She wants to get married."

"I don't know what to say," Katie said.

"Katie, you've met my daughter. She needs to be guided and protected. I'm not getting any younger and I want the peace of mind that she'll be taken care of after I'm gone. God knows, I can't count on Patricia."

Katie swallowed a wince. She knew Patricia regarded Wilhemina as the proverbial millstone around Ivan's neck. "Why me?"

"Because you'll view it as a job, as a challenge."

That sounded like a load of malarkey.

"And there's the bonus," Ivan said with the same gleam in his eye that she suspected the serpent had worn when he was tempting Eve.

"Which is?" she prompted.

"Fifty thousand dollars," he said, and watched her with a cagey expression on his face.

Katie didn't breathe for a full moment. When she finally did squeeze in a millimeter of oxygen, she couldn't have formed words if her life depended on it.

"Okay, to hell with it. A hundred thousand dollars if you

can find a husband for Willie who meets the approval of my security specialist."

A hundred thousand dollars. Katie's world spun on its axis. A hundred thousand dollars could change her life. It could change her brother Jeremy's life. Katie was bound and determined to make sure he received the special help he needed. She took a deep breath. "Let me get this straight. You will give me a bonus of one hundred thousand dollars if I am able to find a husband for your daughter. This husband must meet the approval of your security specialist."

Ivan nodded crisply and extended his hand. "Do we have a deal?"

"I'd like the agreement in writing," Katie said, fully aware that she was negotiating with Ivan the terrible, one of the craftiest men in America. "Expenses in addition to the hundred thousand must be covered, and they will be nonrefundable. I also want the guarantee of my current position if I can't—"

"Never say can't," he said, wagging his finger at her. "Can't is a four-letter word."

"Regardless of the outcome of this endeavor," she said, slowly searching for acceptable words, "I want a guarantee that I will retain my current position."

"Of course," he said, looking as if he was certain he'd gotten the better end of the deal. He extended his hand again, but a knock sounded at the door.

"I'll get that," Katie said, quickly stepping past him.

Ivan stuck his arm in front of her, blocking her. "It's Wingate. I've been waiting for him," he said, surprising Katie with his eager bolt to the door. Ivan opened the door, again wearing his shark smile. "Michael, my boy," he said in a hearty voice. "Come in, come in."

Michael was not a boy, Katie immediately concluded as

she watched the tall, dark man slowly stride into Ivan's office. He wore his dark suit far better than Ivan wore his. His leather shoes gleamed from a scrupulous buffing. His red silk tie contrasted with his crisp white shirt. Katie scrutinized him. His square jaw was perfectly shaven, his mouth held just a hint of sensual curve. High cheekbones framed a roman nose. His eyes were cool, dark, and observant and his short hair meticulously groomed. Katie wondered if he was a marriage candidate for Wilhemina. If so, Katie suspected the poor girl would have her hands full trying to keep this man under control.

"It's good to see you again, Mr. Rasmussen. I'm glad you called," Michael said, smoothly accepting Ivan's pumping handshake.

"Call me Ivan. Michael Wingate, this is my personal assistant Katie Collins. The two of you will be coordinating a special project together."

"Special project?" Michael tossed Ivan a cautious sideways glance as he leaned forward to offer his hand to Katie. He flicked his dark gaze over her and she felt his instant assessment and brief flicker of curiosity.

She had the uncomfortable sense that this man might see more than she would like. Katie gave his strong hand a brief squeeze. "Mr. Wingate," she murmured.

"Miss Collins," he said, and turned back to Ivan. "You mentioned a special project, sir."

Ivan lifted his chin and gave a nod. "Yes, I told you I have an interesting business proposition for you."

"But you wouldn't elaborate when I asked," Michael said in a silky smooth voice.

Ivan smiled coyly. "I like your drive, boy."

Katie's stomach twisted. Someone got the shaft whenever Ivan was coy. She prayed it wouldn't be her. She looked at the broad-shouldered back of Michael Wingate and had a niggling suspicion that this was not a man who liked to play.

She noticed Michael remained silent. A negotiation strategy, she suspected, having watched Ivan engage other men. He who speaks first loses, she'd once heard Ivan say.

Ivan cleared his throat. "I have a family matter that requires your services. I'd like to see my daughter settled and married. While my wife and I are away on a cruise, my assistant, Miss Collins, has agreed to help Wilhemina. I would like you to handle the security details."

Complete silence followed again, although this time, a hushed quality of shock filled the air. Unable to deny her curiosity, Katie surreptitiously took a half step forward so she could view Michael Wingate's face. He did not look pleased.

"Mr. Rasmussen, I appreciate you thinking of me, but I no longer provide bodyguard services myself. Perhaps I could assign one of my employees to assist you. I was interested in providing a security program for your company."

"I know," Ivan said. "But I've used the same security for three years. Except for some dated equipment, they've done a decent job. If I'm going to change security companies, I've got to be sure you're going to do a better job than they do."

"I've shown you our employees' résumés and you know our record is exemplary," Michael said, and Katie noticed the slightest twitch of impatience at the corner of his right eye.

"But your other clients are small potatoes compared to Ivan Enterprises," Ivan said, waving his hand in a dismissive gesture. He swaggered, as much as a short, portly man could swagger, over to his desk and withdrew a Cohiba Esplendido cigar from the wooden humidor. He offered one to Michael. "You and I both know that if you win my security contract, you'll be moving in a totally different league. If you want a shot at my company business, you have to prove you can take care of my family business."

One day, Michael Wingate promised himself as he accepted the cigar, he would be able to tell Ivan Rasmussen to stick his prized Cohiba Esplendido up his ass. Not now, though, he thought as he watched Ivan make a show of trimming and lighting the cigar. As much as he hated the fact, the truth remained that Ivan Rasmussen not only offered Michael the opportunity to take his business to the next level, an association with the manipulative little bastard would give Michael the chance to gain back a measure of his respect. That combination kept Michael from dropping his Cohiba onto the floor and grinding it into Ivan's antique oriental rug.

Instead Michael drew no pleasure as he trimmed his cigar and puffed. From the time he was a child, Michael had known the art of cigar smoking was a necessary evil among Philadelphia's elite. Since he'd become an adult, he'd learned the size of the cigar correlated with the wannabe dick size of the smoker.

Ivan wore a thoughtful, cagey expression. The man knew he held all the trump cards. Michael fought the sensation of chains closing around him. He could take this or leave it, he told himself. He could walk out of here. But Ivan's offer included too many benefits, none of which included working with his strange assistant. Michael wouldn't be worth a nickel as a security specialist if he hadn't learned how to assess a person in sixty seconds or less. With the exception of her killer legs, the woman was so plain Michael wondered if she had gotten an un-makeover. Her drab shapeless dress, unflattering hairstyle, and glasses made her look older than she was. He wondered why she wanted to look older. There was always a reason. In his profession, he'd learned everyone had secrets. He wondered what secret the deliberately painfully plain Miss Collins hid. Her unlined skin and watchful blue eyes gave her youth away. He could feel her watching him even now. He pegged her age at twenty-six, her sexual appeal, intentionally zip. For a sliver of a second he wondered if she was one of those women who dressed like plain-Jane, but made love like a man's favorite bad-girl fantasy. He pushed the thought aside.

"What are the terms?" Michael asked, returning his attention to the more important matter at hand.

Ivan smiled broadly. "I knew you would be interested. You're hungry," he said. "I like that. It's a piece of cake. Miss Collins will provide prospective candidates for my daughter to marry. You will thoroughly screen them. No ex-convicts, no freeloaders, no disease carriers, and no rednecks. I can't accept a redneck for a son-in-law. And you're to provide protection for Wilhemina and my home in my absence."

Michael had learned the hard way to detest vague agreements. "What is the duration of the assignment?"

"Just until Patricia and I return from the cruise," Ivan said with a shrug.

"And we agree that if I handle the security for your daughter, then my company will handle the security for Ivan Enterprises beginning on the date of your return," Michael clarified.

Ivan frowned. "Well, we might have to negotiate the start date for your company. After all, I'll have to give the current security company notice."

Michael felt as if he were nailing a slimy worm to the wall. "What exactly would the start date be?"

Ivan rolled his shoulders in a near-squirm. "How about six months after I get back from Europe?"

"How about two weeks and in writing?" Michael returned. He was nobody's fool.

Ivan stretched his neck and gave an uneasy chuckle. "You and Miss Collins have a bit in common. You both drive a hard bargain. She wanted the agreement in writing too. No problem. I'll have my attorney draw up the papers."

"That's not necessary," Michael interjected, not distracted by Ivan's false flattery. "I'm sure your attorney is busy with other matters. I'll have my attorney draft an agreement." He pulled out his Palm Pilot and flipped through his calendar. "Shall we meet Thursday at ten A.M. or three-thirty?"

"Ten A.M., but my attorney will want to look over the agreement before I sign it," Ivan said with a wary glint in his beady eyes. He wore the expression of a man having second thoughts, as if he knew he'd dangled a juicy T-bone in front of a starving dog, and if he wasn't careful, the dog would take a few of his fingers along with the steak.

Michael would have to say that Ivan's uneasiness was warranted, he thought as he stubbed out his cigar in a crystal ashtray. After getting the shaft from his former business partner four years ago and getting dumped by his fiancée at the same time, Michael might not be a desperate man, but he was damn well determined. He'd learned never to depend on anyone, and his painful education, which had started at an early age, had turned all his soft spots to steel.

One week later, Ivan and Patricia were making last-minute preparations for the trip. Katie was to move in the following day, but she knew from Ivan's schedule that her boss had planned a meeting that afternoon with his attorney. She'd met Ivan's attorney, Gaston Hayes, before, and the beady-eyed, sharp-nosed man reminded her of something from the dark underworld. He gave her the creeps.

But he was important to Ivan, and since Katie had just entered into a legally binding agreement with Ivan, she suspected she had better stay informed. She wasn't normally snoopy and was scrupulous about respecting her employer's confidentiality, but this time she felt she had to make an exception.

Checking her watch, she saw that Gaston was due in two minutes. He was always prompt. Katie could hear Ivan trying to escape a discussion about packing with Patricia. Looking behind her and in front of her, she crept into Ivan's office and walked directly to the closet. Suddenly hearing voices, she opened the closet door, stepped inside, and closed it.

A hand closed over her mouth.

*"It is better to be on the receiving end of a shocked stare
than a bored yawn."*
—SUNNY COLLINS'S WISDOM

Chapter 2

Terror filled her throat and Katie opened her mouth to scream.

"Be quiet. We're both here for the same reason," Michael Wingate said, still holding his hand over her mouth.

Her heart pounding a mile a minute, she shook her head to free her mouth with no success. Panicking, she stepped backward onto his foot.

He swore and removed his hand. For two seconds. She sucked in a quick breath, and he covered her mouth again.

"I'm not going to hurt you. Be quiet so we can hear. If I take my hand away, you have to promise that you'll be quiet. Nod your head if you promise."

She nodded. He removed his hand and she tried to step away from his tall, overpowering frame. She started to trip on something she couldn't see, and he pulled her upright against him.

"Just be still for God's sake!" he whispered tersely.

"Excuse me for not knowing the etiquette for sharing a closet with a man I don't know or trust," she whispered just as tersely.

"Be quiet. They're coming."

Katie heard Ivan's and Gaston's voices as they entered

the office and held her breath. If she could see her face right now, she was sure it was fire-engine red. She was completely mortified to be caught eavesdropping.

"I don't know where Katie went," Ivan said.

"Maybe to the rest room or on a coffee break," Gaston said. "Isn't that where female employees usually spend most of their time?"

Ivan chuckled. "You're right about that."

Katie growled.

Michael pinched her.

She elbowed him in the ribs.

"Have a cigar, Gaston."

"Thank you very much. You have the best."

"Only the best," Ivan said, and Katie could easily picture the old man puffing out his chest.

"Suck up," she muttered, hearing the faint sounds of trimming, torching, and puffing.

"What did you need this afternoon, Mr. Rasmussen?"

"I'm going out of town tomorrow for an extended trip and I want you to check on the house every now and then."

"Because of your arrangement concerning Wilhemina," Gaston said.

"Exactly. I trust Katie as much as I trust any female employee. She's got a good head on her shoulders, but like most women her heart will ultimately win over her head. I still can't believe she's going to try to do this job for one hundred thousand dollars. Orly of Beverly Hills charges two hundred thousand for matchmaking."

Katie bit her tongue. She'd thought she'd done pretty well. Ivan's denigrating words stung.

"Well, Miss Collins is a rank amateur in this area. If you'll forgive me, sir, I'm surprised you chose someone to help Wilhemina who appears to have no fashion sense."

"Katie is motivated. She may wear ugly clothes and be plain as beige, but she wants to make money. I've always tried to work that kind of motivation in my favor."

"Which is why you're so successful, Mr. Rasmussen," Gaston said.

"I'm going to be sick," she mouthed, entirely too aware of Michael Wingate's muscular body brushing against hers. His cologne smelled ten times better than those stinky cigars.

"Now Wingate is a different matter. He's motivated by money, but I don't entirely trust him."

"Then, if you'll pardon me, why did you hire him, sir?"

"Because my security company refused to accept the job," Ivan said in disgust. "I'll cut them loose for that. Michael was the most persistent security specialist to contact me. Most importantly, he was available to watch over Wilhemina while I'm gone." He made a puffing sound. "Don't get me wrong. His record is squeaky clean."

"Except?"

Ivan chuckled. "Very good, Gaston. Nobody's perfect."

Michael held his breath while he waited to hear Ivan's comments.

"His black mark is his family. His parents were mentally unstable."

Michael felt a knot form in his gut. Would the black cloud from his parents' weaknesses ever leave? He gritted his teeth.

"A shame," Gaston said with polite insincerity.

"Yes, it is. That's why I'd like you to stop by the house every so often. You don't mind, do you?"

"I'd be honored, sir."

"Good, I'll give you a number where I can be reached in case of emergency," Ivan said, and the intercom beeped.

"Ah, that's Patricia again." He sighed. "Thank you for coming at such short notice. Do you mind seeing yourself to the door?"

"Not at all, sir."

Michael heard a clicking sound. "Coming, Patricia," Ivan said, then heavy footsteps followed.

"Wait ten seconds," he said in a low voice to Katie Collins. It was a wonder the woman hadn't maimed him when he'd tried to keep her quiet. Her hair smelled good, he'd noticed. Like a mixture of sunshine and flowers.

She moved forward to open the door and turned the knob to no avail. "It's locked!" she whispered in a horrified voice. "What are we going to—"

Michael put his hands on her slim waist and moved her aside, feeling the brush of her breasts against his arm as he set her down. For a half second, he wondered what her body really looked like without the ugly clothes.

Quickly setting the thought aside, he pulled out a credit card and unlocked the door. Katie followed him out in a rush.

Looking from side to side, she inhaled a deep draft of air and took a few tentative steps toward the outer office. She peeked through the doorway and waved him on. Michael stood right behind her and she turned, searching his face. The color of her blue eyes was unusually intense, he noticed. A man would have to stand close to notice, the same way he'd noticed the scent of her hair.

"I don't usually snoop," she told him in a quiet voice. "But this thing with Ivan—"

Michael cut her off, his mouth still filled with bitterness at Ivan's assessment. "No explanation necessary. I was doing the same thing you were. Protecting myself."

She frowned, obviously still uncomfortable with it. "Maybe, but it—"

"You don't owe me any explanations," Michael said.

She studied him. "Okay. What he said about your parents . . ."

"I don't discuss my parents, especially with someone I don't know," he interjected coldly. He didn't want tea and sympathy from Ivan's plain assistant.

Her mouth parted as if she wasn't sure what to say, then she closed it. "Well, you obviously don't need to know my thoughts, but I've worked with Ivan for a year. His personal assessments of people are less than astute, and he's truly a world-class prick."

She adjusted her glasses and walked away, leaving Michael to try to put the woman in a neat little box. He narrowed his eyes and tilted his head to one side. Something about her didn't fit.

Ivan and Patricia bid bon voyage from the *Queen Elizabeth 2*, and Katie moved into the Rasmussen mansion. She told herself not to get used to it. Katie had never slept in such luxurious surroundings except when she'd cared for her previous employer Lana Fitzpatrick during her final cancer-stricken weeks.

Lana had been odd, but so obscenely wealthy that no one cared. Katie had originally cleaned Lana's house. When Lana's personal assistant had left abruptly, Lana had temporarily moved Katie into the position. Temporary turned to permanent, and Katie still had tender feelings for the woman. Lana had taught her much, and she still missed her. Lana had been responsible for opening new doors to Katie, and in a crazy way had looked out for Katie after her death.

Katie supposed her upbringing with her unconventional

mother had prepared her for dealing with eccentric people. The problem with Katie's mother, however, had been that her eccentricity had caused a lot of trouble and heartache. Her mother had given birth to four children by four different fathers, and had lost custody of two of them due to her wacky ways. Katie still missed her sisters, but she knew they were in better homes.

She missed a lot of people, she told herself, shaking her head. But she didn't have time to wallow in it, she thought, sending up another silent thank-you to Lana. Whoever said *the rich are different from the rest of us* knew what they were talking about. In Philadelphia high society, it was a matter of pride to gain an employee as a result of the death of a well-established family. Katie didn't understand it. She just knew that Ivan and Patricia considered her a small badge of honor because of her employment association with one of the long-time matrons of Philadelphia society, Lana Fitzpatrick.

Katie ran her fingers over the fine cotton blue sateen duvet on the cherry queen-sized bed in her temporary room and pushed gently on the firm mattress. The cherry dresser and wardrobe gleamed from the fervent attention of a house cleaner. The lush white carpet gently cushioned her feet as she walked across it to glance out the window to the Rasmussens' meticulously manicured lawn. Her surroundings oozed comfort.

"Don't get used to it," she whispered, and picked up a pad of paper. It was time to meet Wilhemina for tea. They'd met formally and Katie had gotten an earful about Wilhemina, but she'd never had the opportunity to just sit down and talk with her except for the time she'd gone to the grocery store and bought Popsicles when Wilhemina had the flu.

As soon as Katie entered the lady's parlor, Wilhemina

immediately stood in gracious, but ridiculous splendor. She wore a chartreuse suit that appeared one size too small for Wilhemina's plump frame. Around her shoulders, she draped a fox boa, the animals connected mouth to tail. She capped off the ensemble with a black hat with silky fringe. The combination made Katie slightly nauseous, but she couldn't ignore the dejected vulnerability she sensed in Ivan's daughter. Something about Wilhemina evoked a feeling of protectiveness inside Katie that she usually reserved for her brother. Wilhemina knitted her fingers together uncertainly; her heavily made-up eyes darted away from Katie's gaze. "Hello, Katie. How do you do?"

Katie wondered why she felt ancient compared to Wilhemina when there was barely one year's difference between their ages. Unable to suppress a feeling of pity for Ivan's daughter, Katie crossed the room and shook Wilhemina's hand. "I'm fine, thank you. I'm glad I'm getting a chance to talk with you."

Wilhemina gave an uncertain smile. "Shall we sit for some tea?"

"Great, thank you. I'll pour," Katie said, pouring the tea from the sterling silver set and sinking onto the hard antique settee. Katie took a sip, then set down her cup. She opened her mouth to speak, but paused as she saw the most hideous creature on the planet enter the room.

"Chantal," Wilhemina said in delight to the Canadian hairless cat. She patted the seat beside her. "Come join us."

The only person in the household more attached to Chantal than Wilhemina was Ivan, and Katie knew Ivan's interest in the animal was purely financial. A rare breed, the cat was worth a fortune. Katie just didn't get it. The poor animal looked as if someone had taken a razor and shaved nearly every hair from its body. Unfortunately, Chantal's disposition didn't compensate for her appearance. The sight of the animal never failed to make her wince. She deliberately looked away.

"Wilhemina, have you been told about my assignment with you?"

Wilhemina bobbed her head, making the fringe on her hat dance. She absently stroked the cat. "Daddy said you're going to help me find a husband."

Try to help you find a husband, Katie thought, finding the assignment more daunting with each passing moment.

Wilhemina bit her lip. "I haven't had very good luck with men or matchmakers. This is embarrassing to say, but we've tried just about everything. I've worked with three professional dating services and all of them eventually quit. I went out on a few first dates, but there were only two men I went out with more than once. We found out one of them was a cross-dresser, but the absolute worst was the man who was being *paid* to date me. I also tried an on-line dating service, but the most promising prospect was in a penitentiary. I got the impression he was a guard, but it turned out he was incarcerated because of an armed robbery charge. I'm sure he was innocent just like he told me, but Daddy refused to let me continue to correspond with him."

Katie stifled a sigh. Wilhemina obviously didn't know that they were *all* innocent. "I know it's been difficult," she said, not wanting to linger on the disaster zone of Wilhemina's courtships. If Katie dwelt on the subject too long, she would throw in the towel before she got started. "I thought it would be a good idea for me to learn more about your likes and dislikes and your hobbies. That way, maybe we could find the best possible match for you."

Wilhemina gave her a blank look. "I don't really have a lot of hobbies. I took piano lessons, but I wasn't very good.

When I took horseback riding lessons, I fell off a lot. I like to volunteer." She bit her lip and lowered her voice. "I'm not pretty. Patricia mentioned plastic surgery."

"No," she said abruptly, her anger rushing to her head. She bit her lip to keep from calling Patricia a few choice names. "I think we need to focus on what kind of man you might like, and when you meet the right man, he will feel so lucky he'll have to pinch himself."

Wilhemina's eyes softened. "Daddy said you're kind and sensible. I'll never forget the Popsicles you brought me when I was sick." She paused and looked down. "I'm just not sure I can be very selective."

Katie digested Wilhemina's response and felt her stomach twist. She couldn't recall meeting a woman with lower self-esteem than Ivan's daughter, unless she counted her mother. She'd gotten the Popsicle tip from her mom, who had always given Katie and her sisters the frozen treats when they'd had sore throats. Katie fought an overwhelming mix of emotions about her mother, about Wilhemina, about herself. *Who was she to think she could find a good husband for Wilhemina when so many others had tried and failed?*

Katie thought of the hundred thousand dollars and her brother. Jeremy had special needs and it was up to her and nobody else to make sure those needs were met. Katie knew she had to try. She positioned her pen over her notepad. "Lots of women have bad experiences with men. It's obvious that you just haven't met the right one yet. I would still like to know more about you. What do you like?"

"I like food," Wilhemina confessed. "Too much."

Katie smiled. "What foods do you like best?"

"Anything chocolate and any kind of pie. I love pie." She slid her gaze away from Katie. "Patricia has made the cook swear not to prepare chocolate or pie while she and Daddy are gone."

Katie stopped midmotion with her pen. Patricia's ancestors may have come over on the *Mayflower*, but Patricia was a five-star witch. Katie tapped her pen thoughtfully on the notepad. "At one time or another, most people struggle with their diet," she said. "It's one of those goals people keep trying to regulate like exercise."

"You don't have to," Wilhemina said, her gaze taking in Katie's slim frame. "You're thin," she said in a softly accusing tone.

"Size isn't everything," Katie said, although her mother had repeatedly informed her that with men, size mattered. But that was a different matter. "What else do you like?"

"Animals. I like animals. I like music." Wilhemina paused, then leaned forward as if sharing a secret. "Don't tell Patricia, but I love country music."

Katie felt a sliver of amusement. "I won't tell. If you could have any kind of man for a husband, what would he be like?"

Seeming to hold her breath, Wilhemina locked gazes with Katie, and Katie could practically see a cauldron of secret wishes bubbling inside Ivan's daughter. She flexed her pen in preparation for a lengthy list.

"I want a man who wants me so much he can't live without me," Wilhemina said breathlessly.

Katie felt a lump in her throat at the fragility of Ivan's daughter. She hadn't expected their meeting to be so, well, emotional. Absently pushing her glasses up her nose, Katie tried to detach herself. It wasn't her job to get overly involved with Wilhemina. Her assignment was to find Wilhemina a husband. If fate was kind, she would accomplish her assignment and Wilhemina's husband would grow to love her.

"I understand that you've been invited to a cocktail party at the Rogers' home on Saturday," Katie ventured. "Have you thought about what you'd like to wear?"

Wilhemina shook her head, sending the fringe on her hat into a tizzy. "I usually just pick something out at the last minute. Like today, the suit is new, but the fox wrap belonged to my mother."

No disrespect to Wilhemina's deceased mother, but the fox wrap should have been buried with her. Katie nodded, but kept her mouth shut.

"And the hat belonged to my third stepmother, Maria. She was a flamenco dancer," Wilhemina said with a shy smile.

Katie nodded again. "I know you've had professional fashion consultations. Would you like to shop for something new to wear to the Rogers' party?"

"That would be fun. You'll get something too, won't you?" Wilhemina asked.

Confused, Katie shook her head. "I really don't need anything new."

"But you're going with me to the party, aren't you? Daddy said you would also be my companion." Wilhemina scrutinized Katie's olive dress. "You can't wear anything like that to the Rogers'."

Katie paused, stuck on the prospect of attending a high-society cocktail party. Fish out of water didn't begin to cover how she would feel. "I, uh, I had thought you would want to attend alone so you could mingle with the eligible men."

Wilhemina shook her head. "The only reason the Rogers

invited me is because they didn't know Daddy was going out of town."

Katie swallowed a groan. "I really hadn't planned—I'm not sure I'm prepared to attend the Rogers' cocktail party."

"Well, maybe we can have makeovers together. That would be fun," Wilhemina said, warming to the idea. "And I can lend you some of my accessories."

Katie bit back a moan. "Oh, I couldn't let you do that," she said for more than one reason. "Besides, we need to keep the focus on you since we're looking—"

"Excuse me," a male voice said from behind her. "Am I interrupting?"

Katie immediately tensed. Michael Wingate. *Yes, you're interrupting*, she wanted to say, but restrained herself. She turned to see him stride into the room, his hand outstretched toward Wilhemina.

"Miss Rasmussen, I don't believe we've met. Michael Wingate of Wingate Securities at your service."

Wilhemina's cheeks turned pink. "Pleasure to meet you, Mr. Wingate. Please call me Wilhemina."

"Wilhemina," he said with a gentle nod of deference, then cast a brief, curious glance at Katie. "Miss Collins."

Katie nodded, his curiosity making her uncomfortable. She noticed the perfect cut of his suit, perfect knot of his tie, and perfect confidence he oozed with every minute gesture. Her mother's voice whispered through her mind, *Now that's one man's trousers I wouldn't mind climbing inside.* The bawdy thought embarrassed her, and she snuffed out her mother's uncensored comments from her brain.

"Katie and I were just discussing the Rogers' party on Saturday night. I thought it would be fun if Katie got a makeover and went with me," Wilhemina said.

Katie felt Michael Wingate run his cool, dispassionate

gaze over her from head to toe and knew she didn't measure up to whatever his standard was. Not that she gave a tinker's damn.

"Excellent idea, Wilhemina, both for security purposes and for your comfort. I'm certain Miss Collins would be delighted to get a makeover with you. She'll need different clothing for a party at the Rogers'."

"Oh, and you'll be joining us, won't you?" Wilhemina asked.

Katie watched Michael's perfect composure slip a millimeter and felt an inordinate satisfaction. "Joining you for what?" he asked.

"For the cocktail party," Wilhemina said, brimming with enthusiasm. "It will make me feel safer to have a bodyguard with me, and it'll be so much more fun if all three of us go together."

"*Fun*," he echoed, rolling the word in his mouth as if it were foreign to him.

Katie would bet the concept of fun was foreign to Michael Wingate. Although she hadn't engaged in a great deal of fun during the last two years, she could at least identify it.

"I'm not sure my job assignment is intended for me to have fun," he said to Wilhemina, his jaw tight with a restraint that suggested his patience was being stretched.

"But I'd be much more comfortable if you would join Katie and me," Wilhemina said, a world of vulnerability in her eyes.

Katie watched Michael Wingate and waited. His confidence irritated her. His intensity bothered her in weird ways she didn't understand. His response to Wilhemina would determine exactly where Katie placed him on the prick scale for men.

*"Anyone can be a butterfly.
A butterfly is just a moth with eyeshadow."*
—SUNNY COLLINS'S WISDOM

Chapter 3

Michael looked into Wilhemina's guileless gaze and felt his *no* back up in his throat. It would be easier to kick a puppy.

"How can I say no?" Michael finally said. *How in hell could he refuse,* he wondered, tamping down the familiar rumble of frustration. He was caught between a rock and a hard place until Ivan returned.

Although Michael considered this assignment so frivolous it made his teeth ache, he had decided Ivan's bargain was worth the pain. Michael couldn't bear feeling his time was being wasted. He had too much to accomplish, too much to rebuild, he thought, a fuzzy vision of his father sliding through his mind like smoke. Pushing the image aside, Michael tried not to dwell on everything his father had lost all those years ago, but he couldn't deny he burned to regain at least a portion of it. Add to that his own professional disaster that would have buried plenty of men. Between a fiancée who had dumped him in his blackest hour and a partner who had double-crossed him, Michael had learned not to count on anyone. He had worked nearly twenty-four hours a day during the last four years to position his company for this kind of success. With a contract for Ivan's security business needs firmly under wraps in just months, Michael might be able to finally take a breath. Sometimes he wondered if he really wanted time to take a breath.

Wilhemina beamed at him, nodding her head and making the fringe on her ridiculous hat shimmy. Ivan's daughter was an unarmed amateur in the Philadelphia society scene where men and women wielded their tongues with the professional ease of hit men using a switchblade or Uzi. Wilhemina was unfashionable in both temperament and appearance. She would never be able to affect the cool required of the social elite.

Finding a husband for Ivan's daughter in Philadelphia would require a miracle handed down from God, and Michael seriously doubted Miss Collins was up to the challenge. Michael, however, had made certain his agreement with Ivan was not dependent on Miss Collins's success. Michael was merely responsible for Wilhemina's safety to the extent that her life was not threatened and to thoroughly inform her and Ivan of the background of all potential suitors.

Michael suspected his greatest challenge during the next two months would be to keep himself from leaping out the window of his antique-laden bedroom on the second floor from complete boredom. Michael had learned that keeping busy kept the ghosts away, the ghosts of his father and the loss. He wondered how in hell he would be able to keep busy during this insane assignment. Ivan had been unwilling to budge on the issue of Michael's residence. The man might come across like an asshole, but he was a pit bull where his daughter was concerned.

"Wilhemina," Michael said in a voice he reserved for good children. "I haven't had a chance to brief Miss Collins.

It won't take a moment, and I can talk to her in the office across the hall. Would you excuse us?"

"Of course," Wilhemina said. "I'll just drink my tea. Have you met Chantal yet?" she asked, moving her hand toward a cat that looked as if it had been skinned.

"This is the Canadian hairless," Michael said, keeping his tone as neutral as he could. Ivan had slipped the cat's protection into his contract at the last minute. If his colleagues knew he was not only heiress-sitting, he was also cat-sitting, he would be laughed off the east coast.

"Yes. Amazing, isn't she," Miss Collins said in the same neutral voice he had affected.

He saw a sliver of wry amusement in Miss Collins's gaze and felt the slightest click of a connection. She didn't think much of the cat either. They agreed on one thing. He just needed to make sure they agreed on a few others.

He bent to touch the animal, but the cat snarled. He pulled back. "Amazing," he repeated. "My thoughts exactly. If you'll excuse us, Wilhemina," he said, then glanced at Ivan's assistant. "Miss Collins."

He thought he spotted a trace of rebellion in the woman's eyes, but she turned her head before he had a chance to study her. Leading the way to the office, Michael stood inside the room and closed the door as soon as Miss Collins entered.

"I realize you have an ominous task in front of you," Michael began, pulling at his tie. "And desperation drives all of us to take insane action," he said darkly, because he believed Ivan's offer was insane. "But don't include me on your list of prospects for Wilhemina and don't encourage her to include me on her social outings."

Miss Collins's lips parted in surprise. She blinked, then drew a deep breath. "Mr. Wingate, I wouldn't have dreamed of including you on a list of prospects for Wilhemina. After meeting her, my top criterion for her husband would be kindness. As for her desire to include you on her outings, I have no control. If she feels more comfortable with her assigned bodyguard, I certainly wouldn't want to stop her."

Michael's attention hung on the slight edge of her voice when she'd mentioned kindness before she'd called him a bodyguard. The insult scored him. "I am not a bodyguard. I am the owner of Wingate Securities, a professional agency that specializes in commercial and computer security."

Miss Collins shrugged. "Just as I'm not ordinarily a companion or a matchmaker."

Michael felt his temperature rise. "You still don't understand. I will personally screen all of Wilhemina's marriage prospects, but I'll be conducting some of my own business while I stay at the Rasmussens' home. I employ bodyguards who can protect Wilhemina during her excursions."

Miss Collins nodded slowly. "What you're telling me is that you have more important things to do than be Wilhemina's bodyguard."

"Yes," he said, relieved the woman finally had comprehended him, although he couldn't help thinking his complete lack of relationships during the last year had done serious damage to his communication skills. He'd done his damnedest to make himself an island and had succeeded in all the ways that counted.

"That's fine," she said cheerfully. "I'll let you explain it to Wilhemina. It's far too complicated for me. Was there anything else you wanted?"

Michael ground his teeth. He knew part of the reason Miss Collins got on his nerves was because she'd heard Ivan's take on his parents. He ruthlessly pushed aside his discomfort for the moment. "You'll need to supply me with the names of your prospects if or when you find them along with advance notice of Wilhemina's schedule."

"No problem," Miss Collins said. "Now if you'll excuse me—"

"One more thing," he said, her breezy attitude grating on him. "Even if you can't find anyone for Wilhemina, I still intend to get Ivan's business. This is no game for me."

In one blink, the glint in her eyes shifted from contrary to deadly serious. "Then we agree. This is important to me too," she said crisply.

Her resolve echoed inside him with such force that he had the feeling he had just met his match in the determination department.

"I need to get back to Wilhemina. I'm sure I'll see you later," she told him in a dismissive tone that indicated she was as thrilled with their enforced association as he was.

Feeling her anger burn high in her cheeks, Katie marched back into the parlor. "Self-serving, superior sonofabitch," she muttered under her breath. She felt her mother's drawling perspective ooze through her. *Damn shame. A fine specimen of masculinity until he opens his mouth. If he's gonna open his mouth, he should make use of it in a totally different manner.*

Katie rolled her eyes and quelled her mother's voice. She bit her lip and tried to calm herself as she spotted Wilhemina stuffing two cookies into her mouth. This would be worth the trouble, she told herself. It wouldn't be easy, but it would be worth it.

Wilhemina looked up at Katie with a guilty gaze and gulped down the remainder of the cookies. She followed with a quick swallow of tea. "Did Mr. Wingate brief you?"

"Yes," she said, certain his briefs were constantly in a twist.

"Isn't he gorgeous," Wilhemina said with a sigh.

As long as he doesn't open his mouth, Katie thought and made a noncommittal sound.

"Such a shame about his family," Wilhemina said and made a clucking sound.

Curious despite herself, Katie took the lure. "His family?"

"Patricia told me the Wingates used to live on Society Hill, but Michael's father lost all their money to poor investments and they were ruined."

That sounded like the kind of information Patricia would be eager to impart.

"If that weren't bad enough, after he lost all the money, Michael's father killed himself, so there was no life insurance for Michael or his mother. Patricia says his mother has been mentally unstable ever since."

Katie felt a drop of sympathy for the man. Although her mother had never been declared insane, her actions had yielded a truckload of embarrassment for Katie when she'd hit adolescence. "How old was Mr. Wingate when he lost his father?"

"Eight or nine, I think. He was bounced around between distant relatives and foster homes. Then he went into the military," she said, her gaze turning dreamy. "I bet he looked great in a uniform."

"Looks aren't everything," Katie said, dismissing the disturbing Michael Wingate from her mind. She had more important fish to fry. "You want to marry a man who will treat you well."

Wilhemina nodded. "Patricia says money and breeding

are the top two qualities of a good husband, and between the two, money can overcome breeding."

Katie stifled a sigh. Lovely advice from the *Mayflower* barracuda, who wanted Wilhemina out of the house.

Katie leaned forward and took Wilhemina's hand. "No matter what anyone has told you about what kind of man you should choose as your husband, you'll need to combine the very best of your heart and head to make your decision. After all, you are the one who will have to live with your choice."

Wilhemina nodded again, her eyes solemn as the ridiculous fringe on her hat swayed. "Do you really think you're going to be able to find someone to marry me? I'm not like a lot of the people who attend these parties."

Try as she might, Katie couldn't keep that signed check for one hundred thousand dollars in sight when Wilhemina's vulnerability might as well have been placed before her on a tray. "I think it might be a very good thing that you're not like a lot of the people you meet at the parties."

Two days later, Michael finished making notes on his laptop for a security proposal for a midsize electronics company, then turned to write the monthly check for his mother's care. He felt a slight twist of guilt. It had been a while since he'd visited her, but she had started calling him by his father's name, and Michael could take a lot, but not that. He told himself to treat his visits to her as if they were a business appointment, but he'd never quite succeeded. His mother's mental problems represented one more reason why he shouldn't depend on anyone but himself.

The sound of feminine giggles floated up from the bottom of the stairs. The sound was a welcome distraction from his dark thoughts. He leaned back in his leather chair and shook off the trapped sensation that had haunted him since he had moved into the green room. Heavy cherry furniture topped with knickknacks crowded the large room. If it were left to him, he would remove a third of the furniture and all of the objects d'clutter. That response, he was sure, was generated by his days spent in the military where he'd learned the true meaning of minimalistic decorating.

The giggling continued and he recalled that today was makeover day with the legendary Fernando for Wilhemina and Miss Collins. What a challenge the man had faced, the Mt. Everest of makeovers, Michael thought and rose, giving in to his curiosity about the results.

He made his way down the stairs and found Wilhemina and Miss Collins chatting in the foyer. Wilhemina's makeup was much more subtle, and she wore a pink dress with some sort of jacket that concealed her penchant for cookies. Unfortunately, the effect was somewhat destroyed by a hat with a large red feather.

Miss Collins's hair was still upswept in a tight twist, her eyes still shielded by black-framed glasses. Her dress, though a drab pale gray in color, fit her frame more closely, and Michael wasn't entirely surprised to learn that the woman was more curvy than lumpy. He remembered how small her waist had felt in that closet. Not only that, the hem of the dress stopped just above the knee, accenting the legs he'd already assessed the first time he'd seen her.

"Good afternoon, ladies," he said. "Did you enjoy your makeovers with Fernando?"

"Oh, yes," Wilhemina said. "Fernando was fabulous, but we did have a few disagreements with him."

"Really?" he said, placing mental bets on the areas of disagreement.

"He didn't like my hat," Wilhemina said. "He wanted Katie to wear her hair down and he chose a different color for her dress and suggested different glasses frames."

Katie shrugged. "He was too flamboyant for me, but if Wilhemina's happy, that's what is important."

"And I am happy," Wilhemina said. "Two new outfits. I'm taking them upstairs to find hats to go with each of them. My big decision is which to wear on Saturday night." She smiled. "Ta ta for now."

Wilhemina swept past him up the stairs in a swirl of designer perfume. He watched the feather on her hat bob along the hallway. He turned to Miss Collins. "So Fernando couldn't get her to ditch the hat?"

Miss Collins shook her head. "It belonged to her mother. It would have been a kindness for someone to burn the collection, but apparently no one had the heart."

"And Fernando couldn't get you to let down your hair," he said, curious. "Afraid of change?"

She slid a sideways glance at him and moved away from the stairwell. "The makeover was for Wilhemina's benefit. I was just along for her comfort."

"But it would have been a great opportunity for you to—"

He paused at the frosty glance she threw him. Her mouth tightened and she led him into a small office.

Turning to face him, she lifted her chin. "Mr. Wingate, my focus is helping Wilhemina find a man. Superficial self-improvement efforts for myself are way down the list."

Michael shrugged. "You could consider it a perk for taking on the mission-near-impossible."

Her eyes flashed with anger. "I don't consider it a mission-near-impossible. I believe Wilhemina has many good qualities."

"Not the least of which is the fact that her father has almost as much money as God," Michael said.

"Wilhemina has other good qualities. She has a good—" She broke off with a sigh and shook her head. "I don't expect you to understand. You don't need to understand," she muttered under her breath as if she were speaking to herself instead of him. She met his gaze. "You requested a list of prospects. I have one," she said, and pulled a sheet of paper from her desk.

"Already," he said, impressed at the number of names on the neatly typed list. Miss Collins definitely wasn't letting any grass grow under her feet. He pulled out a pen to eliminate three of the names. "Where did you get these names?"

"These men will be attending the cocktail party on Saturday. I got the guest list through a professional connection," she said.

He raised an eyebrow. "Professional connection?"

Miss Collins lifted her chin. "I'm acquainted with the head housekeeper at the Rogers' house, and the head housekeeper is good friends with the social secretary."

Michael's lips twitched at Miss Collins's prickly attitude, but he couldn't fault her resourcefulness. She was definitely going to need it. He crossed out two more names and returned the list to her.

Miss Collins frowned. "Why did you mark off these men?"

"The first one gambles, the second is snorting his inheritance up his nose, the third doesn't prefer women. Ivan would never allow the fourth, because his father was once Ivan's rival. The fifth is getting out of rehab for the third time."

Miss Collins gave a thoughtful sigh. "Why the question mark beside Jason Page?"

"Gut feeling," he said. "Rumor. Where there's smoke . . ."

Miss Collins gave him a look of disbelief. "I'm supposed to eliminate a candidate because of your gut feeling or an unsubstantiated rumor? You'll have to do better than that."

Michael shrugged. "When something doesn't smell right to me, it's usually rotten under the surface. You should trust me on this."

"Trust you," she repeated, as if the concept was completely foreign to her. "I think it would be best if we stick to facts."

Her attitude got under his skin. Who was she to call his integrity into question? "I'm not crazy about this arrangement, but the job will be easier if we cooperate with each other."

"I agree," she said. "But you need to understand that I'm not going to roll over on a prospect just because you have an unexplained case of indigestion. You do your job and I'll do mine, and we'll get along just fine."

He heard the barest trace of an accent in her voice as she left him catching a whiff of her soft, elusive scent. Some kind of soap, he decided, because it wasn't strong enough to be a perfume. Fresh and clean with a hint of something darker, almost sensual. Sensual? He snorted at the impossibility. With the tight bun and cold attitude, Miss Collins was clearly a man-hater. She was probably the kind who would cut off a guy's genitals in his sleep. But the accent niggled at him. He narrowed his eyes. He couldn't quite put his finger on that trace of an accent, but it definitely wasn't Pennsylvania.

Two days later, Katie stood next to a marble column in the shadows at the Rogers' elaborate poolside cocktail party. Lily pads floated in the pool, citronella candles ensconced in decorative holders warded off encroaching mosquitoes, liquor and champagne flowed freely, and tables covered with crisp white cloths groaned under the weight of hors d'oeuvres, desserts, and ice sculptures of swans.

Katie didn't really care about the decor or the food. She was much more interested in the fact that Jason Page had given Wilhemina his undivided attention for the last thirty minutes. Katie felt a sliver of hope. Even if Jason didn't work out, his attentiveness gave Katie a reason to believe that finding a husband for Wilhemina might not be so impossible after all.

If only she'd been able to talk her out of the red hat.

"You might want to see if you can coax Wilhemina into talking with another prospect. I still don't feel good about Jason Page," Michael said in a low voice as he joined her.

Katie felt her stomach give a quick twist. She didn't want Michael to be right. "Any additional facts on Jason?" she asked.

He crossed his arms over his chest and leaned against the column. "Not yet, but my gut hasn't steered me wrong."

"I'll address your concerns when you have facts," Katie said, continuing to watch over Wilhemina. "She looks pleased and almost at ease. I'm not going to interrupt them just because you have some feelings you can't back up with facts."

"Don't say I didn't warn you. You couldn't talk her out of the hat?"

Katie stifled a sigh. "I tried, but she's very attached to the collection. I think it's like always having someone with her who loves her. This one was given to her by her second stepmother. At least it's smaller."

"It looks like she could carry water in it," Michael muttered.

Katie frowned. Michael's evaluation might be true, but

he didn't have to say it. "But the black suit with the trendy flower pin looks wonderful on her. Jason obviously agrees," she said, hoping that would silence Michael. The man had been like an irritating, well-dressed shadow all evening.

"Speaking of dresses, is there a duller color?" he asked, looking pointedly at her light gray shift.

"I'm not sure," Katie said with a secret smile of satisfaction. "But if I find one, I'll be certain to buy it."

"I have to ask. You wear your hair so tightly wrapped. Does it hurt your head?"

Katie closed her eyes at his intrusive question. What business was it of his how she wore her hair? "You must be extremely bored if you're commenting on my hairstyle. Many people dress to make up for their personal insecurities. I've never had that problem," she told him, and deliberately ran her gaze over him from his perfectly knotted tie, down his perfectly cut Brooks Brothers suit, to his perfectly shined leather shoes. She wanted to tell him where to stick his attitude, but counted to ten. She glanced at Wilhemina and saw that Jason was no longer by her side. "Excuse me while I speak with Wilhemina."

Her mother's voice echoed through her mind as she made her way to Wilhemina. *Such a shame. The man looks damn good until he starts talking. Maybe a good blow job would improve his disposition. Never met a man who didn't smile after getting a thorough French kiss on his—*

Katie mentally cut her mother off. "And I'm sure you kissed just about every man you met," she muttered under her breath and dismissed her.

Wilhemina's gaze met hers and Katie saw the woman's eyes sparkle. Katie smiled. "Are you enjoying yourself with Jason Page?"

"Yes," she said, brimming with excitement. "He asked

me to join him at his family's lake house tomorrow. He said he wanted to get some more champagne for me. I'm so excited I need to use the bathroom."

Katie smothered a chuckle. "Then you should go," she said, guiding Wilhemina toward the terrace.

"But I don't want to lose him," Wilhemina said, biting her lip as she trotted beside Katie.

"I'm sure he can wait long enough for you to use the rest room," Katie told her, leading her down a hallway toward the Rogers' powder room. Urging Wilhemina inside, Katie stood outside the door like a sentry. She crossed her fingers that Michael Wingate was wrong.

In seconds, Wilhemina appeared, her lipstick hastily reapplied. "A little too much," Katie said and grabbed a tissue from her purse. Another guest squeezed past her and Wilhemina, leaving them in the darkened hallway. "I need more light," Katie said. "Let's try somewhere else."

Katie wound through the hallway and took another turn. She opened a door and pulled Wilhemina inside.

"Where are we?" Wilhemina asked.

Katie shrugged and glanced around. "I don't know. It looks like a study. The important thing is that it has light," she said, switching on two lamps. She scrutinized Wilhemina's mouth again. It was a mess.

"How bad is it?" Wilhemina asked, clearly a bundle of nerves.

"Not that bad," Katie fibbed and began to wipe one corner. She heard the low voices of men talking to each other outside the door.

"Why are you spending so much time with the Rasmussen cow?" one man asked.

Katie paused midwipe. She looked into Wilhemina's eyes

and saw that the woman had overheard the comment. The vibrant spark dimmed.

"Wilhemina's nice," another man said. "And lonely."

"Are you that hard up?" the first man asked.

"Things are a little tight for me right now. I lost a ton in the stock market, and my old man refuses to give me any more money."

"So what you really want is some of daddy Ivan's spare change?"

"He's got plenty to spare. I figure if I pay Wilhemina some special attention, she might feel generous."

"How special? You're not really gonna take her to bed, are you?" The man made a sound of disgust. "Her father might be loaded, but she's a dog, pure and simple."

Katie watched Wilhemina's eyes fill with disillusionment and disappointment. Her stomach twisted with a combination of empathy and anger. Ivan was such a jerk Katie rarely felt a drop of sympathy for him, but Wilhemina was different.

"With the right motivation, a lot of Scotch, and the lights turned out, it won't matter what she looks like."

Katie watched the light go completely out in Wilhemina's gaze and felt something inside her snap. She whipped open the door and looked straight into the handsome weak-chinned face of Jason Page. "I'm afraid you overestimate more than your charm and abilities, Mr. Page." She pulled his glass of champagne from his hand and tossed the contents into his crotch. His eyes rounded and he yelled in shock. He immediately covered his pants with his hands.

Her heart pounding a mile a minute, Katie caught sight of several curious guests drawing near. "Omigoodness, Jason, it looks like you didn't make it to the bathroom in time," she said loudly. "And I'm so sorry to hear of that defect with your private part. Incontinence must be embarrassing enough, but one inch—" She made a sound of false sympathy. "How terrible for you. We should go, Wilhemina," she said, grabbing Wilhemina's arm.

Katie felt Wilhemina's stare of wonder as she dragged Ivan's daughter down the hall.

"Bitch!" Jason Page called after her.

Wilhemina gasped as they rounded the corner. "Did you hear what he called you?"

Torn between fury and shock at her own actions, Katie shook her head. "I've been called worse."

*"I'm a feminist. I just believe a good push-up bra
has done more for me than Congress has."*
—SUNNY COLLINS'S WISDOM

Chapter 4

Wilhemina rode home in her father's Mercedes caught between a mixture of misery and awe. With the exception of a Slavic housekeeper her father had briefly employed, she'd never seen a female cut a man to ribbons the way Katie had. It had been a glorious sight to behold. She had wanted to tell Michael Wingate all about it, but Katie had signaled her to keep silent.

The silence allowed her to mull over all Jason Page and his friend had said about her. *The Rasmussen cow. Dog.* Jason Page had been so charming, so attentive. He hadn't even seemed to mind the story of her hat. Her stomach rolled and she covered her face. He had just been playing her for a fool. He only wanted her father's money. She would never find a husband at this rate. Although, if she ever trusted someone, she would tell what she really wanted even more than a husband. She wanted a baby. She wanted a child to nurture and to love. A child wouldn't care that she was different, and Wilhemina was convinced that she might not be able to do a lot of things, but she could love and protect a child.

But she wasn't sure how she could make that happen.

Her stomach turned again, and she wished she had

thought to swipe a dessert from the Rogers' table before she'd left.

She just wasn't cut out for the Philadelphia crowd. For years, people had been trying to wedge her into clothes that didn't fit and into crowds of people that didn't want her. At the best times, she'd felt like a stranger. At the worst times, she'd felt like a failure.

Tonight, she felt like both.

Michael drove her father's car past the gate, then held the door for her and Katie to get out of the car. The humidity of an impending storm hung in the air. She felt Michael's curious gaze and would have loved to give him an earful, but Katie still looked angry enough to spit glass.

"Thank you, Michael," Wilhemina murmured and allowed Katie to guide her up the steep steps and through the heavy door that bore her father's family crest.

She stepped inside and Katie led her up the stairs to her room. "I'm sorry you had such an unfortunate experience with Jason Page, but there are many others on my list. I've arranged for you to attend another party on Monday night at—"

Alarm welled up inside her. "Oh, no. I can't face them again so soon. Not after tonight."

Katie paused and met Wilhemina's gaze. "Are you embarrassed because of what I did to Jason?"

"Oh, no. I just feel completely embarrassed and totally foolish because I believed he was interested in me." She cringed at the humiliation dripping through her veins. "I'm sure I've been this embarrassed before. I just don't want to remember when. I can't face seeing those people again, and I know some of the same ones will be wherever you're sending me."

"When you fall off a horse, the best thing to do is get right back on," Katie said firmly.

Wilhemina's stomach churned. "I think cookies would be better for me right now. I hid two packages in my room before Patricia and Daddy left. I may eat both of them tonight."

Katie sighed, and her eyes filled with sympathy. Wilhemina appreciated the kindness, but she was tired of people feeling sorry for her. Her throat closed up and she felt her eyes burn with the threat of tears. "Please don't pity me," she whispered.

Katie bit her lip. "You are a good person, Wilhemina. Any man in his right mind would be lucky to have you. You deserve to be treated much better than you were tonight." Katie paused. "Which is why you and I are going to have a margarita party."

"Margarita?" Wilhemina echoed. "I don't believe I've ever had one."

"Then it's definitely time," Katie said. "You get into your most comfortable pajamas, pick out your favorite music, and I'll be back up lickety-split."

"Lickety-split," Wilhemina echoed at the slight drawl she heard in Katie's voice.

Katie's eyes shifted, and Wilhemina couldn't quite read the expression. "An expression my mother occasionally used. She's dead," Katie said before Wilhemina could ask.

"I'm sorry," Wilhemina automatically said.

"That's okay. Dying hasn't kept her from voicing her opinions," Katie muttered and turned away, leaving Wilhemina in a state of confusion.

Fifteen minutes later and dressed in a nightshirt, Katie thumped Wilhemina's door with her foot while she juggled the tray of margaritas and water. The strains of Lee Ann

Womack plaintively singing about her latest heartbreak wafted through the door.

Wilhemina opened the door to her suite and gaped at her. "You look pretty with your hair down. You should wear it that way more often."

Katie shook her head and set the tray down on an antique mahogany table beside a chaise longue. "I like it up. Keeps it out of my way." She picked up one of the margaritas and presented it to Wilhemina. "Try it. It will turn your head around," Katie said.

Wilhemina took a big gulp and her eyes widened. "That's strong," she said, licking the salted rim of the glass. "But good. I like the salt."

Scanning the room as she picked up her own drink, Katie noticed a half package of cookies already demolished. Wilhemina must be feeling pretty miserable, and Katie couldn't blame her. She also, however, didn't have the luxury of time to allow Wilhemina to fall into a funk. Katie was still determined to find a man for Ivan's daughter, and she was not looking forward to admitting to Michael Wingate that he had been correct about Jason Page. She always felt like she had to be on her toes around him. He seemed to enjoy goading her, and his superiority drove her to the edge. She was starting to have wild fantasies about mud splattering his perfect suits and shoes. She would love to see a gravy stain on his tie.

Darlin', if you're gonna have fantasies about that man, I can make a few suggestions, Katie heard her mother say, and rolled her eyes. *Shut up, Mom.*

Katie took a long drink from her margarita and placed a glass of ice water on a coaster on the antique table. "Sip some water every now and then. It'll keep you from becoming dehydrated," she said and noticed Wilhemina looking at an old photograph of a beautiful brunette. "Who's that?"

"My mother," Wilhemina said. "Isn't she lovely? I wish I looked like her."

Katie looked at the photograph and Wilhemina. The two bore very little resemblance. "I think you've got her eyes," she said, telling herself the tiny stretch of truth wouldn't hurt anyone. "And maybe her smile."

Wilhemina beamed and swallowed the rest of her first margarita. "I wish I'd known her. She was the love of Daddy's life. He waited five years before he remarried."

Katie felt a twist of sympathy. "She died when you were born?"

Wilhemina nodded sadly, and the two women sat without talking for several moments. Katie offered Wilhemina a second margarita and continued to sip her own. She hadn't thought of her father in a long time. Her mother had always described him as her knight in shining armor, but her mother hadn't always exhibited the best judgment in men.

"I never knew my father," Katie slowly revealed. Wilhemina wouldn't use the information against her, she thought.

"I can't imagine what life would have been like without my father. What was your mother like?"

She was a slut.

Katie swallowed the revelation along with her margarita. "She was very pretty. A lot of men were attracted to her."

She gave birth to four children fathered by four different men.

She bit her tongue and felt a faint twinge in her heart. For all her mother's loose living, she'd always tried to make Katie believe she was special. Her mother had even gone so far as to tell her she had magical powers. Katie could have used a wand more than once during the last couple of years.

Once upon a time . . . Katie heard her mother's voice play through her mind. She looked at Wilhemina and sighed. What could it hurt? It was clear Wilhemina could use a fairy tale tonight to offset the ugly reality blow she'd suffered earlier. "Every night, my mother used to tell me a story about a little girl who felt lonely."

Wilhemina eased back into the chaise longue. "What was the story?" she asked. Katie looked into her trusting eyes and wondered if she'd ever had one-tenth of Wilhemina's capacity for trust.

"The little girl lived in a trai—" Trailer. She broke off, deciding to edit the story for Wilhemina's benefit. "The little girl lived in a castle and she often felt as if she didn't have a friend in the world. Every night, the little girl would make a wish on a star that someday she would find someone to love. She grew older, but she still lived in the castle. And every night, she made a wish before she went to sleep. One morning, she woke up and left the castle. She traveled to a faraway kingdom and saw new and exciting sights. During her journey, she found a knight wounded on the side of the road. Although she was a little afraid of him, she was more afraid that he would die if she didn't take care of him. So she rode with him to his castle and nursed him back to health."

Wilhemina swallowed the last of her margarita and closed her eyes to the sound of Katie's story. She wondered if wishing on a star would help her. She heard a roll of thunder. The storm must have finally hit. Her mind meandered in lovely contentment. "Where was the faraway kingdom?" she asked, feeling drowsy and woozy.

"Texas," Katie admitted with an edge of amusement in her voice. "My mother was from Texas."

"Texas," Wilhemina repeated, conjuring visions of cattle and rodeos. "He must have been a cowboy knight."

"Yes," Katie softly said.

"What was the rest of the story?" Wilhemina asked, giving in to the relaxed, carefree feelings that oozed through her.

"The knight fell in love with the girl and he told her that he had been wishing on a star every night of his life for her."

"Oh, that's wonderful," Wilhemina said, smiling.

"And they lived happily ever after," Katie said.

"And had wonderful babies," Wilhemina murmured, because more than anything, more than she wanted a man, she wanted a baby. She knew she wouldn't feel useless if she brought another life into the world and nurtured it and loved it with all her heart.

Katie watched Wilhemina breathe evenly as sleep took over her. She felt conflicted about their little margarita party. The tequila may have been fine, but Katie wasn't certain it was a good idea to nourish wishes wrapped in fairy tales. Real life, she'd learned, was much more harsh.

Sighing, she rose and turned off the CD player and heard a loud crack of thunder. She noticed Wilhemina remained asleep and smiled. The margaritas must have done the trick.

Thunder rolled again, and the lights flickered. Katie covered Wilhemina with a light blanket and loaded the tray with the empty glasses. She turned off the light and crept down the stairs.

Halfway down, another loud crack of thunder split the air. The lights flickered and went dead. Black silence followed. Katie's heart pounded and she took a calming breath. Just a storm, she told herself. Just thunder. Staying close to the wall, she took slow, careful steps down the long staircase. Praying she wouldn't trip, she walked down the hall-way to the kitchen. She pushed open the door with her elbow. All she wanted to do was set the tray on the closest counter.

Suddenly a hand whipped around her waist. Another covered her mouth. The glasses on her tray toppled, but she kept a firm grip. She felt a man's hot breath on her cheek and tried to scream, but his hand prevented it.

"Who are you?" he demanded in a low voice, his hand searching her abdomen, then grazing the underside of her breast.

Instinct took over. Katie bit hard into the man's palm and jabbed his shin with her heel. He released her with an oath and she plunged forward.

"What the hell—"

Katie recognized Michael Wingate's voice and felt a strange relief. "Mr. Wingate?" she said into the darkness.

Silence followed. "Miss Collins?"

The lights flickered on and she blinked. Michael Wingate, dressed in lounging pants that dipped below his navel and wearing a scowl on his face designed to make her cower, stood before her in half-naked splendor. His hair was deliciously sleep-mussed, his chest a distracting display of tanned skin over taut muscle. If Katie didn't know better, she would swear her mother let out a wolf whistle.

She felt his gaze travel from the top of her head down-ward, taking in her eyes minus the heavy black frames that usually protected her. His eyes nearly burned a hole in her sleep shirt where her nipples stood against the cotton. She was helpless to cover herself as she held the tray. His gaze continued a journey of discovery over her hips and legs all the way down to her toes.

Pushing aside her odd jittery feeling, she stomped her

foot in frustration. "Why do you keep doing this? Quit grabbing me!"

He glanced at his bleeding hand and swore. "You bit me," he said in amazement.

"You groped me," she retorted.

He met her gaze. "I wouldn't have groped you if I hadn't thought you were an intruder."

"An intruder carrying a tray?" she said, setting the tray down on the counter. She wrapped her trembling arms around herself.

He narrowed his eyes at her. "It was pitch-black. I couldn't see the tray." He paused a half beat and gave a slight incredulous shake of his head. "You look a helluva lot better in a nightshirt in the middle of the night than you look in a dress in the middle of the day."

"That's interesting. You must be charm-free twenty-four hours a day."

"I was paying you a compliment," he said quietly. "You're pretty."

Katie felt her heart give an odd jolt. "Oh, thank you," she said, still not quite certain she believed him.

He opened his mouth, then seemed to chuckle to himself. "I heard about your little exchange with Jason Page."

Katie didn't think she could stand to hear *I told you so.* "Who told you?"

"Personal connection," he said vaguely. "Sharp tongue when the moment calls for it. I'm trying to figure out the accent. It's from somewhere below the Mason-Dixon line. Where are you from, Miss Collins?" he asked in a velvet voice as he moved toward her.

Katie felt a trickle of perspiration run down her back. "Nowhere important. Remember I'm nobody important to you."

"But I'm a curious man, and I like getting answers to my questions."

"You like getting paid for getting answers. Believe me, no one is going to pay you for getting answers about me. It's been an interesting evening, but I need to go to bed. I'm up early tomorrow to run an errand," she said, and brushed past him.

His hand shot out to stop her. "Hey, wait. What about Wilhemina? She's not gonna be in great shape tomorrow."

Katie glared meaningfully at Michael's hand on her arm. "Wilhemina only had two margaritas. She should be fine. I always take Sundays off. It's in my contract. Tomorrow is no exception."

Michael released her, and Katie breathed again.

"But—"

"Good night, Mr. Wingate," she said, and fled to her bedroom.

The next morning, Katie woke up knowing she would see her brother today. Every life had a purpose, and Katie had concluded that her purpose was Jeremy. She took the train to a town forty-five miles away from the heart of Philadelphia. Then she hopped on a bus, which carried her three more miles. She walked another mile and a half. The weather was kind after the storm from last night. Springtime in Pennsylvania. The dogwoods bloomed and the trees and lawns were beginning to turn green.

Rain, snow, sunshine, or bitter cold, she made the walk every Sunday. She didn't mind it today. With the sun on her shoulder, and with each step she took, she shook off the cares and craziness of the Rasmussens and moved toward her goal.

She made a turn down a long paved narrow driveway and

saw the old house in the distance. The large house with the rambling front porch reminded her of a sturdy elderly woman determined to retain her usefulness.

The house was a school for the hearing impaired.

Both home and learning institution to twenty active children with special needs, the school was loaded with the latest electronic technology for the hearing impaired and staffed by professionals who taught her brother everything she couldn't, such as how to read lips and sign. It was one of the best schools of its kind and Katie was never certain how she would afford the next semester. She would have tried to visit Jeremy more often, but the teachers had gently informed her that unexpected visitors created excitement, and excitement wreaked havoc on the structure the residents desperately needed.

Spotting a brown-haired boy on the front steps, Katie quickened her pace. Her heart lifted at the sight of her brother. Jeremy represented everything good that was possible in a world full of disappointments. He thought she visited him out of the goodness of her heart. What Jeremy didn't realize was that she needed their visits, perhaps more than he did. She needed to see the one good thing in her life to keep her going. She needed to see Jeremy.

She stepped into the yard and his ten-year-old blue eyes met hers. Grinning from ear to ear, he jumped up from the porch and raced toward her. He flew into her arms and she closed her eyes at his sweet, familiar scent. Her heart twisted as he clung to her.

He looked up at her face, his gaze searching hers. Excitement mingled with distress in his eyes. "I heard Mama talking to me again last night."

Katie's eyes burned with tears because she knew her brother was nearly deaf from the accident that had taken her mother's life. Both Katie's world and Jeremy's world had changed in the explosion that had occurred two years ago. Using sign language more as practice for herself than for him because he was determined to master reading lips, she moved her fingers to reassure him. "It's okay, sweetheart," she signed, admitting to her brother something she would tell no one else in the universe. "She talks to me too."

Chapter 5

Frowning, Jeremy tugged her hair loose from the tight knot. "It's ugly that way," he said.

She chuckled. "That's the idea," she said, slowly signing her words. "I don't want to be noticeable at my job."

"It works," he said, hooking his arm through hers and pulling her along for a walk. "Have you gotten my birthday present yet?"

"Your birthday? You have a birthday soon?" she teased, knowing perfectly well Jeremy's birthday was just a few weeks away. "What was it you said you wanted? A football? Was it a bike?"

He gave her a playful shrug. "You know I want a new video computer game." He paused and looked at her earnestly. "Is it too expensive?"

Her heart broke a little. Jeremy shouldn't have to be concerned about money. She shook her head. "Not at all. What kind of cake do you want?"

"Chocolate with lots of icing. And ice cream with gummi worms," he added.

She wrinkled her nose. "Sounds gross, but you're the boss, at least for that day. How are your classes going?"

"Ms. Kimball says I'm her Speedy Gonzalez except for

signing." He stomped his toe into the dirt. "I want to read lips."

His diction was nearly perfect, she noticed. Katie had needed to learn a lot about Jeremy's disability, and she'd learned that one of Jeremy's advantages was that his speech was normal because he'd spent years talking before he'd lost his hearing. Just after the accident two years ago, he had tended to yell, but he'd learned to control his volume.

"Sign language is a backup. Everyone can use a backup," she said, squeezing his shoulder. "What did Mama say to you?"

"She sang 'You Are My Sunshine,' " he said and rubbed his stomach. "I'm hungry."

Her heart twisted. Her mother had sung the same song to her often at bedtime. Katie headed back to the porch. Jeremy wasn't saying anything, but she could feel his turmoil. It was tough being a boy trying to learn how to be a man, especially when you've lost just about everything.

She looked down at him and carefully signed at the same time she spoke. "Would you like to bake cookies?"

"You just asked me if I'd like to bake a newspaper. Priss, your signing really stinks."

Chagrinned, Katie frowned. She clearly had a long way to go with signing. "Newspaper? I meant to ask about cookies."

"I know because I was watching your mouth."

"Smarty pants. Did you know that you are the bravest boy in the world?"

He met her gaze with innocent eyes as old as time. "Does that mean you'll get me the computer game, Priss?" he asked craftily.

She swatted him and laughed. He was the only one she allowed to call her Priss. "We'll see. Birthdays are all about surprises," she said, even though she'd bought the game just this past week.

The rest of the day flew. Jeremy engaged her in a cookie dough fight that required extensive cleanup and they played computer games. He stomped her every time except one, and she was pretty sure he'd let her win that time. A few of his friends joined in the fun. His popularity with the other students eased some of her worry for him. She barely caught the last bus a mile and a half from the school and replayed the treasured moments all the way back to Society Hill. Being with Jeremy made her feel like a real person, and she often felt she had a tougher time leaving him than he had waving good-bye.

Katie noticed the interested gaze of a man on the other side of the aisle. He smiled and she remembered she needed to pull her hair back. When the train pulled into the station, she jumped out and slipped into a ladies' room to face the mirror. She quickly fixed her hair, plopped her glasses on her nose, and dodged raindrops during the last quarter mile to the Rasmussens' home. She walked through the door and Michael Wingate immediately greeted her.

"We have a crisis," he said.

Instead of a suit, she noticed he wore jeans that faithfully covered his hips and powerful thighs and a black pullover shirt emphasized his broad shoulders. Her stomach took a strange dip. The casual clothes better matched the raw, rugged look in his eyes.

Crisis. Her brain kicked in along with panic. "Wilhemina? Did something happen to Wilhemina?"

He shook his head. "Worse. That animal they call a cat got out."

Katie winced. "Uh-oh. She catches colds easily."

"Wilhemina wants to go look for her."

Katie shook her head. "Wilhemina catches colds easily too," she said and didn't like the look in his eye. "Don't say it. Wilhemina is much nicer than that cat. Even you have to agree."

He shrugged. "Just make sure Wilhemina stays inside. I'm heading out to find Chantal now. Any places she particularly likes?"

"The trees in the backyard and the next-door neighbor's sandbox."

He grunted and left. Katie quickly sped up the stairs and knocked on Wilhemina's door. It took a couple of moments, but Wilhemina finally cracked the door. "Yes?" Her eyes rounded. "Oh, good. It's you. Chantal is missing, so I have to go look for her."

"It's dark and getting nasty out there. Mr. Wingate has already left to find her."

Wilhemina's eyebrows knitted with concern. "But he doesn't know where to look for her."

"I told him her favorite places to go," Katie reassured her.

"But Chantal might not come to him when he calls. He's still a stranger to her."

Katie swallowed her impatience. "Would you feel better if I looked for her too?"

"Well, at least Chantal knows you," Wilhemina said.

"Okay. Promise me you won't come outside looking for the cat."

Wilhemina paused a full five seconds. "I promise I won't go outside to look for Chantal."

Something about Ivan's daughter's tone bothered Katie. "You're sure?"

"I promise I won't go outside to look for Chantal," she repeated.

"Okay," Katie said, and turned toward her room.

"Katie?"

She turned around to look at Wilhemina. "Yes?"

Wilhemina laced and unlaced her fingers together. "Thank you. Thank you for everything."

Katie felt a tug at Wilhemina's solemn gratitude. She'd known Wilhemina was attached to Chantal, but she hadn't known she was that attached. Impulsively, she stepped forward and embraced her. "It's nothing," she said. "Don't worry. Mr. Wingate and I can handle this."

In a couple of moments, Katie pulled on a rain slicker, grabbed a flashlight, opened a can of tuna, and headed out the door. The rain was pouring.

"Here, kitty-kitty," she called, waving the can of tuna as she meandered through the backyard. "Here, Chantal." She repeated the calls and continued walking between the trees farther away from the house. "Here, kitty-kitty—" She broke off when a loud thump sounded behind her.

Her heart stopped at the black figure, until she realized it was Michael. "You scared me to death. Do you always have to sneak up behind people?"

"I wasn't sneaking," he said, his dark hair glistening from the rain. "I was looking in the tree for the cat. Do you really think that animal will answer to *kitty-kitty*?"

"What am I supposed to say? Bonsoir, Chantal!" She shrugged. "I need to let her know I'm out here. I was hoping she would respond to the combination of my voice and the smell of tuna. Did you have a better idea?"

He sighed in disgust. "This isn't my area of expertise. I can't believe I'm wasting my time looking for a cat."

"You can go back inside," she suggested, thinking she would prefer he left if all he was going to do was complain.

"No," he said, his expression dark. "I'm here for the duration. I'm not just out in the rain looking for a pussy. I'm looking for the ugliest pussy in the world."

Katie locked gazes with him for a long oddly-charged moment, then looked away. She wasn't going to touch that pussy comment with a ten-foot pole. She continued to call for Chantal and Michael climbed up at least half a dozen trees. They circled the perimeter of the yard another time.

"This isn't looking good. I think we may need to try the Hathaways," she said, glancing at the stone wall separating the two estates.

He nodded. "Okay. Put your foot here." He laced his fingers together and cupped them like a stirrup.

Surprised and strangely touched by the offer, Katie just stared at him. "I-uh-I-don't—"

"Would you move it? I'm not getting any younger."

She blinked, the sliver of a tender feeling disappearing in an instant. Stepping into his hands, she grabbed on to the wall and hitched herself up to the top, successfully saving the can of tuna. She slung her legs over. Before she had a chance to slide down, Michael appeared on the other side of the wall, his hands outstretched.

She immediately fell on top of him.

He made an *oof* sound and fell to the ground, protecting her from the fall. His body was hard beneath hers, his arms strongly supporting her. She couldn't remember a time when anyone had broken her fall. Her face suspended above his, she stared into his dark eyes and felt an odd sensation in her stomach. The scent of rain and man swam in her head.

"Your hair," he murmured.

Katie blinked, noticing that her hair had come loose from the tight knot. She felt it damply clinging to her cheeks. Her glasses were missing. They must have flown off her head.

Swearing, he shook his head and lifted a finger to one of

the strands. "Why in hell do you look better wet in the rain than perfectly dry in the daylight?" His gaze demanded an answer. "Why do you deliberately make yourself look plain?"

"It's my job to look plain." Pushing aside the jittery breathless feeling inside her, she pulled back and gingerly stood.

"What do you mean?"

"I mean if I want to keep my job, I need to be nearly invisible, nonthreatening to Ivan's wives, completely—"

"Asexual," Michael finished for her.

The term jarred her, especially after she'd just felt the strength of his body cushioning hers. She gave a slow nod. "I was going to say ordinary, but I think you get the picture."

"You're so afraid of losing your job that you make yourself look ugly to keep it?" he asked in disbelief.

"Ugly is a harsh term," she said, her ego smarting. She began to look for her glasses.

"That wasn't the point," he said. "I meant you must be damn scared of losing your job to go to such lengths."

She didn't like his description *damn scared*. It hit too close to the truth. She felt his hand on her arm and tensed, rounding on him. "I have a damn good reason to keep my job. That's all you need to know."

He frowned, lifting his hand to her hair. He pulled something from it and lifted it to his nose. "Sugar? You spent your day off making something with sugar? You are one weird cookie."

She lifted her lips in a forced smile. "Exactly. You have me perfectly pegged. I'm weird, strange, and asexual. I give new meaning to the word plain. We can look for the cat now. The mystery of Katie Collins is solved. All your questions are answered."

"Not by a long shot," he muttered, still gazing at her in a way that made her feel like she was Chantal and he was the hunter. "But you're right about the cat. Where's the sandbox?"

An hour later, they temporarily gave up and stomped back to the side door that led to the kitchen. Katie ditched her shoes and slicker in the mudroom. When she saw Michael pull off his shirt, she quickly skedaddled down the hallway to the kitchen, hearing her mother's sultry singsong voice in her head. *Nothing wrong with looking, Priss. And he's definitely worth looking at.*

"The way I calculate it, Mama, the earliest I can think about sex is in seven years. Jeremy won't graduate until then," she muttered under her breath and was immediately filled with the sense that she had just shocked her mother into complete silence. Considering the fact that not even death had silenced her, that was pretty amazing.

Making a face, Katie dumped what remained of the tuna into the garbage and washed her hands. As she turned, she caught sight of a note propped on the table.

Katie, I found Chantal hiding under the sofa. I would have told you, but you made me promise to stay inside. Sorry for your trouble. Thank you again for everything. Gone to bed. Sweet dreams, Wilhemina.

"What is it?" Michael said from just behind her, nearly making her jump.

Katie's heart pounded at his closeness, and her eyes really wanted to look at him, but she kept them trained on the note. "We're in luck. Wilhemina found the cat under the sofa."

"Figures," Michael said. "Maybe I can get a barrier bracelet to use for that animal's collar. Come to think of it, it might be a good idea for Wilhemina too."

Katie frowned at him. "Wilhemina doesn't wear a collar and she's not a prisoner."

He met her gaze and Katie did her level best to keep her focus above his impressive chest. "She wouldn't have to wear a collar. She could wear it like a watch."

"That's inhumane."

"Not if she were kidnapped," Michael said.

Katie felt a chill.

"The flip side of having more money than God," Michael said. "That's why the security business is booming."

"Good for you I guess," Katie said, her gaze slipping and taking in the beautiful strength of his bare chest.

He shrugged. "Yeah. And I bet you're thinking capitalistic guys like me are taking advantage of wealthy victims like Wilhemina."

She supposed she could allow him to think that. After all, she didn't pretend to care what Michael's opinion of her was, and he obviously didn't care what she thought of him. The notion bothered her, though, for some reason she couldn't define. "Actually I was thinking that guys like you give Wilhemina a decent shot at not becoming a victim."

A glint of surprise flickered in his eyes and he gave her an assessing glance that felt as if he were poking beneath the surface, searching for her secret. His gaze made her nervous. "I've had a long day. I'm going to bed. Good night," she said and headed out of the kitchen.

"Katie, why didn't you bring whatever you baked today here for the rest of us?" Michael asked.

She tensed, but at the same time fought a ripple of amusement. "Because I only give my sweets to my sweethearts," she answered, shocking herself with how close that comment was to something her mother would have said. She bit her tongue and raced up the stairs. She didn't know if her mother's spirit was attempting to inhabit her body or Michael Wingate's effect on her body was causing her to forget to be invisible, but she needed to refresh her memory lickety-split.

By noon the following day, Katie began to feel uneasy. Wilhemina hadn't appeared from her room even for breakfast, and to Katie's knowledge, Wilhemina never missed breakfast unless she was very ill.

Concerned, Katie knocked gently on Ivan's daughter's door. No answer. She called Wilhemina's name several times, but again there was no answer. Fighting a trickle of panic, she discreetly got the key to Wilhemina's suite from the housekeeper and opened the door. The lounging area of the suite was empty. No surprise there, Katie thought, and tapped on the door to Wilhemina's bedroom. No answer. Her concern heightening to outright worry, Katie entered the bedroom and scanned the room in an instant.

Wilhemina wasn't sick or unconscious in her bed.

Wilhemina wasn't there at all.

As if he were peering from a jail cell, Michael looked out from his bedroom window at the Rasmussens' house. He was on hold with the vendor who manufactured barrier bracelets. He'd be damned if he was going to tramp through the rain looking for that damn cat again.

His door burst open and Katie Collins appeared in the doorway, her face pale, her eyes huge with panic. She waved a piece of paper. "Omigod, she's gone! We've got to find her. She's run away."

"Who? The cat?" he asked, refusing to believe the cat had written a note.

"No. Wilhemina," she wailed, rushing toward him.

"Wilhemina," he repeated. The vendor returned on the line, but Michael disconnected the call. He could feel his blood pressure rising. "What are you talking about? What happened?"

"I thought Wilhemina was sleeping in this morning, but she wasn't. When I checked her bedroom, she was gone and she left a note. She has run away," she said, looking as if she were going to hyperventilate.

Michael saw his juicy contract with Ivan slipping from his grasp and shook his head. He wouldn't let that happen. He couldn't. "Where did she go?"

"I don't know," Katie said, thrusting the note at him. "She didn't say. But, Michael, this woman is helpless. To my knowledge, she's never made travel arrangements for herself let alone traveled without a companion. Turning her loose out there is like—" She shook her head. "Anything could happen to her. Anything . . ."

Michael studied the note while Katie continued to rail. *Katie, please forgive me, but I must leave. You and I both know I won't find the right man for me in Philadelphia. I just don't fit in and I never will. But your wonderful story has inspired me. It's time for me to venture out on my own to find my future and I have you to thank for giving me the courage. Please don't try to find me. I'll be back before Daddy returns, I promise. Love and kisses, Wilhemina.*

Michael stared at Katie. "What the hell kind of story did you tell her?" he demanded, feeling his head throb with the beginning of a monster migraine. "How did you give her courage? And why did you plant this insane idea in her head?"

"I didn't mean to give her that kind of courage, " Katie retorted, her face regaining some color. "You could tell the poor woman felt lower than snail spit and I just wanted to make her feel better. And I absolutely did not suggest that she go tearing off on her own to find her future."

Michael sucked in a breath and counted to three. That was all he could manage. "Tell me the story you told her," he said in a deadly calm voice.

She pulled back slightly and waved her hand in a dismissive gesture. "It was just a little fairy tale my mother used to tell me when I was a little girl."

"And it went like . . ."

Clearly reluctant, she pursed her lips. "It was about a lonely little girl who lived in a castle who wished on a star every night."

"And?" Michael prompted, not liking where this was headed.

"And the little girl traveled to a far-off land and had many adventures and found an injured knight on the side of the road," she said in one breath, then paused with a wary expression in her eyes. "And the knight and the girl—"

"Oh, no. Let me finish. The knight and the girl fell in love and lived happily ever after."

"Well, those weren't the exact words," she said.

"But the sappy sentiment was the same." He shook his head, a bitter taste filling his mouth at the memory of his own disastrous engagement. His fiancée had been one more person who taught him to rely on himself. "I can't believe you filled her head with these crazy ideas."

"It was either that or she was going to eat two packages of cookies and sink into a funk," she said, putting her hands on her hips. "Besides, I told her the story while she was drinking margaritas, so I figured she wouldn't remember much of it."

"You women and this white knight romance forever crap. Those fairy tales should come with warning labels."

She looked down her nose at him. "Well, I can see why you wouldn't appreciate the concepts of white knight and romance since you're clearly so far removed from chivalry or anything remotely romantic," she retorted.

He heard the drawl in her voice again and tilted his head to one side trying to place it.

"But that's beside the point. We have to find Wilhemina," she said. "And Chantal."

Michael felt the throbbing in his head kick up another notch in intensity. "Oh, hell," he muttered, thinking he didn't know which would upset Ivan more, a missing daughter or a missing cat. Michael just knew his prognosis for getting Ivan's account was in grave danger, to say nothing of Wilhemina's safety. His gut churned at the image of naïve, defenseless Wilhemina on a wild goose chase to find a white knight. She was more likely to find the Hope Diamond in the neighbor's sandbox. And that damned cat. "Tell me she didn't take the cat."

Katie met his gaze dead-on. "She took the cat."

"God will forgive you for bending the commandments in order to earn the money to pay the light bill and feed children."
—SUNNY COLLINS'S WISDOM

Chapter 6

Michael stared at his computer monitor impatiently as the information appeared on his screen. "Bingo," he said. "She bought a ticket on American Airlines for Dallas. She departed late last night," he said, shaking his head in disgust that he'd fallen for Wilhemina's ploy. He hadn't believed Ivan's daughter was capable of deceit. Big mistake. Michael should have remembered that he hadn't met a woman incapable of some measure of deceit.

"She has already rented a car. Texas," he said, scratching his head. "Why in the world would she choose Tex—" He broke off, realization hitting him. He spun around in his chair and stared at Katie. "Your accent. You're from Texas. Are you sure you didn't tell Wilhemina something that would make her choose Texas?"

Katie nearly squirmed, if she'd been the type of woman to squirm. Instead, she looked down her nose at him. "You know all you need to know and I don't have an accent."

Michael sprang from his seat and latched his hand around her wrist. "Oh, no. You practically gave that poor woman a map for her own destruction and now I've got to find her. You'd damn well better cough up the rest of that little fairy tale you told such as suggested locations for finding a white knight on the side of the road."

"There's nothing else to the story," she said. "I told Wilhemina that my mother was from Texas, and Wilhemina decided the knight in the story was a cowboy knight. How did you find out about the airline ticket so quickly?" she asked and looked down at his hand closed around her wrist. "You can let go of me now."

Michael looked into her eyes and glimpsed curious contradictions. Her voice was cold, but her skin was warm, her pulse fast, and her eyes glinted with uneasiness and something darker and more basic. Something about her reminded him of the ocean—different colors, different depths.

He shook his head. Where the hell had that thought come from? His migraine must have been affecting the blood flow to his brain. He released her wrist. "I'm going to Texas."

She nodded. "When do we need to be ready?"

Michael immediately rejected the idea. "What do you mean *we*, Tonto? I can handle this on my own."

"I'm not questioning your detective abilities, but I think Wilhemina trusts me more than she trusts you."

"She didn't tell you she was running away."

She barely batted an eye. "The reason you need me is because you don't understand the appeal of the story I told her."

"And you believe in that fairy tale?" he asked, unable to keep the cynicism from his voice.

"I didn't say I believe in it. But I understand its appeal and I think I understand Wilhemina a little better than you do. Besides, it may be your job to guard her, but it's my job to be her companion. You were hired to do what you do well. I was hired to do what I do well."

Michael fought a ripple of impatience as he pulled a carry-on from his closet. There was some truth to what she was saying. He hadn't spent the last few years working on his people skills and he wasn't looking forward to dealing with a flighty emotional heiress. "You can accompany her when I bring her back to Philadelphia," he said, reluctant to have Katie along.

"How are you going to persuade her to come back if she doesn't want to?" she asked, her gaze turning suspicious. "You're not planning on doing something stupid like abducting her, are you?"

"Abduction is a strong term," he said, pulling T-shirts and socks from his drawer, but still watching her from the corner of his eye.

Katie rolled her eyes. "Abduction should give you big points with Ivan."

"Okay," he said, turning around to face her. "As far as I'm concerned, you're dead weight and you'll only slow me down. Why should I let you come along?"

"Because I understand the way Wilhemina thinks."

"You already said that. Give me one good reason and I'll let you go."

She gave a heavy indignant sigh. "Because I know Texas better than you do," she said, in a drawl that dripped with southern hospitality and a sex appeal so strong he was speechless for at least three seconds.

He stared at her. "I knew you weren't from Philadelphia. Bits of your accent leak into your voice every now and then."

"So give yourself a gold star. When do you want to leave?"

Grudgingly admitting that she might be useful, he shrugged. "Five minutes ago. Pack light and fast."

She barely blinked. "No problem," she said as if she had experience packing light and fast. He would wonder when she'd gotten that experience another time. Now he had to focus on finding Wilhemina. And the damn cat.

Katie was going to hell.

She had always felt that returning to Texas would be her own personal trip to hell. If the airplane crashed and she didn't make it to Texas, then she would probably go to hell for not taking out a life insurance policy on herself to protect Jeremy's future and for telling Wilhemina the fairy tale that had inspired her to run away.

She sat in the center seat of the 737 trying to appear as if she were a seasoned air traveler. She surreptitiously looked through the seat pocket in front of her, poring over the emergency instructions and locating the air sickness bag. Upset to learn there was no parachute, she twisted in her seat between Michael and a pregnant woman with a young toddler on her lap as the plane taxied down the runway.

"White knuckle flyer?" Michael asked, glancing pointedly at her fingers clutching his sleeve.

Embarrassed, Katie immediately jerked her hand to her lap. "Sorry, I thought it was the armrest." She couldn't stop thinking about Jeremy. Although she had a small life insurance policy as part of her employee's benefits, she knew Jeremy's care would be expensive. When she thought about what might happen to him if she should die, she could hardly breathe.

"It's okay. Lots of people are uneasy about flying," he said, surprising her with his charity. "Do you want me to get you a drink?"

She shook her head, fearing that if she tried to swallow anything, she would need to use the airsickness bag. The engines roared and the plane picked up speed, barreling down the runway. Her heart pounding, Katie closed her eyes and prayed. "I know I haven't been perfect, but if you could please just keep me alive until I get a life insurance policy," she whispered.

"What did you say?" Michael asked.

The plane miraculously lifted off the runway and went airborne. She held her breath.

"Did you say something about insurance?" Michael asked.

Still holding her breath, she gave a tiny shake of her head. "It was nothing," she managed, keeping her eyes closed. The plane hit a bump and she grew light-headed.

She felt Michael tug at her arm. "Damn, you look pale. Katie, Katie . . ."

The plane hit another bump and everything inside her turned to gray.

Alarm shot through Michael as he watched Katie's head slump to one side. Reaching for her hand, he touched her wrist and felt for her pulse. Thank God, she had one. She must have fainted, he thought, shocked shitless. If there was one person he would have never expected to faint, it was Katie Collins. She gave the impression she could eat glass if the occasion called for it.

The pregnant woman eyed Katie with concern as she jiggled her toddler on her lap. "Is she okay?"

"I don't know," he said grimly. "I wonder if there's a doctor—"

An elderly woman across the aisle craned to look at them. "Anxiety attack?" she asked, then made a clucking noise. "Poor thing. I have some extra Valium if she needs it."

Michael nodded. "Thank you. I'll take it, but I need to get her awake first," he said. The woman passed the medication across the aisle while Michael flicked his fingers firmly against Katie's palms, then lifted his hand to her cheek. He pulled off her glasses and gently tapped her cheek. "Katie," he said, pressing his mouth against her ear. "Katie." Despite the urgency of the situation, he couldn't help noticing how soft her skin was, and the fresh scent of her hair.

She drew in a deep breath and her eyelids flickered. She met his gaze and blinked as if she were trying to reorient herself. She glanced over at the pregnant woman and offered a weak smile, then looked back at Michael. "What happened? Why is everyone staring at me?"

"You fainted. Why the hell didn't you tell me flying gave you anxiety attacks?"

"Because I haven't had much experience flying," she said, shifting self-consciously in her seat.

Michael got an uneasy feeling in his gut. "Exactly how much flying have you done?"

She hesitated. "Not very much," she said, looking away. "But it's really none of your business."

"It is my business if you're going to faint on me."

"I didn't faint *on* you," she retorted, her cheeks regaining color. "It looks like I did it very quietly right here in my seat."

"How much have you flown?"

She frowned at him. "None."

"This is your first flight."

"My family favored Greyhound," she said in a voice laced with a sexy self-deprecating humor that put him off balance.

"Why didn't you tell me?"

She lifted her lips in a brittle smile. "Because you wouldn't have let me come."

He opened his mouth, then shut it, unable to argue with her. She was right. He wouldn't have let her come. The plane hit an air pocket and Michael watched the color drain from her face again. Shit, he hoped she wasn't going to faint again.

Swearing under his breath, he lifted his hand to press the button for an airline attendant. "You're having an anxiety attack. Are you allergic to any medication?"

She shook her head.

He glanced down and saw her fingernails digging into her hands. Wondering when she would draw blood, he felt an odd instinct to protect her. Weird as hell. He would have to think about that later. "That nice lady across the aisle has shared her Valium with us," he said, waving at the woman. The airline attendant appeared.

"Could you bring us some water? She needs to take some medication."

The attendant frowned with concern. "She looks so pale. I'll bring an extra blanket too."

Katie closed her eyes. "I can't be having an anxiety attack. I don't have time for anxiety attacks," she muttered. "If I were prone to anxiety attacks, I would have been locked away a long, long time ago."

Michael was itching to hear the story behind that statement. He had the sense that Katie Collins had quite a few untold stories locked inside that uptight, compact body of hers. The plane hit another air pocket and she winced. "Are you going to argue or take the Valium?" he asked as the attendant returned.

"Shut up and give it to me," she said with some reassuring starch in her voice.

"You might just want to give her half. It's a strong dose," the elderly woman who donated the medicine said just as Katie swallowed the whole pill.

Katie glared at Michael.

Michael just grinned and shrugged. "Sit back and enjoy the flight." His respect for her strangely jumped a notch.

Okay, so she was terrified of flying. She hadn't let that stop her from doing what she needed to do.

Within thirty minutes, she'd fallen asleep on his shoulder with her hand draped over his chest. Loath to disturb her, he inhaled her clean scent. Her hair was soft against his jaw, and two of her fingers curled inside his shirt.

She would croak if she could see herself right now, he thought, taking in the sight of her abandoned shoes on the floor, one foot tucked beneath her and her ugly navy blue dress revealing one of her thighs. Her breasts pressed against his arm. Snuggling against him, she sighed and her breath tickled his neck.

Michael felt an odd tug inside him, somewhere between his chest and gut. The thought struck him that he hadn't held a woman in a while. There'd been a few passionate meetings of bodies bent on physical release, but no tenderness since . . . since Katrina, and that had seemed eons ago. Katrina had been his fiancée before his business partner had betrayed him. He'd been a different man then. Michael had been cynical since his father had committed suicide and his mother had gone into the mental health facility, but a part of him, a stupid-ass part of him, had believed a little in that same fairy-tale crap Katie had imparted to Wilhemina.

It was dangerous stuff. He'd learned the hard way and there was no way he would go down that road again.

Katie sighed and shifted again. His arm was falling asleep. He should shove her back into her seat. But something stopped him, and he tilted his head back against the seat and willed the rest of him to go to sleep too.

"I need to go to the bathroom," she whispered in his ear, waking him forty-five minutes later.

Michael's brain woke up faster than his arm, which felt as

if it had fallen off. "Just a sec," he murmured, rising to his feet and stepping into the aisle.

Katie pushed her feet into her shoes and stood. Her blue eyes lowered to half-mast, her hair sleep-mussed, she reminded him of hot, steamy, take-all-night-long sex. Michael stared at her, blinking.

Katie wobbled past him, lurching from side to side as she walked to the lavatory. He watched her falter and reached out to steady her. She looked over her shoulder. "Oops. Sorry."

"No problem," he said, walking behind her.

She struggled with the door and he pulled it open, resolving to never give her Valium again. She was much easier to handle when she was uptight and starchy. He waited outside the door, hearing her bump and swear inside the close confines of the small lavatory. He heard the splash of water, then he heard her fumble with the door before she burst out of the room and into his arms.

She murmured a breathless apology. "That pill made me feel funny."

He nodded, hit by a swarm of sensations. She was soft and warm and her defenses were down. He wondered if she had any idea how seductive she was. "Let me help you back to your seat."

"I keep thinking the strangest things," she said, then lowered her voice. "Like how on earth do people get in the mile-high club on a public jet?"

He stared at her, certain he had misheard her. Katie Collins was the last person he would expect to even think such a thing, let alone say it. "Excuse me?"

"The mile-high club," she whispered. "How? Where—"

"The lavatory," he told her.

Her eyes rounded and she glanced back at the small rest room. "You're joking. It's not possible. There's no room."

He chuckled and urged her down the aisle. "Where there's a will . . ."

"I guess," she said doubtfully, meandering forward. She wove her way to her seat and plopped down, immediately kicking off her shoes. She closed her eyes and inhaled deeply.

He sat next to her in his seat and she turned to look at him. He met her gaze warily. *What now?* he thought.

"You know, you're a very good-looking man," she told him.

He swallowed a smile. "Is that so?"

She nodded. "You are. You've got a great body," she said, lifting her hand to his shoulder. "You are hot."

Despite the fact that he knew Katie was under the influence of powerful medication, he felt himself grow warm.

She wrinkled her brow. "I just don't understand why you're so rude." She shook her head. "You would be irresistible if you were just a little bit nicer."

Michael took a moment to digest her statements. How odd. The Valium had obviously lowered her inhibitions and it seemed to have the effect of a truth serum. If there was anything he wanted to know about Miss Katie Collins, then now was the time to ask.

"I would be irresistible to whom?" he ventured.

She shrugged. "To everyone."

"I'll take that under advisement," he said. "Are you from Texas originally?"

"I left when I turned eighteen and only looked back once."

"You didn't like it?"

She turned back in her seat. "I had to get away."

"Rough childhood?"

"Weird. All I wanted when I left Texas was to be normal

and not to call attention to myself." She glanced at him. "A lot of people think being normal is boring, but believe me, normality is highly underrated. My mother was just too—" She broke off and shook her head.

"Too what?" he prodded, his mind drifting to his own mother and her mental fragility. "Did she have a mental problem?"

"That was always debatable," she said dryly. "She was outrageous when she was alive and she's still outrageous. There wasn't much that would stifle her when she was alive and there's not much that will stifle her now."

He frowned, giving her a double take. He wondered if Katie was having delusions. "Is she dead?"

Katie nodded. "Yep, but that doesn't stop her from giving advice. She means well, but she's a pain in the butt."

Michael tensed, questioning Katie's sanity, wishing he hadn't started this line of questioning. "She talks to you?"

She rolled her eyes. "Yeah, but I usually tell her to be quiet. She pipes in with the strangest things at the worst moments." She slid a sideways glance at Michael. "She even has an opinion about you."

He shouldn't ask. He really shouldn't ask. He really couldn't resist. "What's that?"

She crooked her finger for him to come closer. "She thinks all you need to improve your disposition is a really good blow job."

She was crazy. The woman looked like a sensible, uptight lady on the outside, when in reality, she was secretly a nut. But when he looked at her mouth, a hot, wicked visual filled his mind. He shouldn't be turned on by the ramblings of a crazy woman under the influence of mind-altering medication.

He shouldn't, but he was.

*"When traveling, it is important to wear a short skirt
in case you need help with your luggage."*
—SUNNY COLLINS'S WISDOM

Chapter 7

Katie felt as if she were coming off the effects of three margaritas minus the headache. After a layover in Atlanta and a connecting flight, she began to fight the fog that had settled over her brain. Michael grabbed her carry-on bag and after they exited the flight, he led the way down a long concourse to a long line for rental cars. Katie eyed a shorter line. "Why don't we get one from that company?"

"Because this is where Wilhemina rented her car. If the same sales agent is working, we might be able to find out which direction she was headed." He shot her a curious glance. "How are you feeling?"

She shrugged. "Weird."

He moved forward a few steps. "Hmm."

Uneasy, she tried to remember exactly what she'd said to him during the last several hours, but she had slept so much she didn't know what she'd said and what she'd dreamed. Some of her dreams, however, had felt strangely real. She remembered one where her mother had said something to her about the mile-high club. "What does hmm mean?"

"You've been acting kind of weird."

Her uneasiness transformed to a knot in her stomach.

"Did I talk about my—" She broke off, hot with embarrassment.

He squeezed her shoulder. "Don't worry. I don't think you revealed too many state secrets."

Katie didn't feel at all comforted. "But did I say anything about—?"

He leaned closer to her. "Do you really want to know what you said to me when you were under the influence of mind-altering medication?"

Yes. No. Yes. No. Katie took a deep breath. If she hadn't discussed Jeremy with him, then she didn't want to know. "As long as you and I both understand that I was under the influence and anything I said may not be reliable."

"Whatever," he said with a shrug, but she saw a gleam of amusement in his eyes.

Her stomach sank. She wondered if she had discussed the mile-high club with him, or worse yet . . . Katie took a quick, short breath. She would think about that some other time. There was nothing she could do about it now except try to regain her dignity, which was a little tough, considering what she really wanted more than anything was to take another nap.

She glanced around the terminal at the people in the airport. Even here, she could tell she was in Texas. Every now and then, when she inhaled, she caught the combined scents of leather boots, heat, and hair spray. Texas was the land of tall men with tall hats and women with big hair, high heels, and short skirts. She thought of her mother, the master of big hair, high heels, and short skirts, and the men who had moved in and out of her life like revolving doors. Katie felt an itchy sensation.

She and Michael rounded a corner and he turned to her. "Let me ask the questions," he said.

"Okay," she agreed, wondering what the sales agents might have thought of Chantal.

It was their turn and Michael stepped forward.

"How are you? What can I do for you?" a pleasant-looking male sales agent asked with a smile.

"Fine, thanks. I need a car and some information."

The man pulled out a book in front of Michael. "Well, you're in luck. We have a lot of cars. The Camry's on special this week. If you want something bigger, I've got a couple of Cadillacs—"

"I'll take a full-size," Michael said, pointing to a photograph of late-model vehicles.

"Alrighty," the sales agent said. "And would you like insurance on—"

"No insurance. I have insurance."

"Okeydokey. Now what about gas? We have a special plan—"

"I'll pump my own," Michael said. "Do you know who was working last night?"

"That'd be me," the man said. "We're short-staffed, so I'm working ten days straight. It seems like everyone decided to come to Texas at the same time and . . ."

Despite the Valium haze Katie was still fighting to clear, she could sense Michael's tension growing tighter with each superfluous bit of information the sales agent imparted.

Michael pulled out a photograph of Wilhemina. "Did you meet this woman?"

The sales agent eyed the photo, then shot Michael a look of scrutiny. "Well, maybe I did and maybe I didn't. Why do you want to know?"

Michael paused a half beat. "I need to know where she is."

The sales agent shrugged. "I don't know. She rented a car for thirty days. It's her business where she drives it."

Thirty days. Katie practically heard Michael's patience snap in two, and long sworn-off instincts came crashing in. She leaned in front of Michael. "You'll have to excuse him. He's in charge of his sister's safety and he gets upset at the thought of anything happening to her," she said in the Texas drawl she had sworn would never infiltrate her speech again. "I can see that you're a good judge of character, so I'm sure you could tell Wilhemina was naive. And her cat—"

The sales agent's eyes grew wide. "Cat? That animal was a cat? She had it in a kennel." He lowered his voice. "I was afraid to ask, but the poor thing looked like it had been skinned."

Katie nodded. "Ugliest thing you've ever seen, isn't it?"

"You're right about that." He gave Michael another once-over. "You're her brother? You don't look a thing like her."

"Different fathers," Katie said smoothly.

Michael jerked his head toward her so quickly he wondered if he would get whiplash. What had Katie turned into? With a Texas drawl that flowed like honey and a smile that could charm the skin off a snake, she moved her body like a woman who fully understood her attributes.

"Wilhemina was very upset when she left." She leaned closer as if she were confiding in him. "A guy dumped her. We don't want anything to happen to her. We really need your help," she said, stroking his ego the same way this guy would wish she was stroking something else. "Did she give you any idea where she might be headed?"

"Well, I did give her a couple of maps. She said she wanted to know where the cowboys were."

Michael swallowed a groan.

"And I'm betting you already know we have several different kinds of cowboys in Texas."

Katie nodded and smiled. "You're so right. Rodeo cowboys, nightclub cowboys, ranch cowboys."

"That's right. I told her she might try some nightclubs in Dallas and Cowtown. Then she might want to head on down to Bandera, the cowboy capital of the world. I gave her this list of hotels, bars, and dude ranches." He smiled at Katie. "I wish I could do more for you."

As the sales agent assessed her breasts, Michael knew exactly what the man wanted to do for Katie. Tamping down a shot of impatience mixed with something dark and vague, he extended his hand and a business card. "We both appreciate your help. Thank you. Do you know what kind of car she's driving? And her license plate number?"

"White Cadillac," the sales agent said, and glanced at his computer screen. He scratched out a number on a piece of paper and gave it to Katie. "Here you go."

"If you should remember anything else or if Wilhemina should contact you, please don't hesitate to call me."

"Yes, please do," Katie said. "You've been a tremendous help."

"Anytime, honey," he said.

Michael led the way out of the terminal to the shuttle and turned to look at her.

Katie looked at him, glanced away, then met his gaze. "What are you staring at?" she asked, no trace of Texas in her voice.

"I'm just wondering if you're inhabited by some southern belle alien that pops out at strange moments."

She crossed her arms over her chest. "I could see you weren't likely to get anything out of him. It may be a pain in the butt, but it's still a truth that you catch more flies with honey than vinegar."

"Is that something your mother said?"

She paused a moment, her expression turning guarded. "What makes you say that?"

"You mentioned her on the plane," he said, wondering exactly how much she recalled from the flight.

"Great," she muttered, looking away.

"The sales agent looked like he was ready to sit down and beg. That's quite a talent you have."

She scowled at him. "It's not talent."

"Female power play?" he returned, curious. The woman made him damn curious.

"It's a coping mechanism born of desperation. Under-educated, financially strapped women use all their available resources for the purpose of survival." She slid a sideways glance at him. "Resources such as a smile, breasts, legs, and flattery can get a bill collector off your back, can get you an extra gallon of gas, can get questions answered."

"But you hate it," he said, seeing the flash of anger in her eyes.

"Yes, I do. I swore I wouldn't come back to Texas and I swore I wouldn't use my *resources* the way I'd been taught, but I'll do just about anything to find Wilhemina."

Michael looked at the quiet, fierce resolve on her face and felt a click inside him. She was just as determined to find Wilhemina as he was. She might be kooky, but she was strong, the first truly strong woman he'd ever met. He wondered why she wanted Ivan's bonus. He wondered why she was willing to do so many of the things she obviously feared or hated. He wondered, and he knew he would get his answers eventually. But first, there was Wilhemina.

*   *   *

Wilhemina looked around the large dance hall filled with cowboys and was sure she had arrived in heaven. She'd successfully gotten herself down to Texas, rented a car, and used her credit card to get a cash advance. Although she'd gotten lost three times and learned that rush-hour traffic made her nervous, nothing could stop the euphoria racing through her. Not even her twinge of concern that Chantal was going to shred the curtains in the hotel room while Wilhemina was out tonight.

Wilhemina was on her first unescorted adventure, and she was going to make the best of it. Sitting at the end of the bar, she sipped a margarita and watched the dance floor longingly.

"How are you tonight, sweetheart?" a male voice ventured to the woman sitting next to her.

Wilhemina continued to watch the dance floor, wondering if she had the nerve to try to two-step. She'd never been particularly coordinated. She took another sip of her drink.

"Aren't you going to talk to me?" a man asked, moving into her line of vision.

Wilhemina looked to either side of her, then back at the man with the black hat and dimples. He was talking to her. Her heart raced. "I'm sorry. I didn't know you were speaking to me."

The man tipped his hat and grinned, flashing his dimples. "'Sokay. I'm Chad. Pleased to meet you," he said, extending his hand.

"I'm Wilhemina," she said, so nervous she hoped she didn't spill her margarita.

"You've been eyeing the dance floor. You want to give it a spin with me?"

She bit her lip. "I haven't danced much."

"Then you need to get started," he said, setting her drink on the bar and offering his hand to her.

Liking his combination of pushy charm and manners, she accepted and allowed herself to be led on to the floor. She hoped she wouldn't embarrass herself. He took her in his arms and her heart pounded so hard she wondered if she would faint.

"You're not from around here, are you?" he asked.

Wilhemina concentrated on not stepping on his feet. "No, I'm from Philadelphia."

"Here on business or pleasure?" he asked, his gaze dipping to her cleavage.

Stunned, Wilhemina felt a shot of feminine delight. She couldn't recall being the object of any man's lust. Men lusted after her father's money, not her. "Pleasure."

He nodded. "What do you do in Philadelphia?"

Her mind went blank. She stared into his blue, blue eyes. "I-uh-I serve on the board of a charitable foundation." That was true, she thought. Her father had arranged the appointment. Wilhemina attended all the meetings, but somehow she was never assigned any tasks.

"Well, that sounds like a nice thing to do," he said as he gently led her in a slow, easy shuffle. He touched her hair. "You have such pretty hair and your skin is so smooth. Is your husband here with you tonight?"

Flattered, Wilhemina felt her cheeks heat. "I'm not married."

He turned his head and looked at her, shaking his head. "A pretty girl like you? I don't believe you."

"I'm not," she said earnestly. "I haven't found anyone that wanted—" She broke off. "That I wanted to, really."

He nodded, looking deep into her eyes. "I understand. It

takes the right person. The right touch. The right voice. The right everything."

Wilhemina felt a knot of nervous excitement form in her throat. "You sound like you understand."

"Oh, honey, I do. I've been looking for the right person too," he said, and drew her closer to him and spun her around. He lowered his head to hers. "You never know when you're going to meet the right person, do you?"

Exhilaration pumping through her veins, Wilhemina hung on for dear life. She liked the feel of his strong muscles and his shoulder beneath her hand. She liked the way he looked at her. As if he liked what he saw and wanted to see more.

The song ended, and she was immediately crushed. She didn't want Chad to leave, but there were scores of other women at the bar. She bit her lip, trying to think of a way to make him stay.

"Can I buy you a drink?" he asked.

Relief rushed through her. She took a careful breath. "Yes, I'd like that very much."

"Let me find us a place to sit together," he said and she felt literally caressed by his gaze.

He slid his arm around her waist and led her to a corner of the room. "You stay here and I'll get us a drink. Promise you won't leave," he said.

She smiled with delight at his concern. "I'll be right here."

He leaned over to her and lifted his fingers to her chin. "You haven't ever been to Texas before, have you?"

"No," she admitted.

"I think I'd like to show you around a little bit," he said, his gaze falling to her lips. "You think about that. Okay?"

His intensity made her light-headed. "I will," she said.

Pulling back, he tipped his hat. "I'll be right back."

The rest of the evening passed in a lovely margarita- and Chad-filled blur. He was so attentive to Wilhemina she kept pinching herself. He didn't even seem to be looking at other women. He told her all the places they could go together and danced all the slow songs with her. By midnight, Wilhemina struggled with wooziness from the margaritas, but she didn't want to miss a minute with Chad. He brushed his mouth over hers and her heart sped into overdrive. She stumbled, and he caught her, pulling her against his long, lean frame.

"You're looking a little tuckered out. You think maybe we should get you home?"

Loath to see the evening end, she lifted her shoulders. "I'm at the Marriott just a couple miles down the road."

"Well, I can drive behind you to make sure you get there okay."

Her heart twisted. "That's so sweet. You've been so nice all evening. I don't think I've ever met anyone like you."

"My pleasure, Wilhemina," he said. "Let me escort you to your car."

Wilhemina allowed him to walk with her to her rental car. He gave a whistle at the white Cadillac.

"Nice ride," he said, glancing at it in approval.

"It's a rental," she said.

"What do you usually drive?" he asked.

"I don't usually—" She broke off, not wanting to reveal her lack of independence. "One of those little BMW convertibles," she said, naming the car she would like to drive.

He grinned. "Roadster. I can see you in that. You sure you can drive?"

"I'll be fine," she assured him, impressed again by his kind concern.

"Okay. I'll be behind you in my truck. It's red and kinda

beat-up-looking, but it's temporary. I've had a little bad luck lately. You know how that goes."

Wilhemina nodded. She completely understood about bad luck, although bad luck had never affected her mode of transportation. She unlocked her car door and Chad reached to open the door for her.

"Thank you," he said, standing so close his aftershave played havoc with her senses. "I'll be right behind you."

Wilhemina stepped into her vehicle and smiled while he closed the door. As soon as he stepped away, she fanned her face. Whew! That man made her hot. It took a couple of minutes for her to collect herself enough to start the engine and get the car into gear. Her mind reeling, she pictured all the places Chad had told her about.

Driving back to her hotel, she spotted his pickup truck in her rearview mirror. His left headlight was out, she noticed and made a mental note to tell him. She pulled into the parking lot and chose a space with no cars on either side. Wilhemina wasn't very confident of her parking skills.

Her heart pounding in anticipation, she quickly rose from the car. She hoped Chad was going to ask to see her again. He pulled in beside her and was at her door just as she stepped outside.

The intent look in his eyes made it hard for her to breathe. She swallowed over a nervous lump in her throat. "Thank you for following me," she whispered.

"My pleasure," he said, gently nudging her back against the Cadillac. "The whole evening has been my pleasure. I hate to see it end," he said.

"Me too."

"Maybe it doesn't have to end," Chad said, lowering his mouth to hers. He pressed his lips against hers, slow and easy, as if he were waiting for her to protest.

Wilhemina's heart pounded so fast she hoped she wouldn't faint. He slid his tongue inside her mouth and she opened her mouth in shock. She felt his hand squeeze her waist and hoped he didn't think she was too chubby. He moved his hand up her rib cage to the bottom of her breast and she couldn't stop a sound of surprise from the back of her throat.

"Like that?" he asked in a sensual tone. "I've got what you're looking for, Wilhemina."

Her head in a fog, she stared into his blue, blue eyes. Could this be happening to her?

"I can give you what you want," he said. "And I'll give you a real good price."

Her body still churning with desire, Wilhemina blinked. *Real good price?* She shook her head. "Price? Good price?"

He nodded, licking his lips as he skimmed his hand down to her wrist and fondled her diamond tennis bracelet. "I'll take you anywhere you want to go and give you anything you want for a hundred dollars a day. You're rich and lonely. I'm broke and available. You've got the money, honey. I've got the time. We're a perfect match."

"Don't take a man back once he's done you wrong. It's like hoping the milk is still fresh after it's been sitting in the heat all day."
—Sunny Collins's wisdom

Chapter 8

Shock stopped her speech for a full moment. She shook her head. "You want me to *pay* you to spend time with me?" she asked, incredulous.

He shrugged. "It could be a nice arrangement for both of us." He grinned, flashing his dimple. "Think of me as your very own boy toy escort."

Wilhemina felt as if she'd been kicked. Her throat tightened and she felt the threat of tears. Was she so weird that it would be impossible for someone to genuinely want to be with her? Why did she attract so many jerks? She'd had such hopes for this trip.

She looked at Chad and something inside her snapped. She was sick and tired of being disappointed. She remembered years ago in elementary school when a fellow student taped a sign on her back that said "Kick me." She wondered if she was still wearing that sign. A spurt of hot anger broke through her cold shock. Her fingers itched to slap him. She inhaled a quick breath of air. She wondered what Katie would do in this situation. Her father, she knew, would haggle over the price. "Boy toy escort," she echoed, pulling back slightly.

"I could show you a really good time," he promised with a nod of pride.

"For one hundred dollars a day," she repeated again, wondering where he had acquired such arrogance. Filled with hot outrage, she backed farther away from him. "How do I know your equipment meets my specifications?"

He gave a lazy yet confident grin. "My equipment's fine. I've never had a single complaint."

"But that's just your word," Wilhemina said, her heart pounding with fury and exhilaration as she turned the tables on him. "I need proof in order to pay you a hundred dollars. A hundred dollars is a lot of money."

The barest hint of uneasiness crossed Chad's handsome face. "Well, I might be willing to negotiate. I'm a reasonable man. How about seventy-five dollars a day?"

"I don't know. I still don't know if you have the right stuff," Wilhemina said, wondering why she hadn't seen how slimy he was from the start.

"Well, what do you want me to do? Show you?" he demanded, hands on hips.

She bit her lip, resisting her overwhelming urge to laugh. "You know, I think that may be best. It's always better for both parties to have full knowledge and agreement before proceeding into a partnership, no matter how temporary the partnership," she said, reciting what she'd heard her father say a gazillion times before. She backed another step away.

Frustration and desperation warring on his face, Chad looked from side to side. He sighed. "Okay," he said, unzipping his jeans and dropping them along with his briefs to his knees.

Wilhemina bit her lip as she pretended to study his organ, which appeared to be shrinking in the night air. Already moving away, she glanced back up at his face. "I think I'll pass," she said and walked briskly toward the lobby of the hotel. She heard Chad scream profanities at her and she picked up her pace.

Stumbling inside the lobby, she raced to the elevator and stepped inside. Pressing the number for her floor, she waited until the doors slid closed, then leaned against the back wall, her heart pounding a mile a minute.

She couldn't believe what she had just done. She wondered where she'd found the nerve. She'd spent her life feeling like a weirdo, like a victim.

The rush of power made her light-headed and she began to laugh so hard her eyes watered. She would never forget the look on Chad's face when she'd rejected his offer. Sniffing and wiping her damp cheeks, she walked to her room and entered to find Chantal mewing balefully. Tensing, Wilhemina quickly checked the curtains and felt a trickle of relief that Chantal hadn't done anything destructive.

Freshening the cat's water bowl, she chuckled again at Chad's indignation. She sank down on the bed and the cat jumped up beside her. Wilhemina absently rubbed Chantal's hairless little head. "Chad definitely was not any cowboy knight," she murmured, wondering if such a thing existed. "Maybe I should just go back to Philly. Katie's probably sick with worry."

She sighed, discouragement seeping through her veins. What if she was on a crazy wild goose chase? Something inside her balked at the thought of returning with her tail tucked between her legs. Wilhemina felt as if she'd spent most of her life discouraged and defeated. She couldn't bear the idea of seeing pity in Katie's eyes. No, she wasn't ready to return, she decided. Whether she found a cowboy knight or not, she was going to have her own adventure.

Nothing was going to stop her.

*   *   *

After visiting three nightclubs in Dallas, all Katie wanted was to go to sleep, but she wouldn't dare let Michael know how tired she was. She'd already embarrassed herself with that anxiety attack on the plane and heaven knows what all she'd told him after taking the Valium.

They headed for Fort Worth, also known as Cowtown, and arrived at a huge bar just after midnight. The place was still jumping. Michael flashed a photo of Wilhemina to the main bartender and he shook his head.

Michael returned to Katie's side. "Let's try one more tourist trap bar, then find a place for the night. We can start calling hotels on the list," he said, raking his hand through his hair. "We'll find her. She'll stick out among all these cowgirls."

"The same way you do," Katie said, unable to squelch her thoughts.

He narrowed his eyes at her. "What do you mean?"

"I mean you definitely don't look native Texan. You look and sound pure Philly."

He shrugged. "I'll put on a pair of jeans tomorrow, but I draw the line at boots and a ten-gallon hat." He scrutinized her. "You look like you're about ready to fall over."

"I'm okay," she lied. "It's just been a long day. Why don't we try another bar?"

He hesitated as if he were reconsidering, then nodded. "Let's go."

The bar yielded no leads, and Katie and Michael checked into separate rooms at a chain hotel close by. Michael insisted on carrying her bag to her room. "Thank you," she said as she pushed open her door. "I wouldn't have expected you to be so . . ."

"So what?" he asked, the intensity of his gaze unsettling her.

"Gentlemanly, considerate," she said, and wincing at her bluntness, she rushed to explain herself. "I can tell you're very goal-oriented and when you're focused on solving a problem, it's sometimes hard to remember things like—"

"Manners," he finished for her. "And kindness. You mentioned my lack of kindness before. I think you also said something about me being charm-free twenty-four hours a day."

Katie winced again. "I guess that sounded a little harsh."

He shrugged. "Maybe. Maybe not. I've been working twenty-four/seven for the past few years. I haven't had time for charm school. For that matter, almost all of my communication has fallen into the category of necessary business communication."

She frowned. "Why have you been working so much?"

He appeared to stifle a sigh. "That's another story for another time. Too long for tonight. You need your sleep. I want to be out of here by seven A.M."

"No problem," she said. "Is it okay if I meet you downstairs?"

"That'll work. Sweet dreams, Katie," he said, surprising her with his civility.

"You too," she said and entered her room. She eyed the bed with extreme lust. Her body begged for the immediate gratification of clean sheets and a soft pillow.

Tsk. Tsk. Your body's begging for what just walked down the hall, Priss.

Resisting temptation, Katie shook her head and grabbed her toothbrush and toothpaste from her duffel bag. "This time you're dead wrong, Mama. There can't possibly be any sex good enough to compete with the pleasure of sleep tonight."

Spoken like a true virgin, her mother's voice echoed inside her with amusement.

Katie turned the water on full force to drown out the sound. Her mind bounced between Wilhemina and Michael as she brushed her teeth. She wondered where Wilhemina was, if she was barhopping or heading for the open road. She wondered if they were looking for a needle in a haystack. After all, Texas was a big state and Michael wanted to keep their search low profile so Ivan wouldn't find out.

She wondered what had made Michael work so hard during the last few years. She still couldn't believe he'd carried her luggage for her. Remembering he had caught her as she fell on the plane, Katie felt her stomach take a dip. She frowned at the sensation and spit into the sink.

It was the aftereffects of the Valium and lack of sleep, she briskly told herself and stripped out of her clothes. Pulling on an oversized T-shirt, she set the alarm clock on the bedside table. She slid between the sheets and moaned in pleasure. She vaguely recalled the sensation of waking up draped over Michael's body. His body had been warm, his muscles strong, his masculine scent appealing.

Wrapping her arms around the spare pillow, Katie inhaled the clean, crisp scent. "The bed is better," she told herself and mentally turned off her mother's protest.

The following morning, Michael sipped his third cup of coffee as a tall, lean blond woman in jeans walked toward him. She set her duffel bag next to him. He blinked, not recognizing her for a full moment.

"Sorry I overslept," she said breathlessly. "I can grab a bagel and coffee and I'll be ready to go."

He noticed her hair was still damp and she wore not a

smidgen of cosmetics on her face. "We've got a few more minutes."

"Three," she corrected.

"Three?"

She pointed to her watch. "Three minutes. You said you wanted to leave by seven."

"We can wait a few more. I'm mapping out the plan for the day."

She shrugged. "Okay."

Still blinking, he watched her bound toward the self-serve counter. He took in the sight of her hair falling down her straight back, her curvy bottom and long legs. It occurred to him that Katie had a very nice ass. He watched her tap her foot impatiently as she toasted a bagel. She grabbed a miniature container of cream cheese and poured a large cup of coffee, then put it all on the table across from him. She spread cream cheese on half the bagel, lifted it to her mouth to take a bite, then paused. "Why are you staring at me?"

"You look different."

"My hair's wet," she said with a trace of self-consciousness.

"And you're not wearing an ugly gray dress or your ugly glasses. You look eighteen."

She chuckled, and it was a husky, sexy sound. "I'm not," she said and took a big bite of the bagel. She chewed it, then followed with a long sip of coffee. "Hot," she said, pursing her lips and inhaling to cool her tongue. "I felt about eighty after yesterday. What about you? Did you sleep well?"

"I didn't hit the sack until three," he said with a shrug.

Her eyes widened in surprise. "Why?"

"I called all the hotels on the list the car rental agent gave us."

"And?"

"And Wilhemina stayed at a Dallas Hyatt night before last, but checked out yesterday morning. She's apparently on the move. She took out a big cash advance on her credit card, so we won't be able to track her that way anymore."

"Should we visit the Hyatt to see if she talked to anyone about her plans?"

"That's on the list, but I have a hunch we'll just be backtracking. If Wilhemina is serious about finding a cowboy, she'll head away from Dallas."

"True. Are you sure we're going to find her?"

"I have no doubt," Michael said, ready to tear apart the entire state if necessary.

"I'm glad you ditched the suit. Are you sure you won't try a Stetson?"

His lips twitched at her faintly teasing tone. "I'm fine. Are you ready to go? I've already covered the bill for both rooms."

She nodded. "Ready," she said and reached for her duffel bag.

Michael automatically grabbed it first. He caught the look of surprise on her face. "You're not used to having a man carry things for you, are you?"

She shook her head. "I'm a worker bee. It wouldn't occur to Ivan to—"

"I wasn't talking about Ivan," Michael said.

She looked at him blankly for several seconds, then realization occurred and she laughed. "Oh, well that would entail me having the time and inclination to meet men, and I haven't had either."

"You have Sundays," Michael pointed out.

Her face closed up like a candy shop at the end of the day. "My Sundays aren't for meeting men."

They rode to Dallas in an uneasy silence. Michael sensed

he'd stepped over the line when he'd asked about Sundays. Her reaction only made him more curious, but he needed to focus on finding Wilhemina.

"Since part of your argument for being here was because you understood Wilhemina, what do you think her attitude toward Dallas would be?"

"I think she would like it. For a while anyway. Great shopping, the arts. In some ways, she would feel right at home. There's a lot of wealth in Dallas. But if she views this as her great adventure, and I think she does," Katie said with a sigh, "she won't hang around here long. I think you're right when you said we're backtracking."

"You lived in Texas for a while. Do you know anyone who lives here?"

Katie hesitated a half beat too long. "Not anymore," she said with an odd sadness in her voice.

"Where did you live?"

"In a little town in the middle of nowhere. It pretty much got blown off the map a few years ago when a tornado hit," she said, clearly reluctant to discuss it. She pointed ahead. "Is that the Hyatt we're looking for?"

Michael nodded and parked the car in the parking garage. "I'll talk to the front desk—"

"I know," she said. "You'll ask the questions. I'm just here for reference along the way and negotiations when we find Wilhemina."

They walked to the lobby and Michael interviewed the crew at the front desk, the concierge, and the bellman. Several of the employees remembered Wilhemina, and the bellman had given her a few suggestions for places to visit.

Michael glanced around for Katie, but didn't see her. He strode toward the restaurant and caught sight of her chatting with a woman in the gift shop at the same time she was flipping through a telephone directory and scratching down a number. Her gaze and finger hovered over a listing.

"Find something?" Michael asked.

Katie glanced up and immediately shut the directory. "Not much. I was just talking to Anna Lee. This is Michael Wingate."

"Nice to meet you," Anna Lee, a middle-aged woman with big hair, said, accepting his handshake. "Wilhemina was such a nice girl. I hope you're able to find your sister."

Michael blinked, then remembered Katie had proclaimed him and Wilhemina brother and sister. "Thank you. Both of us are anxious to find her."

"Anna Lee said Wilhemina bought some cookies from her and asked where to find cat food. Anna Lee also recommended a few rowdy bars in Fort Worth," she said in a gently teasing tone.

Anna Lee giggled. "They're not too rowdy. Just fun." She glanced at the phone directory. "Did you find your friend?"

Katie shrugged with so much discomfort he could feel it from five feet away. "Too many with the same last name. You know how that goes. Maybe next time. Thank you again for your help," she said, and they left the tiny shop.

"We're going to have to kill some time before these bars open," Michael ventured. "Are you sure there isn't someone you want to look up?"

"I'm sure," she said, her mouth drawn in a firm line.

"Okay. Did you write down the names of the bars?"

Katie nodded and passed him the sheet of paper. "Anna Lee recommended three."

Michael scrutinized the list. "What's this fourth address?"

Katie's eyes widened and she tried to snatch the paper

from him. "It's nothing—" She reached for it again, but he folded it in his hand. "It's nothing about Wilhemina. Just let me rip off the bottom of it."

"If it's nothing, then why did you write it down?"

She shrugged as if she didn't care, but the way she gnawed her upper lip gave her away. "I don't care. Let's just go."

His curiosity aroused, Michael walked toward the rental car with Katie quietly stewing beside him. He opened the car door for her.

"Thank you," she murmured, not looking at him as she slid into the seat.

Michael got into the driver's seat and plugged an address into the complimentary global positioning system on the dash. Katie continued to look out her window, her silence filled with so much tension he wondered how she kept from exploding.

Navigating through the downtown streets of Dallas, he took a turn into an affluent neighborhood full of large homes with wrought-iron gates and circular drives.

Katie glanced at him suspiciously. "Where are we going?"

Taking another turn, he slowed as he rounded a curve and identified his target. "907 Hawthorn Avenue. The address you copied from the phone book," he said, looking past the wrought-iron gate to the front door of a large, elegant home. He caught sight of a blond teenage girl scooping up a terrier and snuggling it just before she passed it to a woman in a black maid's uniform. Michael glanced at Katie and saw a look of hunger on her face.

She lowered the window, her gaze fastened on the teenager as the girl bounced into her red Miata convertible. "She looks so beautiful," Katie murmured and a bittersweet smile lifted her lips. "And she always loved animals. I wonder how many pets he lets her keep."

"Who is she?"

She was silent so long he thought she might not answer, and Michael had learned that the only thing that made Katie talk when she didn't want to was mind-altering medication.

Her gaze clung to the sight of the teenager as she revved the engine, drove out of the driveway, and roared down the street. "My little sister," she finally whispered.

"When you have a terrible day, drink a margarita,
eat chocolate and dance in the kitchen.
Things will look better in the morning."
—SUNNY COLLINS'S WISDOM

Chapter 9

In less than a moment, it was a hot summer day in a little county in the hill country. Katie was twelve years younger and everyone she knew called her Priss.

"Can I take 'im with me, Priss?" Lori Jean asked as she gripped a brown dog of indeterminate breed under its front haunches, leaving the back legs dangling. Lori stretched her little-girl legs to make the big porch step just outside the front door of their mobile home. Lori Jean's father, oil baron Harlan Granger, stood beside his white Cadillac impatiently waiting to take custody of his daughter. Her mother refused to speak to the man. She was infuriated that Harlan was taking Lori away and had already hugged Lori good-bye.

Thirteen-year-old Priss was devastated. Kneeling down, she looked into the tear-filled eyes of her seven-year-old sister and tried to be brave. Harlan Granger wanted nothing more than to purge his daughter of any memories of her life before he'd recognized her existence. Harlan held such contempt for her mother that Priss wouldn't be surprised if the man wanted to give Lori a blood transfusion and complete deprogramming. Priss always had a hard time understanding how her mother's boyfriends could want her bad enough to make a baby with her, yet hate her afterward. Priss knew there was no way he would allow Lori to bring a flea-infested mutt into his fine house in Dallas, but she tried to gently spin the truth for Lori. "I bet your daddy is going to let you have all kinds of pets at your new house."

Lori glanced over her shoulder, her face pinched with fear. "He looks mean," she whispered. "I don't want to go with him. Can't I stay with you?"

Priss's heart hurt so much she could barely breathe. Her mother denied it, but Priss suspected this could very well be the last time she saw her little sister with the lopsided pigtails. Priss pulled Lori into her arms. "I would love for you to stay, but you're going to a much nicer place. Harlan Granger is going to take very good care of you. You'll have new dresses and toys and friends. It's gonna be great."

"But what about when I want to talk to you?"

Priss felt the threat of tears and blinked them back. Crossing her fingers behind Lori's back for the lie she was about to tell, she pressed her lips into a smile. "We'll visit each other." Hating the lie even though it was necessary, she pulled back and followed with a solemn vow. "If you ever need me, all you have to do is call me. Okay?"

Lori bit her lip uncertainly. "Okay. Will you walk me to the car?"

It was something her mother should have done, but her mother couldn't bear it because their middle sister, Delilah, had been taken away just the day before by her father, a Bible-thumping minister. Lori Jean had been told that Delilah's departure was temporary, but Priss knew better. This wasn't the first time Priss had covered for her mother, and deep inside she felt touched that Lori was so attached. Soon enough, Lori would forget her.

"Sure," Priss said, escorting her sister across the yard and trying not to feel small due to the disapproving gaze of

Harlan Granger. She reached down to press a kiss on Lori's head.

Lori whipped around and buried her face against Priss. "I don't wanna go," she wailed, bursting into tears.

Priss felt as if she were having her guts sliced out of her. She saw a glimmer of concern cross Harlan's face. "But what about the pony your daddy is going to get you?" she impulsively asked.

"Pony?" Lori echoed, her head bopping up.

"Pony?" Harlan said, jerking his head toward Priss.

Priss nodded and smiled. "Did you know that your daddy has enough money to get you a real pony?"

Lori's eyes widened with excitement. "A real pony?"

"A real one, and he is gonna tell you all about it while he drives you to your new house." Lifting her chin, she met Harlan's gaze with far more confidence than she felt. "Lori has always wanted a pony, and I think it's terrific that you're going to get her one."

Harlan raised an eyebrow, but didn't argue.

Lori whipped around to look at him. "Is that true? Are you really going to get me a pony?" She hesitated, then took a deep breath. "Daddy?"

Priss watched balls-of-steel Harlan Granger melt a little before her very eyes and felt the pressure in her heart unwind a notch.

"Of course, I'm gonna get you a pony. But I wanted to wait for you so you could help pick it out," he said, and took Lori's little hand in his big palm and led her to the car. After he helped Lori to the car, he turned to Priss for a half beat and tipped his Stetson. A silent thank-you, but Priss knew his gratitude wouldn't extend to letting Lori come back to visit. This was good-bye.

"Your father is Harlan Granger?" Michael asked, interrupting Katie's reverie.

"No. Lori and I had the same mother," she said, horrified to feel a tear stream down her cheek. Her defenses shot back in place and she rounded on him. "And don't even start making remarks about the fact that my mother was a slut because I've already heard them all. It may be true, but I don't want to hear it right now."

Michael calmly met her gaze. "I didn't say anything about your mother."

So he hadn't, she thought, wishing she didn't feel so out of control. She took a careful breath to calm herself.

"Do you want me to go after her?"

"Who?"

"Your sister. I can probably catch up. If you haven't seen her—"

"No," she said, cutting him off along with the tempting possibility of seeing Lori again.

"Why not?"

She sighed in frustration. "I just— It's not—" She frowned. "This isn't a good time. You and I need to go on to Fort Worth."

"How long has it been since you've seen her?"

"A while," Katie reluctantly said.

"Translate *a while* into months," he said, watching her carefully. "Or years."

"Twelve years, but it's none of your business," she quickly added. "Can we just please go?"

He gave a low whistle, shifted out of park, then made a U-turn in the middle of the road to head in the opposite direction. Katie resisted the urge to glance back one last time.

"Twelve years is a long time. You must be pretty pissed off," he said.

She rolled her eyes. "I'm not pissed off. The reason I didn't see my sister was due to a circumstance beyond my control."

"It's not beyond your control now."

Katie was still too busy dealing with a half-dozen different emotions to give Michael credit for being right. The notion that he could be right just added another emotion to the crazy mix. "I realize that you frequently get paid to be nosey, but trust me, you won't get any money for being nosey about me. Don't bother with me. We both need to focus on finding Wilhemina."

"It's always good to understand your partner's motivation," he said, his voice getting under her skin.

"My motivation is the same as yours. I want the money. That's all you need to know."

Michael fell silent and Katie exhaled in relief. No more grilling, thank goodness. Leaning back in her seat, she took note of some of the changes that had taken place since she'd left Texas. Dallas had already boomed, but the construction continued to sprawl. Fort Worth was expanding too, however Katie noticed a couple of guys on horseback on a back lot.

"Did I just see horses on a city road?" Michael asked.

She nodded with a faint smile. "Fort Worth is that way. It's determined to move forward at the same time it refuses to give up its roots. Rodeos and the arts."

"Rodeos," Michael echoed, meeting her gaze for a quick instant as he headed for downtown Fort Worth. "Cowboys, rodeos," he said.

Katie made a face. "I don't think so."

"Why not?"

"I don't think Wilhemina wants a showy cowboy. She wants a cowboy that represents the western male mystique."

"And what would that be?" he asked, his voice oozing cynical disbelief.

"Honor, strength, self-reliance." *Great butt,* she heard her mother say and bit her tongue before she repeated it.

"She could probably find a willing cowboy toy at a rodeo."

"That's not what she's looking for," Katie said with complete confidence.

"What makes you so sure?"

"I know the fantasy. The cowboy part is just the trimming. She wants a man, not a boy."

"That could depend on the guy's equipment."

"Wilhemina's fantasy isn't really about sex," Katie told him.

"How do you know?"

"I just do."

"Wilhemina may not be as repressed as you are."

"I'm not repressed," she said in a voice that sounded terse to her own ears. She shouldn't be offended. After all, she had dedicated herself to making the world believe she was a sexless wonder. She should be happy she had achieved her goal. "I just have a higher priority."

"Like a nun," he said.

"No. It's not a religious thing."

He pulled into a hotel parking lot, stopped the car, and looked at her with an expression that made her stomach dip. "Wilhemina may not have a higher priority. She has hormones and human needs," he said in a low voice that made her think of tangled sheets and a hot endless night.

Not that she'd ever experienced a hot endless night of lovemaking. Katie opened her mouth to say that she had hormones and human needs, then abruptly closed it.

"So yee-haw," he said with no enthusiasm. "Let's find out when the next rodeo is."

"They're shorter than I thought they would be," Michael said, assessing the male rodeo contestants. "I thought everything was bigger in Texas."

Katie shrugged. "Maybe it's easier to stay on a bull if you're shorter."

He gave a noncommittal nod and adjusted his sunglasses as he scanned the audience. "We should split up. You can check all the ladies' rooms."

"Oh, goody. Bathroom duty," Katie quipped.

He slid a sunglass-obscured glance her way. Even Katie would have to admit he looked sexy with those dark shades, dark hair, and pecs beneath his button-down shirt. "I don't think it would go over well if I checked the ladies' rooms."

"I don't know. If you put on a Stetson and a pair of boots, you might be able to attract a few groupies."

"Should I take that as a compliment?"

His voice was just a little too silky, and the fact that she couldn't read his eyes made her nervous. "If you've ever wanted to be a cowboy, I guess you could," she said in a deliberately breezy tone. "I'll check the rest rooms and the food concessions." She grimaced. "If Wilhemina's not having a good time, she'll eat."

He nodded. "Okay. Meet me here in forty-five minutes."

Katie conducted the rest-room relay twice and double-checked all the food concessions. She had a gut feeling they were wasting their time, but Michael had insisted. Checking her watch, she saw she had a few minutes to spare, so she decided to look behind the scenes just in case Wilhemina may have gotten particularly brave and brazen. She wound her way through dozens of trailers with no luck and turned back. Rounding a corner, she plowed into a hard chest.

"Well, howdy, sweet thing," a tall, young cowboy dressed in chaps said, catching her by the shoulders. "Sorry I didn't see you coming. I just blew my ride."

"Sorry," she murmured. "I wasn't looking where I was going."

His gaze fell over her from head to toe, and he gave a crooked grin. "You wanna make it up to me?"

Katie went blank. "Make what up to you?"

He shrugged his broad shoulders in a way that probably mesmerized other women. Katie felt completely immune. "I thought you might wanna console me. A lot of the girls who come back here are looking for—"

Shock raced through her. "Oh, no. I wasn't looking for—"

"She's not looking for action," Michael said from behind her and pulling out a photo. "She's looking for this woman."

The cowboy scrutinized the photo. "Sorry I can't help you. I haven't seen her." He glanced at Katie and tipped his hat. "If you change your mind, my trailer's on the back row."

At a loss, Katie shook her head. "Good luck with your next ride."

Michael pressed his hand against her back, nudging her toward the stadium. "Now that's an irresistible invitation. Meet me at my trailer on the back row," he cracked, shaking his head. "I still don't get this cowboy thing. Is there something romantic about horse manure that I'm missing?"

Katie couldn't swallow a chuckle. "I told you it's more about the mystique, the legend. But the chaps don't hurt."

He glanced at her. "What's so great about chaps?"

She fought back a twinge of self-consciousness. "They make a guy's butt look great."

He stopped in the middle of a walkway. "And you've noticed guys' butts in chaps?" he asked in disbelief.

Katie resisted the urge to squirm and wished she had her own sunglasses. She felt half-naked. "It's a normal feminine observation. I probably haven't dwelled on it as much as some," she said with a shrug. "But I've noticed."

"I'll be damned."

"What?" she asked, not liking his tone of voice.

"Katie has hormones after all."

"I never said I didn't. I just can't act on them."

"Why not?" he asked, then held up a hand. "Oh, I remember. You have a higher calling."

"Not calling," she corrected. "Priority."

"And that is?"

"Nothing that would interest you," she said, unnerved by his attention. She glanced around. "I'm assuming you came up empty. I'm still betting she's looking for a rancher type."

He glanced at his watch. "I need to check out some things on the computer, then we can hit the bars."

Katie bit back a groan. She could only hope they would hit pay dirt tonight. Texas was a big state. If they didn't find Wilhemina soon, she could be anywhere.

Two days later, Wilhemina had successfully transported herself to Banderas, attended a rodeo, and sat in three different bars. She didn't think she had encountered her cowboy knight on any of her excursions so far. Or perhaps Chad had put a bad taste in her mouth. Every time she thought of him, she wrinkled her nose in disgust.

Perched on a bar stool, sipping a watery margarita, she began to worry that she was on a wild goose chase. What if she didn't find her cowboy knight in Texas? What if he didn't exist?

Tamping down her doubts, she heard a man raise his voice to another man.

"You owe me a hundred dollars!"

"I'm not paying you one cent. I never shook on it."

Wilhemina watched in horror as the two men squared off. One took a punch. She heard the sound of a fist impacting a jaw and winced. Glancing around, she noticed that most people acted as if they weren't even aware the men were fighting. That could only mean these people were accustomed to fights in the bar. A sliver of fear raced down her spine. Maybe she shouldn't be here.

She watched one of the men take another swing and bit her lip. Fright galvanized her into action. Scrambling off her stool, she ran for the door and raced to her car. Her heart pounding, she slid into her seat, slammed her car door behind her, and pressed the lock button twice for good measure.

She lifted her hand to her throat and tried to calm herself. Her mind spinning, she wondered if she should go back to Philadelphia. Texas wasn't turning out the way she'd expected. Katie would be worried about her and Michael was probably upset. Plus Chantal didn't like hotel rooms.

The thought of returning to the city where she had never fit in, however, made her stomach hurt. Wilhemina shook her head. She wasn't totally ready to admit defeat. She would check out of her hotel room and drive toward San Antonio. There might not be as many cowboys at Riverwalk, but there was plenty of shopping.

An hour and a half later with Chantal sitting next to her, Wilhemina looked at road signs in vain. About thirty minutes before, she had taken a turnoff for the road she'd believed would take her to San Antonio, but now she wasn't so sure. Frowning at the bumpy two-lane road, she muttered to herself. "This doesn't look right. This doesn't—"

Something gray and furry scampered in front of her headlights and Wilhemina swerved to the right. Her heart racing, she slammed on the brakes, but the car moved as if powered by its own will. Her headlights shone on the ditch just as the car tumbled downward.

"I'd rather be brave enough to do something worthy of wild gossip than be so afraid of others' disapproval that I do nothing at all."
—SUNNY COLLINS'S WISDOM

Chapter 10

Wilhemina instinctively jammed her foot into the brake so hard a searing pain cut through her. The car slammed into the ditch and she banged her forehead against the steering wheel. The teeth-jarring sensation vibrated through her head, face, down to her shoulders.

Her heart pounding a mile a minute, she distantly heard Chantal shrieking. She locked her hands on the steering wheel for two full moments staring at the brown earth one headlight illuminated. Chantal crept up from the floorboard and climbed onto Wilhemina's lap. The cat's plaintive cries snapped her out of shock.

Wilhemina let out a long pent-up breath and gulped in another, loosening her fingers from the steering wheel. She gingerly put the car in park and pushed on the emergency brake with her left foot.

Steam rose from the hood of the car and the engine began to make strange sounds. She bit her lip. "Uh-oh, I don't think that's a good sign," she said, stroking Chantal as much to comfort herself as the cat.

Biting her lip, she took inventory of herself. She rubbed her forehead. No blood. She looked at her hands, clenching and unclenching them. They were sore, but still working.

She wiggled her tight shoulders and breathed a sigh of relief. She wasn't hurt. She'd just creamed the car.

The rental car, she thought with a sinking sensation in her stomach. She would have to call them and have it towed, and her great adventure would be over. There was no way she would be able to hide from Katie and Michael after this.

Disappointment oozed through her. She sighed, reluctantly reaching for the cell phone in her purse. Pausing before she hit the power button, she told herself she had no choice. It was late at night. She was stuck in a ditch. She was going to have to be rescued.

Wilhemina hated that. She felt as if she'd spent her life being rescued. She wanted to be independent, capable, strong instead of helpless. Sighing again, she pushed the power button and waited. And waited. And waited.

No service.

Wilhemina blinked. *No service?* "That's ridiculous," she muttered, turning the phone off and trying again. Still *no service.*

Frowning, she looked outside and wondered if she might get better reception if she climbed out of the ditch. She awkwardly climbed out of the vehicle and put down her right foot. Pain shot through her. She hopped onto her left foot, grabbing the side of the car to keep from falling.

"Ouch! Ouch! How did that happen? When—" She whimpered, tentatively stepping on it again. More pain. Wilhemina felt a shot of panic. She was out in the middle of nowhere in the middle of the night with a creamed car and a bum foot. And no way to get help.

Unless she could get the damn cell to work. Biting her lip, she climbed out of the ditch and turned the power on again. She held her breath, waiting while the phone searched for a signal.

No service.

Her heart fell. She looked in both directions and all she saw was black.

During the next thirty minutes, Wilhemina tried the phone at least sixty times. Her foot was throbbing, but she could put a little weight on it. She hoped that meant it wasn't broken. Not one vehicle passed by her during that time, and she started to think she might be stuck there until morning if no one came along.

Even if someone did come along, who knew if they would be trustworthy. It might be another guy like Chad. A bitter taste filled her mouth and she made a face.

She hobbled back to her car and sat in the leather seat. Chantal climbed into her lap again and gave an accusing meow. The cat seemed to ask, *What were you thinking? What are you going to do now?*

Miserable and afraid, Wilhemina rubbed the cat. "I don't know. I feel like an idiot."

Two hours later, Wilhemina heard an approaching vehicle. She scrambled out of the car to the top of the ditch just as a pickup truck whizzed past. "Help! Help!" she yelled, waving her hands, ignoring the throb in her foot.

The truck slowed.

"Help! Please!" Desperate, she jumped up and down on one foot. "Please help! I'll pay you a thousand dollars if you'll help me."

The truck backed slowly toward her and a tall, lanky man stepped onto the side of the road. He wore a black hat, a white T-shirt, jeans that faithfully followed narrow hips and powerful thighs, and scuffed boots

Wilhemina's heart raced in her throat. She prayed he wasn't dangerous. She prayed he wasn't like Chad.

He took a long look at her rental car in the ditch, then

glanced back to her. His face was tan, and crinkles bracketed his eyes. His jaw was hard as a rock, his lips unsmiling, but his eyes looked kind.

Not that she was a great judge of character, she reminded herself. She bit her lip.

"You okay?" he asked.

She nodded, swallowing and pointing at her foot. "I just hurt my foot a little bit. I don't think it's broken. I don't remember hurting it, just slamming on the brake—"

He nodded. "That's probably when you hurt it. Where are you headed?"

"San Antonio," she said, embarrassed because she was pretty sure she had taken a wrong turn.

His eyebrows furrowed. "This road doesn't go to San Antonio."

"I think I kinda got lost."

He narrowed his eyes as he studied her. "You don't sound like you're from around here."

"I'm not. I'm visiting," she said, not wanting to reveal any more until she was sure he would help her.

He pushed his hat back on his head. "I can tow your car to the next town and drop you off at a motel. If you want to go to a hospital—"

Wilhemina shook her head. "No. I think my foot will be better by morning. I would be very grateful. I'll pay you a—"

"Yeah, I heard you," he said, rolling his powerful shoulders. "Let me hook you up. You can wait here or in the truck. But there are puppies in the backseat of the truck."

"Puppies," Wilhemina echoed.

"Yeah. The mom's a registered golden Lab and she had some problems giving birth, so I took her to the vet."

"Is she okay?"

"Yeah, but we lost one of the puppies."

She felt a twinge of sympathy. "I'm sorry."

He nodded. "Yeah," he said, nodding toward her car. "I'll go ahead and hook you up."

"Thanks," she murmured, watching his wide shoulders as he walked away from her. Wilhemina's mind raced a mile a minute. If he liked dogs, then maybe he wasn't a murderer. One of her stepmothers had said that if a man liked dogs, then he probably had a good heart. Shortly thereafter, she and her father had split up. Her father didn't like dogs, but when it came to women, he sometimes acted like a dog.

Standing on the side of the road, she watched the man attach a chain from his truck to the front of her car. He looked inside her car and gave a double take.

"Holy shit!"

Wilhemina stumbled closer. "What? What's the matter?"

"That animal in there. What is it? Did it get caught in a fire or something?"

Realization hit her. "Oh, Chantal. I forgot all about her. I should probably bring her in the truck."

"Chantal," he said. "What the hell is that?"

Wilhemina opened the car door and pulled Chantal into her arms as the cat hissed and scowled. "Sorry, darling. I was so excited to find help I forgot all about you."

Feeling his gaze on her, she looked up into his face. "She's a hairless cat. A rare breed."

He cocked his head to one side and shook it. "I can see why it's rare. That's the sorriest-looking cat I've ever seen."

Wilhemina winced. She'd always felt an odd kinship with Chantal because she knew she wasn't particularly attractive. "She grows on you."

"A little fur would help," he muttered, slipping into the

car and putting it in neutral. "Let's go. It's been a helluva night."

"I couldn't agree more," she said, following him. She couldn't help noticing that he had the best butt she'd ever seen.

She felt a rush of heat at the wayward thought. She needed to be careful. He could still turn out like Chad.

He did, however, open the passenger door for her and helped her into the vehicle. Wilhemina glanced into the backseat at five puppies and the sleeping mom. Chantal squirmed to get free, but Wilhemina shook her head. "Absolutely not. You might claw them."

Her rescuer opened his door and swung into the vehicle. He started the car and put it into low gear.

She was accustomed to her father's brand of power, built on money. This man had a quiet competence, a natural strength that drew her. "What is your name?" she asked.

He glanced at her. "Doug. Doug McGinley. And you?"

"Wilhemina," she said, thinking he wasn't nearly as pretty as Chad, but compelling in a different way.

"Wilhemina what?" he asked.

His direct gaze unsettled her. He might not have any idea who her father was, but she didn't want to take any chances. "Smith," she told him.

His eyes glinted with disbelief, but he nodded. "Wilhemina *Smith*, nice to meet you."

Doug successfully towed the car from the ditch and drove several miles down the road. He pulled into a small one-story motel, which bore no resemblance to any of the finer national chains Wilhemina had frequented. She told herself it would just be for one night.

"I'll talk to Wilbur, the owner. He's almost always got room," Doug said, getting out of the car.

"Thank you," she said, surprised at his chivalry. He could have just dumped her at the front door with her crippled foot and crippled car. Her mind wandered to the story of the cowboy knight, but she pushed the thought aside. So far, Doug had been kind, and she was relieved not to be sitting on the side of the road, but he could still turn out to be an axe murderer.

Doug returned to the car wearing a disgruntled expression as he adjusted his hat. "Bad news. Wilbur's only got two rooms available. The plumbing is broke in one and the other one needs to be treated for rodent infestation."

Her stomach turned. "Mice?"

He nodded. "I don't know what to tell you. There's not another hotel for sixty miles." He sighed and looked at her for a long moment. "I've got room at my house, but—"

Apprehension trickled through her. "There must be something," she said, feeling desperation grow inside her.

He shrugged. "I dunno what. If you don't mind the plumbing problem, you can stay. Only problem is the carpet's wet too."

She bit her lip, not liking her options. "If only that animal hadn't run in front of my car," she said.

"That's what made you run into the ditch?" he asked.

She nodded, wondering what her father would do in this situation. He would probably pay the hotel owner triple the rate to oust a guest and let him stay in the room. Wilhemina had the money, but not the nerve. What would Katie do? she wondered. Katie would have walked on her hurting foot and slept underneath the stars. Wilhemina was too tired, hungry, and shaken.

She looked at Doug McGinley. "I really hope you're not an axe murderer."

He chuckled, his face breaking into a smile for the first

time since she'd first seen him. The change was remarkable. His face and eyes lit with warmth and a laid-back sensuality. "No, I'm just your average hog farmer. I breed dogs on the side." He met her gaze. "How about you? Are you an axe murderer?"

She blinked in surprise. "I've never touched an axe in my life."

"Good," he said, climbing back into the car. "I'll rest easier knowing I probably won't wake up with a blade in my head."

On edge, she sat quietly as he drove back down the road and turned off on another road, then another. With each passing mile, she felt more isolated and more afraid. Two dozen what ifs played through her head, and she began to sweat.

"This isn't anywhere near the main road," she said as he pulled into a long dirt drive.

"Yeah, it's a lot quieter back here."

She swallowed over a lump of fear in her throat as he pulled in front of a two-story farmhouse. "Does anyone else live here with you?"

"Nope," he said, cutting the engine and getting out of the truck. He rounded the vehicle and opened her door.

She could taste the metallic flavor of fear in her mouth. Biting her lip, she slid out of the truck. The second she stepped on her right foot, she pitched forward.

"Damn," Doug said, catching her in his arms.

Her heart hammering in her chest, she instinctively clung to him.

Doug frowned. "You might need to get that foot checked tomorrow. In the meantime . . ." He swung her up in his arms, rendering her completely speechless.

Distracted by his wide shoulders and the sensation of his

well-developed muscles bunching beneath her hands, she said, "That's not necess—"

"Just easier than having you fall all over the place," he said without a pause.

Wilhemina couldn't remember the last time anyone had carried her. She knew she was no lightweight. "But I'm—" She broke off, not wanting to draw attention to her weight.

"You're what?" he asked, climbing the porch steps.

"I don't want you to get a hernia," she blurted out.

He looked at her and roared with laughter. "Darlin', I've lifted three times your weight."

Darlin'. Her stomach turned. She remembered that Chad had called her darlin'. But Doug had been so kind. She'd thought the same thing about Chad.

Doug carried her into a bedroom downstairs. "You can take my room for the night. I'll take a bed upstairs," he said, allowing her to slide to her feet just beside the bed.

Torn between severe attraction and severe doubt, she searched his eyes.

"I'll get your bag and the cat, then I'll bring in the puppies. I'll check on you before I head upstairs."

She nodded and sank down on the bed.

True to his word, he returned with her bag and Chantal. Wilhemina washed her face and brushed her teeth in the connecting bathroom. Surveying his medicine cabinet, she unfastened the top of a bottle and smelled his aftershave. It was a clean, sexy scent. She returned to his big bed and sat there for several moments, not knowing what to do. She couldn't undress yet. A few more moments passed and she glanced at his nightstand. A periodical on hog farming lay on top. The drawer was cracked open and Wilhemina spotted a package of condoms. The sight of it unnerved her and she pushed the drawer closed.

A knock sounded at the door and Doug strolled inside the room. She noticed he took up a lot of space. He seemed to suck the very oxygen from her lungs.

"You okay?" he asked, hands on his lean hips, his crotch nearly at her eye level.

She deliberately looked away. "Yes," she managed. "I have to say this. I absolutely refuse to pay you for sex."

Four days. Michael had been searching for Wilhemina for four days with zero results. Michael was starting to sweat, and he had the unsettling sensation that the trail was growing cold. Katie had been uneasy since she first set foot on the plane and he could tell that she was getting worried about Wilhemina. Michael also knew that Ivan's slimy attorney, Gaston Hayes, had been calling the house. In another situation, he could have filed a missing persons report and received some much needed assistance, but Ivan would find out and Michael would lose his opportunity to win the account.

He might lose it anyway. The knowledge was a burr under his skin, but he refused to think about it. Do the job. Deal with the consequences later.

Katie sat across from him in the lobby of their hotel. She wore a distracted expression on her face. Michael had seen the ghosts come and go in her eyes. Texas was clearly a tough place for her to be, and he couldn't help admiring her determination to find Wilhemina despite the fact that she wanted to be anywhere but here.

"Since she's obviously using an assumed name at the hotels, we should call back and ask about a woman with an unusual cat. Nobody forgets Chantal," he said. "We can split a list and . . .

He broke off as he watched Katie staring at a woman trying to communicate with the front desk clerk. The woman's speech was deeply slurred. A little girl clung to the woman's cotton dress.

"What? I can't understand you," the clerk said.

Katie surprised the hell out of Michael as she rose from her chair and approached the woman. Katie began to move her hands and fingers, and Michael quickly saw that she was speaking in sign language.

The woman smiled and began moving her hands in a flurry.

Katie laughed and motioned for her to slow down.

She was a surprise a minute. Michael narrowed his eyes. He wondered where she'd learned sign language. And why. He had been staying up late every night trying to trace Wilhemina through credit card usage or bank withdrawals with no luck. Last night he'd been tempted to run a check on Katie to satisfy his curiosity, but he'd ditched the idea. He'd never met a woman who tried so hard to hide her every emotion. Her eyes, however, gave her away. They told stories of pain and love and unspent passion. Stories that were none of his concern.

The same way the drama in front of the desk clerk was none of his concern. He watched Katie talking to the front desk clerk, but the man firmly shook his head. Katie glanced over her shoulder and met Michael's gaze.

In that half moment, he felt her asking for help. Michael felt an odd twist in his gut at the micro-glimmer of trust in her eyes. He knew she didn't trust easily, and that she'd turned to him meant something. It shouldn't, but it did.

She seemed to catch herself and turned back to the clerk who continued to shake his head. Michael held an internal debate that lasted twenty seconds. He preferred to avoid messy situations, and this one looked potentially messy.

With a sigh, he rose from his chair and walked toward the front desk. "Problem?" he asked Katie in a low voice.

She jerked around and met his gaze. He felt a flash of electricity zap between them. He put it down to static electricity in the carpet, or maybe in her hair. "This is Rosa. She's been hearing disabled since birth. She got a letter telling her she had won a trip for two to the rodeo for twenty-five dollars. She sent in the money and received a contest confirmation, but it looks like it's a hoax. The hotel manager doesn't know what she's talking about. Plus the hotel is full for the rodeo. So now, she has spent money on bus tickets and there's no hotel room or rodeo tickets."

"You have no rooms at all?" Michael asked the desk clerk in disbelief.

The clerk shook his head. "Everybody's booked for the rodeo. I've got prepaid confirmations for people coming into town today. You two are lucky you've still got your rooms."

He'd known this was going to be messy. He wasn't responsible for fixing Rosa's problems. It wasn't his job to wipe the disappointed expression off the little girl's face either. He was surprised Katie had allowed herself to be dragged into this. He'd gotten the impression she was almost as much of a loner as he was.

He could crab all he wanted, but Michael couldn't stop his brain from trying to solve the problem. It didn't take long. *Rooms. Plural.* Michael glanced at Katie. He stepped back and crooked her finger for her to join him. "How much do you want to help Rosa and her daughter?"

Her eyebrows furrowed. "What do you mean?"

"I mean how much are you willing to be inconvenienced in order to help them?"

Her eyes turned wary. "I don't know. What did you have in mind?"

"You could give up your room for the night," he suggested.

"And stay where?"

"With me," he said.

Her eyes widened. "With you, but that's not—I don't think—" She gave a little huff and lowered her voice. "I don't think it's a good idea for us to, well, sleep together."

"Why not?" he asked, pushing her a little because she so rarely lost her composure.

She glanced away and crossed her arms over her chest. "Because we have a professional association. Nothing more."

"Nothing has to happen," Michael told her.

She stared hard at him. "Are you sure about that?" she asked skeptically.

He chuckled, but fought an undercurrent of discomfort. "I haven't acted like I'm trying to get in your pants, have I?"

She paused and glanced downward. "No," she finally admitted. "But . . ."

"But what?"

She looked up at him and he saw it again, the combination of fire and darkness in her eyes that made him think she would be hell on wheels in bed. In another life, he would have been tempted to find out. This life was reserved for rebuilding his reputation. This day was reserved for finding Wilhemina.

Impatient, he shrugged. "Make your decision. We've got other things to do. It's up to you. You want to play fairy godmother or not?"

She bit her lip. "Okay."

"Okay what?"

"Okay," she said softly with a world of reluctance. "I'll stay with you."

"Fine," he said. "Just don't hog the bathroom or the covers and we'll be fine."

Her eyes widened. "Covers? Don't you have two beds in your room?"

He shook his head. "It's a king."

She bit her lip again. "I didn't know you only had one bed. I thought—"

"Well, now you know," he said. "We need to get moving. I don't care what you do. Just make a decision and let me know." He turned his back to walk away.

No sooner had he turned than he felt her hand on his arm. He paused, but said nothing, just looked at that small capable hand.

"I'll stay with you." She hesitated. "Thanks," she whispered so softly it could have been her breath and not a word.

The combination of that one little word and her touch made him feel weird, taller, stronger, almost better. He frowned at the odd feelings and shrugged them off.

Michael made a list of the hotels in the area, and gave Katie a list she could handle on foot while he took the car. By the end of the day all he wanted was a beer and a mind-numbing baseball game on television, but he knew he and Katie would have to hit the honky-tonks tonight.

As soon as he walked through the hotel's double doors, he spotted a woman across the lobby bending to sip from the water fountain. She wore a short denim skirt that revealed a pair of legs designed to make a man sweat. High heel sandals arched her legs, and a tight little shirt accentuated her perky breasts. Her hair hung in a shimmery dark blond curtain to her shoulders. As she pushed her hair behind her ear, he saw her purse her lips to sip the water.

He felt an immediate visceral response.

Quickly followed by shock.

The woman stood and turned to face him. She walked toward him with lethal determination in her blue eyes.

Was that mascara? he wondered. He stared at her mouth, which was painted what had to be bad-girl red. Michael couldn't speak for a full moment, so he was damn glad it took her that long to arrive in front of him.

"I don't want to hear any stupid remarks from you," Katie said.

"I think you need to define what you mean as stupid," he said, tearing his eyes away from her legs.

"Anything," she retorted. "Anything about my appearance. I don't want to hear how trashy these shoes are, that the mascara makes me look like a slut, and that the skirt is too short and the shirt is too tight. I don't want to hear it."

"Okay," he said with a shrug. "I have a question."

"What?" she returned in a short voice.

"Why the makeover?"

She sighed, then looked back at him. "Because we've been here four days and we're not getting anywhere. Nobody trusts you because you sound and act like you're from Philadelphia. One of us had to do something."

He shook his head and stifled the urge to whistle. "Well, I'll tell you, Katie, if one of us had to get a makeover, then it's probably best that it was you, because I don't think I would look one-tenth as good in that skirt as you do."

"Girls, there's no such thing as having too many men on second string . . . just in case your star hitter starts practicing on another field."
—SUNNY COLLINS'S WISDOM

Chapter 11

One woman, seventeen men.

Michael nursed his beer in amazement.

In the three bars they'd visited, Katie had danced with seventeen different men. Not that Michael was really counting. He'd just happened to notice.

He had to concede that her new look had loosened tongues. Bartenders talked to her more. The rest of the men's tongues were hanging out of their mouths as they studied various parts of her anatomy. She two-stepped like she'd been born to it, and he wondered how bad her feet were hurting in those sexy, but most likely uncomfortable shoes.

The twangy country tune ended, and she smiled and squeezed her partner's shoulder, then exited the dance floor. "I need a beer," she said and strutted past him.

No winces, he noticed and was impressed. She walked in those high heels like she'd been doing it since she reached puberty, and he knew damn well she hadn't been, at least during the last month. He narrowed his eyes. More surprises. The woman was full of them.

Michael watched her smile at the bartender and pull out

a photo of Wilhemina. When the bartender pulled his eyeballs out of her shirt, he studied the photo and nodded.

Michael did a double-take. He'd shown the same bartender a photo of Wilhemina and the guy had blown him off. The bartender chatted a few more moments, occasionally stealing glances at Katie's breasts, then he poured a beer for her.

Michael waited until the bartender had moved onto another customer, then approached Katie. "You got a lead," he said.

She took a long sip of beer. "Uh-huh."

"Amazing what breasts can do," Michael muttered.

She shot him a dark look, then closed her eyes and took another sip. "Headlights."

"Headlights?"

"Yes, sir, headlights," she said, opening her eyes and meeting his gaze. "My mother always said stand up straight and stick out your headlights."

He couldn't swallow a chuckle. "She sounds like she was a character. Where'd you learn to dance?"

"From her. As soon as I could walk, she was teaching me to two-step."

"It shows," he murmured. "I suppose she also instructed you in the art of walking in heels and applying makeup."

Katie nodded. "Yes, indeedy. My mother believed a woman should use all God-given and retail-enhanced resources to survive. She made sure all of us knew how to dance, walk in heels, and apply makeup. It just would have been nice if she'd also taught us how to balance a checkbook. Who knows," she said, skimming her finger down the sweaty beer glass, "if she'd known how to balance a checkbook, then maybe she wouldn't have had to rely on her other charms." She lifted the glass to her tempting mouth, then met his gaze. "Enough about me. You and I need to have a little chat with a man named Chad. Al told me Chad danced the night away with Wilhemina a few nights ago. He also told me that Chad is greatly attracted to wealthy lonely women."

"Is he here?"

She nodded toward the dance floor. "Working the crowd. Blond, slick guy in the middle of things wearing a black shirt and a rodeo belt I suspect he bought at Wal-Mart." She tilted her head. "Oops. Song's over. That's my cue," she said, and turned away from the bar.

Michael snagged her hand. "Your cue to do what?"

She gave him a wry smile and batted her eyelashes. "To work my wiles."

His lips twitched at her facial expression, but as soon as she turned and Michael was treated with the crotch-tightening view of her backside and the sinuous motion of her walk, he felt his temperature rise. He heard a low wolf whistle behind him and felt a quick surge of protectiveness, which confused the hell out of him. The men thought Katie was hot, but he knew she wasn't. Sure she looked hot, but Michael knew she had put a ban on sex. He understood it because although he hadn't banned sex during the last couple of years, it had not been a high priority. He hadn't met anyone who got under his skin and that was fine with him.

He watched Katie smile at the good-looking man. Chad stood straighter and puffed out his chest. She led the man to one of the few available tables on the other side of the dance floor, then glanced up at Michael. She didn't say a word but he knew by her expression that she wanted him in on the discussion. Striding toward the table, he saw her pull out a photograph of Wilhemina.

Chad glanced at it and scowled.

Michael sat across from the two of them. Chad eyed him suspiciously. "Let me get your beer," Michael offered, taking the sympathetic, commiserating approach. "I understand you met Wilhemina a few nights ago. I hope she didn't give you any trouble. She can be sweet, but she's not quite—"

"Right," Chad said with a big nod. "The woman is not quite right. You know I thought that woman had a mental problem. That's the reason you're looking for her, isn't it?"

Katie stared at the man in amazement. Michael gave a wry grin. "You catch on fast, don't you?" He glanced at Katie. "Sharp guy, huh?"

"Amazing," she said, but Michael knew she meant amazing in a totally different way.

"Katie feels responsible for Wilhemina because they're sisters," Michael began, spinning the flip side of the story Katie had told the car rental agent.

"Sisters," Chad echoed in disbelief, his gaze falling over Katie in unabashed appreciation. "You two don't look a thing alike."

"Different mothers," Katie said with a smile. "But enough about me. Do you remember if Wilhemina told you about her plans?"

Chad took several long draws from his beer and shrugged. "She mentioned something about wanting to see cowboys, Bandera, maybe go to San Antonio. I made several suggestions when I offered to be her personal driver and escort, but she—"

Katie blinked. "Personal escort?"

"Well, yeah. I've been told I'm nice to have around for a lot of purposes," he said with a wink. "If you know what I mean."

"Really?" Katie said.

"Yeah. I knew something was wrong with Wilhemina

when I told her she could have had me cheap and she turned me down."

Michael cleared his throat to cover his chuckle. "I'm surprised she turned down your proposition. Do you know where she was staying?"

"Marriott on King Street. It's just out of the city limits," Chad said and glanced at Katie, or more precisely Katie's cleavage. "I'd be willing to waive my fee for you."

Katie sucked in an audible breath and threw Michael a wide-eyed glance. "I don't know what to say. I'm so flattered, but I'm—"

"With me," Michael instinctively said, surprising himself as he spoke the words. "She's with me."

Chad narrowed his eyes skeptically. "Then how come I seen her dancing with a bunch of different guys all night?"

"He can't dance," Katie said. "And he didn't want me to sit and be bored all night."

"She can dance with other guys, but she'll be in my bed tonight," Michael said.

"Hmm," Chad said, then glanced at Michael. "Well, I'll give you a little advice. With a woman that looks like she does, you better learn to two-step or some other man is going to dance away with her. And I'd be first in line." Chad stood and tipped his hat to Katie. "Evening, ma'am. Pleasure to meet ya."

He left and she scowled. "What a slimeball. If Wilhemina turned him down, my hope in her is restored."

"But this guy was obvious."

"Probably not in the beginning, not to Wilhemina," Katie said and met Michael's gaze. "Thanks for your help."

"What help?"

"When Chad made his generous offer of waiving his fee."

"I didn't say anything that wasn't true. You're with me and you'll be in my bed tonight," he said and felt a strange coil of tension in his gut.

Her gaze still fastened to his, she bit her lower lip. "But not the way Chad thinks."

"Right," Michael said, standing and pulling her to her feet. He couldn't resist the urge to tease her. "I wouldn't even make you pay for it."

She gaped at him.

"Gotcha. Let's get out of here. If we're lucky we can find someone at the Marriott who had a chat with Wilhemina."

As they wove through the crowded bar, Michael would have had to have been deaf and blind not to notice the leering gazes and suggestive comments men made as Katie passed by. With each step, she seemed to draw into herself. Her face grew taut with vulnerability.

A man with whiskey on his breath bumped between them and put his arm around her shoulder. "Hi, Sugar," he said in a slurred voice. "I been watching you all night and I gotta tell you I'd really like to bury my bone in your backyard."

Katie recoiled. Rage swept through Michael and of its own volition, Michael's arm flexed and he punched the man in his face so hard he fell to the floor.

Katie stared at Michael in shock. Michael stared at his bloodied knuckles in shock. He couldn't remember the last time he'd hit another human being. Hearing murmurs of surprise from the crowd, he shook his head and grabbed her elbow. "Let's get out of here," he said and dragged her out the door to the rental car.

The night air was cooler, but he was still hot with anger and a bunch of other emotions he didn't understand.

"I must really look trashy to inspire that kind of remark," she muttered as she climbed into the car.

Michael slid into his seat, started the engine, and peeled out of the parking lot. "No. You just look hot. You need to consider the source. The guy was drunk. It's pathetic, but that was probably his attempt at flattery."

She rolled her head back against the headrest. "I want my ugly clothes back. I want my too-tight bun and orthopedic shoes," she said, knowing her new look was a matter of using feminine resources she'd ignored. Her appearance had helped loosen tongues and given her and Michael a sorely needed lead. She had to concede that her mother's instruction had served her well. *Okay*, she silently whispered to her mother, *thanks. I couldn't have done it without you.* Something inside her eased.

"Well, I have to agree that your before look was a lot easier on my knuckles."

She sat up then and looked at him, full of mixed feelings. She couldn't quite believe he had punched that man who had insulted her. The knowledge did strange things to her heart.

"What?" he asked, stopping at a traffic light.

Her gaze fell to his hand, then traveled back to his face. "How bad does it hurt?"

"The guy had a hard head, but I'll survive." The light changed and he accelerated.

A couple blocks later, Katie waved her hand at a fast-food joint. "Could you please pull in there?"

He glanced at her in confusion. "Why? Are you hungry or—"

Her mouth tightened with impatience. "Just please pull in the drive-thru. It won't take but a minute."

Shrugging, he pulled in. When the clerk's voice came over the speaker at the drive-thru, he turned to her.

"A large cup of ice please," she said, digging in her purse for change. "They charge for cups."

"You don't have to pay for—"

"Just drive through and give him the money," she said, pressing the coins into his palm.

Michael collected the ice and handed Katie the cup. She pulled off the plastic lid, then positioned the cup on the center console between the seats. "Here, put your fingers in the ice."

He stared at the cup, then looked at her in surprise. The gesture had been . . . nice. He'd seen glimmers of compassion, but she'd never extended herself to him. He felt an odd sensation in his gut, not unlike indigestion.

"Hello? Didn't you hear me?" Glowering at him, she tugged at his hand and plunged his fingers into the ice. "It'll keep the swelling down."

"Thanks," he said.

She nodded and finally looked at him. "Thank you."

Her clear, honest gratitude kicked through him like adrenaline. He suspected she didn't give it easily. She wouldn't put herself in a position to need anything. Damn odd combination in a woman. Mouth like a siren, eyes like a child.

A car horn beeped behind them, signaling him to move forward. Damn odd combination in a woman, he thought again as he drove out of the fast-food parking lot.

Wilhemina *Smith* was one weird lady, Douglas thought as he returned to the house from the barn. He was still shaking his head over her. *I refuse to pay you for sex.* No one had ever said anything more insane to him in his life. And he couldn't imagine why Wilhemina would say such a thing. Sure, she wasn't the prettiest woman he'd seen, but she had nice eyes and a shy but ready smile. Doug had never gone for bony women. Wilhemina would probably slap him into next week, but he wouldn't be a man if he hadn't noticed she had a helluva rack.

He opened the front door and she peeked around the corner from the kitchen. "I-uh-fixed a sandwich for you for lunch," she said. "I don't know much about cooking, but I can put together a sandwich."

"You didn't have to do that."

"I know, but you've been very kind to me," she said, sliding the diamond pendant on her necklace from side to side in a nervous motion that unknowingly drew his attention to her ample cleavage.

Her little display of nerves was both sexy and sweet to Doug. He suspected she had more money than she could spend, but she didn't put on airs.

"What'd you fix?" he asked.

Her lips twitched. "I noticed you didn't have ham, so I fixed deli turkey. What do you want to drink?"

"A beer sounds good," he said and watched her slight limp as she headed for the refrigerator. "I can get that." He easily caught up with her and grabbed the door. "Looks like your foot's still bothering you. I should probably take you to a doctor."

She shook her head forcefully. "Oh, no. I'll be better in no time. It's just a little sore."

"If you're sure." Doug grabbed two beers from the fridge. "You fixed yourself a sandwich too, didn't you?"

She nodded. "I was hungry," she confessed.

"No need to apologize. I don't want you to starve while you're here."

"I don't think there's any danger of that," she muttered more to herself than to him.

He sat down at the table and motioned her to sit across from him. "What do you mean by that?"

Her cheeks turned pink. "I'm not exactly tiny."

"From where I sit, you've got a damn good body."

She gaped at him in surprise. "Excuse me. A damn good body?"

"Yeah. No disrespect intended," he quickly said, remembering her odd comment about paying him for sex.

She shook her head, still wearing a surprised expression. "None taken," she said. "Did you really mean that?"

"Yeah. Why?"

She bit her lip, clearly self-conscious. "Well, I'm just not tiny."

"Not all men like their women tiny."

Her gaze locked with his for a long moment, and he felt a sizzle that reminded him of a branding iron. Her eyes darkened with a hint of sensual mystery, and her gaze wandered over his shoulders. "That's good to know."

He watched her take a sip of beer and make a slight grimace. "You don't like beer much, do you? You look like you might be more the champagne type."

"Or tea," she said. "But it's too hot for hot tea. I'll tell you what I really like," she said, leaning toward him with a confiding tone.

His gaze dipped to her breasts. Hell, he was a man and it had been a while. He forced his gaze back to her eyes.

"I really like margaritas."

There was something primed and ready to go about Wilhemina *Smith*. He got a niggling feeling that she could be trouble, but Doug hadn't dabbled with that kind of trouble in a long time. He wouldn't take advantage of her, but there was nothing wrong with having a little fun. She was clearly of age. "You're not married, are you?"

Her eyes rounded. "Oh, no."

"Me neither. I got some tequila."

Her eyes lit up. "You do?"

"Yeah. It's a little early for margaritas, though. Maybe tonight?"

"That would be nice," she said with a shy smile. "How long do you think it will take the mechanic to fix my car?"

"Probably at least another day or two, but your foot can heal in the meantime." He lifted his beer to take a long swallow while he studied Wilhemina. There was something innocent and vulnerable about her that tugged at his conscience. He'd been taught to protect innocence. He shouldn't take advantage of her, he thought and decided that he wouldn't.

Unless she convinced him she wasn't so innocent after all.

Katie wouldn't approve.

Neither would her father.

Wilhemina ducked her head and wallowed in guilt for a moment. Her chest felt tight and heavy, her stomach twisted. She could hear her father rail against her, accusing her of a lack of gratitude. Was she insane to do such a thing? Wilhemina felt like a wicked, terrible, undeserving person. For two moments.

Snapping her head up, she stared into the mirror in Douglas's bathroom and sprayed her neck with perfume that she hoped would act like a sex potion.

No one would accuse Douglas of being smooth or sophisticated. She suspected he hadn't gone to college, and hog farming wasn't a prestigious career. But he was kind and he had a body that made every feminine hormone inside her want to stand up and scream. Plus he didn't know who her father was. All of this added up to the chance of a lifetime.

Katie might not approve, and her father would be appalled at the notion of her losing her virginity to a hog farmer, but with the way things were going, Wilhemina was starting to fear that she might keep her virginity for the rest of her life. Douglas was the best candidate to move her into the realm of being an experienced woman.

Whatever that was.

She'd known he was different from Chad when he'd looked at her as if she'd grown an extra head when she'd told him she wouldn't pay him for sex. She believed him when he said he thought her body was damn good because he'd appeared to have difficulty keeping his gaze away from her breasts. For some reason, his awareness of her as a woman didn't feel lewd. It just felt honest.

When he looked at her, she didn't feel slimy. She felt hot. Hearing the screen door slam, she felt her heart kick into overdrive. She pressed her hand against her chest, feeling a ripple of panic. Could she do this? Could she be wicked and seductive? Or would she wimp out?

Wilhemina glared into the mirror. "You will not wimp out." She enhanced her lips with red lipstick, stiffened her spine, and marched out of the bathroom to the kitchen.

Douglas was mixing something in a blender. Taking in the sight of his broad back and shoulders, she felt a sudden attack of shyness.

"Hi," she said, but he couldn't hear her over the blender. She stepped forward and repeated herself. When he still didn't hear her, she gingerly tapped his shoulder.

He whipped around so fast she stumbled backward. Wilhemina felt her feet fly out from under her. She was going to fall. She opened her mouth to scream, but no sound came out. She was going to—

She felt herself jerked upright against the front of Douglas's long, hard frame.

"Oof." The air went out of her lungs while her heart raced like a car in the Indy 500. Her breasts were smashed against his chest and her thighs cradled his. His arms wrapped around her like steel.

When the I'm-gonna-fall feeling of panic melted away, Wilhemina decided her current position had plenty to recommend it.

Douglas cleared his throat. "Sorry. You took me by surprise. I was making margaritas." He slowly eased his arms away from her. "I thought you might like to drink one while I get my shower."

"That would be nice," she said. "I wish I knew more about cooking, but—"

Douglas shook his head. "No problem. I've got a couple of steaks. I thought I would grill."

She smiled. "I'd like that."

His gaze brushed her breasts, then he deliberately lifted his eyes to meet hers. "You smell really good. A lot better than I'm sure I do," he said, stepping to the side.

"I hadn't noticed. But you've been working and I've just been taking it easy trying to keep Chantal from getting too curious."

"She's probably seen one of my barn cats, Flash, roaming outside and she wants to see what he's doing. You better keep a close eye on her. You don't want Flash to get ahold of her."

"Do you think he would hurt her?"

He paused for a moment. "No. But there are two things Flash likes to do besides sleep. Catch mice and uh . . ." He frowned as if he were searching for the right word. "Propagate."

"Oh," she said because she couldn't think of anything else to say.

"Chantal might be ugly as hell, but she's still female."

Wilhemina's stomach tightened. "Is that all it takes?

She can be ugly as long as she's female and he'll still want to—"

"Flash isn't choosy."

Her stomach twisted into another knot and she nodded. She felt a little queasy and wanted to ask if Doug shared Flash's philosophy, but she couldn't fathom a way.

"But that's one of the differences between humans and animals. For animals, it's all about primitive drives," he said, pouring some of the liquid from the blender pitcher into a glass. "Take a sip and tell me how I did."

Wilhemina accepted the glass and tasted it. Cool and cold with a kick. She took another drink. "Very good."

His mouth tilted in a crooked grin. "Good enough. You can nurse that while I'm in the shower. I'll put this in the fridge. If you want any more, help yourself. Okay?"

She nodded. "Thank you, but I'm sure this will be enough to start."

As she watched him climb the stairs, however, Wilhemina couldn't help imagining what Douglas looked like in his shower, the water rippling down his long, strong naked body. She remembered what he'd said about primitive drives and felt a surge of heat run through her veins. She finished the first margarita while the shower was still running and decided one more wouldn't hurt.

By the time Douglas had grilled steaks and they'd eaten dinner, Wilhemina had drunk two more margaritas in search of her liquid courage and her nose was numb. Douglas offered to teach her poker and she agreed, although the numbers were blurry.

Joining her at the kitchen table, he dealt five cards to each of them. She frowned at the cards. "Blurry," she muttered to herself.

"What'd you say?" Douglas asked.

"Nothing. Would you mind repeating the basics again?"

"Sure. Royal flush beats straight flush beats four of a kind beats full house beats straight beats flush beats straight beats three of a kind beats two pair. Got it?"

She nodded, although she was still computing what he'd said. She was supposed to be seducing this man, but she felt as if she were stuck in a stomach-jerking amusement park ride. Taking a deep breath, she blinked to clear her vision. "I'll take three cards." Looking at her new cards, she was pleased to see that she now had two of a kind. Her head swooned and her stomach rolled. She took another deep breath, hoping it would pass.

"Did you know that the odds of drawing a royal flush are one in six hundred fifty thousand?"

Wilhemina shook her head. *Big mistake.*

"Yep. The odds of drawing a straight flush are one in seventy-two thousand two hundred. Four of a kind, it's one in four thousand two hundred. You got a one in seven hundred chance of drawing a full house . . ."

Wilhemina's stomach rolled violently and her head felt as if the Liberty Bell were clanging inside it. She feared the statistical odds that she would be sick within two minutes or less were one in one. Embarrassed, but fearing she might embarrass herself further, Wilhemina stood in the middle of his discourse. "Excuse me, Doug. I'm sorry, but I have to leave. I'm going to be sick."

Fleeing from the room, she made it to the bathroom just in time to lose her dinner. Hearing Doug's heavy approaching footsteps, she closed the door and locked it. She didn't want him to see her this way, at this most unseductive moment in her life.

Disgusted with herself, she cradled her head in her arms and sat on the floor.

"Wilhemina," Doug said, tapping on the door.

She wished he would go away. "I'm fine," she said, even though her stomach continued to roll.

"You had too many margaritas, didn't you?" he asked.

Due to both her and him. "Probably."

"I should have stopped you after two. You must not be used to drinking much liquor."

She wasn't used to ingesting much of anything except too much pie and too many cookies. The thought of pie and cookies made her stomach turn. She moaned.

"Wilhemina, are you okay?"

"I will be," she said, voicing more optimism than she felt. At the moment, she felt as if death were imminent. "Don't drunk people usually pass out?"

She heard his husky chuckle. "Only when you're lucky. Wait there a minute. I'll be right back."

"No chance of me going anywhere," she muttered. She gave in to another wave of nausea and rinsed her mouth and face.

"I have something for you," Doug said through the door.

I have something for you. Sinking to sit on the floor again, she thought about how those words would have been music to her ears if she didn't feel so awful.

"Open up," he told her.

"That's okay. I'd rather ride out the misery alone if that's okay with you."

"It's not," Doug said. "Since you're staying in my home, you're my responsibility."

She blinked as he jiggled the doorknob. "No, you really don't—"

"Hope you're decent," he said and pushed open the door.

Surprise rushed through her, almost overriding her nausea. "I thought that door was locked."

"It was, but it's got a lousy lock. Here," he said, extending a damp washcloth toward her. "Put this on your face and you'll feel better."

Too weak to protest, she draped the washcloth over her forehead and cheeks. The cooling sensation soothed her. When her skin warmed the washcloth, she flipped it over and sighed. She couldn't ignore that it had been a nice thing to do, especially when she felt so stupid for overindulging.

"I don't usually drink too much," she told Doug, still too embarrassed to look at him.

"I got that impression," he said, swiping the wash cloth from her and putting it under the running faucet. "You want to lay down?"

"I'll get up in a couple of minutes." The room was still spinning and she didn't want to risk it.

"I can help you."

She shook her head, then stopped because the movement caused unbearable pain. "That's not necessary. Not really. Not—"

She broke off in surprise when she felt him lift her from the floor and cradle her against his chest. Her racing pulse warred with her nausea. "Do you ever take no for an answer?"

He looked at her with an inscrutable expression. "Only when it's really important," he said, and lowered her to the bed, then placed the washcloth on her forehead. He left for a moment, then she heard his footsteps on the hardwood floor of the bedroom and a click followed by the whirring sound of a fan. She took a deep breath and willed herself to relax.

After she was sure she wouldn't need to dash for the bathroom again, she lifted a corner of the washcloth and looked at him. "Thank you. You've been very nice to me."

He nodded, standing with his hands on hips. "No problem."

She continued to stare at him, wondering about his motives. "Why?"

His eyebrows furrowed. "Why what?"

"Why have you been so nice to me?"

Shrugging, he shoved his fists into his pockets. "I dunno. You looked like you needed somebody to be nice to you."

"So you felt sorry for me," she said, her stomach knotting, but not with nausea. More than anything, she didn't want Doug to pity her. She'd been the recipient of enough pity to last two lifetimes.

"Well, a little," he admitted, his lips twitching. "You wrecked the Cadillac, hurt your foot, have the ugliest cat in the world, then drank too much tequila. This probably hasn't been the easiest couple of days of your life. Plus there's something about you that—" He broke off and a self-conscious expression crossed his face. "Nothing," he muttered.

Curious, she slowly shifted to her side. "No. Finish. There's something about me that?"

He glanced away from her and moved his shoulders as if his shirt felt too tight. "There's just something about you that makes a man feel like you need to be taken care of." He shot her a quick glance. "Don't get upset about it. My father always said my urge to take care of things would be my downfall. I've always been this way with puppies and birds and . . ."

"Women?" She wasn't sure what to think. She'd just been placed in the same category as puppies and birds.

His gaze shifted and he gave her a quick but thorough once-over that she suspected was purely instinctive. He shook his head. "Not women," he said, and something about his tone shimmied down her nerve endings. "You want to listen to some music?"

She shook her head. "I like the quiet and the fan."

"Me too. I lived away from home for a while after I turned eighteen because I needed to be on my own, but I always missed the quiet. When my parents were killed in a pileup on the highway, it made sense to move back here."

"I'm sorry. When did they die?"

A trace of grief darkened his eyes. "Four years ago. You never know how much you're gonna miss 'em till they're gone."

She felt his loss echo inside her. "My mother died when I was born."

He frowned. "That must have been tough. What about your dad?"

"He's very much alive," she said. "Just married his sixth wife."

He raised his eyebrows and gave a slight grin. "Busy man."

"Yes, he is," she said, thinking how easy it felt to talk to Douglas. "I like the quiet out here, but it's so isolated. Do you ever get lonely?"

He shrugged. "You can be lonely with a hundred people around you. I've learned there's a difference between being alone and being lonely. I've been both." He cracked a grin. "Depending on the people, there are times when I prefer my own company."

She smiled in return, remembering how lonely she'd felt at all the parties she'd attended.

"Can I get you a glass of water before I head off to bed?"

Wilhemina wrinkled her nose. Her stomach was still iffy.

"I'm *not* giving you any more margaritas," he said firmly.

"I don't want any. I don't really want anything."

"As soon as you can, though, you need to drink some water. It cuts the dehydration factor and will make you feel a little better."

"That's what Katie said."

He cocked his head to one side. "Katie?"

Her stomach knotted at the prospect of explaining her life and the embarrassing fact that her father had hired someone to help her find a husband. She closed her eyes. "She's a friend."

"Does she know where you are?"

The knot tightened. "She knows I'm in Texas."

"But does she know you're staying on a hog farmer's ranch?"

Feeling a spurt of anger override her guilt, she opened her eyes and met his gaze. "I don't have to tell her everything. I don't have to tell anyone everything. I'm an adult."

He raised his eyebrows. "Okay. Just thought there might be someone worrying about you. If not Katie, then maybe a man."

She immediately thought of Michael. But his interest in her was purely professional. "There's no man waiting for me," she said, conveying her availability in the clearest possible way. She wished she hadn't drunk so much. She wished she could seduce Douglas. But she felt horrible.

She saw something flicker in Doug's eyes as he nodded, a recognition of the message she was trying to send. It occurred to Wilhemina that seduction was a lot like playing catch, not that she'd ever been athletic. She threw the ball and waited for Doug to throw it back. If he did, then the game continued. If he didn't, it was over.

"Feel better. G'night now," he said, and the game was over.

For tonight.

"Don't waste your time on a man
unless his kiss makes you forget your name."
—SUNNY COLLINS'S WISDOM

Chapter 12

No big deal. She was just going to share a bed with
Michael. Nothing else. No naked bodies entwined in the
darkness writhing in sexual pleasure.

Katie adjusted an air conditioner vent so that it blew on
her full blast. She should think about something else.

She and Michael had gleaned very little from the hotel
front desk employees at the Marriott except for the fact that
Wilhemina had checked in under a different name and paid
with cash. Michael said they would leave for Bandera the
following morning.

Nothing was going to happen, she told herself, but the
closeness in the dark interior of the car made her more sensitive to him. His hands on the steering wheel, the subtle
scent of his aftershave, the way he rolled his wide shoulders
as if to release the tension of the day.

She was certain she didn't appeal to him, which was a
huge relief. She wondered, however, in the secret darkness
of the car, what it would be like if Michael wanted her.
Funny how she'd hated the way the men in the bar had
leered at her, but she didn't feel that way at all about how
Michael looked at her. She knew he could be surprisingly
chivalrous. She wondered what kind of lover he would be.

Would he be passionate? Would he have to control every-thing the way he controlled the rest of his life? Would he take his time? She wondered what a woman could do to make Michael lose his control. A forbidden image of French kisses filled with a combination of teasing and seduction made her feel warm and oddly restless.

Katie frowned at the sensation. A shot of alarm raced through her. Where had all that come from? Those were things she would expect her mother to think.

Like mother, like daughter.

The prospect made her stomach knot.

How about you're human? she heard her mother ask. *What's wrong with that?*

Everything if it got in the way of doing what she needed to do. She wished she weren't cooped up in this car with him. Lord help her if proximity to Michael was affecting her this much now, she was going to feel as if she'd been dipped into a boiling cauldron when she got into bed with him. Swallowing her self-disgust, she slammed the door shut on her unsettling thoughts and concentrated on where Wilhem-ina might be. She wished she had mental telepathy. At the rate they were going, Ivan would return before she and Michael had recovered Wilhemina.

"Are you worried that we won't find her before Ivan gets back?" The question bubbled out of her throat.

Michael glanced at her. "No."

"Why? Are you just obscenely confident in your tracking abilities or what?"

"I'm confident in my tracking abilities, and I'm confident that Wilhemina will have to use her charge card or withdraw some money from a bank before long. When she does, I'll know it and we'll find her." He paused. "Worst-case sce-nario is Ivan comes back before we rein Wilhemina in and I lose his contract. I won't be happy, but I'll survive. If I play things right, I'll do better than survive. He may be the big fish I wanted, but there are others."

Katie digested his words and wished she could say the same. If her worst-case scenario happened, she wouldn't get the bonus and it was likely she would lose her job. Her stomach twisted. And what would happen to Jeremy then?

"You're so tense you could give off the same electrical energy as one of those bug zappers. What are you so afraid of?"

"I don't have your options," she admitted in a low voice. "I don't want to get fired."

"If you get fired, you can get another job."

"It may not be that easy," she said, gnawing her lip.

"You're young, unencumbered, bright, attractive when you ditch the plain-Jane look. The world is at your feet."

"You're not much older, but you don't act like the world is at your feet."

His mouth tightened. "I've got more than my history to settle."

I do too, she thought, but kept her mouth shut. She might be starting to think she could trust Michael, but there was too much at stake to bet on it.

He pulled the car to a stop. "Time to hit it," he said. "You can have the shower first."

Her throat tightened at the notion of continued proximity with him. "Thanks," she managed and nodded.

They walked in silence to Michael's room and Katie felt the knot of tension inside her grow tighter with each passing second. This was ridiculous, she chided herself. Michael wasn't interested in her. It wasn't as if he was going to turn into a raving sex maniac once the lights went out.

You would be so lucky, she heard her mother murmur.

Katie rolled her eyes and took her bag into the bathroom. When she finished bathing, she dressed in a T-shirt and shorts, then headed for the big king-sized bed.

His shirt stripped from his upper body, Michael sat glued in front of a laptop computer. She was momentarily glued to the sight of his bare chest and broad shoulders. She watched him lift his hand to rake it through his dark hair and saw the slight flex of his pecs. A strange quiver jiggled through her stomach. The odd sensation caught her off guard, but she quickly pushed it aside.

Be matter-of-fact. As if it's no big deal to share a bed with a man like Michael. "Finding anything?"

"Not a damn thing yet," he said and turned off the computer wearing an expression of disgust. "Tomorrow we go to Bandera. I'll make some calls to the hotels tonight asking if a woman with a weird cat checked in."

Katie couldn't hold back a chuckle. "I can't help wondering how Chantal is enjoying her visit to Texas."

"She's probably so traumatized that Ivan will have to take her to a cat shrink when she gets back to Philadelphia," Michael muttered, shaking his head. "I know she's a rare breed, but why anyone would want such an ugly pet is beyond me."

"Ivan looks at everything with a measuring stick of prestige or money."

He shrugged. "I don't have to like him. I just want his business. I'm taking a shower, then hitting the sack."

Katie nodded and looked again at the big bed. Another spate of nerves jiggled through her. Brushing aside her silly reservations, she pulled the covers back on one side, slid in, and hugged the edge. She took several deep breaths and the sound of the shower finally lulled her to sleep.

Sometime later, she awakened to complete darkness and

the sense that Michael was in bed beside her. He hadn't crowded her, but she could feel his warmth. She listened quietly and heard the even sound of his breathing.

Her mind sped into hyperdrive. What was he wearing? Was he naked? Was his hair damp from his shower? How could he fall asleep so easily with her in the bed beside him? Should that offend her?

No. That was good.

Katie willed herself to go back to sleep, but her brain was too busy, her skin sensitized. Maybe a different position would help, she thought, and carefully rolled over. She closed her eyes and began to count sheep, but a vision of Michael's chest and sexy, intent eyes crowded out the image of white, fluffy animals.

Sexy.

Katie frowned at the unedited thought. He wasn't sexy. He was single-minded and disturbingly perceptive. He could be chivalrous, but he could also be a pain. He was strong, reluctantly dependable. He had allowed her to help the deaf woman. He was sharing his bed and not climbing all over her.

She had slept alone for so many years that she wondered what it would feel like to fall asleep in someone's arms.

She sighed and turned again. She flipped her pillow over to put the cool side to her cheek. Why was her cheek so hot?

She turned over again.

Michael sighed. "What's the problem? You're making more turns than meat on a rotisserie."

She winced. "Sorry. I didn't mean to disturb you. I'm just not used to sleeping with—" She broke off, not wanting to reveal more.

"Not used to sleeping with anyone," he knowingly finished for her. "Neither am I."

"Then how did you go to sleep so easily?"

"I'm tired."

"Oh," Katie said and bit her lip.

"Something on your mind that's keeping you awake?" he asked, shifting in bed.

"Not really," she said, then asked what had been on her mind all evening. "Why did you punch that man when he hit on me?"

A long pause followed, and the silence between them grew charged. "I didn't think you deserved it. You weren't asking for what he wanted to give."

"But I was dressed like I was asking," she said.

"But I knew you weren't asking."

"Do you often punch people?"

He gave a rough chuckle. "I haven't punched anything in four years, and that was a wall. I broke a damn finger."

"Why did you punch the wall?"

"Because my partner double-crossed me."

"Oh, I can see how that might bother you."

"Yeah, it did." He paused. "Do you have a ritual?"

She stared into the darkness, wishing she could see more than the outline of his frame. "What do you mean?"

"I mean, do you have a ritual for when you can't go to sleep?"

She thought for a moment. "I read sometimes."

"Did you bring a book?"

"Yes, but—"

"Then why don't you read?"

"Won't the light bother you?"

"I'll turn away from it."

She hesitated a second, then grabbed the opportunity. There was no way she was going to fall asleep in the same bed with Michael while she counted sheep. She flicked the light on low and he immediately rolled over. The covers slipped revealing his bare back.

She tore her gaze from his smoothly muscled skin. "Are you sure this won't keep you awake?" she asked, pulling a book from her duffel bag.

"I'm sure," he said, glancing over his shoulder to look at her. "But I have a favor to ask."

Her stomach tensed. Was this when he asked her to take off her clothes? "What?"

"Read aloud."

The simple request surprised her. She cleared her throat. "But what if you don't like what I'm reading?"

"It doesn't matter," he said with a shrug and rolled over. "Just read in your natural voice. I like your voice."

He murmured the request in a low, intimate tone that tickled her nerve endings. At the same time, however, he'd rolled over as if he had no intention of, well, doing anything but sleeping.

Trying to push aside her hypersensitivity, Katie flipped open the classic tale of Macbeth and began to read. She continued for several pages, darting a glance at Michael every now and then. Soon, she began to relax. Pausing, she looked at him and listened. His breathing was even, his chest rose in a peaceful rhythm.

She swallowed a chuckle. Why had she been worried? She hadn't turned Michael into a raving sex maniac. She'd only made him sleep like a baby.

He was as hard as a rock.

Her voice slid through him with a combination of Philadelphia proper and slow easy drawl that affected him like a caress across his groin. He deliberately made his breath even, so she wouldn't know. The woman was about ready to jump out of her skin, let alone his bed.

She was such a contradiction. One minute she was giving up her room to strangers taken in by a scam, the next she was freezing him with a stare so cold a winter in Antarctica would feel balmy.

She'd made him curious. He shouldn't be, didn't have time for it, but she had layers and he wanted to look beneath them. A little searching on the net had told him her mother was Sunny Collins, the mother of Katie and her two sisters. The records had been a little murky, but it appeared Sunny's daughters had been fathered by different men. Sunny had lost custody of two daughters within two days. Michael suspected Sunny had known how to use her feminine wiles to her advantage, or necessity as Katie had said, and Katie had been living that down her entire life.

Katie wasn't exactly what she seemed, starting with her name. He wondered what she would do if he called her Priscilla. With her voice drifting over him, his mind began to wander. Underneath the tough uptilted chin and chilly exterior, she was soft and warm. He wondered how she tasted, what sounds she would make as he slid between her legs.

She made him curious.

And hot.

Michael and Katie visited three popular bars in Bandera, and she quickly grew tired of fending off passes while Michael quizzed the bartenders. She cast a quick hopeful glance in Michael's direction, but he just shook his head. Another dead end. She sighed, and the man dancing with her lifted his hand to her hair.

"What's wrong, sweet thing? If you're tired, I can take you home with me," he said.

Forcing a smile, which she suspected looked more like a grimace, she shook her head. "No. I was just looking at my boyfriend. I've been trying to talk him into learning to dance, but he refuses."

The man frowned a second, then chuckled. "Well, I'm disappointed you won't be coming home with me, but maybe I can persuade him to take you for a spin. You think it would help if we made him a little jealous?"

A trickle of panic raced through her and she shook her head. Darn. Wrong move, she thought. "It's nice of you to offer, but there's no use trying. He's just not the jealous type."

Her dance partner gave her an appreciative once-over. "Well he should be. If he's not careful, someone's liable to steal you away."

Katie gave an uneasy chuckle. "Oh, that will never—"

Before she could finish, her dance partner planted his lips on hers. Katie stiffened. "What—" she tried to say, but the man pushed his tongue into her mouth. She nearly bit it. "No," she said, pushing at his shoulders.

"Trust me," he muttered against her mouth. "Stop struggling. He'll be here any min—"

Katie felt the man abruptly pried away from her. She stumbled backward, instinctively wiping the man's kiss from her lips with the back of her hand. Michael steadied her as he glared at the man. "The lady isn't interested in your advances," he told the man. "Any fool could see that."

"Any fool could see she wants to be dancing with you. What's your problem?"

Katie froze as Michael scored her with a questioning gaze. "I-uh-I told him that I wished you—my boyfriend," she clarified, feeling her cheeks heat. "I told him I wished you would dance with me, but you refused."

His blue eyes didn't waver from hers and she felt the sizzle of something electric crackle inside her. "I didn't know it was so important to you," he said in a silky voice that did strange things to her insides. "You should have told me. I'll dance with you," he said and pulled her into his arms.

"I told you so," she heard her dance partner say, but then the rest of the room seemed to fade.

"Teach me," he said in a voice that got under her skin.

She saw something different in his eyes and her breath hitched in her throat. He tugged her against him, and she let him. She lifted her hand to his shoulder while he took her other in his. She was extremely aware of his hand pressing at the small of her back. His gaze didn't waver from hers and she felt a million emotions she'd never felt before.

Another couple brushed against her and she blinked, trying to regain her equilibrium. She shook her head to clear it. "You-uh-move your feet like this," she said and demonstrated. He followed, catching on quickly. Too quickly.

She searched his face suspiciously. "You've done this before."

"I was in the military and country music was popular at one of my posts."

She shook her head again. "I never would have thought it possible. You're just so—" She broke off when she couldn't come up with the right description.

"So what?"

"Anti-fun," she said when her muddled mind would produce nothing else.

He tilted his head to the side and his eyes held a dangerous glint that made her heart trip. "I haven't had time for fun," he told her, then whipped her around in a fast twirl.

Surprised, she rushed her steps to keep from tripping. "Neither have—"

"Trouble keeping up?" he asked with an arched brow when he dragged her against him.

She inhaled and his scent went straight to her already dizzy mind. "Absolutely not," she retorted, but her voice was too breathless.

"Okay," he said and shot her a rare, potent grin. He twirled her again and again, then pulled her back against him.

Determined to meet the challenge in his gaze, she clung to his shoulder and let her feet follow the training her mother had drilled into her. She could dance while she was asleep and dreaming, and at the moment she felt as if she were in the middle of a dream.

His hands made her feel warm and secure, his gaze made her giddy. The combination was breathtaking. After everything they'd been through during the last few days, she could almost trust him. She instinctively squeezed his shoulder and wondered what it would be like to be held by him, to be able to rely on him. To not have to be alone. The notion was so tantalizing it nearly blew her circuits.

She'd never considered the possibility of not being alone. It had been too dangerous. She'd never met a man on whom she'd thought she could truly rely. He pulled her against him so that she was flush against his front, soft against hard. The desire to be closer rolled through her like gasoline on fire. Closer, close enough to . . . She looked into his eyes, and saw his gaze drop to her mouth. Her lips burned as if he'd kissed her. He stopped moving, but her heart was hammering at breakneck speed. Anticipation stole her breath. She waited.

Michael inhaled audibly. He stepped back slightly with a reluctance she could almost taste. He looked at her with an expression of stunned wanting.

Her insides echoed the same emotion.

"The song's over," he finally said, breaking the spell.

Katie blinked and noticed he'd dropped his hand from hers, but she was clinging to him. A rush of self-consciousness raced inside her. Her cheeks burning with embarrassment, she pulled her hands away from his as if he were a hot stove. "It is. We should leave, shouldn't we?" She glanced at her watch just to give herself something to do.

Avoiding his gaze, she walked with him out of the bar to the rental car. He opened her door and she slid in. He rounded the vehicle, got in, then started the engine. The silence between them was thick with forbidden possibilities that Katie tried to chase from her mind.

From her peripheral vision, she saw him pull out his cell phone and check his messages. His eyes narrowed and his jaw began to twitch. She couldn't squelch her curiosity.

"Problem?" she asked.

"Not with this case," he said.

"Another client?"

He shook his head and narrowed his gaze. "Not with work." He shot a glance at her and worked his shoulders. "My mother has a medical problem. She sometimes confuses me with my father."

Katie remembered Wilhemina had told her the story about how Michael's father had ruined the family finances, then committed suicide. "I'm guessing you don't like that," she ventured.

His mouth tightened. "Considering the fact that he managed to lose millions of dollars, then take a hike into the hereafter because he didn't want to deal with the consequences, he's not my favorite person."

She nodded slowly. "Not everyone can be strong."

"But everyone eventually needs to accept responsibility for their actions."

Katie heard the edge of bitterness in his voice and felt an odd urge to soothe him. "What did she want?"

He paused, then glanced at her. "For me to come see her. No, I meant to say for my father to come see her."

"How long has it been since you visited her?"

"A month," he muttered. "Every week I check with the nurse's station at the facility where she stays." He rubbed the back of his neck. His guilt was tangible.

"She wants to see you."

"She wants to see my father, and I can't pretend to be him."

Katie remembered how she'd avoided seeing her own mother after she'd left Texas. She identified with the conflict of his sense of obligation and his desire to avoid any association with his father. "I understand," she said softly. "If I were you, I think I'd go anywhere but Philadelphia."

"I did when I was in the service, but running wasn't going to solve my problem."

Now that she was back in Texas, Katie couldn't disagree with him. She wasn't sure what she'd accomplished by leaving. She only knew she'd been certain she would suffocate if she stayed.

"Did running solve yours?" he asked.

"When I left Texas, I could be someone else. I wasn't known as Sunny Collins's daughter who was bound to turn out just like her mother."

"So now you're known as Katie Collins with the tight hair and plain clothes. Is that who you really are?"

His question made her uncomfortable. She'd never felt safe enough to be whoever she was. Sometimes she wondered who the real Katie Collins would be. But not for long, because she didn't have time for that kind of wondering. "I think I may plan to find out who I really am when I turn thirty," she said and chuckled. "Maybe things will level out by then.

He tossed a glance of disbelief at her. "Thirty?" he echoed.

"Yeah, I've got too much to do." She looked at Michael and his strength made her stomach dip. She wondered if she would be able to wait until thirty to have sex. She shrugged at the thought. Men like Michael didn't come along every day. As soon as he moved on, temptation would too.

"What would make your life level out? If you could have anything in the world right now, what would it be?" Michael asked.

She tensed at the question. "I want to find Wilhemina, then I want to help her find a husband."

"So you can get the bonus," he concluded. "Money."

She didn't want to care that her answer may have sounded shallow to him. "Money can't buy love, but it sure can solve some problems." Relief swept through her as Michael pulled into the parking lot of the single-level motel where they would stay.

"You wait here and I'll get the rooms," he said when he stopped the car.

Katie nodded and watched him walk toward the small lobby. He walked with purpose, she thought. No swagger, just a determined masculine stride. Something about him gave the impression that he could walk like that forever. Nothing would stop him. He counted on himself and other people could rely on him too. For a woman who'd never been able to count on anyone, the notion was too seductive for words. Strange feelings coursed through her, leaving her hot and cold, making her heart race.

Hormones, she thought and snorted. Hormones had gotten her mother into trouble.

The kind of trouble that produced four beautiful children, Katie heard her mother say from the hereafter.

Which wasn't all bad, Katie thought. Frowning at her conflicting thoughts, she rubbed her forehead wishing she could rub away her confusion the same way.

The car door whipped open, interrupting her internal debate. Michael tossed her a key. "We're right around the corner." He started the car and moved it to a parking space in front of two rooms. He rounded the car to open the door for her, but she stepped out first. It was crazy, but she didn't want to give him too many opportunities to be chivalrous or kind. He might make it easy for her to forget her wait-till-thirty rule.

"I'll get your bag," he said when she followed him to the trunk.

"That's okay. I can—"

"I've got it," he said, lifting his bag and hers along with his laptop.

Her nerve endings jumping, she walked briskly to her door and put the key in the loose doorknob and opened it.

Michael dropped the luggage beside him. "Wait a minute," he said, pulling the door shut and removing the key. He jiggled the doorknob and the door opened without the key. "Damn," he muttered. "Let me try mine."

He stepped next door and found his doorknob more secure. "You're staying in here."

Katie's heart slammed into her rib cage. She couldn't spend another night in bed with him. She wouldn't sleep. She would . . . want. Even if he didn't make a move, she would want. She shook her head. "I can't sleep with—"

"You stay in my room. I'll stay in yours," Michael said.

Katie blinked, staring at him for a full moment.

"Okay?"

She lifted a shoulder in a half shrug. "But what about you? The door."

"No big deal. I'll just put a chair under the doorknob." He carried her bag into his room, flicked on the lights, checked the closet, the bathroom, and all the windows.

Checking for her safety. Her stomach took another dip. How long had it been since anyone gave a rip about her safety?

He returned to the front of the room to stand in front of her. "It's not the Ritz, but it should be okay."

She nodded, crossing her arms over her heart hammering against her chest. "Thanks."

His gaze wrapped around her, and lifting his thumb and forefinger to a strand of hair, he gently tugged.

It would have been easy to pull back. She wouldn't have felt a bit of pain. Her hair would have slipped through his fingers.

But Katie wasn't inclined to pull back. Everything inside her seemed to be pushing her toward him. She bit her lip at the barrage of feelings rushing through her.

He skimmed his thumb over her lip, soothing it away from her teeth. He looked into her eyes for a long, potent moment, then lowered his gaze to her mouth. Katie forgot to breathe. Inch by excruciating inch, he lowered his head and his lips brushed hers.

She closed her eyes at the sweeping sensation inside her. She felt his fingers stroke her cheeks and jaw as if he wanted to know her bone-deep. A shiver ran through her and he slid his tongue across her bottom lip just inside her mouth. Tilting her head, he probed deeper. His fingers slid from her jaw to her head, and she felt like a flower blooming under his caress.

But it wasn't enough. Her head was spinning, but she knew she wanted more and she dropped her arms to her sides and she stepped closer until her body brushed against his. Her breasts skimmed his chest, and she would almost swear something crackled in the air.

She felt his hand slide down her back, urging her closer to him. He was hard, and his arousal made her knees feel like butter. Her nipples turned stiff against the fabric of her bra, and she felt a coil tighten between her thighs. Needs rose like volcanic lava, some basic, some deeper, and thickened the air between them.

He rocked against her, intimating a more erotic intimacy, then pulled his mouth from hers. He swore under his breath and pressed a kiss to her neck. "I want inside you," he told her in a voice low and swollen with need. He slid a finger just beneath her tank top onto her bare skin and moved it with agonizing slowness down her chest to the top of her breast. A little lower and he would touch her nipple.

He stopped and Katie bit back a moan.

"I want to go as deep as I can go," he said, and the roughness lacing his voice made her want to do something crazy like rip off her clothes. "But you're not ready."

A protest bubbled up from deep inside her, but she clenched her teeth to keep it from spilling out. He helped her not to ask for more when he pressed his mouth over hers again in a warm French kiss that made dark, hot promises.

She'd just begun to taste him when he pulled back. His eyes were nearly black with the same arousal beating inside her.

"Night, Priss," he said.

The name hit her like cold water. She sucked in a quick,

shallow breath. He knew. With his deftness at conducting investigations via the computer, she shouldn't be surprised. But how . . . "How did you dig that up? You couldn't have learned that on the Internet."

His gaze narrowed, then he raised his eyebrows. "Lucky guess."

Lucky for who, she wondered. She felt naked, and wondered how much more he knew. "I don't know what all you've dug up, but I'm not like my mother," she told him.

"Damn right you're not like your mother," he said, the directness of his gaze nearly knocking her over.

She blinked, and a wave of more feelings she couldn't identify swam over her like high tide. He had just aroused her to the point of her nearly begging him to take her, yet at the same time, he'd assured her that he knew she wasn't a tramp. The combination confused her at the same time it made her feel lighter than air.

She rubbed her head. Too much. Her body was thrumming, her heart was tight, and her mind raced.

"Night," he said again, lifting his finger to her cheek for a quick stroke. Backing away, he cocked his head toward his room. "See ya in the morning."

"Good night," she managed and watched him walk out of her room. She stared at the door for a full moment before she could move her feet. She double-checked the lock and secured the chain, took a deep breath and tried to clear her head.

Mud, Katie thought. Thick brown mud. That was her brain. Kicking off her heels, she went to the bathroom and splashed water over her face, then looked in the mirror. Her eyes were still nearly black with desire, the way Michael's had been. She touched her lips, swollen from his kisses.

Curious in the same way she would be if she were looking at a train wreck, she pulled her shirt over her head and unhooked her bra. Her breasts were flushed, her nipples still stiff. She touched them, amazed at how little he'd done and said and how much her body had reacted. Lower still, she felt wet and swollen in other places.

She waited for some kind of *I told you so* comment from her mother from the hereafter, but the only noise she heard was the echo of Michael's voice.

I want inside you.

Damn right you're not like your mother.

She suspected it was going to take a month of Sundays to figure it all out, but she wondered if Michael knew he'd given her a gift she'd wanted as long as she could remember.

"It's a funny thing, but for a special kind of man, making a woman laugh is almost as gratifying as getting her into bed."
—SUNNY COLLINS'S WISDOM

Chapter 13

"I think I can. I think I can," Wilhemina whispered to herself as she sprayed perfume to her throat. She wondered if *the little engine that could* would be offended or delighted to be the basis of her inspiration to seduce Douglas.

Her heart fluttered in her chest. For once, she just might be successful. Douglas had visited the house for lunch. Although she'd fixed him a sandwich, her stomach had still been a little queasy. Douglas had gently teased her, but she hadn't minded. He hadn't been mean, just funny in a sweet way.

She tugged on her hair, pushed at her plump cheeks, and sighed, wishing she looked different. This was as good as it was going to get, she thought, adjusting the one hat she'd brought with her. She wondered what he would say when he saw it. It bothered her that she still hadn't quite figured out how to broach the subject of getting him into bed. Biting her lip, she hoped inspiration would strike later.

She heard the screen door slam and her heart nearly bolted out of her chest. Taking a deep breath, she slowly walked to the hallway.

Douglas glanced up at her and his face froze. "Are you leaving already?"

She shook her head. "No."

"But you're dressed like you're leaving. You're wearing a hat, for Pete's sake," he said, pointing to her head.

Wilhemina felt a rush of embarrassment. "I just wanted to look nice. You know, dressing up can make you feel better."

He frowned in concern. "You still sick?"

She bit back a groan. "No. Uh, this was my mother's hat."

"Really," he said, moving closer to take a more thorough look. "It's nice."

She smiled. "You really think so?"

"Sure," he said. "I just like your hair better. You got pretty, long brown hair."

Her heart gave a hiccup. No man had ever complimented her hair. "Well, thank you for saying that."

"Just the truth," he said with a shrug. "I think I should warn you it's only gonna be burgers tonight. I can't eat steak every night. Too expensive."

"Burgers would be great," she said, still reeling over his compliment.

"Okay, and no margaritas."

"No argument from me."

He grinned. "Good. See ya after I wash up."

As soon as he left, Wilhemina returned to the bedroom and pulled off the hat, staring into the mirror. She'd never thought anything about her was pretty. Smoothing down her hair, she was very glad she'd come to Texas. With each passing moment, Douglas was looking more and more like her cowboy knight.

She joined him while he grilled the burgers, which they ate with chips and lemonade. Afterward, they took a little walk since her foot was better. When they returned to the house, she asked to see photos of his family.

Happy to comply, Douglas sat beside her on the sofa, his long, lean thigh pressed against hers while he told her story after story.

After a while, he glanced up at the clock. "Hell, it's almost ten o'clock. I'm boring you to death."

She shook her head. "Not at all. I loved it."

"You're too kind," he said dryly. "It's almost my bedtime."

Anxious for the evening not to end, Wilhemina bit her lip. "I'm not sleepy at all."

"You're not?"

She shook her head, searching for an idea. Any idea. "You know we didn't get to play poker very long last night. Do you think we could try again?"

"Sure," he said and grabbed a deck of cards from a drawer in the walnut end table. He dealt the cards and Wilhemina tried to concentrate.

He easily beat her in the first game.

She performed a little better in the second when an idea occurred to her. "Don't people usually bet something when they play poker?"

"Yeah, but I'm not sure you're ready for that," he said, laying down a straight.

She surprised him and herself when she set down four of a kind. "I'm getting a little better, aren't I?"

Glancing at her cards, he nodded and grinned. "Not bad for a beginner. What do you want to bet? Pennies?"

She paused for a long moment, then chickened out.

"What?" he prodded, curiosity glinting in his eyes. "What were you thinking?"

She felt her cheeks heat and almost wished she could

drink a margarita except for the fact that she didn't ever want to see another bottle of tequila. "It's nothing. Silly."

"No. C'mon. Tell me."

"You'll think I'm crazy."

"I won't think you're crazy. Tell me."

"Do you promise?"

He raised his right hand. "Promise."

"Well, there are lots of things I haven't done," she said, staring down at the sofa and rubbing her fingers over the upholstery.

"Such as?"

"Well, I haven't ridden a horse in a western style saddle."

"What does that have to do with poker?"

"Nothing really," she said, stifling a groan at her awkwardness. She squished her eyes closed, held her breath, and blurted it out, "I haven't ever played strip poker."

A long, long silence followed.

Panic burned through her, and the worst embarrassment of her life followed right after. "I told you that you would think I'm crazy. I told you," she said, hating the way her voice grew high and tight. "Just forget I ever said—"

Douglas covered her fidgeting hand. "I don't think you're crazy. I was just surprised." He hooked his thumb under her chin and coaxed her gaze to meet his. "You haven't known me very long."

Her heart pounding in her throat, Wilhemina took a careful breath. "No, but I trust you."

He cleared his throat and chuckled. "I'm not sure that's such a good idea."

"Why?"

"Because . . ." He shook his head. "Because I'm a man. I may live by myself, but I'm not a priest or a monk or anything like that."

"Have you ever played strip poker?"

"Once," he said.

"Did you like it?"

"It was okay," he said, his eyes dark, but not angry.

She took her courage in hand. "Do you think you might like to teach me to play strip poker?" When he didn't answer in three seconds, she regretted asking him. "That's okay. Just forget I said—"

"Hold on," he interjected, pulling back to rub his hand over his face. "I didn't say. You didn't give me time to say anything. Give me a minute," he said, closing his eyes. The minute lasted forever. Wilhemina considered slinking away, but she was determined to wait it out.

He opened his eyes. "You know that strip poker doesn't necessarily end with cards."

Sex. He was talking about sex. Wilhemina's pulse tripped. She swallowed over the lump in her throat. "Why don't we see what happens?"

His gaze took a quick trip to her breasts, then he shifted slightly and met her gaze. "Okay." He shuffled the cards, then looked at her again. "Ready?" he asked, as if he were giving her an opportunity to back out.

No chance of that. "Ready."

She lost the first game and removed . . . one sandal. But she did it slowly. Feeling Douglas's gaze on her, she unfastened the buckle, released the strap, tucked her finger under the strap across the bridge of her foot, and eased it off her foot. When she glanced up, she saw Doug's gaze linger on her bare foot and couldn't resist the urge to wiggle her toes.

He grinned. "Good choice. You have cute feet."

"Thank you."

"Ready for the next hand?"

"I am," she said, and lost her other sandal and the belt to

her skirt in no time. When she lost another hand, her accessories were all gone. They were getting down to business now. Wilhemina feared that if Doug saw her without clothes he might just change his mind about being attracted to her.

She had to stop being so cowardly. This was the opportunity of a lifetime. She needed to be woman enough to take it. Biting the inside of her lip, she looked away from Doug and unbuttoned her sleeveless blouse and pushed it down her arms.

Douglas was quiet so long she nearly put the blouse back on.

"That's the prettiest bra I've ever seen."

She glanced up at him in surprise. "Really? You like it? I can't get a lot of the skimpy ones because I'm not . . . small."

"Nothing wrong with that."

"Thank you," she said and smiled.

"Thank *you*." He paused. "You wanna stop?"

"Do you?"

He shook his head.

"Neither do I," she said and he dealt another hand.

It took a little longer, but she lost again. This put Wilhemina in a huge quandary. She could remove her skirt, but the idea of exposing her full white thighs to Douglas sent her into a full-fledged panic. Her only other choice was to remove her bra and bare her naked breasts to him. Oh, Lord, she wondered if she could, and she mentally recited, *I think I can. I think I can.*

Keeping her eyes firmly on a rust-colored stripe in the sofa, she lifted her hands to her back and tugged at the catch of her bra. She felt it the second it was released. Taking a deep breath, she lowered the straps and slid the bra from her breasts.

Daring a glance at Douglas, she saw his eyes fasten onto her nipples. He stared and took a deep breath, then he met her gaze. "Wilhemina, I hope you don't mind me saying that you have got the most beautiful breasts I've ever seen in my life."

"You don't think they're too big?"

He shook his head vigorously. "Not at all."

She felt her nipples grow taut under his gaze. Her skin felt hot.

"They're just beautiful," he said, wiping his hand across his forehead as if he, too, were hot.

When he continued to stare, she felt the slightest ripple of amusement. "Well, are we going to play another hand?"

Douglas blinked, looking up at her. He nodded. "Yeah," he said. "I need to deal. Here we go."

He dealt the cards and this time Douglas lost. He removed his shoe.

Wilhemina soon learned that all she had to do was move her upper body just a little bit and Douglas seemed to lose all concentration. Using her edge, she won five more games in quick succession.

"I'm not doing too good," he grumbled. With his socks, shoes, and belt surrendered, he had to move onto something more substantial.

Wilhemina couldn't wait.

With a trace of self-consciousness, he quickly unbuttoned his shirt and shed it.

Wilhemina stared, enraptured by his hard muscular chest. In some distant part of her brain, she registered him dealing another hand, but she couldn't take her gaze from his chest. More than anything, she wanted to touch him. With her mind halfway on the game, she discarded and drew her cards. Before she knew it, she had lost.

Which meant she would have to remove her skirt. "Oh, damn," she muttered, fighting a trace of panic.

"What'd you say?"

"Nothing," she said, reluctant to continue, but determined. She considered her options. The only items left were her skirt and panties. If she removed her skirt, then she would have her panties. Or. An idea struck her. It would only buy her time and a little modesty. She smiled and stood, lifting the back of her skirt and sliding her panties down to her feet. Kneeling, she picked them up and tossed them onto the sofa.

Douglas stared at her panties as if he'd been scalded. His Adam's apple worked as he audibly swallowed. "I didn't expect that."

She shrugged and his gaze fell to her breasts. "Another game?"

He sucked in a shallow breath and nodded, his eyes hazy with desire. *Desire for her.* The realization went straight to her head and every other feminine pulse point in her body.

"Coming right up," he said, and dealt the cards.

She barely beat him, but she did and he ditched his jeans. Wilhemina bit back a moan at the sight of his strong thighs. She couldn't not look at what was between them. Wilhemina was so hot she felt as if she were in an oven.

Douglas dealt another hand and it took a long time to play. She got so distracted looking at him she would forget to discard and draw. He seemed distracted too. He kept wiping his jaw. Finally, he won.

"Oh, shit."

"I heard that," he said with a rough chuckle.

"I wanted you to have to—" She broke off, the fire in his gaze making her lose her voice.

"You wanted me to have to what?" he asked with just a hint of a taunting tone. "Take it all off?"

She nodded, fighting nerves and arousal.

He must've seen both. "I'll take something else if you want to give it," he offered.

"What?"

"A kiss."

A kiss. A thrill raced through her. Just a kiss or more? she wondered. Nodding, she moved closer to him and offered her lips. His mouth descended and she felt the room turn upside down. Her achy unfettered breasts brushed his hard chest and he groaned. The delicious sound vibrated in her mouth. He slid his tongue inside to taste her and she felt herself begin to melt. He caressed her lips and tongue and before long, she felt his arms wrap around her, drawing her against him.

Her head cloudy with arousal, she wrapped her tongue around his and he groaned again. The sound generated a buzz between her thighs where she felt damp and swollen. She felt so many different sensations she couldn't catalog them all. She instinctively rubbed her sensitive breasts against Douglas, craving more, and his mouth nearly devoured hers.

He pulled back slightly, gasping as hard as she was. His eyes dark and sexy, he looked like a man on the edge.

Wilhemina was so worked up that the notion didn't frighten her at all. "I don't want to play poker anymore," she told him in a voice that sounded breathless to her own ears.

"What do you want to do?"

"I want you to kiss me again," she said, her heart beating so loud she was sure he could hear it.

"If I start kissing you, it's gonna be a long time before I

stop," he warned her, giving her yet another chance to run away.

"Promise?" she asked, and watched his eyes turn to midnight.

Letting out a growl, he pulled her against him. "I promise," he said, just before he took her mouth again.

He kissed her for so long she felt dizzy. She felt as if she wanted him to touch her breasts forever. When he finally did, a moan bubbled up from her throat, surprising her.

He used his fingers on her nipples, then followed with his lips and tongue, and Wilhemina thought she would die from the pleasure. The pressure building between her thighs was indescribable.

His mouth still laving one nipple, Douglas slid his hand under her skirt, up her thigh to where she was wet and achy. He stroked her intimately at the same time he gently nibbled her breast. The combination tightened the coil inside her until she could barely stand it.

Unable to stop herself, she began to moan.

Douglas continued to stroke her and Wilhemina felt a spasm of pleasure so intense she jerked with it. She felt as if she'd been pitched over the edge of a precipice and she was flying through the air. "Ohhhh, yessss," she moaned, completely out of control of her faculties. She moaned again.

"Oh, Wilhemina, you're killing me," Douglas said. "Touch me, baby."

It took a full moment for her to comprehend what he was asking. He placed her hand on the bulge beneath his briefs and she rubbed him, not knowing exactly what to do. He didn't appear to mind. Closing his eyes, he tilted his head back, his face the picture of sensual pleasure. She slid her hand beneath his briefs and touched him. He groaned. "Oh, hell. I'm not gonna last."

Clamping his hand over hers, he met her gaze. "We're finishing this in my bed."

Her heart pounding, her head swimming with renewed desire, she nodded. He stood and picked her up, surprising her. She bit her lip to keep from protesting. He swept her into his bedroom and onto the bed, dug out the condoms from the bedside table and ditched his briefs.

His size gave her pause.

"You look worried," he said, settling beside her and pulling her skirt down inch by inch.

"You're big," she said, pulled between uneasiness and arousal.

He dropped a kiss on her lips and slid his hand between her thighs. "You're wet," he whispered. "And ready for me."

He kissed her and played with her and she forgot her uneasiness. Before she knew it, he had pushed her thighs apart and he kneeled over her. What a glorious sight he was in full arousal.

He plunged inside her and her eyes about popped out of her head.

"Shit! You're a virgin."

Wilhemina bit her lip against the quick, overstretched sensation. "Not anymore," she said breathlessly.

Douglas's nostrils flared. "Well, hell. Why didn't you tell me?"

"I got distracted," she said, feeling helpless and not so desirable.

Douglas swore under his breath.

"Do you think you could move slow?" she asked.

He let out a long sigh mixed with a chuckle. "If I don't die first. I feel like I'm gonna bust."

Reassured and wanting to please him, she wiggled experimentally. "We can't have that."

He shook his head. "Oh, Wilhemina, don't do that. Honey, don't—"

"Doesn't it feel good?" she asked, continuing to move as her body adjusted to his.

"Too good," he said roughly.

"Don't you like feeling too good?"

He groaned and gave her a look of surrender. He began to thrust inside her in a rhythm that rendered her totally mindless. She felt the pressure inside her begin to build again. Her body began to reach and search for release. Feeling herself get closer and closer, she began to moan.

His gaze, filled with desire for her, and the primitive movements of his strong body taking her were too much. She felt the pleasure snap through her again and a scream of passion soared from her throat.

Douglas bucked inside her, his body bowed in hot scalding release, he muttered her name over and over again. Rolling over, he brought her with him, clutched against his side.

Wilhemina was still whirling in space and time, unable to stifle her moans of satisfaction.

"Oh, God," he muttered, his big body quaking with aftershocks. "Oh, God. Big breasts, and she's a moaner *and* a screamer. I've died and gone to heaven."

*"A woman's curves can pack more punch than
a double-barrel shotgun."*
—SUNNY COLLINS'S WISDOM

Chapter 14

It was a mean crowd.

Michael glanced at Katie every half minute. During the alternating thirty seconds, he'd watched three fights break out within the last hour. Going to Slim Jim's Saloon had partly been an act of desperation. He and Katie had combed every other bar and dude ranch in the area with no luck. The rough, basic furnishings, predominant male clientele, and advertisement for topless floor show suggested an atmosphere where Wilhemina wouldn't have felt comfortable.

But there was a thunderstorm coming down like the wrath of God, so the rodeo had been called off. Cowboys full of unspent energy crowded into the small building. Someone gave Michael a hard shove that he returned with a hard look.

He glanced over at Katie again and she pointed to her hand. Michael gave a slow nod. Just before they'd walked into the bar, she'd taken his hand and told him not to use his fist tonight. The protectiveness got under his skin at the same time that it made him uncomfortable. He wasn't accustomed to anyone interested in his health and welfare. He didn't need that kind of interest, but some part of him liked it.

He had wondered if she would return to her glacial state after he'd kissed her last night, but she hadn't. A flicker of amusement raced through him. She just seemed to be trying her best to pretend that it hadn't happened. That was one thing he liked about Katie. She almost always tried her best.

Brushing aside his preoccupation with her, he strode to the other side of the bar and approached a reasonable-looking man. "You come here often?"

"Often enough. Why?"

Michael pulled out a photograph of Wilhemina. "I'm looking for this woman. She's missing. Have you seen her?"

The man pinched his chin and scrutinized the photograph while the man beside him elbowed in. "Whatdoeshewant?" he asked, slurring his words.

Even from three feet away, the man's breath was so strong, Michael thought the place would start on fire if someone struck a match too close to his mouth.

"He asked me if I come here often and if I've seen this woman," the first man said.

The drunk man frowned. "Well, it's none of his business whether you come here often or not."

Great, Michael thought. A reasonable man with a drunk friend. He knew better than to argue. He pulled out his card and gave it to the reasonable man. "If you recall seeing her—"

"Now just hold on a minute," the drunken man said. "Where're you from, anyway? You don't sound like you're from around here."

"I'm not from around here," Michael said without answering the man's question.

"Snooty too, huh?"

"Frank, he's just looking for a woman," the reasonable man said.

"Well, he can find one somewhere else," Frank said.

Michael turned around to walk away and shook his head to himself. Suddenly he felt a hard push at his back and he pitched forward, barely stopping himself from falling. "What the—" He turned halfway and a man's fist came out of nowhere, smashing into his jaw. Pain vibrated through his face and head.

Reeling, Michael stumbled backward, running into another man.

"Hey, watch where you're going," the man said and shoved him hard.

"Nobody turns his back on me," Frank said. "Especially some damn northerner."

"Haven't you heard? The Civil War was over a long time ago," Michael muttered, feeling a twinge in the back of his neck as two men joined Frank. They all looked like they were itching for a fight. If he wasn't careful, the whole bar would turn on him.

"You didn't turn your back on Frank when he was talking to you, did you?" one of the men standing beside Frank said.

"Hey, boys," a familiar feminine voice drawled from behind Michael. He whipped his head around and saw Katie standing on top of a table. Damn, he had to get her out of here. She tossed him a let-me-handle-this look and gave a slight jerk of her head.

"I see y'all hold a wet T-shirt contest every Wednesday night. I was wondering if you think I might qualify."

Michael watched, stupefied, as she lifted her shirt and flashed her breasts. A chorus of wolf whistles ripped through the bar. His first instinct was to jump in front of her, but she gave him another hard glance with a jerk of her head.

Michael finally grasped her message. She was distracting

these men so he could get out of the bar alive. Pushing back the impulse to snatch her off the table, he sighed in disgust at how the situation had gotten out of hand and slipped out the door.

The rain fell in sheets. Michael walked toward the car, then stopped. There was no way he was leaving without Katie. He barely turned back, and she flew out of the bar door like a bat out of a cave.

"Hurry up!" she called, running toward him. "I think I distracted them long enough that we can get away."

"Can't imagine why you would think that," he said, still boggled by the fact that she had flashed half a restaurant full of men. "How did you get out of there?"

"I tossed them my bra. They were fighting over it when I ran out."

"You tossed them your bra?" he yelled, fighting the oddest urge to return to the bar and retrieve her undergarment. "You tossed your bra to that pack of wolves!"

"It was a cheap underwire and very uncomfortable. If fate is kind one of them will put it on and get struck by lightning."

He shook his head. "I can't believe you—"

Her hair plastered to her head, she tightened her mouth. "I had to distract them."

"Distract is putting it mildly," Michael said, pulling her toward the car. Unlocking the door, he tucked her into the car, rounded the front of the vehicle, got in, and looked at her. She was wound tighter than an overstretched string on a violin getting ready to snap. He hated the hollow vulnerability he saw in her gaze.

"If you make one comment about my breasts, I will hurt you," she said, not meeting his gaze.

Michael started the car and peeled out of the parking lot.

"That wasn't the first thing on my mind. Why in hell did you do that?"

She crossed her arms over her chest. "They were going to pulverize you."

"I appreciate your confidence in my ability to protect myself, but—"

She shook her head. "You don't understand. They were going to gang up on you because you're an outsider and they were going to beat you up."

"So why didn't you leave my sorry ass there and let them?" he asked in a low voice as he turned down the road that led to their motel.

She bit her lip and looked away. "If you get beat up, there's no way we'll find Wilhemina."

He suspected she would sooner cut out her tongue than admit that she cared about him. The knowledge that she would go to such lengths for his safety boggled his mind and tugged at other parts of him. "So it wasn't personal," he said, unable to keep from baiting her.

"Of course not," she said with a sniff.

"So, except for the Wilhemina issue, you couldn't care less whether I live or die," Michael said, impatient with whatever had been popping and buzzing between them since the first time they'd met. He turned the car into the motel parking lot, which was riddled with potholes full of water.

She opened her mouth as if she were going to agree that she didn't care about him at all, but she looked at him and something in her eyes sparked, then softened. She sighed. "I didn't say that."

"So it is personal," he continued, not totally certain what drove him to push her. He'd watched her dole out smiles and kindness to strangers, and all that watching had made him feel deprived. And greedy.

"You're not quite as much of a jerk as I thought you were."

"And you care about me."

"Well, I care about Chantal," she said with a testy smile.

He leaned closer. "But Chantal doesn't turn you on."

Her eyes widened.

"You don't want to kiss Chantal."

She opened her mouth, but when he brushed her lips with his, he could practically hear the protest stick in her throat. "I think we've danced with denial just about long enough, Priss," he muttered and took her mouth. He tasted her surprise and arousal and something sweet that made him think of violins. He tasted vulnerability and strength, and everything he tasted made him hungry for more.

The rain beat a pounding rhythm on the car as the kiss went on and on. She lifted her hand to his arm, clinging to him, never taking her mouth from his, stoking the fire that burned inside him. He felt her breasts brush against his chest and despised the wet clothes between them. He had never wanted to feel every inch of a woman's flesh more than now. His desire for her felt like the rain, forceful, inevitable, and unstoppable. Her wild, heroic gesture at the bar had put him over the edge. No one had ever rescued him.

But Katie tried to stop, pulling back and drawing in deep, shuddering breaths. Her eyes were dark with the same wanting that permeated him. She shook her head ever so slightly.

"Tell me you don't want me," he said.

A long moment passed where the electricity zinged inside the car like a wayward bullet looking for a place to lodge.

Katie tried to form the words that would save her from him. Michael was like a tornado, powerful and fascinating, but she feared what would happen to her if she allowed herself to slide into him. But she felt as if she was scrambling up a rocky ledge and the rocks were breaking beneath her. She had nowhere to go, but to him.

"I can't," she said, her voice low and unsteady to her own ears. "I can't tell you I don't want you."

In a flash, he tugged her from the car and swept her to her doorway. She somehow produced her key and he took it from her to unlock the door and push it open. No sooner had the door closed than he pushed her against the wall and surrounded her with his body and kiss.

She felt the insistent hum of needs she'd buried her entire life. His mouth was full of passion and that same need. She could feel his drive to take and give. She wanted to sink all the way into his passion. She wanted to forget everything she shouldn't do and do what she needed to do. What she needed was Michael. He knew at least some of her secrets. He knew her as more than Katie Collins, personal assistant, and he knew she was more than Sunny Collins's daughter destined for no good. He knew some of her secrets and she wanted him to teach her a few more. Her heart pounded with anticipation. She leaned against the wall and slid her fingertips through his rain-wet hair.

Pushing his knee between her thighs, he skimmed his hand down to adjust her pelvis so that she cradled his hardness while he rolled against her. The erotic motion rolled through her like thunder. He gave a deep moan and pushed her skirt down to her ankles. His hand dipped beneath her panties and he found her wet and swollen.

Katie's breath left her at the riot of sensations that raced through her. He stripped her panties off and she felt a second of self-consciousness, but then he slid his finger inside her. Her inhibitions burning like tissue paper, she pushed her hands beneath his shirt and reveled in the sensation of muscle, heat, and the beating of his heart.

He groaned, pulling his mouth from hers, and swore under his breath. "Oh, God, you feel like silk in my hands."

Katie felt herself melting under his touch, under his words.

He took her hand in his and kissed it. The gesture was so sweet it made her stomach dance. Then he drew her hand down his body to where he was hard and wanting. Her heart stopped at the power of his need. It was almost as strong as hers, she thought. Almost. She hesitated a half beat while he held her with a gaze that searched hers so deeply she felt as if she might drown.

Feeling a hard nudge from inside her to take another step, she unfastened his jeans and slid her hand inside. When she wrapped her palm around him, he let out a hiss of arousal.

Katie stroked his length and he closed his eyes. "You feel so good." His nostrils flared and she saw a fine sheen of perspiration bead on his forehead. "You just feel so—" He broke off as if something inside him were cracking. "Can't wait," he muttered and pulled her shirt up over her head. In one swift motion, he clasped her bottom and lifted her against the wall. "Wrap your legs around me," he told her.

Dizzy with excitement and arousal, she obeyed, and Michael pressed his face to her breasts. Her nipples were already hard pinpoints of sensitivity. He slowly rubbed his cheek from side to side. The rough texture of his whiskers didn't hurt, but instead made her even more sensitive. Her nipples tightened unbearably. He moved his head and took one deep into his mouth.

Katie gasped at the electric sensation that traveled from breast to between her thighs. Shifting her slightly, he stroked her where she grew wet and even more swollen. The restless frenzied feeling inside her spun to fever pitch. A sound of need and frustration bubbled from her throat.

One. Two. Three seconds later, Michael eased her onto him and thrust inside. Her eyes flew open at the invasion. He felt huge inside her. It hurt. And didn't. She saw the surprise in his eyes, felt the slightest pull back and couldn't bear it.

"Don't say anything," she whispered, unable to do anything about the huskiness in her voice. "Just don't . . ."

"Don't what?" he asked through gritted teeth.

"Don't stop," she managed, feeling her body adjust to his, feeling her close around him like an intimate hug.

His lids lowered to half-mast, he began to slowly pump and stretch inside her, filling her with sensation after sensation. She felt the coil of frustration and need inside her tighten with each stroke. The closeness of their bodies did something to her, touched her in a place she'd always kept guarded.

"Give me your mouth," he told her.

She stretched to press her lips to his and he gave her a French kiss that made the room spin. His mouth mated with her in the same way that his body joined hers. She wanted to be as close to him as possible. She never wanted this feeling to stop. The combination of erotic sensation and emotions sent her one step closer to the vague goal she was reaching for.

"Too much," Michael said against her mouth. He stiffened and swore as he thrust inside her once more, his body shuddering with pleasure. The sight and sensation of his climax was so fascinating that it distracted her from her own climb. In that one moment, he was utterly powerful, utterly vulnerable, and utterly hers. Her heart swelled and for the first time in her life, she didn't feel alone.

Michael swore again. "You didn't come."

Trembling, she clung to him. "Well, I didn't go away."

He gave a rough chuckle and drank in a deep breath of air. Their bodies still connected, he lifted his gaze to hers and Katie's lungs stopped at the sensual expression in his dark eyes. He shook his head. "That's not what I was talking about," he chided and shifted her to carry her to the bathroom. He let her slide down the length of his body to her not-so-steady feet, then took a deep kiss.

Katie's knees felt like hot wax.

Michael turned on the shower.

"What are you—"

Without a word, he pulled her under the warm spray with him. She wondered when her brain was going to stop feeling like sludge. She felt as if her body and emotions were flying while her mind was moving in ultra-slow motion. She tried to shake it off, but Michael kissed her again like he couldn't stay away from her and she allowed herself to sink into the sensation of the warm water and his strong body and his kiss. He moved her around so that the water streamed down her scalp and hair. When he pulled back to reach for shampoo, her surprise must have shown on her face.

"I like your hair," he said, lathering her hair and massaging her scalp.

The care he took made her stomach feel funny. "I didn't know that."

"I like you to wear it down," he said, pushing her under the spray to rinse the soap away. He drew her against him again and before she opened her eyes, he was lathering her breasts with soap.

She rubbed the water from her eyes to stare at him.

"What's wrong? Hasn't anyone ever washed you from head to toe?"

"It's been a while," she admitted.

"How long?" he prodded.

"A while," she said because he knew he was her first.

His soapy hands slid down her belly to between her thighs. He stroked her where she was sensitive, still swollen, reminding her of that vague something she'd been headed for earlier. He lowered his lips to hers and she loved the feeling of his wet mouth and the warm shower. She felt his hands stroke her back and bottom, always returning to the place between her thighs.

Katie felt the restlessness inside her escalate. She moved against his hand, wanting more. He gave a murmur of approval and French-kissed her.

Dizzy, she felt him pull back, then skim his mouth down over her breasts. She arched into his mouth and the combination of his fingers inside her while he tugged at her nipple made her crazy.

A helpless, desperate, needy sound escaped her throat.

"I'll take care of you, baby," he murmured, moving his mouth down her rib cage to her belly, and then he was between her legs. His tongue found her and stroked her with relentless, maddening precision.

The pleasure was so intense she felt herself flush with heat. She felt herself reaching, reaching, climbing, and then Michael sent her flying through the air. Her body rocked with spasms of pleasure. But it wasn't enough for him. He continued to take her so completely with his mouth until her knees buckled and he caught her.

Pulling her up with him, he held her under the shower until she began to breathe normally. Her heart, however, still hammered unevenly in her chest. She felt both full and devastated. Her brain was still chugging along like quicksand. She couldn't think of a thing to say.

The water turned cold and he quickly pulled her from the

shower. He wrapped a towel around her and dried her with such gentleness that it almost hurt, but she was too wasted to protest. After he brushed some of the moisture off his own body, he carried her to bed and followed her under the covers.

He tucked her body against his.

"Don't talk," he told her.

Good, she thought. *Because I can't.*

"Don't think."

Her feelings were so big she was having a hard time thinking.

"Just sleep."

Katie closed her eyes and followed orders.

Michael slept like the dead, but when he awakened in the darkened room, the tension was palpable. Katie sat at the edge of the bed, naked, her arms huddled around her knees. His heart twisted at the sight. This was more than regret. He knew it and it put a bitter taste in his mouth.

He rose and moved across the bed to her. He put a hand on her shoulder and she shot up from the bed, her arms over her breasts.

"We didn't use anything."

Her voice was filled with fear and misery. Michael took a moment to digest what she'd said. Surprise, uneasiness, trickled through him. He hadn't been thinking last night. At least not with his brain. He'd acted purely on instinct, an instinct so forceful it had knocked practicality into outer space. They hadn't used protection. She obviously wasn't on the pill because she was a virgin and she hadn't expected him to nail her against the wall.

Michael swore under his breath and rubbed his forehead. "It was only once."

She gave a husky chuckle edged with pure terror. "That's what parents say."

"I don't know what to say. I should have been thinking, but I wasn't."

"I can't believe I did this," she said, her voice filled with self-loathing. "This is something my mother would have done." She paused a moment. "This *is* something my mother did. Four times." She dropped her head into her hands. "I can't believe I did this."

Something inside him could hardly stand her despair. Ignoring the wall she was rebuilding around her, he moved toward her and put his arms around her. "It's not definite that you're pregnant. I may have rotten swimmers."

She glanced up at him with disgust in her eyes. "I'm twenty-five, prime time for pregnancy and I suspect your swimmers are just fine." She pushed away from him. "This isn't a joke."

"*If* you're pregnant, and at this point it's a big *if*, the situation could be worse. You and I are both reasonably mature adults. I'll take care of you."

Katie's sob rent the air, surprising the hell out of him, cutting at him. "You can't take care of me," she wailed. "You can't afford me."

Completely confused by her extreme reaction, he shook his head. "What in hell are you talking about?"

She turned back to him, grabbing his arms and shaking him. "I can't be pregnant," she told him desperately. "I have to take care of Jeremy."

"Jeremy? Who's Jere—" He broke off as the name rang a bell from an old newspaper article he'd read on the net. "Your mother's last child. I thought he died in the explosion."

She shook her head solemnly and rubbed her wet cheeks

with the back of her hand. "No. He survived, but his hearing didn't. He's deaf."

"That's why you know sign language," he said, his mind spinning. There were too many pieces still missing to this puzzle. "So where is he?"

"At a special residential school for the severely hearing impaired about thirty miles away from Philadelphia. I visit him every Sunday." She hesitated, then looked down. "It's a very expensive school."

"That's why you took Ivan up on his offer to find a husband for Wilhemina."

She nodded. "It would make a big difference in Jeremy's life. In my life. I might actually be able to fall asleep at night without worrying." She bit her lip and gave the saddest smile he'd ever seen. "He is totally terrific and I can't let him down. I can't be pregnant."

Michael put his hands on her shoulders. "Priss, one night of unprotected sex doesn't guarantee a pregnancy."

"In my family it does," she muttered.

"We'll see. But this is too early to tell. You still have options."

"Oh, I can't even think about that. I can't think about having an—" She broke off as if she were unable to say the word.

"I wasn't talking about that," he said, avoiding the word out of his own discomfort.

"And who gave you permission to call me Priss?" she asked him in that cold voice he hated.

"I don't need your permission to call you by your real name."

"I'm not that person anymore. I left that girl behind a long time ago."

"You are that person," he corrected. "You're just not your mother."

Her face turned pale. "I never wanted to be like her."

"Well, that's a lie. You probably wanted to be just like her when you were little."

She closed her eyes and shook her head. "No I didn't. I never ever—"

"Just like I wanted to be like my father," he interjected quietly.

She opened her eyes and stared at him. She fought what he was saying, but he saw something click in her eyes. He didn't know when she would admit that he was right, but he saw the recognition of the truth in her eyes.

"Most of us start out wanting to be like our parents until we get a reason to change our minds."

She looked away from him. "It doesn't matter. I just can't be pregnant."

"Well, if the worst scenario happens and you are, then I'll take care of you and the baby. I can," he told her. "And I will."

She looked at him with a healthy dose of skepticism he wanted to wipe away. "That's the same thing they told my mother."

Her disbelief enraged him. He ground his teeth so hard he thought he might break his jaw. "I'm not a coward. I don't walk away from my responsibilities." He was so furious he wanted to punch a hole through the wall. "I'm going to my room. If you need anything, call me."

"There's nothing wrong with enjoying a man's attention. The only problem is if the attention results in contractions nine months later."
—SUNNY COLLINS'S WISDOM

Chapter 15

When Michael knocked on her door early the following morning, he was all business. "A charge came through on one of Wilhemina's credit cards. It's a garage in a town a couple hours away from here. We need to leave as soon as possible."

"I'm dressed. It won't take me but a few minutes to pack my stuff. Is fifteen minutes soon enough?"

He nodded and turned away.

Katie felt a gnawing sensation inside her at his cool attitude toward her after they'd been so close. But she wasn't brave enough to close the gap. She'd been wrestling with her own demons since Michael had left her two and a half hours ago, nearly wearing out the carpet in the small hotel room pacing from one end to the other. Every once in a while in the midst of blaming herself for her foolishness and praying that she wouldn't get pregnant, Michael's face would slide into her brain. She could see the haunting pain in his eyes. If he actually followed through on his promise to take care of her, then she wouldn't be the only one impacted. His life would be changed too. His goals would be set back too.

If he followed through.

That was the big question. She had watched him follow through on all his other promises, but this was different.

The distance she'd felt between them made her feel alone. Again. She took a shallow breath at the odd pain just inside her rib cage. She had spent years learning not to rely on anyone but herself. There was no real reason to change that.

She studied herself in the mirror for a moment. There was no need to put on lipstick or wear clothes that flattered her figure and would draw Michael's eyes to her. She could put her hair in a bun and pull on glasses, she supposed, and do an un-makeover. She lifted her hair and twisted it into a bun. It felt too tight. And stupid. Who was she trying to hide from now? She brushed her hair and put gloss on her lips since they were chapped from his kisses. True to her word, she packed her belongings and joined Michael outside. It was still raining. He grabbed her bag and hustled her into the car.

He had done that from the beginning, she thought. Latent gentleman tendencies that always surprised her. He got in beside her and checked his GPS, then pulled out of the parking lot. The silence between them was thick with a dozen different emotions Katie didn't want to examine. When he turned on the radio, she closed her eyes and pretended to sleep. After an hour on the road, she felt the car stop.

"Damn."

She glanced up and saw at least two feet of water streaming across the road in front of them. A barricade of patrol cars stretched across the road. "Flood," she said more to herself than him.

"It's not supposed to flood in Texas. Texas is supposed to be in a perpetual drought. Aren't they always whining about water rights?"

Katie's lips twitched at his assessment of her native state.

"We're in the hill country. It rains in the hill country. If it hasn't rained for a long time and then it rains too much, there's often a flood because the dry land can't absorb the water quickly enough."

He glanced at her and raised an eyebrow.

"Texas Geography 101."

A policeman dressed in a long, gray rain slicker tapped on Michael's window. Michael pushed the button to open it. "The road's closed, sir. You'll have to turn around."

"I need to get to Calvert County. Any other route?"

"At least two other ways," the policeman said. "But they're flooded too. Only other way is flying and since it doesn't look like you have wings . . ." He shrugged and cracked a half grin.

Michael sighed, clearly not appreciating the officer's humor. "Any idea when I'll be able to get through?"

The policeman shrugged. "Tomorrow if you're lucky."

"Tomorrow!"

"Listen, son, I can tell you're not from around here, but I'm gonna give you a little bit of advice. You can't fight mother nature. Go get yourself a room and a hot meal at Laralyn's bed & breakfast in Chadburn." He nodded toward Katie and rain streamed off his hat. "That's a pretty lady in the car with you. You should be able to think of some way to pass a rainy afternoon."

Katie felt her cheeks heat at the implication and glanced away. Michael muttered something unintelligible and turned the car around. It was too late for breakfast and too early for lunch, so Michael followed the officer's suggestion and got a room at the bed and breakfast.

"They only had one room left," Michael told her as he returned to the car.

Katie's stomach tightened. How in the world was she

going to sleep in the same bed with him without . . . She swallowed a scream of frustration. "Did Laralyn recommend a place to eat?"

"A diner in town. We can try it now," he said, pulling out of the large driveway.

"Good. I'm starved."

"I should have stopped earlier for breakfast, but I wanted to get to Wilhemina."

"You and me both," she said. The sooner they collected Wilhemina, the sooner Katie could get back on the road to finding a match for her. Plus, Jeremy's birthday was right around the corner and she had promised him she wouldn't miss it.

The diner was packed, and the waitress who served Michael and Katie was so harried she'd poked her pencil in and out of her teased red hair at least ten times when she'd taken their order.

As soon as she left, an uncomfortable silence descended on Katie and Michael. She cleared her throat. "Did you call the auto repair shop where Wilhemina placed her charge?"

He shook his head. "I didn't want to tip my hand. When I saw the size of the bill, I did call the local hospital."

Katie's stomach clenched. "You think she was in an accident?"

"I wouldn't be surprised. That was a brand-new Cadillac. Nothing major should have gone wrong with it."

Katie knitted her fingers together. "Oh, I hope nothing terrible has happened to her."

"We'll have to wait until tomorrow to find out," he said grimly.

The redheaded waitress returned with burgers, fries, and sodas. "Hope that's right," she said, ripping the ticket out of her book and putting it on the table. "Sorry I can't chat, but we're running short on help. Thank goodness they're setting up a shelter and spaghetti kitchen at the elementary school."

"Spaghetti kitchen?" Michael echoed.

"Yep. Spaghetti stretches and when you gotta feed a lot of people cheap, it's the food of choice. I bet they'll be serving into the night. Thank y'all for coming. Y'all take care now."

"I've never heard of a spaghetti kitchen," Michael murmured, taking a bite of his sandwich.

"I think I'd like to go," Katie said, warming to the prospect of a distraction.

He looked at her in disbelief. "You want to serve spaghetti to a lot of people you don't know in a town that's not yours."

She wiggled her shoulders. "It's not like we have anything else to do," she said, trying not to think about the officer's suggestion.

He opened his mouth to disagree, then appeared to think better of it. "Okay," he said. "I'll drop you off after we eat."

"Thanks," she said and devoured her meal.

They quickly finished eating and Michael got directions to the elementary school. He pulled next to the front door. "Are you sure you want to do this?"

"Absolutely," she said, already pushing open the door. She couldn't wait to escape his brooding glances and the memory of what they'd done last night. Every time she thought about how he'd made love to her, her bones turned to butter, and Katie suspected she was going to need a backbone of steel to get her through the coming days and weeks.

Michael spent three hours catching up on office work via E-mail and phone. The bed and breakfast was nice, but the sight of the romantic canopied bed got under his skin after a while, so he decided to check on Katie. He returned to the elementary school and the sight that greeted him nearly gave him a heart attack. She was feeding triplet baby girls.

He got a strong feeling like the worst case of heartburn he'd ever experienced in his life. What if Katie was pregnant with triplets? The thought of being responsible for one baby was enough, but multiples . . . Gulping, he forced himself to remember that the statistical probability was very low, and something told him that if anyone could handle triplets it would be Katie.

Brushing aside the disturbing thought, he walked toward her. "Practicing?"

She whipped her head around and threw him a dark look.

"Not funny. Here," she said, giving him a spoon and a jar of baby food.

Michael looked at the baby food in disgust. "Where's mom?"

"Chasing two toddlers," she said. "She told me she uses the rhythm method of birth control. People who use the rhythm method are called parents," she said, throwing him another dark glance.

Michael sighed and contorted his legs so he could sit down on the chair designed for an elementary school age child. "Damn, how do you keep from getting a cramp?"

"Watch your language in front of the girls," she said.

He chuckled and dipped the spoon into the carrots to offer a bite to the baby with the orange face in front of him. "What? You afraid that'll be their first word?"

She rolled her eyes. "You don't know much about children, do you?"

"I used to be one," he said, offering the baby another bite. "Who am I feeding?"

"Charlotte. Diaper time after feeding."

Michael wrinkled. "That's definitely a job for next of kin."

"Real men change diapers," she said with a light of challenge in her eyes that did strange things to his gut and other places.

"Real men who can't get out of it change diapers." He offered Charlotte another bite and she worked it around in her little mouth. She was pretty cute considering her cheeks matched her orange hair. "Do you like carrots?" he asked her.

She smiled coyly and dipped her head.

"She's flirting with you," Katie said.

"Really," he said, oddly pleased with himself. "I guess I'm just irresistible to women of all ages."

"She doesn't know any better," Katie told him.

"At least she smiles at me," he said, offering her another bite. Charlotte backed her head away. "One more bite, sweetheart." Michael poked it past her pursed lips. Charlotte held it in her mouth for three seconds, then spit the carrots right back at him.

Baby carrots splattered his chin and shirt. Michael grabbed some napkins and mopped at the orange mess. He heard Katie snicker and glanced at her.

"You think she might be finished?" she asked in an arch voice.

"I think that like most females, she's a living, breathing booby trap. All smiles one minute, spitting on you the next."

"Well since feeding time is over, you know what time it is?"

Diaper time. "Not for me. Where's the mother?"

Katie gave a heavy put-upon sigh. "Never mind. If you're that afraid, I'll do it myself."

"I didn't say I was afraid," he said.

"Then here," she said and tossed him a diaper bag. "Wipes, diaper, and changing pad inside. You can change her over there." Katie pointed to a small vacant corner of the cafeteria.

"I'm supposed to change her in public?" he asked in horror. "Won't that scar her or something?"

"I doubt she'll remember it," she said in a dry voice as she continued to rotate spoons into the two mouths of the other babies. "Especially if you're fast."

Great, Michael thought, feeling a tight itchy sensation at the back of his neck. *I'm not only supposed to be good. I'm supposed to be fast.* He couldn't remember feeling this much pressure since timed tests in the military. Mentally swearing, he shook it off.

"If I change this diaper, then I want something in return."

Her gaze turned wary. "What do you mean?"

"I mean if I change this diaper, I don't want to hear any more remarks on how inferior men are in the area of child care." He didn't know why it was so damn important to him that she didn't think he was a complete washout with kids. He'd have to think about that later.

"Deal. But not if she cries."

"Okay. She won't cry," he said with far more confidence than he felt. He wiped off Charlotte's cheeks and hands, then lifted her from her infant seat and carried her away. "You might have to help me with this, sweetheart."

Mentally hearing the starting gun, he reached the corner and tossed the changing pad, diaper, and wipes from the bag. He knelt down and put Charlotte on the pad. She immediately put both her fists in her mouth.

Good start. She would have a hard time crying if her fists were in her mouth. Hopefully. He spread out the diaper and looked for the front and back. He frowned. They both looked the same. Charlotte started to kick.

The clock was ticking. Michael felt that tension in the back of his neck return. He pulled a wipe from the container and set it on top, then examined Charlotte's clothing. "Snaps," he muttered, popping them open. "Clever." He unfastened the diaper and was greeted with a big surprise.

"Oh, Lord," he said, wondering how a cute little baby could produce so much . . . He started wiping and quickly realized he was going to need more than one. Charlotte started to kick again, getting her foot in the mess.

"Oh, shit." Michael scrambled to clean her foot, then trapped both legs and used baby wipe after baby wipe. Her little arms started to flail and she was making moderately displeased noises.

Michael felt a trickle of sweat run down his back. He whipped the diaper underneath her bottom and made a calculated guess as to where to put the tabs, careful not to attach them too tightly. Charlotte continued to kick and started to whine.

Out of desperation, Michael made car noises while he struggled with the teensy snaps. The whining paused, so he continued more loudly. The damn snaps resisted, but he finally conquered them and gave a sigh of relief. He picked up Charlotte and turned around to a group of five women. They applauded.

"Well done," one said.

"The noises were a great touch," another said.

"The diaper's a little loose," another one warned.

"You might want to tighten it or you could end up with a surprise."

A surprise. Michael tensed. He could only imagine. "Can I do it without unfastening the snaps?"

She shook her head in sympathy.

Sighing, he mentally girded himself. Still holding Charlotte, he undid the snaps, then he carefully pulled loose the tabs, but the plastic from the diaper stuck to the adhesive.

"New diaper," the woman coached.

Charlotte began to kick again.

Michael began to sweat and make car noises. He dug out another diaper and situated it around Charlotte's bottom, then secured the tabs and pushed the snaps together. Just as Charlotte began to make fussy sounds, he pulled her up against him.

The woman gave a nod of approval. "You'll get the hang of it. You're a good father."

"Oh, I'm not her father," he said. "I'm just helping out."

The woman's eyes nearly popped out of her head. "Oh, my. Amazing. Listen, I have a younger, single sister I would love for you to meet. Can I get your number?"

Michael shifted Charlotte in his arms. "I'm not from around here. Just temporarily delayed due to the flood."

"Well, that's okay. Maybe you two could—"

He shook his head. "You're too kind. Thanks for the diaper-changing advice," he said and walked triumphantly toward Katie.

She lifted her brows when he stood in front of her. "I must confess. I'm surprised. I didn't hear any screaming or crying."

"Nothing to it," he said, wondering why he felt exhausted.

"No problem at all?" she asked doubtfully.

"None. Didn't you see those women cheering for my performance?"

"I thought they were looking at your butt."

He blinked, affronted and flattered at the same time.

"They were impressed with my diaper-changing ability. One of the women even wanted to hook me up with her sister." He hesitated a half beat. "I didn't think you'd noticed my body."

Her lips parted in surprise and the you-caught-me expression flashed in her eyes. Her glance slid away. "I'm not blind."

It would be pulling teeth to get the woman to pay him one lousy compliment. Except when she'd been coming apart in his arms last night. The vivid sensual memory made him warm again.

"Did you get rid of the dirty diaper?" she asked, clearly eager to change the subject.

"That's next. I need to get directions to the nearest toxic dump." He set Charlotte in her infant seat and slid her closer to Katie.

"So you really had no problem changing her diaper?" Katie repeated, a speculative gleam in her eye.

"None at all."

"Then how about changing Emily's?" she asked with a grin.

"Oh, no. I don't want to deprive you of the thrill of that accomplishment. I did mine. You do yours."

"But what are you going to do?"

Something less stressful like detonate a bomb. "Serve spaghetti. Those people look like they need a break. Ciao, Priss." He waved and deliberately turned so she could get a good look at his backside while he walked away.

Katie tried hard not to steal glances at Michael and his very nice rear end the rest of the evening, but if she were being graded on the percentage of time she looked away from him versus the time she looked at him, she would have flat-out flunked.

It wasn't just that Michael was attractive. That was no news. It didn't help, however, that she knew his body much more intimately, so that when she looked at his chest, she knew how it felt against her bare breasts. She knew how his thighs felt pushing hers apart. She knew how his tongue felt when he kissed her mouth, nipples, and lower. She knew what it felt like to have Michael inside her and some insane part of her had never felt more complete. That same insane part, she reminded herself, was probably hormone-driven and could very well be related to the drive to reproduce.

And Katie definitely didn't want to reproduce. Her mind wandered to Jeremy and the brief call she'd made a few days ago. The school was equipped with special telephones that enabled the students to see the caller's conversations in text, but not being able to see his face had been hard. She'd heard the disappointment in his voice when she'd apologized for not being able to visit him on Sunday. She'd promised she would be there for his birthday even if she had to ride a donkey from Texas to Pennsylvania.

She glanced at the sleeping triplets, then her gaze was drawn again to Michael. He was smiling at an elderly woman as he served her a sandwich. Katie was surprised at his friendliness and willingness to serve for so long. After all, the spaghetti line had long since closed and it was almost nine o'clock now.

He caught her looking at him and she almost looked away, but couldn't muster the energy to hide her curiosity. He gave her a long look that sent a zinging sensation through her, nodded, then continued to dole out sandwiches.

After a few more moments, the line died down and he walked toward her. "You look tired. Are you ready to go?"

She was tired, but she wasn't ready to face sharing a bed with him. "I'm okay."

"Why were you staring at me?" He looked down at his shirt. "Do I have spaghetti on me or something?"

"No, just rejected strained carrots," she said, unsuccessfully smothering a chuckle when he rolled his eyes.

He crumpled his long frame into a tiny chair beside her. "Then why were you staring?"

She felt her stomach take a little dip and she shrugged. "I don't know. I guess you surprised me."

"How?"

"Well, you've been—" She paused at the inevitable word that came to mind. "You've been charming today. You almost seem like you've enjoyed yourself helping with Charlotte and the spaghetti line."

"It wasn't bad. I just followed your lead."

"What do you mean?"

"There's nothing I can do about finding Wilhemina. I'm stuck. Might as well make the best of it."

"I think it's the first time I've seen you when you didn't have a one-track mind. You haven't been Dick Tracy today."

"Same with you," he said, his gaze wrapping around her like a hug she'd needed all day long.

"Same with *me*?"

"Yeah, since you accepted Ivan's mission impossible, you've had a one-track mind. Matchmaker, matchmaker."

That stopped her. "I don't know what to say. I hadn't thought of myself that way. I was too busy trying to keep my job and make sure Jeremy was taken care of."

"I haven't breathed in several years either. It's funny what you notice when you stop for a minute, isn't it?"

"Yeah," she said, feeling an odd warmth suffuse her as she thought again of Michael changing the baby.

"Of course part of your problem is that you've been afraid I would try to get in your pants," Michael added, jerking her out of her gooey moment. "The other part of your problem is you were afraid of wanting me to get in your pants."

She opened her mouth to protest, but stopped at his arched brow. "I have reasons for not wanting to get pregnant."

He nodded. "Good reasons." He covered her hand with his and laced his fingers through hers. The gesture reminded her of how their bodies had twined together last night, and his hand wrapped around hers felt more intimate than it should have. "Don't worry, Katie Priss. I won't make you do anything you don't want to do."

That was the problem. She wanted to hold him and be held by him. She wanted to feel him inside her again. She wanted, but she shouldn't. There was no future to it and there shouldn't be. It would only muddy the waters and she was already swimming upstream.

An hour later, they entered the lovely room at Laralyn's bed and breakfast. Amid the elegant Queen Anne furniture, the canopied bed took center stage. Fresh fruit and wine with two glasses sat on a bedside table in silent invitation. Katie cast a questioning glance at Michael.

He shook his head. "I didn't order it. It came with the room."

"Okay," she said, her awareness of him heightened with each passing second. She ducked into the bathroom to draw a quick breath of air and calm herself. A clawfoot porcelain tub big enough for two sat on a gleaming tile floor. Fresh flowers and toiletries graced a small brass table beside the pedestal sink. She felt Michael move behind her and stiffened.

"Did I tell you this was the only room they had left?"

"Yeah." She nodded, staring at that big tub and trying not to visualize Michael and her in it.

"Did I tell you it's the honeymoon suite?"

The realization nearly knocked her over. No wonder the room was so romantic. It was designed for couples determined to consummate their wedding vows. Most of them, repeatedly, she thought and chuckled to cover her awkwardness. "Figures," she said and returned to the room.

"Well since it's here, do you want some wine?"

She nodded. "Might as well, thanks."

He poured the wine and gave her a glass and she couldn't help wondering how Michael would act on a real honeymoon night. The fact that she was even thinking such a thing bothered her so much she gulped down the wine.

"Thirsty, huh?"

"Yes. Do you mind if I take a quick bath?"

"Go right ahead."

"Thanks," she said, wondering if she should drink a second glass to take the edge off her nervousness. Katie walked into the bathroom and scowled at herself. There was no reason for her nervousness. The only thing she was going to do in that bed was go to sleep.

After she took her bath, she pulled on a long T-shirt. Anti-sex clothing, she assured herself and went into the bedroom. Michael had ditched his jeans and shirt and was reclining on the bed in a pair of athletic shorts. Her gaze moved over his tousled dark hair and dark magnetic eyes down to his broad shoulders and muscular frame. Her heart tripped at the look in his eyes as he rose on one elbow. He reached behind him and pulled something out of the bedside table.

"I just want you to know that I'm ready if you decide you want to be with me again," he said, and put two boxes of condoms on the bed. "It doesn't have to be tonight."

Katie stared at the condoms and worked her mouth, but no sound came out. She gulped. "Isn't that a lot?"

"Enough to get started," he said and looked as if he wanted to do a lot more than just get started with her.

Her skin heated and her heart hammered against her rib cage. She cleared her throat. "I'll-um-I'll keep that in mind."

"You do that," he said and put the boxes back in the drawer. He rose from the bed and walked toward her and her heart raced even faster. If he kissed her, she didn't know what she would do. Could she possibly say no to him?

He walked past her so that she caught a draft of his scent. "My turn in the bathroom. Sweet dreams, Katie Priss."

He disappeared into the bathroom and Katie stared at the drawer that held *all* those condoms. Waiting until she heard the water running, she walked over to the table and opened it. Good Lord, he couldn't possibly want to . . . that many times. Could he?

Sliding a gaze at the bathroom door, she then looked back into the drawer and opened one of the boxes. She wouldn't use it, she told herself. Wouldn't need it. Michael wouldn't force her and she certainly wouldn't initiate. Still, she couldn't forget what had happened last night.

She tore one of the packets loose and carefully replaced the others back in the box and closed the drawer. She took the condom and put it in her little purse and quickly slipped into bed. It was just in case of emergency.

"God created passion.
Denying passion will only make you cranky."
—SUNNY COLLINS'S WISDOM

Chapter 16

Just in case of emergency, she chanted.

She wasn't dying to explore Michael's body and mind more thoroughly. The thought of feeling his hands all over her didn't make her warm as toast, she told herself, but kicked off the bedspread. She absolutely wasn't picturing his naked body in that oversized tub . . . where she could be right now if she chose.

Liar, liar, pants on fire. Katie heard her mother's voice from the hereafter. *Stop fooling yourself. You want him and if you would stop denying your womanhood, you could have him tonight. All night.*

Groaning, Katie pulled the sheet over her head to hide from her crazy feelings. She hadn't heard her mother's voice in days and she wasn't delighted with Sunny's reappearance in her brain. *Womanhood?* Katie rolled her eyes. That sounded like Sunny's excuse to give in to her hormones.

Call it what you want, but—

The bathroom door opened and Michael walked into the room. If her mother was still talking, Katie couldn't hear her for the beating of her heart. She heard Michael's footsteps on the floor and his heavy sigh. When she felt the mattress dip under his weight, she held her breath. She heard him click off the lamp by the bed, then slide under the covers. He sighed again and she willed her heart to stop beating so loudly. Surely he could hear it.

He rolled first one way, then another. Couldn't get comfortable, she thought. Neither could she. She could feel his frustration even from beneath the covers.

She could take care of that frustration. The wicked thought slid into her brain like smoke. And she couldn't blame her mother for this one. She inhaled a shallow breath and swallowed a groan. She needed to get a grip.

Michael moved closer. She felt his heat as he drew closer to her back. Her heartbeat started to hop and skip. He moved closer and suddenly he was pulling her back against him. Her bottom was cradled into his crotch and there was no mistaking his arousal. She supposed she should tell him to stop and pull away. Her body and vocal cords called a mutiny.

He lifted her shirt and she stopped breathing. He curled one of his big hands around her waist to her belly and held her there for several seconds when she should have been scrambling out of the bed. He pulled the sheet from her head and tucked it under her chin, then returned his hand to her belly.

"It's okay," he rumbled in a sexy voice next to her ear. "Just go to sleep."

She stared bug-eyed into the darkness. "But you're—you're—" She couldn't finish it.

"Hard," he said for her. "I get that way a lot when I'm around you. Just go to sleep, Katie Priss."

Never. Not in a million years. Even though she'd kept herself relentlessly busy all day, she felt awake enough to paint the entire bridal suite and bathroom. There was no way she would fall asleep with Michael wrapped around her like a sexy cocoon. No way.

But five minutes later, she fell asleep.

The following morning, Katie awakened curled against Michael. Bothered by the fact that she hadn't instinctively moved away from him during the night, she sprang out of bed, grabbed her duffel bag, and dashed to the bathroom before he could say anything.

Or before she gave in to the temptation to wave one of those condoms like a flag of surrender and jump on him. She repeatedly splashed her face with cold water and considered banging her head against the wall to knock some sense into it. Knowing he would want to get on the road to Wilhemina, Katie quickly washed up and brushed her hair. She debated putting on eye shadow for ninety seconds, then rejected the idea. She was not going to try to seduce him.

She heard her mother humming in the background of her mind and stuck out her tongue at her reflection in the mirror. She dressed and left the bathroom. Michael stood in the middle of the bedroom wearing only a pair of shorts slung low over his lean hips.

Katie's mouth went bone dry at the sight of his near nakedness. She swallowed a moan. The morning wasn't starting out well. Determined to ditch her crazy conflicting feelings, she pasted a smile on her face. "Good morning. I'm ready when you are."

Michael met her gaze with a gleam of sexual intensity that stabbed right past her pretense. "Ready when I am," he echoed. "That could mean a lot of things."

"I'm ready to go," she said quickly. "To go find Wilhemina."

"Okay, let me shave. It won't take long."

Can I watch? She bit her tongue to keep from asking the terrible question. As soon as he closed the door to the bathroom, she scowled at herself. She couldn't even blame her randy mother for these thoughts. *She* was producing them all on her own with no assistance. She wondered what, besides Michael, was making her act this way. Maybe it was Texas.

They left within twenty-five minutes after grabbing toast and coffee in the kitchen of the bed and breakfast. As soon as they got out of town, Michael turned on the radio, relieving Katie of the necessity to make conversation. The only problem was that he chose a smoky, sexy jazz station that played songs that made her think of hot skin and that hot shower they'd shared. She lowered her window, but the temperature was already climbing into the eighties.

"Too warm?" he asked, reaching to adjust the thermostat.

"I just wanted some air."

When they reached Calvert County, Michael paid a visit to the car repair shop and took the indirect route. He asked the shop owner about the Cadillac he'd seen in the lot a couple of days ago. He wanted to know who the owner was because he was interested in buying. The helpful shop owner said the Cadillac was brought in by a lady friend visiting Douglas McGinley.

Within fifteen minutes of leaving the car repair shop, Michael had hooked up to the Internet via his cell phone and downloaded a surprising amount of information on Douglas, most importantly where he lived.

"Let me talk to Wilhemina," Katie said to Michael as they turned down a narrow country road.

"Why?" he asked.

"Because I think she might respond better to me."

"Why? She pulled the wool over your eyes just like she did me."

Katie felt a twinge of irritation. "Well, what were you planning on doing? Showing up and saying, Time to go?"

He shrugged. "Not much else to say," he said as they pulled within sight of a farmhouse with a truck parked out front. "How do you think Ivan would react to the prospect of Wilhemina hooking up with a hog farmer who drives a Ford with a gun rack?"

Her stomach knotted. "Not well."

"Not well," Michael said and chuckled. "Try, Katie and Michael, you're fired and I will not rest until I ruin you."

She felt her stomach turn. "He wouldn't waste his time ruining us," she said. "I don't think." She didn't want to think it. "But Wilhemina may not have hooked up with Douglas. She may be hurt and he's just letting her stay here."

"Or not."

"Maybe he's ugly."

"Or not."

She sighed. "Maybe he's gay."

Michael shot her a look full of doubt. "Or not. She has stayed here for several days without trying to call anyone for help. She is looking for her cowboy knight."

"I don't think we should jump to conclusions."

"I agree. We'll see soon enough," he said as he pulled into the driveway. They got out of the car and walked to the front porch. Michael rang the doorbell and they waited. No answer. He repeated, then banged on the door. Still no answer.

He sighed and glanced around. "Let's walk down this path and check things out."

After a short walk, Katie saw a barn in the not-too-far distance. She and Michael picked up the pace. Drawing closer, she heard laughter.

"Stop that," Wilhemina said, giggling. "You're distracting me. We've got to find Chantal. This is the third time she's gotten out of the house."

Katie strained to hear the low murmur of a masculine voice. She heard an unintelligible feminine moan and tripped over a stone in the path. Michael slipped his arm out to steady her.

"That sounds like Wilhemina," she said.

"Yeah," he said in a noncommittal tone, while his eyes said *I told you so.*

"Ohhhh, Douglas, let's do it in the barn again," Wilhemina said. "Ohhh, you feel so good. I love it when you—"

Katie covered her ears.

Filled with dread, she stopped walking abruptly and looked up at Michael. "I don't think Douglas is gay," she whispered. "What do we do?"

"Haven't you heard of coitus interruptus? They provide the coitus. We provide the interruptus," he said grimly, pulling her along.

"I'm not sure I want to see this," Katie said, wondering if she should cover her eyes.

"Call out her name," Michael told her.

"Me? Why me?"

"You said you wanted to talk to her."

"Yes, but not when she's in the middle of—"

"Okay. Don't say I didn't give you your chance. Wilhemina," he yelled.

Silence followed, then a muffled squeak of distress.

Michael glanced at his watch. "Wilhemina, Michael and Katie here. We've been worried about you."

Katie started to move forward, but he put out his hand to stop her. "Thirty seconds more," he whispered, pointing to his watch. "Do you really want to catch them naked?"

Katie winced, shaking her head.

After another glance at his watch, Michael walked to the barn door and slowly pushed it open. He gave Katie a nudge. "Call her name," he said in a low voice.

"Wilhemina," she said and walked into the barn.

Wilhemina stood several feet inside the barn with straw poking out of her hair. The man standing just behind her appeared to be struggling with his zipper. *Oh, no.* This could be a mess.

Folding and unfolding her hands, Wilhemina smiled nervously and bounded toward Katie. She might be nervous, but she was also glowing. She threw her arms around her. "It's so good to see you, but I told you not to come."

Katie hugged Wilhemina in return. "Michael and I were too worried."

Wilhemina pulled back. "Oh, I've been fine. Well, except for when I got lost at night and an animal pulled out in front of me and I landed in a ditch."

Katie's stomach turned. "In a ditch! Are you okay?" she asked, looking at Wilhemina for signs of injury.

"I'm fine. I hurt my foot, but it's much better. And Douglas," she said, looking at the man behind her with gooey, sweetie-pie eyes, "rescued me."

"Is that so?" Michael interjected, extending his hand to Douglas who had finally managed to pull up his zipper. "Thank you for your kindness to Wilhemina."

He gave an awkward nod. "My pleasure."

I'll bet, Katie thought, assessing the man. He was tall and strong with kind eyes. She checked for any physical signs of weakness or general sliminess and didn't find any. Yet. It was still early.

"Well, Wilhemina, you can certainly say that you've had a genuine adventure."

Wilhemina giggled.

"That's right," Michael agreed. "After all your excitement, I'm sure you're ready to go home."

Wilhemina's smile fell. "Well, actually—"

"Since your father will be coming from Europe in the next few weeks, I know you'll want to be ready for his return," Michael added.

Katie watched the air go out of Wilhemina's balloon right before her eyes.

"So soon," Wilhemina said in a forlorn little voice. "I didn't realize how much time had passed."

"I'm sure your mind has been occupied with your traveling," Katie said, feeling sorry for Ivan's daughter. "I imagine it was challenging with Chantal along."

"Yes, it was. Douglas and I were just looking for her," she said, blushing. "But we got sidetracked. Chantal!" she called and the cat pranced out with a huge barn cat bringing up the rear.

Katie tensed at the cozy sight of Ivan's pedigreed cat with the barn cat. She glanced at Michael and saw him rake his hand through his hair. He met her gaze and she knew he was thinking the same thing she was. She just hoped that barn cat was female.

Michael clapped his hands together briskly. "Well, Katie and I are ready to get you and Chantal to the airport so we can all go back to Philadelphia. I'm sure Katie will be happy to help you pack."

Wilhemina frowned. "Well, there's no rush, is there? I mean, why don't we all have dinner together?"

"There's been a flood and some of the roads closed," Michael told her. "We should travel during daylight."

"But I'm not—I'm—" She broke off helplessly and looked at Douglas.

Douglas put his arm around Wilhemina and met Michael's gaze. "Wilhemina wants to stay a little longer."

Katie watched Michael bristle. She could practically smell the testosterone flaring between Douglas and Michael. They were both tall, well-built, physically fit men. Michael didn't want his authority challenged and Douglas was protecting his newfound territory.

"I'm responsible for Wilhemina until her father returns from Europe. I'm her bodyguard," Michael said.

Douglas frowned and looked down at Wilhemina. "Is that true?"

Clearly upset, Wilhemina twisted her hands together. "Yes."

"Who in the world is your father that you would need a bodyguard?"

Michael gave a short laugh of disbelief. "I realize this is the middle of nowhere, but everyone has heard of—"

Seeing Wilhemina's eyes fill with distress, Katie elbowed Michael in the rib cage and cleared her throat. "I think," she said, meeting Michael's hard questioning gaze, "that Wilhemina wanted to be the one to discuss that with Douglas."

Wilhemina shot Katie a look of pure gratitude. "Yes, that's right."

"I think she may want to do that very soon since we really do need to return to Philadelphia," Katie said firmly.

Wilhemina sighed and reluctantly nodded.

His brow still furrowed with displeased confusion, Douglas shrugged. "Well, I guess that means you two will be staying for the night. I would offer you a room, but I only have one extra and Wilhemina's using it. I suppose you could use the mobile home I have on the other end of the farm. I keep it for temporary employees to sleep over during the busy season."

Mobile home. Visions of her childhood assaulted Katie. "Isn't there a hotel some—"

Douglas shook his head. "I tried one for Wilhemina, but the plumbing's messed up and the owner's taking his time getting to the repairs. It's not a bad trailer." He cleared his throat. "I just need to take a couple of the *Baywatch* posters off the wall."

Katie swallowed a moan and looked at Michael.

He sighed. "It'll just be for one night," he said, throwing both Wilhemina and Douglas a firm glance. "We'll leave tomorrow."

After dropping their bags at the small trailer, Katie and Michael put fresh sheets on the beds and dusted and cleaned. It truly wasn't that bad, Katie thought and tried not to give in to bittersweet memories of her childhood. Douglas took them on a tour of the farm and showed off his prize hogs. Luckily he didn't go into an in-depth description of the fate of the hogs, but Katie still wasn't sure she'd be able to look at a ham sandwich exactly the same way for a while.

Wilhemina complimented Douglas and flirted with him shamelessly, and he didn't seem to mind at all. Douglas barbecued burgers on the grill while Katie helped Wilhemina prepare potato salad.

"I don't know how to do anything but boil water," Wilhemina confessed to Katie. "You're so lucky you know how to cook. Douglas has had to cook for me every night."

"It's not difficult if you can read and follow instructions, and you can do both."

"Do you think you could help me bake a cake for him?" Wilhemina asked. "As a thank-you for all he's done for me."

Katie didn't want to think about all Douglas had probably done to Wilhemina. She felt uneasy about the looks they shared. She was concerned about Wilhemina's feelings, but she was also concerned about getting Ivan's daughter on the plane back to Philly. "Sure. I think I remember a simple recipe for a dump cake and we can put it together in no time."

Wilhemina looked doubtful. "Dump cake? How does it taste?"

"Don't let the name fool you. It's chocolate, and it's great hot. I bet Douglas has the ingredients," she said, looking through the cupboards. "If we hurry, we can get it in the oven and bake it while we're eating dinner." It took a little extra time to give Wilhemina the instructions and allow her to put the cake together, but seeing the sense of accomplishment on her face pleased Katie. Wilhemina might have one of the richest fathers in the world, but she'd been deprived of so many things that could have helped her self-esteem. She wondered how Wilhemina might have turned out if she had been raised in a more normal home.

Katie paused. Not that she knew what a normal home was.

Just as Wilhemina carefully set the cake in the oven, Douglas and Michael brought in the burgers.

"Hi," Douglas said, nearly drowning as he gazed at Wilhemina.

"Hi," Wilhemina said breathlessly.

The two looked so sappy Katie glanced down at their feet to see if they were melting into the floor. Hearing Michael's put-upon sigh, she looked up and saw him roll his eyes.

Katie bit back a chuckle, but couldn't help thinking that there was something sweet about their adoration for each other. She cleared her throat.

Douglas blinked and glanced at Katie and Michael self-consciously. His gaze traveled back to Wilhemina. "That potato salad sure looks good. I thought you said you couldn't cook."

Wilhemina blushed. "Thank you, but Katie helped."

"I can't wait to taste it."

Michael walked to Katie's side. "That isn't all he wants to taste," he muttered in her ear.

If Katie didn't do something, she wondered if Wilhemina and Douglas would throw the food aside and jump on each other. "The table's ready and I'm hungry. Let's eat," she urged.

The four sat down to dinner and Katie and Michael were forced to endure glances brimming with lust and longing and lengthy distracted silences. Katie remembered to get the cake from the oven and Douglas made over it as if Ivan's daughter had made him a gourmet delicacy. When he asked what kind of cake it was, Katie didn't have the heart to tell him dump cake.

"*Chocolat special*," Katie improvised in a French accent she could only say she'd learned from Pepe LePew. "She did a great job."

"Sure did. I think I want some more."

Wilhemina's face colored prettily in delight and she quickly rose to take care of Douglas's request.

Unable to endure their verbal foreplay any longer, Katie grabbed Michael's hand and dragged him to his feet. "Michael and I will do the dishes," she said, ignoring Michael's glare of displeasure.

"Dishes?" he echoed.

"Are you sure?" Wilhemina asked, returning with Douglas's cake.

"Sure," Katie said. "It's the least we can do. You two have done all the work."

"That's so nice, Katie. Isn't that nice, Douglas?"

"Yeah, it is," Douglas said, his gaze dipping into Wilhemina's cleavage.

"Get the plates," Katie muttered and cleared the table in record time. Michael followed her to the sink, but she could feel his dark unspoken grumbles at her back.

"Why the hell—"

Katie covered his mouth with her fingers until she saw that Wilhemina and Douglas had adjourned to the den. "Because I was going to scream if I had to witness one more minute of the loopy way they were acting."

"It's better that they have supervision. He's probably banging her right now."

Katie covered her ears. "Don't say that."

He covered her hands with his and pried them away from her ears. "We have to decide if we're going to try to keep them apart or not."

"Wouldn't it be easier to change the force of gravity?"

He looked at her, then rubbed his forehead. "We still have to decide if we're going to try to chaperone them or not."

"Don't you think they've already—" She broke off, wanting him to fill in the blank.

"Been at each other like rabbits."

But not quite that way. She looked up at the ceiling.

"Yeah, I think they have. The question is whether he gets her pregnant or not."

Shock raced through her. She gaped at him. "Preg—Preg—Preg—"

Michael frowned at her in concern. "Are you hyperventilating? Do I need to get a paper bag?"

She shook her head and forced herself to breathe slowly. "I'm the one who might be—be—"

"Pregnant." His gaze gentled and he brushed his hand over one of her shoulders. "You're gonna be okay."

Her stomach dipped at the steadfast assurance in his eyes, and she wondered how the moment had changed in less than a heartbeat. She shook her head and swallowed over a strange lump in her throat. "We got off track. You were talking about Wilhemina."

He nodded. "One of us needs to make sure she's using contraception."

"And exactly how are we supposed to do that?"

"Someone needs to talk to her."

"About contraception," she said. "I'm not sure I'm the best candidate for that job in light of the fact that I completely forgot to use any when you and I—" She broke off, wondering why all roads of this conversation kept leading back to the same uncomfortable place.

"Then I can talk to her. I can talk to Doug too."

Katie saw visions of Michael with broken bones and Wilhemina sobbing with tears of embarrassment. "I'll talk to her," she said quickly, not at all sure what she would say.

"Okay," he said and waited.

"After we do the dishes," she clarified.

"Are you sure you should wait?"

"It can't be that urgent."

"Listen," he said.

She heard a combination of feminine moans and low groans and slapped her hands over her ears again.

Chuckling, he pried them loose again. "I'll load the dishwasher."

"The most important thing you can do in life is to be your best you. You wouldn't have been born if the world wasn't needing you for something."
—SUNNY COLLINS'S WISDOM

Chapter 17

Katie frowned at Michael, then made her way to the den. The sighs and moans of hot and heavy foreplay made her want to cover her ears again, but she stiffened her spine. She had a job to do.

She cleared her throat, but the love sounds continued. Katie sighed, wondering if she would need a whistle or a water hose.

"Wilhemina," she called from the hallway. "Can I speak with you for a moment?"

Katie heard the rustle of clothing being rearranged and a nervous feminine twitter. Katie counted to ten. "Wilhemina?"

"Just a second, Katie," she said, then appeared in the hallway, her cheeks flushed and her eyes sparkling.

"Is there somewhere you and I could talk?" Katie asked.

Wilhemina shrugged. "How about the front porch?"

"That will be fine."

"Douglas, I'll be back in just a few minutes," Wilhemina called and walked with Katie outside.

Katie remained standing while Wilhemina sat in one of the old rockers. "What did you want?"

Katie searched for the words. "It appears that you and Douglas have gotten close in a short amount of time."

Wilhemina's gaze turned guarded. "Yes, we have. He's been very kind to me."

"I'm glad he's been kind," Katie said and cleared her throat. "But there are other concerns when you get close with someone."

Wilhemina frowned. "What do you mean?"

"Well, you will be leaving and while I'm glad for you to have a good—" She broke off again searching for the right word. "A good experience with Douglas, I wouldn't want you to have to face any unpleasant repercussions."

"Unpleasant?"

Katie decided to be blunt even though she felt like a complete hypocrite. "Pregnancy or a sexually transmitted disease."

Wilhemina's eyes widened. "Oh, that. Douglas uses a condom every time. Even when I get in a hurry and just don't want to wait for him to put—"

Katie was hearing far more than she wanted to. "That's good," she cut in. "That's good to know. I know you haven't had a lot of experience with men, so I felt like I should just remind you to take care of yourself."

Wilhemina stood and took Katie's hand. "That's so sweet of you. You're right. I haven't had much experience with men, but I've been doing my best to make up for it the last few days."

Again. More than she wanted to know. Katie forced her lips into a strained smile. "You just keep making sure you protect yourself, then." She patted Wilhemina's shoulder. "That's all I wanted to tell you."

Wilhemina smiled. "Okay, I'd like to get back to Douglas now."

Katie nodded, hating the necessity of taking some of the

sparkle from her eyes. "Remember, Wilhemina, we are all leaving tomorrow."

Wilhemina's smile fell. "Yeah. I guess so. Are you coming back in?"

"Just to finish cleaning the kitchen. Then Michael and I will probably go to the trailer. We've had a long day. Please tell Douglas we appreciated the meal."

"I'll do that," Wilhemina said, and hotfooted it back to her hog farmer lover.

Katie sighed and returned to Michael in the kitchen. He had loaded most of the dishes and was wiping off the counter. "I'm impressed," she said.

"With what?"

"It takes a real man to do the dishes," she said, unable to prevent a smile.

He rolled his eyes. "I seem to recall a similar statement about changing diapers. Dishes and diapers? Sounds like pansy material to me."

"Not with your body," she murmured.

He stopped and looked at her, something electric coming from his eyes. "What a surprise. That kind of remark could make me think you'd like to do a lot more than *look* at my body."

Katie's stomach twirled at the velvet invitation in his voice. He was taunting her, and she probably deserved it. She struggled with a strange undercurrent of danger and excitement. She liked his attention entirely too much. "You're full of it. You're not surprised. You walk around with your shirt off every chance you get just to distract me."

She barely got the words out of her mouth before he backed her up against the kitchen counter. "Is it working?"

Her nerve endings jiggled up and down, but she lifted her chin. "I don't have to answer that."

His lips lifted in a sexy, but maddening grin. "You just did."

She scowled at him and pushed at his muscular chest, barely resisting the urge to allow her hands to linger on his muscles.

Michael chuckled, stepping back slightly. "So are we chaperoning or not?"

"Not."

He lifted his brows. "So Douglas wears a sock?"

She nodded. "Every time even when Wilhemina gets—" She gave him a pained look. "Eager."

"Eager," he repeated, his lips twitching with humor, but his eyes dark with an undercurrent of something hungry and wild. "Maybe I need to ask Douglas his technique for making women eager," he ventured.

She groaned and started walking. "That's it. I'm going back to the trailer. I've had all of this loony bin I can take." When she heard him laugh, she walked faster, stepping swiftly to the door and letting it fall as she skipped down the stairs. She needed some fresh air. Her brain was getting all gooey with Michael. She'd barely taken a few steps on the dirt road before Michael swooped up behind her and grabbed her hand.

"Was the discussion with Wilhemina that rough?" he asked.

"It's just the whole situation. She and Douglas walking around like they're going to rip each other's clothes off any minute and make those never-ending sound effects."

He pulled her around and took her mouth so fast her head spun. He gave her a swift, hot kiss that gave her a glimpse of his need. And hers.

He pulled back and inhaled. "Feeling deprived?" he asked, then didn't give her a chance to lie. "I am."

She took a mind-clearing breath, but still felt dizzy. "Why me?"

"I could ask the same of you."

"That's not an answer."

His gaze flicked over her. "You're strong, you're tough, but you have a lot of soft spots. You're sexy even when you try not to be. I wanted—" He broke off and shook his head.

"What?" she asked, dying to know what he was going to say. "What?"

"I watched you with Wilhemina and that deaf woman. You were passionately protective of both of them. I think you would do just about anything to help them. I'm betting you're the same way about your brother."

She felt somehow naked by his assessment of her, but she couldn't deny it. She nodded. "I would."

"I've never met anyone like that. Like you."

She felt her heart swell in her chest. "But you said something about wanting."

"You make me want a lot of things. Do you really want me to go into all of them?"

Katie felt her insides heat up several degrees. *Whew!* "Maybe not tonight," she said in a breathy voice and began to walk. "Lots of stars out. Did you notice?"

"Yeah." He walked beside her. "Do you remember a lot of nights like this from your childhood?"

She nodded. "My sisters and I used to catch fireflies and when they went to bed, I would let them go."

"How much baby-sitting did you do when your mom went out at night?"

"A lot. Sometimes she worked as a waitress. She was always looking for the man who would make her life perfect. I liked to think she was always looking for someone as good as my father, but I never knew him, so I'm not sure what he was really like. She was always talking about wanting to go back to Myrtle Beach, but heaven knows, we never had enough money for that. That's where she met him." She always felt both hopeful and silly when she thought about her father. "She said that was where I was conceived. I know she had this romanticized version of it in her mind, but I can't help wondering if it was some kind of spring break fling. My mother saw potential when most other people would see a big question mark."

"It's hard when you want answers to questions and the people who can answer aren't around anymore."

Katie nodded, looking at Michael and remembering what had happened with his father.

"I've heard about your youngest sister's dad. What about the middle sister?"

"Ah, Delilah," Katie said, smiling at the memory of her sister. "Delilah was three years younger than me. Prissy, but she liked frogs too, so that saved her from being a pain. Her father was from a well-to-do family. He got involved with my mother when he was part owner with the local bar owner. My mother won a wet T-shirt contest and he was smitten. Temporarily. When his mother found out he was carrying on with a waitress in a bar, she had a stroke. Literally. He felt so guilty that he repented of his sins, ditched my mother, and went to seminary."

Michael stared at her in disbelief. "You're joking."

"Nope, and my mother was too proud to go after him, so she had his baby and named her Delilah just to drive him and his mother crazy if they ever found out."

"And they did."

Katie felt her humor fade. "Yeah, he took her away one day before Lori left."

"That must have been rough on you."

"It wasn't fun. That was when I started dreaming about running away. I didn't really hate my mother. I just hated the situation and how people whispered about me behind my back.

"I didn't understand a lot of the things they said, and when I grew to understand what they were saying, it felt like a box was closing in around me. I couldn't wear a dress without someone commenting on the length. I never dated. I was too afraid of what guys would expect. According to just about everyone, I was destined to be white trash just like my mother."

"But you weren't," Michael said and his voice soothed some of the rough spots she was feeling.

"I guess not. I don't feel like I've really had a chance to be normal."

He gave a half smile. "What's normal?"

She closed her eyes and revisited the daydream she'd had when she was a child. "Having a dad who fussed at you if you were late and who grilled your potential boyfriends. Having a mother who does *not* draw wolf whistles and cat calls when she walks down the street. Having a mother who is home every night."

"She must have done something right."

Katie opened her eyes and looked at him. "Why do you say that?"

"You turned out pretty well."

"When she was there, she was always affectionate. She hugged and kissed us nearly to death. She was always play-ing with our hair," she said, smiling at the memory. "She made everything fun, even taking out the trash and doing the dishes. Cleanup was a relay and the one who did the most in the shortest time got the first ice cream sandwich." She paused. "Even when we probably deserved it, she never spanked us. She called us her little flowers and she told us we were beautiful even when we weren't."

"You missed her when you left, didn't you?"

Her eyes filled with sudden dampness that caught her off guard. She blinked. "I did, even though I left the day I turned eighteen," she admitted in a low voice. "She sent me postcards and asked me to come back to visit, but I just couldn't," she said, shaking her head. "I was nobody in Philadelphia, but nobody was better than the somebody I was in Texas."

Feeling strange about all she'd revealed, she hesitated a moment, then lifted her chin. "Don't feel sorry for me."

He chuckled, lifting his thumb to her jawline. "Not likely, Katie Priss."

She frowned. "Why do you call me that?"

"Because you're both," he said.

"No, I'm not."

"Yes, you are, and when you accept it, things will be easier for you."

"And what makes you such an expert?"

"I've watched you a lot during the last month."

"Yeah, well, I've done the living and I know who I am, and it's not Priscilla," she insisted, feeling an itchy, hollow sensation even as she made her declaration. "I need to go to bed. I have a feeling tomorrow's going to be a long day. We've got to get Wilhemina on a plane soon." She briskly walked the rest of the way to the trailer. She wanted to walk fast and go to sleep fast to get away from the thoughts whirring around in her brain. Just as she opened the door, Michael called to her.

"I have something for you," he said, jogging up the pathway.

She turned and her heart gave an involuntary flutter. "What?"

He joined her on the porch. "Give me your hand."

She noticed his hand was in a closed fist. "Why?" she asked, warily.

"Trust me. You'll like it."

She didn't want to trust him. She didn't want to rely on him. That was edging too close to other feelings she didn't want to be feeling. But she would feel like a shrew if she said no. Sighing, she extended her palm. "Okay."

He took her hand and opened his fist to shake three fireflies into her palm. A spurt of nostalgic little-girl delight pulsed through her. "I didn't see them."

"Too busy running from Priss."

She refused to reply. Regardless of his comment, she couldn't help smiling as the fireflies crawled on her palm while he kept them trapped. "You're a city boy. What do you know about fireflies?"

"After my mother got sick, I was moved from relative to relative. One of my aunts had a place in the country, so I caught them. We weren't as nice as you. We would pull off their lights and make designs on the front porch."

Katie wrinkled her nose at him. "That's gross."

"We thought it was like hunting. You bring a rack to display your hunting success. You stick the lights on the porch to show off your—"

"Sick cruelty to helpless insects. My sisters loved it when I caught these for them. They didn't ever understand how they got out of the jar by the next morning." She looked at him, then shook her hand and released them. "I don't want you giving in to the temptation of pulling their lights off to show off your hunting success." She watched them fly away, their little lights flickering. With mixed feelings, she looked at him. "Thanks."

"That hard to say?" he said with a half chuckle.

"It's easier for me when you're a jerk."

"Easier how?"

She thought about that lonely condom burning a hole in her little purse. "In every way. G'night."

"Good night, Katie Priss," he said and she felt as if he'd slid past another locked door. She wondered how she was going to continue to keep him out.

Wilhemina heard a knock at the front door and nearly hyperventilated. Lifting her hand to her chest to calm herself, she glanced at her unpacked luggage. The tapping sounded again.

Her heart in her throat, she forced her lips into a smile as she opened the door to Katie. Katie smiled in return and Wilhemina's stomach turned with guilt.

"Ready to go?" Katie asked.

"No. I'm not ready to go." Her voice broke and she felt her eyes well with tears. "I don't want to go back!"

Katie's eyes widened in alarm. "Wilhemina," she began.

Wilhemina shook her head, not wanting to hear Katie's practical words. "I love Douglas. I've never been so happy. I don't want to go." Unable to hold back her emotions, she began to cry.

"Katie?" Michael's voice carried from the porch.

Katie's eyes widened and she made a panicky sound. "Talk to you later," she said to Michael, then shut the door in his face. Wincing at her rudeness, she turned a concerned gaze on Wilhemina. "Oh, Wilhemina, you've gotten yourself all upset," she said, giving her a hug. "You need to catch your breath. Let me get you some water."

Wilhemina inhaled deeply and shuddered with relief in Katie's arms. She felt so confused and afraid, but she didn't want to leave Douglas. She breathed again and a little of the tight heavy feeling in her chest lifted.

Katie patted her on the back and urged Wilhemina toward the kitchen. "Come on. A drink of water will make you feel better. You sit down," she said, pointing to a chair

Pulling a glass from the cabinet, she filled it with water and a few cubes of ice. She lifted her lips in a sympathetic smile and sat across from Wilhemina after she gave her the glass. "You know you haven't known him very long at all," Katie said.

"Yes, but he's different than anyone I've ever met," Wilhemina told her, wanting desperately for her to understand. "He thinks I'm pretty. He doesn't think I'm stupid. And he didn't know who my father was. He just really wanted me," she said, her voice breaking slightly. She took a quick sip of water. "Me. He wanted me," she said, still almost unable to believe it.

"But, Wilhemina, how can you possibly really know him after just a few days with him?"

"I know he's been so kind to me. I know he's good."

"That is really good, but it's not everything. I know this is going to be hard for you to hear, but you and Douglas are from different worlds and that's part of the attraction. I think the novelty of being a hog farmer's wife will be likely to wear off."

"I can't imagine getting bored with Douglas," Wilhemina insisted.

"What about when he gets extra busy with the farm? What about when he gets tired of cooking and taking care of the hogs?" She sighed. "I'm glad Douglas has been kind to you. I'm glad you've had a good experience with him, but,

Wilhemina, you can't avoid the fact that you are from totally different worlds. You're like a princess, and Douglas is—"

"Don't call him a commoner."

"I was going to say that Douglas knows nothing of your world."

Wilhemina bit her lip, refusing to give up. "He knows about my heart, and that's what's really important." She swallowed over her nervousness. "I'm not leaving him. Not yet." *Not ever.*

Katie patted her hand. "Just take a breath. We can talk about this later. I-uh-should probably better go and let Michael know we won't be leaving right away." She patted her hand. "You'll be okay, Wilhemina."

Wilhemina blinked to keep from tearing up again. "You don't understand what it's like to need somebody, Katie. You're so strong. You just don't understand what it's like to find someone and want to be with them more than any-thing."

Wilhemina watched a flash of vulnerability cross Katie's face, an expression of longing so deep it made her look twice. But Katie glanced away. "You're stronger than you think," she said. "We can talk later."

Wilhemina watched her rise from her chair and walk to the front door. She waited to hear Michael's voice, knowing he would be angry. The thought of it made her want to hide. Katie mercifully closed the door behind her and left Wil-hemina alone with her thoughts and the feeling that she was still on borrowed time.

Katie nearly walked straight into Michael as she stepped outside the front door. His jaw was tight and his gaze watchful.

"Why isn't Wilhemina out here with her luggage?"

Katie tugged him down the front steps to the rental car. "This may be a little more difficult than we anticipated."

"What?"

She lowered her voice. "She thinks she's in love with Douglas."

"What?"

Katie winced. "Keep your voice down. She's freaked out enough as it is."

His nostrils flared as he inhaled slowly. "Let me get this right. Just because this hog farmer has been keeping her in bed since they first met, she thinks she's in love. You told her there's a difference between marrying love and fun sex, didn't you?"

Katie's stomach tightened. She couldn't help wondering if she fell into the fun sex category with Michael. Which should be totally okay. "I didn't put it exactly that way, but I did convey the message."

"And?"

"And she's not ready to leave. She thinks she's in love with him."

"She thinks he is her cowboy knight," he said, cynicism making his voice edgy.

"She didn't say that," Katie said, trying to figure out how to manage the situation. "I can't totally blame her for not wanting to go back to Philadelphia. She hasn't fit in there at all."

He shot her a wary look. "You're not seriously considering letting her stay."

"No, but none of this is feeling right at the moment."

"Feeling right? I think you'd better explain."

"I mean, what if Wilhemina is really in love with Douglas? She's happy here. Is it really right for us to drag her back to Philadelphia where she's miserable and doesn't fit in?"

Michael shook his head. "Have you forgotten your agreement with Ivan? My agreement with Ivan? Have you forgotten the money?"

"No, and I know I need the money more than you do."

"That's a matter of opinion."

"You want the money for your ego. I need the money for a deaf child."

He narrowed his eyes, his anger visible in the set of his jaw. "You think this is about my ego. It's about honor. My honor."

"Well, what kind of honor is there in dragging Wilhemina away from her chance at love?"

Michael rolled his eyes. "Lord save me from the romantic insanity of women. For one thing, the distinction between true love and sex is a little murky here. Have you forgotten that the reason we're down here is because of that little fairy tale you told Wilhemina?"

His words dug under her skin. . . . *distinction between true love and sex is a little murky . . .* "What makes you the expert on the distinction between love and sex? From everything you've said and done, you're only an expert on sex."

He stared at her, then gave a short, humorless laugh. "I'm not sure if I should thank you for complimenting me for being an expert on sex or if I should ask you if you're comparing Wilhemina's relationship with Doug to ours."

Katie felt hot with embarrassment. She hated that he had nailed her concerns so easily. She glanced away. "I wasn't talking about us, so—"

"If you are comparing our relationship, I think you might want to bear in mind that we have both fought it, and continue to fight it. We both know more about each other than we want the other to know, but in a weird way, you trust me and I trust you. You would also be right if you said I want you in bed like I've never wanted anyone, but I'll be damned if I'll push you. Maybe it's ego. Maybe it's something else but I want you to come to me one hundred percent willingly."

It was her turn to blink. The intensity of his words and his gaze stung her from head to toe.

"Nothing to say?" he asked, his voice filled with an edge of rough emotion and need.

That same emotion and need echoed inside her. But she was way out of her depth and too much of a scaredy-cat to admit it. Unable to tear her gaze from him, she swallowed and shook her head.

"Didn't think so," he muttered and swore. "This is looking worse than the *Titanic*. Ivan will come back and after he destroys you and me, he'll rip into Wilhemina. If she has the insane nerve to defy him and stay with Douglas, can you imagine what Ivan will do to a hog farmer?"

Katie shuddered at the image. "Do you really think Ivan would bother with a hog farmer?"

Michael looked at her as if several of her mental lightbulbs were missing. "If his daughter was involved. Have you forgotten his feelings about rednecks?"

Katie felt a deep ripple of uneasiness. "This is going to be difficult."

"Unless we just put Wilhemina in the car and leave. She's been brainwashed by sex."

"I wish you would quit saying that. I was a virgin before last week too."

"Yes, but I haven't succeeded in brainwashing you."

"How do you know you haven't?"

"Because you haven't used the condom you took from the box."

Katie felt her cheeks heat. "How did—"

"I counted."

She hated that he knew so many of her secrets. "We're getting off the subject of Wilhemina. We can't treat this like some kind of cult intervention. She's going to have to reach the right conclusion on her own."

"Fat chance with Douglas banging her every other—"

Katie lifted her hands to cover her ears. "Stop." She breathed in and exhaled slowly, then met Michael's gaze. "I'll talk to her later this afternoon."

"Why not now?"

"Because she's all worked up. This will give her a chance to settle down enough to hear me. If we're lucky."

Michael scowled. "Luck," he echoed, then broke off when his cell phone rang. He pulled it from his pocket, glanced at the incoming caller ID number, and shook his head. "Michael Wingate," he said into the receiver and paused. "How is she physically?" he asked, and waited. "Is she on suicide watch?" he asked, then sighed. "I'm out of town and I can try to see her within the next two days. Make sure you tell her that. Connect me with her and I'll tell her the same, but I think you need to put her on watch until I can get there. I'll hold while you transfer."

Michael looked at Katie and the ghosts in his eyes tore at her. "Hey, Mom," he said. "I hear you're having a rough spell." He nodded as he listened in silence. "I can't come see you today and probably not tomorrow, but I'll try to come the next day." He paused again and sighed. "I can't, Mom. I'm in Texas. Two days. I'll be there in two days." He raked his hand through his hair. "Two days," he repeated. "Chin up. You'll be okay. I love you, Mom." He punched the power button and jammed the phone back in his pocket.

"Does that happen often?" Katie asked.

He shrugged. "She has a lot of breaks with reality. Sometimes it's harder for her when she remembers what really happened and that she has a son. She starts to panic. By the time I see her, she may not remember who I am."

Her heart hurt. She wondered what it was like for him for his mother to be technically alive, but so unreachable. "How soon after your father died did she get sick?"

"She had several episodes, but her family committed her about two years after my father killed himself. Even though I was only ten, I always felt like I should have been able to make things different."

"You felt responsible," she said. "You weren't. And you're not now. And I'm betting you don't want to talk about it anymore."

"That would be right," he said. "My mother gets enough psychoanalysis for ten people. She can have my share."

Katie laughed. "Sounds kinda like something I said."

"What?" he asked, curiosity lighting his eyes.

She shook her head. "No. It's an inside joke."

"With whom?"

"Inside me."

"Stingy."

"Maybe. So what are you going to do now? Go back to the trailer and work?"

"Guess so," he said, eyeing the house with a dark expression and walking toward the trailer. "Since Wilhemina's in crisis."

"I'll talk to her in a while." She walked beside him.

"What are you going to do in the meantime?"

"Go swimming," she said, knowing she was treading on

dangerous ground. She should allow Michael to find his solace in his work. He'd obviously been doing that for some time and it had worked. That should be fine with her, but it wasn't. She knew what it was like to want to just take off and do something fun to forget her problems. Every once in a while she allowed herself to go do something crazy. Sometimes you have to do something a little crazy to keep from going crazy. This might be the craziest yet, she thought as she looked into his dark eyes.

He gave her a double take. "Where?"

"There's a pond beyond the trailer."

"I didn't know you brought a bathing suit with you."

"I didn't," she said and let him chew on that while she walked in front of him.

*"Love makes us do amazing, wonderful things . . .
and really stupid things too."*
—SUNNY COLLINS'S WISDOM

Chapter 18

She tore his heart out and stomped that sucker flat when she didn't go skinny-dipping.

Michael followed Katie from a distance as she shucked her tennis shoes, but not her shorts and T-shirt. There was no way he was going to glue himself to his computer screen after she dropped her little bomb. The sun shone on the water and her hair bounced in a ponytail pulled high on her head. In his mind's eye, he could see her as a child, eager to wash away whatever was bothering her by taking a swim. He'd done the same a few times when he'd had the opportunity.

Katie walked to the edge of the pond and turned around with her hands on her hips. "Are you just going to stand there and watch or are you going to join me?"

Smart mouth woman. It would serve her right if he let her stand there and yell while he hiked back to the house.

"Are you afraid you can't beat me in a race, city boy?"

She was obviously goading him. It was working. Michael strode to the lake and pulled off his shirt, then started on his belt.

Katie's eyes widened. "You're not taking off your pants."

"I can't race in slacks," he said, pulling down the zipper.

"But—but—" She turned to the lake and jumped in.

Michael laughed when she surfaced with her head turned firmly away from him. "Who's afraid now?"

"I'm not afraid," she said vehemently. "I just didn't think you would take off—"

"Everything," he finished for her, then jumped into the water wearing just his boxers unbeknownst to her. He surfaced and swam to her side. "Just because I'm a city guy doesn't mean I've never been skinny-dipping."

She gave a double take. "Oh, really. When did you—" She broke off as if she realized her curiosity had gotten away from her. "Never mind."

"You forgot. I told you one of my aunts lived in the country and they had a pond."

She tossed him an assessing glance. "How long since you've been swimming?"

About a week since he'd visited the gym. He shrugged. "I haven't been dunked in a pond in years."

She smiled. "Race you to the other side and back?"

"I'll give it my best shot."

"Okay. On-your-mark-get-set-go," she said in one breath and got two strokes in front of him.

Michael shook his head and felt the lick of excitement and something lighter inside. He took off after her, catching up in a short time. He reached the other side of the pond just before she did and headed for the finish line, surprised when she nearly caught him at the end.

Gasping for breath, she flipped onto her back and floated. "You tricked me."

"No, you just *ass*umed that since I was from the city, I hadn't spent much time swimming. Wrong assumption."

"I figured you were the weight-lifting machine sort. I figured you wouldn't want to get wet. So how often do you swim?"

"Three or four times a week. You?"

"Four," she said, shooting him a quick glare.

Michael was too distracted by the outline of her breasts on her wet T-shirt to pay much attention to her scowl.

"What are you grinning at anyway?" she asked, then glanced down at her shirt and gave a little shriek. She abruptly sank into the water up to her chin.

"I've seen you before," Michael said. "Why the sudden modesty?"

"I don't know. This is different."

"Since you're not rescuing me from a bunch of drunk rednecks."

"Don't remind me."

"And I'm not making love to you."

She opened her mouth, then shut it as if she couldn't remember what she'd intended to say.

"We can change that last one," he said, moving closer to her.

"Or not," she murmured. "Do you have cannonball experience?"

"Limited."

"Are you telling the truth?"

"Swear. Why?"

"We could have another competition." She frowned. "Except you're naked."

"No I'm not. I'm wearing my boxers."

"Oh," she said, her expression a combination of disappointment and relief. "We can have a jumping competition. Whoever makes the biggest splash wins."

"Wins what?"

"Just wins," she said, looking at him as if he were dense. "Isn't winning enough?"

"Sometimes. Okay, I'll play."

"The only thing is that you have to agree not to look at my shirt while I'm jumping."

He hesitated a half beat before he thought of a loophole. "I agree."

She frowned at him. "Are you sure?"

"I'm sure. I won't look at your shirt while you jump."

She waggled her finger at him. "You better not be lying or you automatically lose."

"Lose what?" he asked, unable to smother a chuckle.

"Just lose. You will be a *loser*. Now you go first."

"Why me?"

"Because I'm a generous person."

"You just want to see what you need to do to top me," he said, but pulled himself out of the water. Recalling that summer spent with his cousins, he leaped into the air, folded his legs underneath him, and flung himself into the water. When he arose, he shook the water from his hair and treaded next to Katie. "How'd I do?"

"Not bad," she said with a sniff. "For a novice."

He smiled, enjoying her playful snootiness. He suspected she didn't reveal this side to many people and he felt strangely exhilarated that she'd done so with him. She wouldn't feel safe letting her guard down with most people, but she did with him.

"Remember not to look at my shirt," she told him and climbed out the side of the pond.

Standing on the side, she folded her arms to cover her breasts and squinted her eyes at him. "You're looking."

"I'm studying your technique," he insisted.

She muttered something he couldn't hear, then did a little hip-hip-hop. She went airborne and reared back, landing at an angle on her back with one leg extended and one folded against her belly. A huge spray of water shot around her.

She surfaced, smiling, so pleased with herself that he had a tough time resisting the urge to kiss her. "That was a good one."

"How do you know?" Michael asked. "You didn't see it."

"I felt it. You can't deny it was good."

"It was," he grudgingly admitted. "How does such a small person as you make such a big wave?"

"Technique," she said, tossing him a saucy grin.

"Okay. My turn again. Best two of three."

She shrugged as she treaded water. "We can do the best ninety out of one hundred and I'll still beat the pants off of you."

Her tone got under his skin, and his skin was already way too itchy for her. He swam close to her, pulling her against him. "Is that what you want? To beat the pants off of me?"

She gulped. "It's just an expression."

"Uh-huh," he said, coating his voice with disbelief.

"It is," she insisted. "I was only—"

He cut her off by dunking her. She sputtered to the surface, cursing him, but he just laughed and swam to the edge. Imitating her technique, he threw himself into the water at an angle. It stung like hell, so Michael figured he must have made a big splash.

Katie sniffed. "A little better, but not much," she said when he came up for air.

"What do you mean? I did what you did."

"You tried to do what I did. I told you it's all about technique." She took her turn and delivered another stunning splash. Then he followed with another attempt. Soon, she became so eager to show him her technique that she forgot to cover her breasts. Michael didn't forget to look.

Afterward, she grabbed her towel and covered her shirt and collapsed on the grass. Spreading his shirt beneath him, he joined her. "You lied," she said, her eyes closed and one of her hands slung over her forehead. "You looked."

"I did not look at your shirt," he told her.

Leaning up on her elbow, she shot him a quick glance of disbelief. "I saw you look."

"I wasn't looking at your shirt."

"Oh, yes, you—"

"I was looking at your breasts."

She hesitated, blinking, then narrowed her eyes. "In order to look at my breasts, you had to look at my shirt."

"No, I didn't. The water made your shirt transparent. So transparent I could tell you the circumference of your nipples in centimeters."

She worked her jaw, then clamped her mouth shut and sank to her back. "I still say you cheated."

"Well, I lost the game anyway. It's not as if I had anything else to lose," he said, chuckling as he moved closer to her.

"What about your honor?" she asked sternly, but the way she bit her lip made him think she was pulling his leg.

"When it comes to your breasts, I'm a weak man."

"So I should remove temptation."

"You should remove your shirt, shorts, and panties."

Her lips lifted in a small but sexy grin. "But I'm not wearing panties."

Michael groaned and lowered his mouth to her. She tasted like spring and summer, laughter and sex, and he couldn't get enough of her. He sucked her bottom lip into his mouth and dared her tongue to dance with his. He wanted all of her to dance with him. He caught her sigh and drank it in, then pulled back slightly to catch his breath. He was already hard.

"I like the way you play," he said, staring into her clear, clear eyes. Something told him he could count on the honesty in those eyes.

"I don't have time to play very often," she admitted.

"Neither do I. You did it to distract me."

Her eyes widened, then she looked away. "I did not. I took a swim and you followed me."

"As if I wouldn't when you said you didn't have a bathing suit."

She shrugged. "How could I know that?"

"Good guess," he said, and took her outrageous mouth again. This time, the heat swelled between them and she moved with restless arousal. When she wove her fingers through his damp hair, his own arousal banged like a drum inside his head. He slid his hand beneath the towel to touch the hard outline of her nipple against her wet shirt.

She sucked in a quick breath and drew back, her gaze dark with the same wanting he felt. "I didn't bring the condom."

"You won't need it," he told her, although it might kill him. "We're just going to kiss each other until our brains explode."

At the same time that he wanted more than anything to slide into her and lose himself inside her, he also wanted to take his time. It was strange as hell, but he wanted to give her things she'd never had, and one of those included kissing her until they were both crazy from it.

Late that afternoon, Wilhemina steeled herself for the onslaught of argument and persuasion she knew Katie would make. Although Wilhemina believed Katie was a good-hearted person, she also knew Katie wouldn't get her monetary bonus if Wilhemina didn't marry someone her father approved of. She also knew that Michael wouldn't get what he wanted if she decided to stay in Texas.

The fact that her decision to stay could upset so many apple carts made her stomach hurt, but the idea of leaving Douglas upset her far more. She had never been so happy in her life.

A knock sounded on the door and Wilhemina tensed. She was resolved and nothing Katie could say would change her mind.

"Wilhemina," Katie called, her voice mingling with the whining sound of the screen door opening.

"You can come into the den," she said, poking her head around the corner. "We can sit in here where it's cool."

Katie walked into the den and offered a tentative smile. "You look like you're feeling better."

"I am," she said and sat down. "I still want to stay with Douglas."

Katie sank into a chair and sighed. "I know. I can see that." She looked away for a moment, then met Wilhemina's gaze. "I wouldn't feel right if I tried to tell you to leave. You haven't had the privilege of making a lot of your own choices because your father or someone else has made them for you. I think you should make this choice on your own."

Wilhemina sat in stunned silence. She had expected Katie to threaten, cajole, manipulate. She had expected anything, but this. "But this means you won't get the money."

Katie's eyes deepened with sadness, then she shook her head as if to shake off the emotion. "Yeah, and it's disappointing, but this is complicated."

"What about Michael? I half expected him to put me in a straitjacket to get me to go back to Philadelphia."

Katie winced. "Well, I can't say that Michael is quite at the same place that I am." She opened her mouth and hesitated. "There's only one thing that he mentioned that you might want to think about."

Wilhemina's stomach tightened in a knot. "What?"

"You might be ready for your father's fury, to be disinherited and cut off. You might be strong enough for that, but I don't know Douglas well enough to make that judgment."

Wilhemina immediately rose to Douglas's defense.

"Douglas is very strong. He's the strongest, kindest man I've ever met."

Katie nodded, but she didn't look convinced. "That's great, but your father isn't known for being kind. Your father is known for being ruthless. I don't know if you've seen what he's done to competitors, employees who have disappointed him, and even ex-wives."

Wilhemina's stomach tightened further. "What do you mean? Do you think he would try to do something to Douglas? What could he possibly do to him?"

Katie shook her head. "I don't know. If Douglas has a mortgage, your father might be able to get his hands on it. All I know is that your father has destroyed powerful, highly sophisticated men. I don't know what he would do to a hog farmer."

Wilhemina felt nauseous at the images that raced through her head. "I hadn't thought about that," she managed in a husky voice.

Katie gave a sad smile. "You haven't had time to think. You've had yourself a whirlwind romance with a cowboy."

It was more than a whirlwind romance, but Wilhemina

didn't correct her. Her head began to ache. "I'm going to have to think about this."

Rising, Katie nodded and put her hand on Wilhemina's shoulder. "I understand. Just let me know in the morning. Michael and I need to get back to Philadelphia."

Her heart heavy, she closed her eyes for a second, then met Katie's gaze. "I thought you were going to try to force me to leave."

"I don't envy your decision, Wilhemina, but I trust it."

Wilhemina felt tears burn her eyes. "You know, nobody ever thought I had enough sense to trust me."

"Maybe nobody looked close enough," Katie said with a soft smile.

"You're a good friend," Wilhemina said and really looked at Katie. "You look different with your hair down. Pretty. And the jean skirt looks nice too. You shouldn't go back to the old way of wearing your hair up and plain clothes."

"You know, Wilhemina, I've been thinking about doing just that." She squeezed her shoulder again. "I'll scoot back to the trailer. Okay?"

Wilhemina nodded. "Okay," she said, and her mind returned to how Douglas would be able to survive the wrath of Ivan the terrible. Gentle, wonderful, kind Douglas. Ivan would shred him into little pieces and feed him to the dogs and she wouldn't be able to stop him.

That night she fixed spaghetti with sauce from a jar and Douglas acted as if she'd prepared an elaborate meal. Katie, bless her, had discreetly allowed Wilhemina and Douglas privacy by fixing sandwiches for her and Michael at the trailer. After dinner, she and Douglas danced in the dark in the den to the songs of Mark Wills, one of Douglas's many country music CDs. The feeling of Douglas's arms around her was so sweet Wilhemina closed her eyes to savor every moment.

She cherished their lovemaking that night and the next morning.

"You're leaving, aren't you?" he asked when she couldn't look him in the eye afterward.

She nodded, stroking his shoulders and chest. She wanted to remember every intimate detail, the way his skin felt and smelled, the way he breathed, the feel of his laughter vibrating against her, and the sound of his voice. Something told her everything she'd learned about Douglas during the last few days was indelibly branded on her soul. Her chest felt so heavy and tight she could hardly breathe, let alone speak.

"Not quite good enough for Ivan Rasmussen," he mused, skimming his fingers through her hair.

Wilhemina couldn't hold back the tears. She shook her head. "Too good for Ivan Rasmussen," she corrected.

"That doesn't make a lick of sense," Douglas said with a frown.

"I don't think I can explain it. You just need to know that you are the absolute best man I've ever met."

"In bed," Douglas clarified.

"And out," she said, meeting his gaze.

"Well, if that's true, then you'd be a fool to leave me because I want you to stay. I hadn't realized how lonely I'd been until you came and I didn't feel that way anymore."

She tried to swallow over the lump in her throat. "I don't want to go, but I think it's the right thing to do."

"For whom? Your father."

She fought a deep scratchy irritation that bubbled deep below her skin. "It's not about pleasing my father. It's about avoiding his nasty temper."

Douglas went perfectly still. "He wouldn't dare try to lift a finger to you."

She shook her head and smiled sadly. "No, but I don't like thinking about what he'd do to you."

Douglas frowned at her in confusion. "I can take care of myself. Do you really think I'm so weak that your father could do anything to damage me?"

Wilhemina felt her smile abruptly flatten. "You don't know my father."

Douglas stared at her for a long moment, then rose from the bed. "I think this is a bunch of bullshit," he said, pulling on the jeans he'd left abandoned on the floor.

Wilhemina sat up. "Oh, please, don't be that way. Please," she pleaded. "You are everything I could ever want in a man."

"Except for the fact that I'm a hog farmer."

"I don't mind that you're a hog farmer at all."

"Hmm," he said shortly, his voice brimming with disbelief. "This sounds like a convenient excuse, Wilhemina. You didn't even trust me enough to tell me your real last name. I may be a hick, but I'm not an idiot. I was your good time in Texas. Well, thanks for being such an easy lay. Don't let the door hit you on the way out."

"Douglas!" Wilhemina called out as he snatched his shirt and stomped from the room. She jerked the sheet around herself and stumbled after him, watching the screen door slam just as she rounded the corner. She shoved it back open and called out, "I love you, Douglas."

Already down the steps, he paused. "Would that be Wilhemina Smith or Wilhemina Rasmussen?" he asked without looking at her. Then he continued to walk.

"Wilhemina forever," she whispered to herself. "I wonder if you'll ever figure it out."

* * *

Michael and Katie picked up Wilhemina, dropped off the Cadillac at the nearest rental car facility, then headed for the Dallas/Fort Worth Airport. The four-and-a-half-hour drive was interminable. Wilhemina's sniffles were punctuated by Chantal's mews from her kennel in the backseat. Out of deference to Wilhemina's state, Michael turned the radio station from hard rock to country. That worked for a few songs until a love-gone-wrong tune filled the car. Wilhemina sobbed and Katie changed the station to pop. Before long, however, Enrique Iglesias invaded the small space with his sensual song "Escape." Enrique's words and voice emanated heat and need, reminding Katie of how hot Michael had made her when he'd kissed her by the pond yesterday in the sun.

Her fingers had burned to get that condom from her purse and take it to Michael and ask him to take care of the achy need he was causing in her.

Hearing another sob from Wilhemina, Katie switched the station again, this time to seventies disco.

Michael threw her a look of horror. "Disco," he said in disgust.

Katie leaned across the console and pressed her mouth against his ear. "She needs a distraction. She doesn't need to be reminded of her feelings for Douglas."

He tossed her a dark glance. "But do we need to make her sick to her stomach?"

"It's not that much longer. Look, there's a sign for the airport," she said, pointing ahead.

Traffic slowed to a crawl, and Michael took a detour. After several miles, however, it appeared that they were headed away from the airport instead of toward it. Katie hated to question Mr. GPS, but she wanted to get on the earliest flight possible.

"I don't remember this route," she mused.

"We're making a quick stop," he said, his gaze inscrutable.

His voice held something full and heavy in it, something she couldn't read, but she sat back for a few minutes until the streets became vaguely familiar. The houses grew more grand, the lawns more lush, the driveways protected by ornate iron gates. Her chest tightened in suspicion. "We're not going—" She broke off when he took another turn to the street where her sister lived. "What are you doing? We don't have time for this." She shook her head. "We don't—"

He pulled to a stop in front of the house. "Her car's in the driveway. Bet that means she's there."

Katie looked at him in dismay. "So what am I supposed to do? Bang on the door and say give your long-lost sissy a hug?"

He shrugged. "You can say whatever you want, but we're not leaving until you say something to her."

"Why are you doing this?"

"Because you want to talk to her."

He was right. And wrong. She shook her head. "Not in this situation. Not this way."

"Why are we stopped?" Wilhemina asked between sniffs.

"Katie just needs to say hello to her sister."

"Sister? You have a sister?"

Katie frowned at Michael. "Yes," she reluctantly said. "We haven't seen each other in a while."

"How long?" Wilhemina asked, craning forward to look at Lori's yard.

"I can't go knock on the door," Katie told Michael as she began to sweat. "I'm sure the housekeeper has been told to turn me away."

Michael shrugged. "It's been a long time."

"How long?" Wilhemina asked.

"Twelve years," Katie muttered.

"Twelve years! Why?"

"Long story," Michael interjected for her. "Looks like you won't have to knock. She just came out the door."

Katie looked at her sister and her heart stopped. Fear gripped her. What if Lori snubbed her? She would rather remember her as her sweet adoring sister. Panic twisted inside her. "I can't do this."

"Either you do it, or I will," Michael told her, unlocking the car doors.

Anger and fear bucked through her. "Damn you," she said. "Damn you for interfering. I won't forgive you for this."

Undeterred, he opened his door. Seeing him slide his foot outside the car galvanized her into action. She whipped open her car door, and stood there with her heart beating in her throat. "Lori!" she called, then took a breath. "Lori!"

Her sister paused in the act of opening her car door and glanced toward the gate. "Pardon me," she said. "Were you calling me?"

"Yes," Katie said, her palms damp with nerves. "I-uh-happened to be driving by. You probably don't recognize me."

Lori flipped her long hair behind her diamond-enhanced ears and cautiously stepped closer to the gate. "Who—who—" She broke off and her eyes rounded. "Priss! Priss!" She began to run and unhooked the gate. She threw herself into Katie's arms and Katie bit her lip with relief.

Lori pulled back. "I can't believe it. My father wouldn't let me call. No matter how much I cried and begged, he wouldn't let me. I couldn't stop thinking about you and Mama. Here, I was living the high life and you were stuck—"

She broke off and tears streamed down her beautiful face. "I just turned eighteen last month."

"I know," Katie said. "Belated happy birthday."

Lori laughed, but shook her head. "I've been trying to find you, but you disappeared. Where did you—" She peered through the shrubs to the rental car. "Who—"

Katie waved her hand. "I'm in Philadelphia. Long story. You know Mama died two years ago, don't you?"

Lori's darkened with sadness. "Yeah. My father told me that much."

"Have you seen Dee?"

Lori shook her head. "My father pretty much cut me off. I think he wanted me to forget the first six years of my life." She smiled. "But I didn't. Maybe you and I could go somewhere and talk. I would invite you inside, but if Daddy found out, he would freak."

Katie shook her head. "I really can't stay. I've got to catch a plane. I almost didn't stop, but Michael forced the issue."

Lori's face fell. "But we haven't talked in so long. I really missed you."

Katie felt her eyes water. "I really missed you too." She felt her throat tighten and swallowed hard. "Listen, if you have a pen, I'll write down my number for you and you can give me yours."

Lori pulled some scrap paper out of her tiny purse and they traded numbers. She looked at Katie and touched her hair. "I feel like I've missed half your life. You're a woman now. What do you do?"

"I'm a private assistant to a CEO in Philadelphia. I've been in Texas on a special assignment." *Wild goose chase.*

"Oh." Lori glanced at the car. "Is that man a coworker or your husband?"

"Coworker," Katie quickly said. "I'm not married."

"He's hot," she said, giving Katie a smile that probably made her father lose sleep.

"I need to go," Katie said, ignoring the comment about Michael. She knew exactly how hot the man was. "Before I go, I hate to drop a bomb, but did you know that you have a half brother?"

Lori blinked and dipped her head. "Pardon me? I thought Mama had died. I wouldn't think even she could reproduce after that."

Katie chuckled. "She had Jeremy before she died. He's—" She took in her sister's stunned expression and decided the rest of the story could wait. "He's up in Pennsylvania. I can tell you more about him later. He's ten and terrific."

"My father must have known," Lori said, a dangerous glint of anger flashing in her eyes. "He must have known and not told me."

"He wanted to cut all ties," Katie said.

"He succeeded," she said bitterly, then met Katie's gaze. "For a while. If you don't call me, I'll call you."

Warmth suffused her at her sister's determination. "Good." She hesitated a second, then embraced her, inhaling her sister's designer perfume. "You don't smell like puppies anymore."

"Horses, Priss," Lori said. "I'll smell like horses in a little while."

"You always wanted a pony."

"And you got it for me."

Katie pulled back. "I'm surprised you remember."

Lori's eyes changed in an instant, revealing a deep grief. "I had a lot of time to remember."

Katie nodded. "Take care of yourself."

"You too, Priss. And thank the hottie for making you stop to see me."

Katie ran to the car, slid into the seat, and waved at Lori as Michael pulled away. Wilhemina immediately began to pound her with questions.

"She looks just like you with a makeover," Wilhemina said.

Katie swallowed a chuckle and slid a sideways glance at Michael. He didn't say a word, but his lips were twitching.

"Why haven't you seen her in such a long time?"

"We have different fathers and her father wanted to distance her from the influence of my mother."

Wilhemina sat quietly for a moment. "That's terrible."

It had been. Assaulted by grief from all the lost years and the joy at seeing Lori again, Katie dug her fingernails into her palms to keep from crying. She was so overwhelmed she could hardly breathe. She closed her eyes.

Wilhemina continued to exclaim and speculate. When Katie didn't respond, Ivan's daughter continued to carry on her one-sided conversation as if she had no clue that Katie was silently falling apart in the front passenger seat. That was fine with Katie. She closed her eyes as the tears leaked out. Michael said nothing, thank goodness.

Katie might have decided she had succeeded in becoming invisible if Michael hadn't pulled his sunglasses off and handed them to her. Her stomach dipped at the protective, intuitive gesture. He knew way too much about her and the knowledge that he knew so much made her feel as if she were on a roller coaster. Exhilaration and fear. He could hurt her.

Her heart and head were too full for talking when they arrived at the airport. Michael dropped them at the curb, then returned the rental car. Katie approached a ticket agent and secured seats for the three of them along with Chantal on the next flight. Wilhemina became increasingly subdued as they went through security and got to their appointed gate. Feeling Michael's gaze on her, Katie tried not to look at him. She feared that if she did she would beg him to hold her. Stiffening her spine, she told herself she needed to stop thinking about everything that had happened in Texas and start planning how to get to Jeremy before the day was gone. His gift was at her apartment, but she needed to pick up a cake. And Gummi Worms. And she had no car. Glancing at her watch, she worried. She couldn't disappoint him. She absolutely couldn't disappoint him. Looking at Wilhemina, she saw the lost expression on her face and squeezed her shoulder. Wilhemina began to sniffle again.

She paced the waiting area next to Wilhemina as the ticketing agent made an announcement. "Passengers waiting for Flight 67 to Philadelphia, your flight is delayed due to mechanical problems. We apologize for the inconvenience . . ."

Amid a chorus of groans from other passengers, Wilhemina stood. "I should have stayed with Douglas," she wailed. Chantal began to mew.

Her heart sinking to the floor, Katie whipped around and something inside her snapped. Michael was already striding to the counter. She ran after him with Wilhemina carrying Chantal as she brought up the rear.

"I can't be late," Katie said on the edge of hysteria as she tugged at his shirtsleeve. "I absolutely positively have to get back. I can't be late."

"I knew it was a mistake to leave Douglas," Wilhemina said, her lower lip quivering.

Michael looked at the two human females and one feline female all voicing their shrilling demands and ground his teeth. "Sit down and take that cat out of my hearing range."

"I can't be late," Katie said. "I have to—"

"If you don't get that cat away from here, I'm going to tie its mouth shut. I'll handle this," he said through gritted teeth.

The unholy light in his eyes gave her pause and she grabbed the kennel. "Let's go get a Coke, Wilhemina."

Herding Wilhemina to a fast-food restaurant down the concourse and ordering sodas, Katie tried to put the words together in her mind to explain her delay to Jeremy, but all she could see were his disappointed eyes. Her stomach began to twist and turn. She couldn't stand the idea of not showing. Jeremy had enough to overcome without having an unreliable guardian. Unreliable. Oversexed. She was turning into her worst nightmare. Her mother.

Wilhemina continued to sniffle and Katie absently patted her hand. "I already miss him," Wilhemina said.

Chantal gave a pitiful mewl and Katie didn't know how much longer she could stand their misery.

She rubbed her forehead and Michael's leather loafers appeared in front of her. She glanced up. The grim resolve on his face made her stomach hurt. "No alternate flights?" she asked dully.

"In a manner of speaking," he said, his gaze unreadable.

"What do you mean?"

"I mean we're going to help Ivan spend some of his money. We're taking a charter."

Wilhemina began to cry so loudly that people began to stare. Chantal mewed.

Michael clenched his jaw. "Get ready for the flight from hell, sweetheart, and this time there's no Valium."

*"If your man doesn't dance, then teach him.
If he won't try, then cha-cha on to the next one."*
—SUNNY COLLINS'S WISDOM

Chapter 19

"I need to rent a car," Katie said to Michael as soon as they exited the death ship that had flown them from Dallas to Philadelphia through nearly continuous turbulence and non-stop sniffling and mewing from Wilhemina and Chantal. Her head was still throbbing, but she had no time to waste if she wanted to reach Jeremy before bedtime.

"I'm going to take you," Michael said as he carried duffel bags and Chantal in her kennel.

Katie blinked. "Excuse me?"

"I said I'm taking you. Do you have an objection?"

Her heart pitter-pattered at the intensity of his gaze.

"I-uh-guess not, but don't you think you should take Wilhemina home?"

"Do you really think she should be left by herself right now?"

Katie glanced at the woman in question and saw her dab her pink nose and puffy eyes with a tissue. "I guess not." She searched Michael's face. "Don't you need to go see about your mother?"

"I can do that later tonight," he said.

She wanted to ask him why he would help her, but she couldn't. She sighed and decided to think about it later after

Jeremy had opened his gift. "I'll need to make more than one stop," she warned him.

"Where do you need to go?"

"I need to get a chocolate cake and Gummi Worms and I need to pick up his gift. It's at the Rasmussens'."

"Where is the school?"

She told him and watched him shake his head. "What did you get him?"

"Computer game."

"We should just stop by a department store on the way. You can take the other one back."

Surprised and unsettled, she opened her mouth, then closed it.

"I'll get the car and meet you and Wilhemina outside the door."

"Okay," she said, not knowing what else to say. She watched him leave and felt a strange tightening sensation inside her chest. She wasn't used to being helped. She patted Wilhemina through the next few minutes, mentally planning what she needed to get for Jeremy.

Michael appeared and she and Wilhemina got into the car. After a few minutes, Wilhemina blew her nose and looked out the window. "Where are we going?"

"To a birthday celebration," Michael said.

"For whom?"

"Katie's little brother."

"Brother! Katie has a brother? How many other siblings do you have?"

"One," Katie said. "One sister."

"Where is she?"

"I think somewhere in Texas."

Wilhemina poked her head between the front bucket seats. "Why don't you know where she is?"

"Different fathers," Katie said grimly. "We all have different fathers."

"Oh," she said, sinking back into her seat. "Your mother must have attracted men like flowers draw bees."

Katie nodded. "You could say that." Other people had put it different ways. *Slut, whore, easy, trashy . . .*

"Gosh, I've always wondered what it must be like to have men chasing after me."

"There's a downside. Remember Chad."

Wilhemina blushed profusely. "Ew. I'd forgotten all about him. Douglas made me forget about everyone but him," she added sadly and began to sniff again.

Michael gave a long-suffering sigh and put a CD in the player. "No disco," he told Katie, grinding his teeth. "Enough's enough."

She wasn't going to protest. This man was going to get her to her brother in time. If they were lucky, Wilhemina and Chantal would fall asleep. She closed her own eyes, leaned her head back, and allowed the jazzy music to play over her. The lyrics were sweeter than the kind she would expect Michael to choose. She expected rock music so hard and fast that it prevented thought. It occurred to her that she had pre-judged Michael in a lot of ways. It had felt easier that way. She wondered why she'd worked so hard to believe he was a jerk and didn't like the answer her conscience offered.

He pulled into a Wal-Mart superstore. "I'll get the computer game. You get the cake and Gummi Worms."

She blinked. "How—why—"

"It'll be faster," he told her. "Are you okay? You seem kinda out of it."

You keep surprising me, she didn't say. She moved her head in a circle. "I'm still coming down from the flight. Let's go," she said, then opened her car door.

"Can I come too?" Wilhemina asked.

Katie glanced over her shoulder in disbelief. "You want to go to Wal-Mart?"

Wilhemina shrugged. "It's gotta be better than sitting here. When Chantal whines, it makes me feel like crying too."

Katie held the door. "Then you're welcome to come along."

In short order, they gathered their assigned items and converged at the checkout line. "Ice cream?" Katie said as Wilhemina put it on the counter.

"And decorator frosting so you can draw his name on the cake."

"Thank you," Katie said. "I wouldn't have thought of that."

Wilhemina sighed. "I wish I had a brother and two sisters."

When Katie started to pay, Michael stepped in front of her and pulled out his wallet. She frowned, not wanting his charity. "I can cover this. It's my brother."

"No problem," he said.

"I insist. Jeremy is my responsibility." She tried to elbow her way in front of him.

Michael ignored her, shoving a wad of bills at the clerk.

Katie's temper spiked. "I'm not a charity case," she whispered to him in a voice that sounded more like a hiss even to her own ears.

He threw her a look that mixed frustration and anger. "I never said you were."

They gathered the bag and Wilhemina picked up the cake. "Then why are you acting like it?" Katie asked.

"I'm not. It was just something I wanted to do. Don't get your panties in a twist over it. You can pay me back later."

As soon as Wilhemina scooted into the back seat, Katie slammed the door closed and rounded on Michael. "Okay, what's going on here? Why are you being so damn nice to me? If you think I'm going to have sex with you because you paid for my brother's birthday, you're wrong."

Michael looked at her as if she'd completely lost it, then closed his eyes for several seconds. He had the look of a man who was counting to bring his temper under control. "I have no interest in using your brother's birthday as a seduction." He opened his eyes and met her gaze. "I'm not that hard up."

Katie immediately felt like a crazy person. What had possessed her? She wasn't sure she wanted to answer that question. She took a quick breath. "That was pretty ridiculous, wasn't it?"

He nodded.

"Sorry," she said in a low voice. "I'm just used to having to do everything myself." She paused. "Thanks."

He gave another brief nod, then opened the passenger door for her. "We need to go."

Katie slid into her seat and wrapped Jeremy's gift while Wilhemina added Jeremy's name to the cake. Michael pulled into the drive just as the sun began to set. A group of children burst through the front door onto the porch, curious to see the visitors.

"If you can remember to make sure that Jeremy can see your mouth when you're talking to him, please do. He can't hear hardly anything, but he's determined to be the best lip reader in the world. He speaks well because he lost his hearing two years ago in an accident," she said, dropping the bomb, then scooting out of the car.

"Priss!" Jeremy cried, pushing through the crowd on the porch.

"Priss?" Wilhemina echoed.

"Family pet name," Michael said.

"But Katie isn't prissy."

Jeremy flew down the steps and threw himself in Katie's arms. "What took you so long?"

"Airplane problems," Katie said, hugging him to her. "How has your birthday been?"

"Okay. I'm glad you showed up."

Katie's heart twisted. "I wouldn't miss it."

Jeremy looked past her. "Who's carrying my cake?"

Katie chuckled. "How do you know it's your cake?"

Jeremy rolled his eyes. "Because it's my birthday and you promised and Priss always keeps promises."

Katie squeezed her brother again for the gift of his belief in her. She only hoped she could live up to it. "This is Wilhemina. I work for her dad."

Jeremy's eyes widened. "You're Ivan the terrible's daughter. But you look nice."

Wilhemina smiled, one of very few today. "Thank you. Happy birthday, Jeremy."

"Thanks," he said, then looked at Michael. "Who are you?"

"I work with your sister," Michael said.

"For Ivan the terrible?"

Michael nodded, his lips twitching.

Katie touched Jeremy's shoulder to signal that she was going to say something to him. "Michael fixed things so I would be able to get here tonight. He drove me here and he fixed things with the plane."

"He can fix a plane?"

Katie laughed. "No, he found another plane for us to take when ours was broken."

Jeremy frowned. "I'm glad you didn't fly on a broken plane."

"Me too," Katie murmured, remembering the turbulence during the flight.

Jeremy looked up at her and squinted his eyes. "You look different. Prettier."

She smiled, feeling a little rush of pleasure at his approval. She had been so determined to be plain and invisible for so long that she hadn't known how nice it could feel to look like herself. "Thanks. Don't you want to open your gift?"

"Yeah, come inside. Some of my friends will want some of the cake too. They didn't believe you were coming, but I knew you would."

Katie looked at Michael. He had made it possible. She wondered if he had any idea how important this had been to both her and Jeremy. His gaze met hers and she saw a light of recognition. He knew. What a strange connection she felt with him.

Jeremy tore open his gift and gave approving sounds to the cake. There was a moment of panic when Katie realized she had forgotten to buy candles. Wilhemina had not. Katie impulsively hugged Ivan's daughter in gratitude.

While Jeremy showed Michael the new computer game, Katie spoke with one of the staff who repeated Jeremy's request to spend the summer with her. As much as she would love seeing her brother every day, she wanted a better environment for him. Her apartment was cramped and she worked long hours. Jeremy deserved better.

A staff member gently reminded her that the time for lights out was past and Katie looked for Jeremy. She found him talking with Michael on the front porch. Clearly unac-

customed to speaking to a hearing-impaired person, Michael
turned his head at times during the conversation.

She watched Jeremy catch Michael's jaw between his
hands and position it directly in his eyesight. "I want to hear
what you're saying. Keep your mouth right there."

Katie held her breath wondering how Michael would
react to Jeremy's directness.

Michael laughed and ruffled Jeremy's hair. "You're
going to have to remind me."

Her heart swelled at the sight of the two of them. She
hadn't expected Michael to be so generous. He was a busy
man, a man with a mission, almost a vendetta. No time for
little boys with hearing problems.

"Can we really go to a baseball game sometime this summer?"

She caught the look of delight on Jeremy's face and heard
an alarm bell go off in her mind. She didn't want Michael
making plans with Jeremy that he wouldn't keep. She
quickly stepped onto the porch.

"Sure if—"

"We need to leave," Katie said.

Jeremy swung his head toward her seconds after Michael
did.

"We need to leave," she repeated for his benefit.

Jeremy scowled. "But you just got here."

"I know. I'm sorry, but it's not fair for us to foul up everyone else's schedule." She leaned down to kiss his cheek.
"Happy birthday."

He gave her a hug and they walked toward the car where
Wilhemina waited. "You should take me with you," he said.

"You would be bored. My apartment is small. I'm gone
all day long and the computer at school is much much bet-

ter and newer than mine," she said and tried to sign the words.

"You just signed that whiskey is great for video games," Jeremy told her.

Michael appeared to cough to cover a chuckle.

Katie threw him a chastising glance before she turned back to Jeremy. "Sometimes I think you're pulling my leg because you don't want to spend a lot of time on sign language."

"You signed whiskey."

"If you say so. I'll bring you to my apartment for as many weekends as you can stand this summer. How is that for a compromise."

His eyes lit up. "Great!"

She smiled and her heart squeezed tight. "I love you."

"Me too," he said and gave the sign for *I love you.* It was one of the few phrases he'd willingly incorporated.

Jeremy turned to Michael. "Thanks for bringing my sister."

"My pleasure," Michael said. "We'll have to try to go to a baseball game sometime this summer."

"That would be great." Jeremy peered into the car at Wilhemina as she stroked Chantal. "What is that?"

"It's a cat. Her name is Chantal."

Jeremy frowned. "Cat! She doesn't look like a cat. What did you do to her?"

"Nothing," Wilhemina said, giggling. "She's a hairless cat."

Jeremy shook his head and made the sign for ugly. Chuckling, Katie kissed him and got into the car. Michael slid behind the wheel, started the engine, and pulled away. Katie waved even though she knew Jeremy probably couldn't see her, then sank into her seat. "Thank you both very much."

"You're welcome. He's a sweet boy," Wilhemina said. "I would have stayed at the house longer, but my stomach doesn't feel right. I think I just need to go to bed."

"I hope you're not coming down with something. Maybe you can sleep on the drive back," Katie suggested.

Wilhemina gave an unintelligible murmur and turned quiet. After a few moments, Katie leaned toward Michael. "I really appreciate you talking with Jeremy, but you really shouldn't even mention things like baseball games if you can't—"

"I wouldn't have said it if I didn't think I could make good on it," he said, cutting her off.

She opened her mouth, then bit her lip. "But he won't stop talking about this until the two of you go."

"Then I'll take him."

"Why?"

He tossed a quick glance at her, then focused on the road. "He's a good kid. I liked being with him."

Not knowing what to say, she sank back into her seat. She was so tired that when she closed her eyes, she felt as if her body were spinning.

"You're not the only one who can keep promises, Priss," Michael murmured to her.

In the darkness of the car, it was tempting to lean toward that voice, to lean against his shoulder, to let someone else be strong while she took a breath. A hazy image filled her mind of Michael, Jeremy, and her all together, living and laughing. Another followed of her held in the circle of Michael's arms. Katie rarely indulged in fantasies. They were a huge waste of time, but this one was more tempting than the fantasy of winning the lottery.

*　　*　　*

"Can I go with you?" Katie asked after Wilhemina had gone to bed. They stood outside Ivan's room in the darkened hallway.

Michael shook his head, both touched and uncomfortable with the offer. His mother represented a difficult, painful part of his life that he couldn't control, and he wasn't inclined to share that with anyone. Although, if there was anyone who could handle it, he suspected Katie would be the one. The woman was a rock.

"You're tired," he finally said.

"So are you," she said. "You helped me with my little mission tonight. I'd like to help you with yours."

He raked his hand through his hair. "Yours was fun. Mine won't be."

"All the more reason," she said.

"Someone needs to watch Wilhemina. She might escape again."

Katie shook her head. "She's exhausted and she doesn't feel well. She's not going anywhere. The least you can do is let me ride with you. How far is it?"

"Not that far," he had to admit. "But I don't want you along."

She paused a half beat. "I don't believe you. I'm riding with you," she said, turning toward the stairs.

Frustration cut through him and he went after her. "I meant it. I don't want you going with me."

Her face was set. "Then pretend I'm not there." She proceeded down the stairs.

Exasperated, he followed her down the stairs. "This is none of your business."

"I know," she said, continuing toward the foyer.

"I don't want you to go."

She ignored him and opened the front door. "Lots of stars out tonight, aren't there?"

"You're dead tired on your feet." He grabbed her arm and swung her around to face him. "Why are you doing this?"

She stared at him for a long moment, her eyes filled with a dozen emotions he couldn't read, but he felt somehow warmed. "I'm weird," she finally said.

He sighed and strode toward his car. "I think it's so you won't feel like you owe me. This is your version of payback," he said, and expected her to deny it.

"That's partly true," she mused, sliding into the car after he unlocked the door.

Michael got into the car and looked at her. "You don't owe me anything. I don't want you doing anything because you feel you owe me."

Her eyebrows knitted while she sat for a moment. She met his gaze. "You were a friend to me, tonight. I want to be a friend to you."

The honesty in her eyes undid one or two knots that had been tied tightly for years inside him. At another time to another person, he would have doubled his defenses and said he didn't need a friend. And maybe he still didn't need a friend tonight either, but it felt good for her to care. He didn't know what to say, so he said nothing. He didn't want to go down that road again, that road of counting on someone. Even though he had more than a feeling that he could depend on Katie almost as much as he could depend on himself. Wanting to push aside his thoughts, he started the car, opened the moon roof, slid in an Aerosmith CD, and headed down the road. With Aerosmith playing and the wind blowing, he wouldn't be able to think, and that was okay with him. He didn't talk and neither did she, but he felt her presence with him, almost inside him, throughout the ride.

When he turned onto the road where he could see the lights of the Liberty Mental Health Facility, his chest tightened up. Approaching the gated entrance, he cut Steven Tyler's volume in half and showed the attendant his driver's license. The man checked his list and waved Michael through.

Michael drove directly to a row of visitors' spaces in the parking lot, cut the engine, and looked at Katie. "I won't be long."

"I could go with you."

He immediately shook his head.

"Not exactly the kind of girl you bring to meet your mother, huh?"

Her words jerked him to a dead stop. He searched her gaze and saw the barest hint of vulnerability glinting in her eyes. Swallowing a sigh, he shook his head. "Trust me. This has nothing to do with your upbringing and everything to do with mine."

She nodded, but still looked unconvinced.

"She probably won't even know who I am."

She nodded again, still unconvinced.

"This isn't pleasant. You don't want to go in there."

She gave a half smile. "I've had more than a few unpleasant experiences in my life. On a scale of one to ten, this would probably only rate about a two for me. Don't put words in my mouth. I'd like to go with you."

He squeezed the bridge of his nose. After everything he knew about Katie, he wouldn't ever want to do anything that gave the barest suggestion that he didn't think she was good enough. "Okay, but if she starts screaming, I'm sending you out right away."

"Let's go," she said, reaching for her door. She was out before he could meet her on the other side and Michael led the way to the double doors where a guard allowed them to enter. He checked in at the visitation desk, and after a couple of minutes, they were allowed to take the elevator to the third floor. The halls were darkened for the evening to promote calm, but Michael heard a few voices as they moved toward his mother's room. It was a sad fact that many of the residents struggled not only with mental problems, but also with sleeping difficulties. He inhaled the strong scent of antiseptic and his gut tightened again. He hated that smell. For Michael, it was the smell of his mother gone mad. An aide unlocked the door and allowed him and Katie to enter.

His mother sat up in bed with the television on, her arms tied to the bars alongside her bed. Not a good sign. She was a small forlorn wisp of a woman in that bed. It always surprised him how small and delicate she looked.

She glanced up and her face lit with joy. "I'm so glad you came. I've missed you."

Cautiously, Michael drew closer. "It's good to see you too. I brought a friend with me. This is Katie Collins."

Katie extended her hand, then quickly modified the usual plan by touching his mother's arm. "It's nice to meet you, Mrs. Wingate. What are you watching?"

His mother waved her hand in a dismissing gesture. "PBS. It's the only thing I can stand." She looked at Michael. "Where have you been keeping yourself, darling?"

Michael felt a prickly sensation at the base of his neck. He still wasn't sure if she recognized him or not. "I had an assignment that took me down to Texas."

"The bluebonnets are beautiful there. Unless it was too dry, of course."

"There was so much rain it flooded, so we saw plenty of flowers," Katie said. "Do you like flowers?"

His mother widened her eyes. "Oh, I've always loved a garden. Reginald could tell you that."

"Did Michael ever help you in the garden?" Katie asked.

She chuckled. "He would rather build things, but he liked to play in the sprinklers when the groundskeeper turned them on. It didn't matter what clothes he was wearing. Do you remember that, Michael?"

She'd called him by his name. It took him by such surprise that he didn't say anything for a second. He nodded. "I remember your rosebushes. Didn't you win a lot of ribbons for them with the garden club?"

His mother nodded. "Every year it seemed." Her brow knitted with a frown. "Until I came here." Her gaze grew hazy. "I miss gardening." She looked at Michael. "I've missed you so much, Reginald."

He tensed. In and out. Lucid and not. Hide and seek. He could barely remember a time when she hadn't confused him with his father. He could never remember a time when he hadn't hated it. He felt Katie take his hand and he looked at her. There wasn't pity in her eyes, instead an affirmation that she knew who he was. For the first time in years, something inside him eased.

"I'm sure you're proud of how hard your son works," Katie said.

His mother nodded. "He's always been industrious. He liked computer games. His father—" She broke off as if confused. "His father didn't." She sighed. "I wish I didn't feel so tired. Will you come to see me again soon?"

"I will," he said, then leaned toward her and kissed her forehead.

"It's so good to see you, Reginald."

Michael sighed. "Good night, Mother."

"Good night, Mrs. Wingate. It was nice to meet you."

"Come again."

Katie held his hand as they left the room. She held it while they rode the elevator down to the main floor, and she didn't let go until they reached his car. He got in and was ready to turn on Aerosmith at one hundred decibels, but she stopped him.

"You know why she calls you by your father's name, don't you?" Katie asked.

"She wishes he were still alive."

"Yeah, but it's more than that. You are the man she wishes your father could have been."

"She is delusional."

"But she remembered what you were like as a child. She remembered the difference between you and your father. She looks at you and wishes."

After all the years of dealing with his mother's instability, it shouldn't have made sense, but it resonated inside him. "How do you know I'm not like my father?"

"Was he charming?" she asked, taking him off guard.

"Yeah," he admitted.

"You're not," she said with a smile. He could have been insulted, but the smile prevented it. "You don't have time to be charming. You're too busy being responsible and strong."

At that moment, he wanted her so bad he could howl with the need. She had no idea how significant it was that she had come with him to visit his mother and taken the situation in stride in her compassionate way. "I wish you'd brought that damn condom you swiped from my stash."

Her eyes darkened with the same need he felt and the air in the car thickened in an instant. "I wish I had too. I left it in my purse at the house."

His heart cranked into overdrive. She was ready for him. He was always ready for her. And he didn't have a damn condom. And he'd promised her he wouldn't take her again without protection. He wouldn't die from it, he told himself. He just felt like he would.

"Would you let me kiss you?" she asked, her voice husky and her eyes full of something that made him feel hot and bothered.

Her kiss would only make it worse.

"The more forbidden the candy, the more you want to eat it."
—SUNNY COLLINS'S WISDOM

Chapter 20

"Yeah," Michael said, leaning toward her, and she lifted her mouth to his. Her lips were warm, but her breath was cool from the peppermint she'd chewed just moments ago. Lifting her fingers to cradle the sides of his cheeks, she slid her tongue over his. He liked the way she held his face, as if he were important to her. He liked the way her breasts pressed against his chest, as if she wanted to be closer. She tasted like everything he'd ever wanted and needed, but had spent his life not knowing it. He felt the slow beat of his need pounding through his blood. It was arousal and something more.

Her tongue tangled and teased, her mouth tugged at his lower lip. He plunged his fingers into her silky hair and wanted to sink inside her skin, into her lungs and heart. But skin was as close as he could get, and even that was difficult in the car.

"Damn console," he muttered, pushing his seat back as far as it would go, and pulling her over him so that she straddled him.

Her breasts rubbed his chest while she undulated over the part of him that she had already made rock hard. The air in the car turned hot. He slid his hands beneath her shirt to cup her breasts and she moaned, pressing into him.

There was something tender yet primal about the way she kissed him, and the strange, growing connection he felt with her wrapped around him like a silken cord. He rubbed his thumbs over her tight nipples and she shifted restlessly over him, driving him farther and farther from sanity with each little movement. He slid one of his hands down to touch her thigh, then inside her panties to where she was wet for him. She suckled his tongue deep into her mouth.

She made him so hot he felt as if his brains were sizzling inside his head. Before he could tell her they needed to slow down, she slipped one of her hands inside his slacks.

Michael thought he might explode.

He pulled his mouth from hers and opened his mouth to tell her something that he completely forgot when she wrapped her hand around him and began to stroke.

Her breath whispered over his cheek. "Why isn't anything close enough?" she whispered, with the same gnawing desperation he felt. "Why?" She gave him a French kiss that belied her lack of experience and he felt her tug at the buttons on his shirt. Her open mouth slid over his throat tasting his pulse, cranking up the drumbeat of need pounding in his head. She made him forget everything but her.

She flowed down him like a warm breeze and suddenly her mouth was suspended mere inches from him.

Michael's heart stopped.

Her eyes dark with passion and a desperate need to give, she looked into his eyes, then her gaze skittered down his torso. "I don't-really-know-how," she said in a husky voice that tied him in knots as she moved millimeters closer.

In an instant, her mouth replaced her hand. She kissed him intimately. Her lips were untutored, but eager, and the erotic sight and sensation of her mouth made him sweat. When she took more of him deeper into her mouth, Michael nearly lost it.

Three long wet strokes from her tongue and lips and he pulled away from her.

She looked up at him in sexy confusion, her hair in disarray, her lips swollen. "I didn't do it right?"

He shook his head, still close to the edge. "Too right."

Skimming up his body, she took him in her hand again and French-kissed him and sent him over the top. Still shuddering from the intensity of his climax, he sank his fingers into her hair and pulled her mouth against his. He wanted to drink her, consume her, get inside her, and claim her. The power of his need made him shudder again.

He pulled back and sucked in a long draft of air. Looking into her eyes, he felt himself sinking and swore. He swore, rubbing his hand through his hair. He didn't feel embarrassed, but he sure as hell felt naked. It didn't make a damn bit of sense because although his fly and shirt were only loosened, he felt as if she could see straight through to the core of him. And he wasn't sure if he liked it.

Reaching past her to the glove compartment, he grabbed a few napkins he kept inside and handed them to her. "Okay, I have intimate knowledge of your lack of experience, so I know this isn't something you've done before. You said you wanted to be a friend to me. Why in hell did you—"

"Was I that bad?"

Michael rolled his eyes. "I think the result speaks for itself." He lowered his head so that they were eyeball to eyeball. "Why?"

Her eyebrows furrowed. "Isn't this one of those instances where if you liked it, you can just say thank-you-very-much?"

The woman was going to send him back into Liberty Mental Health Facility seeking his own treatment. "I want to know why?"

She lifted one of her shoulders. "I wanted to?"

Michael waited, knowing there was more.

"I was . . . curious."

He nodded, but still said nothing.

"I just really thought you might need it," she said bluntly.

He blinked. "Pardon? I *needed* it."

"Since I've met you, you've seemed very tense. And tonight after we visited your mother, you held my hand so tightly." She paused a half beat, then lifted her chin. "I didn't force you to accept my . . . attention."

He couldn't hold back a burst of laughter. "No. You didn't force me. What am I going to do with you?" He tucked her head against his chest and kissed the top of it. "I want you in my bed."

She sighed. "The walls in that house have ears and I don't want Ivan to know. He would find some way to hold it over me or you."

Michael didn't like it, but he agreed. "I won't be sleeping at the Rasmussen house much longer. Neither will you."

"It could get complicated."

His heart twisted at her measured retreat. "Are you saying I'm only good for a quickie or a good time in the car?"

She glanced up at him in surprise. "Are you joking?"

"Yes," he said, but something inside him felt tight and uncomfortable. "And no."

The color of her eyes changed colors like a sea of emotions. "You have a goal. You have a mission," she said with a wry smile. "I would get in your way."

His gut twisted. "I'll be the judge of that."

"Your judgment is impaired."

"Why?"

"Because you just got a blow job," she said with a sexy smile intended to distract.

He allowed it, for now. "That I did," he said and kissed the wonderfully wicked mouth that had brought him such pleasure.

"Chantal is sick."

Katie took a long look at Wilhemina and noted the drawn look on her face and her pale skin. "How are you feeling?"

Wilhemina gave a halfhearted shrug. "For the first time in my life, I'm not interested in pie. Is that what romance does to a woman? Makes her not care about pie?"

Katie smiled and put her hand around Wilhemina's shoulders. "I'm sure it depends on the woman. Why do you think Chantal is sick?"

"Well, look at her. She looks so puny."

Michael strode into the parlor and Katie's heart skipped a beat. He looked at her as if they shared a secret. He looked at her a little too long in her estimation, since she suddenly had difficulty breathing. She cleared her throat.

"Wilhemina says Chantal is sick. She says she looks puny."

He glanced at the cat and then lifted a brow. Katie covered a smile. She knew exactly what he was thinking.

"Chantal always looks puny," he said.

"But she really does look worse than usual."

"Hard to imagine," he muttered under his breath. "Do you think you should take her to the vet?"

"Daddy would," Wilhemina said. "To him, she's an investment, not a pet."

"Okay, let me know when you get an appointment and Katie and I will take you." He glanced at Katie. "Have you two discussed the invitations that came in during Wilhemina's absence?"

Katie gave a quick shake of her head. "Wilhemina is still recovering from the trip. I don't think she's ready for social appearances."

"I'll never be ready for social appearances in this town," Wilhemina said flatly. "I've found out that not everyone in this world is as nasty as the people here are, and I refuse to waste my time on the dregs of Philadelphia's elite society." She left the room in a huff.

"I think it's safe to say I won't be getting the matchmaker bonus for Wilhemina."

Michael touched her arm. "Sorry."

She shrugged. "It was a long shot. Not because of Wilhemina," she said quickly. "But because they don't appreciate her. I hate it that she's hurting, but she's definitely different."

"No more hats."

"It's more than that. She's more okay with who she is. I think she's more confident." She looked at Michael and smiled. "That's not bad."

"No. But it doesn't pay for Jeremy's school."

"No. It doesn't, but things could be worse. As long as I keep my job, I can stay one half step in front of the bill collector."

Wilhemina peeked around the corner with Chantal in her carrier. "The vet says he'll see Chantal right away."

"Let's go," Michael said and led the way to his car. He ushered Wilhemina into the backseat and paused before he opened the passenger door for Katie. "You think this is just too funny, don't you?" he asked with a dangerous glint in his eyes.

"You mean because the big, tough security expert has to

be concerned about an ugly cat?" She snickered. "Why in the world would I find that amusing?"

"Keep it up, Katie Priss, and I'm going to have to kiss you."

Katie's heart bumped against her rib cage. What a delicious threat. Except she didn't want anyone at the Rasmussen house knowing there was something between her and Michael, whatever that something was. "In a different circumstance, I would take you up on your offer," she said and opened her own door and slid inside. When Michael got inside, she avoided his gaze. When he turned on the air conditioner, however, she turned her vent on her cheeks. The man made her hot at the most inconvenient moments.

At the veterinarian, Wilhemina insisted on going into the examination room with Chantal. Katie and Michael sat in the waiting room. The vet decided to do blood work. Finally Wilhemina left the examination room with Chantal cradled in her arms. Katie rose when she saw tears in Wilhemina's eyes. "Uh-oh."

Michael rose beside her.

"What is it?" Katie asked, feeling a twist of concern at the expression on Wilhemina's face. "Is she going to be okay?"

Wilhemina nodded and beamed with pleasure. "Chantal is pregnant! And the father is Flash."

Michael made a strangled noise. "Something tells me Flash isn't a purebred Canadian hairless."

Wilhemina shook her head. "Flash was Douglas's barn cat. Isn't this exciting?"

Katie imagined Ivan's reaction and exchanged glances with Michael. He looked slightly ill. "Exciting," Katie echoed. "Yes, it's definitely exciting. We should talk about this on the way home, shouldn't we, Michael?"

He nodded and raked his hand through his hair. "Yeah, we definitely should talk about this."

In the car, Katie cast a worried glance at Michael. A muscle was twitching beneath his right eye. "I think it might be best if we don't mention Chantal's condition to your father for a while," she said to Wilhemina.

"Why not? The kittens will be so cute."

"I wonder if they'll have hair," Michael muttered.

"I think your father was hoping to breed Chantal with another Canadian hairless. He might not be pleased that Chantal has been impregnated by—"

"A fucking barn cat," Michael finished for her.

"But it's Douglas's cat," Wilhemina said.

Visions of the gun rack on Douglas's truck swam in Katie's head. "I'm not sure that would make a difference to your father."

"But even Daddy would like kittens," Wilhemina protested.

"It's about money and status," Katie said impatiently. "Even with the damn cat."

Wilhemina turned quiet. "He's that way about me too, isn't he?"

Katie's heart twisted and she turned to look at Wilhemina. "Not with you," she said, even though Wilhemina's suspicions were at least partly true. Ivan Rasmussen's ego transcended even her imagination.

"You don't think he would do anything to hurt Chantal, do you?"

"I don't think so."

"But it would be unpleasant."

"Well, I don't want Chantal put under any extra stress during her pregnancy," Wilhemina said firmly.

Michael rolled his eyes.

"I wonder if there's another place you could keep her when she gets further along," Katie mused.

"A home for unwed cats," Michael said dryly.

Katie threw him a quelling glance. "Do you have any suggestions? Aren't you concerned about how this might affect your contract with Ivan?"

"There's no pregnancy clause. He tried, but I threatened to walk if he was going to put me in charge of birth control for the cat."

Michael turned onto the street where the Rasmussen house stood proudly at the top of the hill.

"I'm glad we've got a little time before Ivan returns," Katie said, foreseeing a giant explosion in the making.

"Me too," Wilhemina said.

Michael swore.

"What is it?" Katie asked, but she saw the reason for Michael's displeasure before he voiced it.

"Ivan's home early."

Michael managed to hustle them into the back entrance of the house. Eager to avoid answering any questions, Wilhemina took Chantal up the back stairs and secluded herself in her room and Michael retreated to his room. That left Katie to face the lion. Swallowing her nerves, she fixed on her face what she hoped was an expression of surprise, without hysteria.

"Good afternoon, Mr. and Mrs. Rasmussen," she said as she approached the foyer. "What a lovely surprise. I hope you enjoyed your trip."

Patricia scowled. "Ivan had an urgent business matter to handle. We left before I got a second day of shopping in Paris."

"But I'll make it up to you," Ivan said in an oily placating tone. Katie suspected there was already trouble in paradise. She wondered how long Patricia would last. Ivan turned to Katie and studied her. "Something's different," he said. "Your hair. You're wearing it down. It looks nice."

Patricia's nostrils flared as if she were sniffing out a competitor. She narrowed her eyes while her frozen botox-treated forehead remained smooth. "Yes, you have lovely hair."

Katie bit her lip. Ever since she'd come back from Texas, she just couldn't make herself pin her hair back in that too-tight bun. She liked the way Michael looked at her. She liked it when he told her she was pretty. She liked looking in the mirror and feeling like herself. "Thank you," she murmured. "I've always admired yours. It always looks perfect."

Patricia preened.

Ivan guffawed. "It should with the truckload of hair spray she wears."

Patricia's smile fell. "I'm going to rest for a while. Since we're back early, I think a cocktail party would be a good idea. I'll start planning right away. Ciao, darling," she said with an air kiss for Ivan.

Ivan gave a long-suffering sigh, then turned to Katie. "I had a hard time reaching you while I was gone," he said in a voice that made the hairs on the back of her neck stand straight up.

"I didn't think you would have time since you were on your honeymoon trip."

"I always make time for things that are important to me," he said, giving Katie the feeling that she was being circled by a wild carnivorous animal.

She told herself not to panic. "I'm sorry a business emergency interrupted your trip."

He made a face, and something told her there was no

business emergency. That meant he had either come home because he couldn't stand any more time with Patricia or he was concerned about something at home.

"How is the project coming along with Wilhemina?"

She swallowed over another lump of nerves. "It's been challenging. I'm not sure I'm going to be able to find the right person in the amount of time you designated."

"She's that difficult."

"I don't think Wilhemina is the problem," she said, feeling defensive.

Ivan shot her a sideways glance. "What do you mean?"

"I think Wilhemina is a fine person. I think too many people have tried to make her over and she needs to be left alone. You have raised a lovely, lovely daughter."

A naked longing deepened Ivan's beady eyes for an instant, then it was gone. "You're speaking of her heart."

"Partly. She's not self-centered. She's considerate. Unfortunately, I'm not sure those qualities are appreciated in the circles she's been moving in."

Ivan paused. "I have called my home every other day for the past week, but you, Michael, and Wilhemina have never been available. What's been going on?"

Katie's stomach wrenched. Ivan wore that too-calm expression just before someone got the axe. She bit her lip, searching her mind for what to say.

"We went to Texas," Michael said from behind Katie.

Katie's knees nearly buckled with relief. At least she wasn't alone.

"Texas?" Ivan echoed with a deep frown. "Why the hell would you go to Texas?"

"Wilhemina needed to get away. She had a bad experience at a party. A young man led her to believe he was interested, then insulted her behind her back."

"Who was it?" Ivan demanded.

"Jason Page," Michael said, then chuckled. "But Katie pretty much verbally castrated him."

Ivan looked at her in surprise, then nodded. "I still don't understand why in hell you went to Texas."

Wilhemina swung into the room. "Hi, Daddy." She gave her father a hug. "You're back early. How was the cruise?"

Ivan returned the hug, but waved his hand dismissingly at her question. "It was okay. What's this I hear about you going to Texas?"

Wilhemina's face froze and Katie immediately stepped beside her. "We were just catching your father up on how we all went down to Texas together because you needed a little diversion."

Wilhemina slowly nodded. "Right. We-uh-visited rodeos."

"Yes, and learned to two-step," Katie said encouragingly.

"And ate barbecue," Wilhemina said with a nervous smile.

"Right," Michael said.

"Hm," Ivan said, looking at the three of them. "Sounds harmless." He gave a shrug. "Still don't understand why you would choose a hellhole like Texas."

"It's so different," Wilhemina said. "Compared to Philadelphia, it's almost like going to a foreign country."

"Hmm," he said again as if he didn't approve or disapprove. Yet. "Well, you're back now and you can get in the swing of attending some of these social events Katie finds for you."

"Oh, I'm not going to any more social events here," Wilhemina announced.

Katie froze and saw Michael's right eye twitching from the corner of her eye. Complete silence followed.

"Excuse me," Ivan said in that scary too-quiet voice.

Wilhemina didn't appear to give a flying fig. "I'm not going to any more parties. Those people are assholes and jerks and they're just not worth my time," she said, and flounced out of the room, leaving Katie and Michael with the rare sight of Ivan with his mouth hanging open, speechless.

"For some men b-a-b-y is the most terrifying four-letter word in the English language."
—SUNNY COLLINS'S WISDOM

Chapter 21

Ivan Rasmussen always got his money's worth.

Although it made little sense to Katie, Ivan decided he wanted her and Michael to stay at the house until the date he had originally planned to return. Michael fought it, but Katie just figured she was saving a few pennies on her electric and food bill since there was no chance of her persuading Wilhemina to attend a social function let alone interest her in a man.

Katie walked around with the unsettling feeling that the sky was getting ready to fall on her. She felt Michael's gaze on her whenever he was around, and when she turned in at night, he invariably greeted her just inside her room and kissed her until she turned to butter. Then, because he didn't want her to worry about talking walls, he left.

She was getting close to the time that would tell whether or not she was pregnant, and with each passing day, she grew more jumpy. One afternoon, Wilhemina breezed in to see her father. Her eyes were a little too bright, her cheeks flushed with excitement. For a second Katie wondered if she had seen Douglas. Her stomach tightened. "I have something I need to tell you, Daddy," Wilhemina said, her voice trembling with emotion as she stood in front of Ivan's desk.

Sensing Wilhemina was going to say something important, Katie eyed the door. "Let me leave to give you some privacy."

"Oh, no," Wilhemina said, pleading and desperation in her eyes. "I want you to stay."

Katie's sense of unease jumped two notches. "Okay." She spotted Michael approaching the outer office and gave a minute shake of her head. He paused, frowning, and stood just outside the door.

"Daddy, this isn't easy, and you might feel upset in the beginning, but I know you'll be happy later."

Ivan took off his reading glasses and studied his daughter. "What are you talking about?"

Wilhemina twined and untwined her fingers. "I-uh-I want you to promise that you won't yell."

Ivan stretched his neck against his shirt collar, a sign of discomfort. "Why would I yell?" he asked in the scary quiet voice.

Wilhemina swallowed audibly. "Well, I told you that you might be upset at first. But you won't stay that way," she hastened to reassure him. "You're going to be overwhelmed with joy just like me."

He tented his fingers in front of him and nodded. "Okay. Go ahead and tell me."

"You promise you won't yell at me?"

Ivan paused. "I promise."

Katie wondered what in the world . . .

"I'm-going-to-have-a-baby!" she said in a rush, nearly bursting with excitement and joy.

Katie stared in shock.

Ivan furrowed his brow in confusion, still nodding as if he hadn't heard her. "Excuse me. Could you repeat that?"

"I said I'm going to have a baby," Wilhemina said.

Katie felt light-headed. She swung her gaze to Michael. He looked as frozen as she felt.

Ivan began to shake his head. "You can't be. You can't be. You said you didn't like anyone you've met at the parties."

Wilhemina began to worry her fingers again. "I didn't meet this man here. I met him in Texas."

"Texas?" he said with distaste, rising to his feet. "You went down to Texas and carried on with some cowboy—"

"Well, he's not exactly a cowboy. He's a hog farmer, but—"

"Hog farmer!"

"Daddy, you're yelling."

Katie felt as if she were watching a train wreck.

Ivan turned his furious gaze on her. "Katie, you'd better have an explanation for this."

Me? Panicked, Katie tried to make her mind work. "Wilhemina met a man in Texas and she felt very strongly about him and she, uh—"

"Breeded with him," Ivan said with distaste.

Katie winced, thinking of Chantal's delicate condition.

"Katie had nothing to do with Wilhemina's decision to go to Texas and get involved with this man," Michael said, calmly walking into the room.

Ivan turned on him like a snake. "Did you? Why weren't you protecting my daughter?"

"Your daughter was never seriously in danger."

"That's right. Douglas rescued me after I drove into the ditch," Wilhemina said.

Katie bit back a groan.

"Ditch," Ivan echoed. "You two were supposed to watch over my daughter during my absence."

"She ran away after the incident with Jason Page,"

Michael said. "Nothing in our contract stipulates that I was responsible for her safety if she should sneak out of town."

"Contract, shmontract," Ivan said. "It was your job to make sure she was kept safe."

"I did run away, Daddy," Wilhemina confessed. "Katie and Michael had nothing to do with it. The only reason I went to Texas was because of the story Katie told me."

Katie saw Michael grimace and wanted to sink into the floor.

"What story?"

"This wonderful story about a cowboy knight. I was upset and I decided I needed to go seek my future."

"And now you're knocked up with a hog farmer's baby," Ivan said viciously. "He wasn't very careful, was he?"

Wilhemina's head dipped. "You don't understand. I wanted to get pregnant. I wanted a baby, but then I didn't feel it would be right to trick Douglas. He used a condom every time we made love. And trust me, Daddy, it was a lot of times."

Ivan's face turned red. "Oh, God. Spare me the details. This hog farmer probably has an IQ of ten."

"He actually graduated from high school with a 3.5 average," Michael said. "He could have easily gone to college, but he worked in the family business. He's not wealthy. His debts are related to the farm. No criminal record. Regarded locally as an upstanding member of the community."

"With a gun rack on his truck," Ivan said and swore.

"That too," Michael admitted. "But I didn't see any chewing tobacco or snuff."

"This is your fault," Ivan said, growing more visibly enraged with each passing moment. "I told you I didn't want Wilhemina hooking up with a damn hick."

"It's not their fault! And Douglas isn't just a hick. He's—"

"Go to your room," Ivan roared. "You've embarrassed me beyond belief."

Wilhemina burst into tears. "You promised not to shout."

"Go to your room," he shouted, the veins in his neck bulging.

Crushed, Wilhemina fled from the office. Ivan immediately turned his attention to Katie and Michael. "You ingrates. I hired you, paid you well, and look what you did to me. Katie, I can't believe you allowed this."

Katie knew she should keep her mouth shut, but she couldn't. "She's twenty-four. She's not a child. It's time for her to make choices, good or bad. When are you going to understand that she's the best thing in your life?"

Ivan's face turned a mottled purple. "Get out of here. You're fired. You're both fired."

His words hit her like a blast from a furnace. Katie stood with her knees locked for a full moment.

"Get out! Both of you."

As if she were a robot, her feet started to move. She heard Michael's voice as she collected the personal items from her office in a paper bag.

"Pregnancy isn't a valid basis for breaking my contract or Katie's," Michael said.

"You didn't fulfill anything. She was traipsing all over Texas getting pregnant when you should have—"

"It was not a condition of my contract to be in her presence every minute . . ."

Katie climbed the stairs, packed her suitcase in three minutes, and heard Michael and Ivan still screaming when she walked past them. Although she felt as if she were in a dark tunnel, some part of her absorbed the voices. She hoped they didn't have a stroke.

Well, she amended, as she walked out the front door and headed for the train station, she hoped Michael didn't have a stroke. She hoped a lot of things. She hoped pregnancy wasn't contagious. First Chantal, then Wilhemina. Katie felt her first spurt of panic. She hoped she wasn't going to turn out like her mother. Like her unwed mother.

And if she was very fortunate and she wasn't pregnant, she also hoped she would find a new job. Quickly.

Michael called later that night. "Are you okay?"

"I'm not dead." Surprised at how glad she was to hear his voice, she sank onto her bed. "How did you get my number?"

"I'm a security expert. I can find out anything." He paused. "Ivan will change his mind."

"I don't think so," Katie said, remembering the complete rage she'd seen in his eyes. "He was a little ticked. And you're forgetting the fact that he doesn't know about Chantal. What happened with you?"

"I'm still here in the Rasmussen horror hotel."

Katie sat up. "You're joking. Aren't you afraid of being murdered in your sleep? Oh, wait, I forgot. You're a security expert, so you should be able to prevent that."

"Very cute, Katie. I'm here for the duration. I'm not breaching anything in the contract. If he wants to welsh on this deal, then he'll pay for it. I'm not knuckling under to Ivan. I'm not giving him an excuse to welsh on the deal."

Katie made a face. "It wasn't fun being fired and it's probably not going to be fun looking for a job, but I'm glad I'm not in that house at the moment."

"Lucky you in your own apartment."

"Very small, but safe apartment." She sank back onto her bed.

"One bedroom?"

"Yep."

"Where are you right now?"

She paused, and almost didn't tell him. What the heck. "My bedroom."

He groaned. "You just ruined my sleep."

She laughed and rolled her eyes. "Why? It's a very small, very modest bedroom. I'm not wearing crotchless panties and a see-thru bra."

"Thanks for the visual."

"You're not missing anything. I promise."

"Oh, but I am. When are you going to admit that you are too?"

Her stomach twisted at the truth of his statement. "Sleep with one eye open."

"Probably both. I'm burning the midnight oil. I'll come see you when I get out of the big house."

She smiled.

"How are you really?" he asked, his voice deepening in a way that made her heart hammer.

"What do you mean?"

"I mean, uh, health. How is your health?"

She tensed at the same time that something inside her turned oddly mushy. He was nervous about asking if she was pregnant. "Nothing yet. I should know soon."

"You'll tell me."

"Yeah," she said, wanting to get away from the scary subject. "Take care of you."

"You too, and by the way, Katie, I told Ivan he was an asshole for you."

She shook her head. "You might want to focus on watching out for you. I'm a liability right now."

"That's a matter of opinion."

"Go to bed."

"I'm waiting for you to bring me the condom."

Not anytime soon, even if she burned to cinders from her lust. "G'night." His deep chuckle rippled under her skin as she hung up.

The following morning, she jogged to the apartment office to buy a paper, then returned to peruse it while she drank coffee and ate stale cereal minus the milk. She'd been too disoriented to buy food on her way home after being fired. She was busy circling every job possibility when her doorbell buzzed. It was an annoying sound that she rarely heard, thank goodness.

Rising from the table, she peeked through the privacy hole to see Wilhemina toting the cat carrier. Katie quickly opened the door.

"Can I stay with you?" she asked, her face splotchy from tears. "My father wants both Chantal and me to have abortions."

Katie blinked in shock and stood aside. "You're welcome to, but this is a very small apartment, Wilhemina. I'm sure you're not used to—"

"What a cute, sunny, little kitchen," Wilhemina said, quickly entering. She was twirling her fingers, a sure sign of nerves.

"Wilhemina, are you sure you don't want to try to talk things out with your father?"

Wilhemina nodded. "I already talked. I told him to go fuck himself."

Katie blinked again. She couldn't have heard correctly. "You told your father—"

"To fuck himself," Wilhemina finished for her. "He told me he's disinheriting me. I'll try not to be a lot of trouble. Chantal is a bigger pain than I am. I'll learn to cook and help out with the rent."

"How can you help with the rent if he disinherits you?"

Wilhemina smiled sweetly. "I took a cash advance on my credit card on the way over here." She turned serious. "I don't want my baby affected by his negativity and anger."

Despite the insanity of the situation, Katie couldn't disagree. "Have you thought about what you'll do after you have the baby?"

Wilhemina shook her head. "No, but I have nine months to figure that out. Well, make that eight. I'll eventually have to get a job. I have a college degree. It should be good for something."

Katie nodded, feeling for Wilhemina as she came to terms with her responsibilities. It was almost as if Wilhemina was growing up before her very eyes. "Have you thought about contacting Douglas?"

Wilhemina's eyes immediately welled with tears. "He was really hurt when I left. He doesn't want to hear from me."

"Even if you're carrying his baby?"

"I can't think about that today. Can I take the couch?"

"Yes, it's a sleep sofa," Katie said, feeling self-conscious about her modest home. "I wish I had more to offer you."

Wilhemina turned to her with tears in her eyes. She set Chantal's kennel on the floor and took Katie's hands in hers. "You have been something I've never had before. A friend. I couldn't ask for anything more."

Katie felt her own eyes fill with tears. Oh, wow. "You're pretty darn special, Wilhemina. You'll be a great mom."

Wilhemina lifted her shoulders and smiled. "Thanks."

Michael spent that entire night on the Internet.

And the next. And the next.

He was in a war of wills with Ivan, but something else weird was happening to him. He couldn't stop thinking about Katie. He was worried about her. He wondered if she was pregnant. He wondered how her job search was going. He knew Wilhemina and Chantal were staying with her. Lord, the woman had to be a saint.

But he knew she wasn't. He'd known her when she came apart in his arms and made him come apart in hers. She had the oddest ability to pull him apart, yet make him feel whole. He wanted her in his bed, in his life. He'd spent so many years pushing people away that he didn't exactly know how to allow someone in.

Since Ivan was still so angry he was spitting venom at every opportunity, Michael knew he just had to wait the man out. Sometimes he thought waiting was stupid, yet at the same time, he felt as if he'd spent his life living down his father's unreliability and instability, and winning against Ivan would prove to everyone that he was different. This went a lot deeper than his bank account, but today the thought that he should be with Katie instead of battling Ivan had slid through his mind more than once.

While he was waiting, he might as well do something productive with his time, such as conduct security checks for other clients. And search for information on Katie's parents. He learned the name of her father and began the arduous search of how the man had disappeared. Katie had been told he'd died.

Searching death records in ten states for the four months around his guesstimate of her conception, he looked until his eyes were ready to pop out of his head. Remembering she'd mentioned that her mother had always said she'd been conceived in Myrtle Beach, he searched the death records for South Carolina.

When her father's name appeared, he felt his heart stop. Killed in an automobile accident, he'd only been twenty-three, and he'd never gotten to see his daughter. That was only the beginning. He searched for her grandparents and learned that they, too, were dead. Then he found something interesting. An unclaimed inheritance.

This was going to require telephone calls during business hours. Michael rubbed his eyes and rested his head in his hands. His weariness hit him like a sledgehammer. He sat there for a moment that turned into ten, waking when his chin hit the desk.

Swearing, he shook his head. He needed some sleep. Adrenaline and sexual need could only keep a man awake for so long before he crashed. He automatically checked the company E-mail before he signed off. There was a message from a hog farmer in Texas.

Katie answered the heavy knock on her door and stared in amazement through the peephole. "Douglas?" She opened the door unable to think of a thing to say. How had he found her apartment?

"Where's Wilhemina?" he demanded, striding through the doorway. "I know she's here. It was a mistake for her to leave and I'm not leaving until she realizes it." He folded his arms over his chest. "Now where is she?"

Heaving in the bathroom. This was going to get interesting. "Just a second. I'll get her."

"Tell her there's no use in hiding. I'll come after her."

Katie nodded and headed for the small hall bathroom where Wilhemina had spent many of her waking hours during the last couple of days. Wilhemina walked slowly toward the sofa.

"Wilhemina," Katie said.

Wilhemina adjusted the washcloth over her forehead. "In a minute. First, if you don't mind, could you please give me a few crackers and soda? I know that will help it—"

She rounded the corner and shrieked. "Douglas! What are you doing here?"

Douglas puffed out his chest. "I've come to tell you that I'll fight anyone, including your father, for you. You belong with me."

Wilhemina lifted a hand to her throat. Concerned that she might swoon, Katie rushed to her side. "Do you need to sit down?"

Wilhemina moved her head in a circle. "What made you—" She swallowed. "How did you—" She stopped and frowned. "Do you know about the baby?"

"Baby?" Douglas echoed, his voice cracking. "You can't be pregnant. I used a condom every damn time."

Wilhemina stood for a long moment and Katie sensed her quandary. She didn't want Douglas to pursue her out of obligation. She wanted Douglas to pursue her because he loved her.

Katie cleared her throat. "She meant Chantal's babies. Chantal is going to have kittens."

Douglas relaxed a millimeter. "Oh," he said, nodding. "Must've been Flash."

Wilhemina nodded. "I think so."

"I love you, Wilhemina. I want you to come back with me."

Wilhemina bit her lip and meandered toward the tiny kitchen. Douglas watched her every move. Since the apartment was so small, he could have watched her if she went anywhere except for the rooms with doors.

Wilhemina poured herself a soda and took a sip. "What if I'm richer than you'll ever be?"

"I still want you with me," he said, rock solid.

"What if my father has disinherited me and I'm broke?"

"That sonofabitch better not mistreat you—"

"What if I'm broke?"

He shrugged. "I want you. I don't want your money. I want you in my bed, in my house every day for the rest of my life."

Wilhemina looked at him with her heart in her eyes. "Are you very sure?" she whispered, moving back to stand in front of him.

"Surer than I've been of anything."

She flew into his arms and he held her tight. Katie felt the urge to cry.

Wilhemina let out a little sob against Douglas's throat. He stroked her hair. "Don't cry, honey. I'm here. I love you and I'm never leaving you."

"I never thought I'd see you again."

Katie backed toward the bedroom to allow them some privacy.

"Douglas, do you still want me if I'm pregnant with your baby?"

Katie couldn't resist stealing a glance at his shocked, confused expression. "You said it was kittens. You can't be pregnant. I used a condom every time."

"One of them didn't work."

Douglas looked as if he'd been hit in the head with a frying pan.

*　　*　　*

"You sent Douglas, didn't you?" Katie said the following night when she talked with Michael. He called her every other night. She had given up trying not to look forward to hearing his voice. With an amorous about-to-be-married couple proving their love for each other every other hour, she had given up on sanity.

Michael chuckled. "He got there fast. I got an E-mail from him two days ago. I gave him the third degree before I disclosed Wilhemina's whereabouts."

"Well, they're temporarily staying on my sofa bed until Wilhemina can get the wedding planned."

"That fast?"

"I wish it were faster." She heard a sexual groan of pleasure and covered one of her ears. "They're torturing me."

"How?"

"Michael, I swear they go at it like rabbits. I've almost walked in on them three times."

Michael laughed again. "Getting a little too hot around there?"

"Maybe."

"What do you think about when you hear them?"

Knowing he couldn't see her made her bold. "You."

She heard his sharp intake of breath.

"You making love with me on a bed. You and me with all the time in the world."

"I hate Ivan Rasmussen," he said in a rough voice.

"I do too. I got a job offer today."

"You did? With who?"

"I'll be working for a female attorney. She's sane. It was so refreshing. I won't get quite as much money, but they offer educational assistance and an extra week of vacation so I think it evens out."

"Congratulations."

"Thank you. I can't tell you what a relief it is to work for someone sane. Are you sure you want to work for Ivan?"

"It's not just the contract, although the money is part of it. I want him to admit that I met the conditions, that I wasn't weak. I want the admission." He paused, and she could feel his tension through the telephone line. "He brought up my father again today."

Katie's stomach turned at Ivan's ruthlessness. "You're not weak, Michael. You're strong."

He sighed. "I want to come see you tomorrow, but I have this feeling that once I see you, I'm going to have a damn hard time coming back."

Her heart squeezed at his admission.

"Someone is going to come see you tomorrow. You need to try to be there tomorrow afternoon."

"Who is it?"

"I promised I wouldn't tell. Just be at your apartment tomorrow afternoon."

"A mother's love is a gift that keeps on giving . . .
long after she's gone."
—SUNNY COLLINS'S WISDOM

Chapter 22

By three-thirty, Katie had made twenty-three trips to the window.

"Who are you expecting?" Wilhemina asked when she came up for air from kissing Douglas.

"I don't know. Michael wouldn't tell me. It's a surprise." She made a face. "I hate surprises." She shrugged. "Well, whoever it is must have changed their mind. They're not coming. They're not—" She stole another glance and saw a car pull into the parking lot. Anticipation thrummed through her as she watched the car pull into a space. Two women got out. A young woman with long blond hair. Katie's heart raced. "It's Lori and, and—"

She stared at the other woman. Brown hair cut in a hip, choppy bedroom style swung slightly in the wind. Katie glanced over the rest of the woman and couldn't help noticing her hourglass shape. She was dressed in a sophisticated curve-conscious suit and looked like sin waiting to happen. There was something vaguely familiar. She frowned as the two women walked out of her sight.

Then it hit her. "Dee!" she cried. Her middle sister. Twelve years since she'd seen her. Her heart hammering,

Katie flew to the door and pulled it open just as her two sisters appeared.

"Dee! Lori!" She grabbed them both and squeezed. Lori returned the embrace. Dee hesitated.

"Priss," she said, removing her dark sunglasses. Her lips curved in a smile that Katie suspected had caused more than one man to walk into lampposts. "It's good to see ya." She glanced around the apartment. "A little cramped in here."

"She's been spending all her money on Jeremy," Lori chided.

Dee pulled out a pack of cigarettes.

"I'm sorry. You can't smoke."

Dee paused. "Are you allergic?"

"No, but the cat is pregnant," Katie said. "And so is Wilhemina."

"Who's Wilhemina?"

"I am," Wilhemina said, tugging Douglas along with her. "Katie's my best friend."

"Katie?" Lori echoed.

"I don't go by Priss anymore," Katie said.

"And this is Douglas," Wilhemina added proudly. "We're getting married tomorrow."

"How exciting," Lori said.

"Best wishes," Dee said with more politeness than enthusiasm, putting away the cigarettes.

"How did this happen?" Katie asked.

Dee's lips lifted in a genuine smile. "Your man Michael."

"He's not really—"

Dee waved her hand. "Don't be pedantic. He called both of us, and I agreed if I could be the one to tell you the news. I've always wanted to do this kind of thing. Lori and I would have been here sooner, but our plane sat on the tarmac forever. That gave us a chance—" She cleared her throat and gave a wry smile. "A chance to bond since we hadn't seen each other in twelve years."

"And what is the news?"

"Well, Michael has been a busy boy and he has done a lot of research on you." She gave Katie a considering glance. "I wasn't able to establish exactly how much research, but he knows all about Mom and your dad and your grandparents and sisters. He knows we all have different fathers and that Lori and I were taken from Mama twelve years ago. He found out that your father lived and died in Myrtle Beach. Your father was the son of upper middle-class parents, who have unfortunately died. The good news is that his parents—"

"His parents left Mama some money, but she never got the notice," Lori interjected, clearly unable to contain her excitement.

Dee scowled. "I'm supposed to tell this."

"You're taking too long."

"Okay. Michael found an unclaimed inheritance. It was supposed to go to Mama, who in turn left everything, which wasn't a helluva lot, to all of us. That means her children get to split the inheritance, but we are giving our share to you and Jeremy."

Katie's head spun. She could only stare.

"Katie, that's wonderful," Wilhemina said.

"You're not saying anything," Dee said. "Do we need to go over it again?"

Katie worked her mouth, but no sound came out. "How much?"

"Oh," Dee said. "A hundred thousand dollars."

Katie gasped and lifted her hand to her mouth. "I don't believe it. I can't believe it." Her heart began to hurt, her eyes felt like sandpaper. "I've counted so many pennies," she whispered.

Distress filled Dee's eyes. "It's been tough on you, hasn't it? Damn, I wish I'd known."

"It hasn't been that bad. It's just—" She broke off, swallowing over a lump in her throat. "It's just been . . ."

Lori squeezed her shoulders. "Not so much anymore."

"Are you two sure you want to do this?"

"Absolutely," Dee said.

"It's the only thing we can do," Lori said.

"But we both want to meet Jeremy."

Katie nodded.

"Now."

Still reeling from the news, Katie alternately smiled and wiped at her eyes. "Okay, I'll call the school to tell them we're on the way."

Within five minutes they were on the way to Jeremy's school. They shared memories along the way while Lori searched for a suitable radio station and Dee smoked a cigarette.

"That's a disgusting habit," Lori said, wrinkling her nose.

"There are worse habits, Little Miss Perfect," Dee said, and Katie couldn't help noticing how easily the two of them had slipped back into sisterly banter. "What kind of car do you drive, Priss?"

Katie felt self-conscious, then pushed the feeling aside. "It wasn't economically feasible for me to own a car."

Dee frowned and blew out a stream of smoke. "Maybe you can get one now. I don't like the way this went down for you. It wasn't fair."

Katie shrugged. "There are lots of things that aren't fair. I just did what I had to. I imagine you have too."

"I suppose."

"Where do you work?"

"Here and there," Dee said vaguely. "Is this the turn I take?"

Katie nodded. "Yeah." She was getting an uneasy feeling about her middle sister. "How often do you see your father these days?"

"Never. He thinks I am spawn of a devil and a heavenly angel, and the devil won."

"Did he beat you?"

Dee met her gaze in the rearview mirror, and Katie saw the lashings in her eyes. Then her expression grew shuttered. "I survived. This is such a momentous occasion. Let's stick to pleasant conversational topics."

Katie felt sick. She may have had it tough, but she'd never had to endure abuse. She had thought Dee would be okay, and she hadn't been. There was a shell of cool sophistication about Dee that Katie suspected had been erected as a defense. A shield born of necessity. Katie remembered Dee as a sweet, eager young girl and felt another stab of loss. How many would they face? she wondered, and made a silent oath not to let her sisters get away from her again.

"There it is," she said, pointing to the house with the children hanging on the porch.

"I like it. It looks welcoming," Lori said.

"It is," Katie said. "I'm betting Jeremy will call you by name when he sees you."

"But he's never met us," Lori said.

"Yes, he has," Katie said. "Mama talked about you and I told him about you and showed him photographs."

"Those photographs had to be ancient. He won't recognize me," she said doubtfully.

"We'll see. There he is."

"Where?" Dee asked, stubbing out her cigarette.

"Running down the steps. Brown hair." She glanced at Dee. "Like yours."

Her guarded expression melted away for a moment. "He's beautiful," Dee said.

"Oh, wait till you talk with him. Just remember he'll need to see your lips."

"Is his hearing all the way gone?"

"Just about," Katie said. "But trust me, he doesn't want your pity."

The three sisters got out of the car and Jeremy bounded toward them. He hugged Priss, then looked from Lori to Dee. His gaze moved like a Ping-Pong ball between his two newest-to-him sisters.

"Lori and Delilah," he said.

"Oh, he knows my full name. Most people call me Dee. I hear you like computer games."

He nodded, still staring. "Y'all are so pretty."

"A man after my own heart," she said and took his hand. Lori took the other. "Show us your room."

"It's a mess. I wasn't expecting company."

Katie held back a moment and watched the three of them climb the steps. Her chest felt so tight she couldn't breathe. God, how she wished Michael were here. Damn him for arranging this and leaving her to manage the shock on her own. The sight of her brother with her sisters was so sweet she almost couldn't bear to look.

Turning away, she hid behind a huge maple and wept. She begged her mother's forgiveness for not believing in her. After all, Sunny had come through. There'd been some frightening moments, but even in death, she'd managed to take care of her children. Her mother had been far from perfect, but she'd done her best, and Katie's life was the richer for it. Of all her siblings, she suddenly felt the luckiest, because she'd had the most time with her mom. Knowing how to two-step and wear high heels had come in handy, and Popsicles, the song "You Are My Sunshine," and fairy tales took the rough edges off of life.

It took several moments for her to collect herself. Thank goodness, her siblings were distracted. She made a quick dash to the rest room and splashed water on her face, and joined the trio on the front porch.

Dee squinted her eyes at her. "Still a little splotchy."

Katie smiled. "Kind of you to notice."

"Does Mama talk to you?" Jeremy asked suddenly.

Katie watched her sisters' faces freeze in surprise.

"What do you mean?" Lori asked, facing Jeremy so he could see her speak.

"She sings to me. I hear Mama and she sings to me. I can't hear music anymore, but I can hear her sing."

Silence descended on the four of them. Dee dabbed at her eyes. "I assume you already knew about this."

Katie nodded.

"She tells me I'm not alone," Lori admitted. "She tells me my sisters love me." She slid a sideways glance at Dee. "She must be talking about Priss."

Katie chuckled at Lori's gentle joke. "What about you, Dee? You hear anything from the hereafter?"

"She says I'm gonna be the death of her."

"But she's already dead," Lori said.

"My point exactly." She paused a moment. "A few times I wondered if I was going nuts, but I heard her sing too. It was just before I ran away that last time. I would hear her sing every night after he beat—" She broke off and smiled, ruffling Jeremy's hair. "Well, I'm glad to know I'm in good company."

The revelation scored Katie's heart. Oh, how she wished

she could have done something. No wonder Dee was guarded. She bit her lip and glanced at her watch. "It's dinnertime for the students. We should leave."

Jeremy protested. Hugs were repeated all around with promises to return. Katie and her sisters drove to Katie's apartment, but Lori and Dee were scheduled to return to Texas that night.

"You've done well for Jeremy," Dee said.

"Thanks. I would have liked to have done well for you if I'd known."

"Water under the bridge. It's been twelve years, Priss. You can't be responsible for everyone."

But it wasn't enough. "If you ever want to live with me, you can," Katie impulsively offered.

Dee lifted an eyebrow. "It's a little crowded."

"Wilhemina and Douglas will be leaving soon. I mean this invitation," she said, hugging both Lori and Dee. "I don't want to lose touch."

"Me either," Lori said.

"Me either. I'll be in touch." Dee smiled. "You always showed us the right way to do things. You haven't stopped."

Katie felt the threat of more tears. "Trust me, I'm not perfect."

"You didn't ever say what Mama says to you," Lori said.

Katie rolled her eyes and sighed. "Mama tells me to have sex."

Dee laughed. "With Michael, I'll bet. Ah, gotcha. I can see it on your face."

"Shut up," Katie said. "But call me."

"Anytime?" Lori asked with a wide smile.

"All the time."

*   *   *

"I would like to see you at Wilhemina's wedding tomorrow," Katie had said. "I would really like to see you, and no I'm not pregnant."

Her words kept him awake. She kept him awake. Nothing new there. He had half wanted her to be pregnant. That way, it might have been easier to— He broke off his thoughts, disgusted with himself. Staring at the ceiling, he remembered her voice getting tight and choky when she'd talked about her sisters. Then she'd cussed at him for not being there. He'd felt like a heel, or at the very least, an idiot.

He was deliberately locking himself in the Rasmussen prison to prove a point to the prick of the century when the woman he needed more than he needed his next breath needed him with her. The silent knowledge sank through him. God help him, he was head-over-ass in love with her, and he was scared to death she was somehow going to slip away from him. Which made his current choice of holing himself up in Rasmussen's house doubly asinine.

Michael stared at the ceiling and calculated how many accounts he would have to get to make up for Ivan Rasmussen. By early dawn, he reached his decision.

Michael walked into Ivan's office. Ivan glowered at him. "Why haven't you left?"

"I wanted to prove the point that I was stable and reliable, but it occurs to me that I really don't care what you think of me anymore."

Ivan met his gaze. "If that's true, then why don't you leave?"

"I am," Michael said and felt the oddest weight lifted from his chest. "I only have one more week and I could make it with no problem, but there's somebody waiting for me, somebody I care about a helluva lot more than I care about you. So you can keep your security contract wherever you like. I'm going to your daughter's wedding," he said, and walked out of the office.

He hadn't walked ten steps before Ivan appeared at his side. "You can't say something like that and just leave."

"I just did."

"But you can't."

"Yes, I can."

"I order you to—"

"Nuh-uh-uh," Michael said, holding up his hand in a stopping motion. "You can't order me because I don't work for you."

Ivan's brows knitted. "Is she marrying the hog farmer?"

Michael nodded. "He's a nice guy and he thinks the sun rises and sets on Wilhemina. She glows when she's around him."

Ivan sighed and looked away. "She's getting married today."

"Yep."

"Where?"

"Can't tell you."

Ivan looked affronted. "I'm the father of the bride. I damn well deserve to know where my daughter is getting married."

"Not if you're gonna be disruptive."

"I won't be disruptive. I just," Ivan said and stopped. "I just want to see her."

"Okay. Want a ride?"

Michael wasn't certain it was a great idea for Ivan to attend the wedding given his previous attitude, but he had an inkling the old coot was coming around. And when Michael saw Ivan catch a glimpse of Wilhemina in her lace wedding dress, he was shocked to see tears in the man's eyes.

All fine and good, but Michael wanted to see Katie. He searched the small crowd and saw her standing near the minister holding a bouquet of flowers. The sun glinted on her hair, and he could feel her smile from thirty feet away. For that moment, though, all he could do was stare.

She must have felt him looking at her, because she turned and her gaze latched on to his. Her smile broadened and he felt his heart trip over itself. He walked, then ran to greet her, taking her in his arms.

She felt warm and wonderful and like everything he'd ever wanted. "I've missed you," he said.

"Me too. I didn't think you'd come."

"I brought Ivan, but I probably lost the contract."

She pulled back and searched his gaze. "Are you okay with that?"

He nodded. "I needed to see you. You look beautiful," he said, taking in the flowing pastel dress and baby's breath in her hair.

"Thanks. It was nice to buy something that wasn't gray."

"I knew you were pretty even when you wore gray."

"When it came to me, it always seemed like you knew just a little too much."

"I want to know more," he told her, and it was the truest thing he'd ever said.

Her eyes darkened with an emotion that grabbed his gut and wouldn't let go. "I don't have a condom with me," she said in a low voice. "But I'm on the pill."

She was going to give him a heart attack. "Why?"

She looked from side to side, then bit her lip. "Because I don't want any barriers. I just want—" She took a quick breath that undid him, then tied him in a dozen knots. "I just want you."

"You're going to make it difficult to get through this

wedding ceremony if you don't stop talking like that," he warned her.

"How long do I have to stop?"

"Until the minister pronounces them man and wife. Can we get this show on the road?"

The ceremony felt interminable, but in actuality only lasted eight minutes. The minister pronounced them man and wife, and Douglas laid a whopper of a kiss on his new bride. Ivan strode up to the couple and for a second Michael was afraid the old man was going to take a swing at Douglas. That would have been a mistake, given the fact that Douglas stood a good five inches taller. Instead, however, Ivan kissed his daughter, shook his son-in-law's hand, and gave the couple a fat check with a condition. There would always be a condition with Ivan. He made Wilhemina promise they would bring the baby to visit frequently.

Michael and Katie exchanged hugs and good wishes with Douglas and Wilhemina, then Michael pulled Katie away from the crowd. "I want to be alone with you, but I brought Ivan. He'll need a ride home." He swore.

"Let him take your car. We can pick it up later," Katie said.

"How?"

"I bought a used car."

Michael smiled at her obvious joy. Damn, he wished he'd been there when she'd picked it out. "You did?"

"You don't quite approve?" she asked.

"I just wish I'd been there too."

"Can I drive you to my apartment?"

"Yeah, let me give Ivan my keys." Michael gave Ivan the keys and joined Katie in her little compact. He barely refrained from running his hands all over her lithe little body as she drove to her apartment.

*   *   *

"It's small," Katie said apologetically as they entered her front door.

"That's okay."

"Are you sure?"

"I'm not looking at the apartment. I'm looking at you."

"Oh," she said, her gaze growing dark and unbearably sexy. He'd seen that look before when she was aroused.

Unable to wait a moment longer, he picked her up and carried her to the back of the small set of rooms. He thanked his stars that his radar was working. He found the bed with no problem and immediately began to remove her dress. His impatient mouth took hers. Her impatient hands tugged at his shirt buttons. One flew onto the floor. Michael felt as if he'd been hard for two weeks with no relief.

"I want to go slower," he muttered, kissing her with carnal pleasure as he rubbed his hands over her breasts and rib cage.

"Another time," she said in a breathy voice that affected him like an intimate stroke. He pushed her dress and panties to the floor. She felt like silk. She was his most secret dream. He slid his fingers between her thighs. She was already wet.

The knowledge nearly sent him over the edge. He swore. "Too fast. I'm warning you," he said, stripping off his briefs and slacks.

He pushed her down on the bed and stared into her eyes.

She looked aroused and vulnerable. "Promise me that you'll never make a promise you can't keep."

That was easy. "I promise I'll never make a promise I can't keep."

She licked her lips and her lids lowered. "Promise this won't be the only time."

Michael thrust inside her. "I promise this will not be the only time." She moved beneath him and he began to pump.

She was so tight and so wet that it didn't take him long. He had wanted her for so long. If not forever.

Afterward, he pulled her against him. "I will not rush next time."

She laid her head against his chest. "Remember not to make promises you can't keep."

"Well you could help a little."

She looked up at him. "How?"

"If you were less sexy, less beautiful inside and out, less of everything I could ever want."

She sucked in a quick breath. "Careful. You'll turn my head," she said, as if she were trying to keep it light.

"I keep trying," he said, dead serious. He lifted her chin so she would look at him. "I wished you were pregnant."

Her eyes popped wider. "Why?"

"Then I could get you to stay with me."

"You probably could get me to stay with you without getting me pregnant."

"Probably?"

She nodded.

"How would I do that?" he asked, lacing his fingers through hers.

"If you loved me."

He put it all on the line. "I love you, Katie Priss. I want to make promises to you and keep them. I want to be yours and I want you to be mine."

She closed her eyes. "Could you say that again?"

"Which part?"

"The *I love you* part."

"I love you."

She opened her eyes. "And I love you."

And Michael knew everything in his life would be just fine as long as he had Katie.

"Laugh hard enough to make your stomach hurt. Sing loud enough to wake the neighbors. Love as if the whole world's survival depends on it, and you will have a wonderful life."
—SUNNY COLLINS'S WISDOM

Epilogue

One month later, Katie and Michael embraced a few friends and Katie's sisters and brother after they said their vows to each other. Delilah had come a few days before the wedding and insisted on helping Katie prepare. In a strange and wonderful way, that time together of doing girly things like manicures and fittings had been healing. Katie knew Delilah still had a ways to go before she would be able to trust again, but she knew they'd both made a start, and she felt hopeful. But it was impossible not to feel hopeful with Michael around.

Michael kidnapped Katie at the reception and drove all the way down to Myrtle Beach, South Carolina. They stayed in a villa on the far north end, a little off the beaten path.

Katie stood on the beach in the circle of her husband's arms and watched the moon on the water. "Why here?"

"You know," he said, rubbing his lips over her throat.

Her heart flip-flopped every time he touched her that way. He knew it and enjoyed it. She smiled, unable to believe her good fortune.

"Because this is where my mother got knocked up."

He frowned at her. "Because this is where Katie Priss started. A very important place."

Her heart tightened at his fiercely loving expression. She smelled the yellow rose she carried, her mother's favorite. She began to pluck the petals from the rose.

"What are you doing?"

"It's a memorial."

"Huh?"

She tossed the petals over the edge of the waves and let the ocean breeze carry them away. "Thanks, Mom. For everything." She turned into Michael's arms again. "Did I ever tell you that my mother always approved of you?"

"I got that impression."

"Really? When?"

"On that first flight when you took Valium and you told me she thought I needed a blow job."

"I don't remember telling you that."

"I-uh-think that's one of the side effects of mind-altering medication."

"When did you know I would be important to you?"

He chuckled. "When we were in that closet together and you were pissed that you had to stand so close to me. Ivan said that terrible stuff about my family and instead of being nasty to me, you called him a prick. I kept seeing you do nice things for other people. I wanted you to be nice to me."

His longing made her heart ache. The only thing that helped was that she knew that for him, she was like a cool glass of water that he never tired of drinking. She cradled his strong, precious face in her hands. "I never dreamed you were possible. You've been so wonderful to me, to Jeremy." Michael had already kept his word and taken Jeremy to a baseball game. He'd also insisted that Jeremy spend as much time as possible with them.

Taking a deep breath at the emotion that had welled up inside her repeatedly over the last couple of days, she tugged at his collar and buried her face in his throat. "I think you should prove that you're real."

"How do I do that?" She felt his smile against her forehead.

"You start with your clothes."

"And?"

"You take them off."

"Why?"

He was being ornery. "I told you so I can make sure you're real."

"How do you plan to do that?"

"I plan to use all my senses, sight, hearing, touching, tasting—"

Not giving her a chance to finish her plans, he hauled her over his shoulder toward their villa. He would start warning her any minute. She loved that. She wanted Michael Wingate to spend the rest of his life loving her and warning her.

She slid her hand under his jeans to his bare backside.

"I'm warning you, Katie Priss . . ."

About the Author

Leanne Banks is a USA Today best-selling author with over thirty novels and novellas to her credit. She holds a bachelor's degree in Psychology, which she says qualifies her to treat only fictional characters. Winner of multiple writing awards, she never fails to be delighted when readers write her praising her books as fun, feel-good reads. Leanne's debut single title, SOME GIRLS DO, is her response to readers' repeated requests for a longer book. Leanne lives in Virginia with her husband and two children, but can usually be persuaded to take a trip to the beach at the drop of a hat. You can visit Leanne at *www.leannebanks.com*